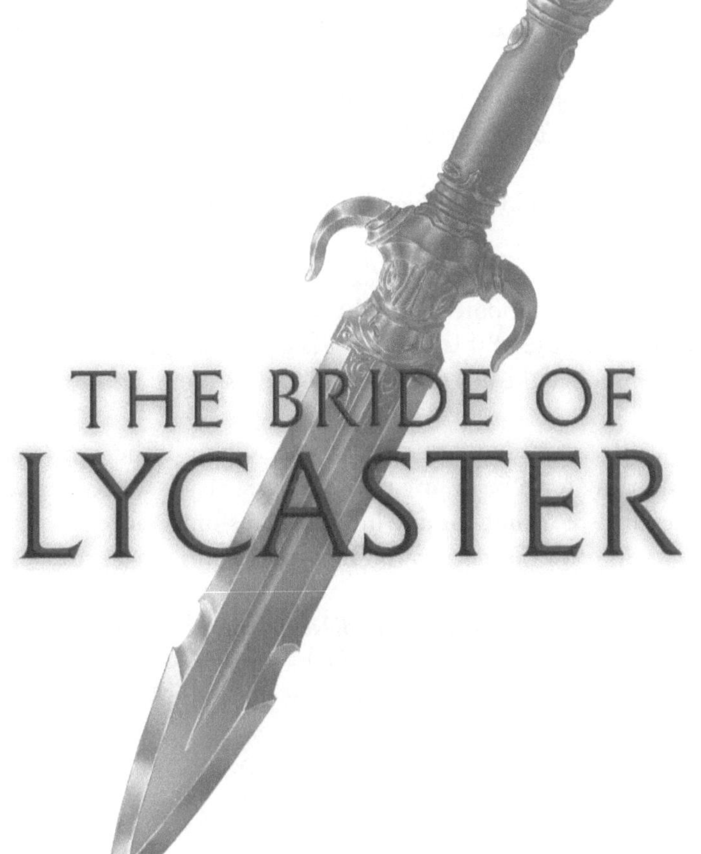

THE BRIDE OF
LYCASTER

First Edition: May 2023

Names: Jay, Perci, author.
Title: The Bride of Lycaster/ by Perci Jay.
Description: First edition.
Audience: Ages 18 and up.
Summary: Serafina Ravenwood must marry, betray, and confront her internal turmoil to find her power in the Dukedom of Lycaster.

ISBNs: 979-8-9881752-0-9 (paperback), 979-8-9881752-1-6 (hardcover), 979-8-9881752-2-3 (ebook)

Printed in the United States of America

For those who shelter in stone.
Let the light in.

Author's Note

This story contains dark fantasy themes and is not recommended for readers under age 18. Although the content is written to uplift and empower survivors of mental illnesses and abuse, reader discretion is advised.

Content Warning: alcohol abuse; anxiety; accidental death; attempted self-sacrifice; attempted murder; blood; death of a family member; depression; emotional manipulation; fantasy violence; grief; familial abuse; implied intimate partner abuse; misogyny; post-traumatic stress disorder; sexual assault by proxy; sexual threat; sexual content; victim-blaming; violence.

Dukedom of Lycaster
N
S
W
E
Fraleigh's Palace
Nordingaard Mountain
Bloodstone Fortress
Ravenwood
Hyton Palace
Bloodstone
Ravenwood Manor
Meadowshyre
Hyton
Odeneye Lake
Elvar
Amberfield
Western Sea
Mydina
Pebblebrooke
Thornebow

Part One

Stone

and

Iron

Chapter One
The Last Ravenwood

I wanted the sun to die.

Three blankets covered my head, but sickly golden afternoon light still crept through the cracks in my defenses and stung my eyes. If I could trade my blankets for bricks and mortar, I would stack a wall into the heavens so high that I would never see sunlight again.

I used to love when the sun stretched across the sky—when my older brothers came home from Heaston Academy every June and they were all mine until September. We would hide in the woods outside of Ravenwood Manor, eat lingonberries in the meadow, and dip our ankles in the rocky stream and scream about how cold the mountain water was.

But then the giants ate my brothers.

I had stopped counting the sunrises after the news of the failed battle against the giants had darkened Ravenwood Manor. Instead, I counted the threads in my green and white quilts, how many times my stomach growled, and the thumps of my heavy heart.

But I did not count my tears. I was too angry to cry.

I pulled the blankets tighter around me as my bedroom lock clicked open. Unmistakable footsteps tapped closer to my nest of torment.

Mother. The liar who promised me my brothers would come home.

She tore the blankets away and yanked me out of bed by my wrist. I did not want to even look at her, but I could not ignore the panic etched in the lines of the corners of her eyes as she spoke. "The Duke is coming."

She let go before I could pull my arm away and directed the maids to make me presentable. They scrubbed days—maybe even weeks—of stale grime from my skin, raked through my matted hair, and smeared a mixture of red berries and beeswax on my cheeks and lips to make me look alive.

Mother had painted her sallow cheeks and dry lips with the same vermillion grease. She had oiled her dark hair so it shined and traded her dingy nightgown for a green velvet dress. She forced her tears behind sparkling emerald eyes and hid her screams beneath perfect red lips.

She became a lie for the Duke and she turned me into one too.

Mother pulled my dark hair back into a golden comb shaped like a raven in flight and gave me a ghost of a smile. "Now His Excellency will see your pretty face."

Liar. People often said I looked just like my mother, but I was only a shadow of her famed beauty. My cheeks were sharp as a starving man's, my hazel eyes were hard, and I was so short and frail I was often mistaken for a much younger girl.

Mother's beautiful mask disappeared as she noticed my scowl. She grabbed my chin and forced my eyes up to meet hers. "Smile, Serafina. We have everything to lose now."

A team of horses trotted on the cobblestones outside the manor. The Duke of Lycaster had arrived. Mother hurriedly swiped perfumed oil across my clavicle and the smell of roses punched me in the nose.

Before I could protest, Mother snatched my wrist and led me downstairs. With each step she took, she straightened her back, brightened her eyes, and held out her chest—completing her transformation from a grieving mother to the beautiful Baroness of Ravenwood.

Father waited for us in the foyer with his dark eyes fixed on the wooden doors of the manor. He was still as a sentinel, seemingly counting down the seconds until the man who sent his sons to their deaths walked into our home. His dark green cape that marked him as a member of the House of

Ravenwood was fastened with a golden pin of the House emblem—a raven looking over its shoulder—that designated him as the leader of our province.

Mother wanted the last three members of the House of Ravenwood sparkling for the man who ruled Lycaster, but Father went too far. He had put on the family jewels like armor and glittered in the thin strips of orange light that slashed across his chest.

Mother put on a strained smile as she dragged me with her to dutifully stand beside Father. Her voice was sweet as a rose hiding its thorns. "Frederick, we are in mourning. Why are you wearing a dozen rings on your hands and eight amulets around your neck?"

Father glanced down at Mother and kept every other part of his body facing the doors. "I am sending a message, dear Adalia. The House of Ravenwood is still mine as long as I breathe. That rat-bastard takes my province, my home, and my daughter over my dead body."

"And if you anger him," Mother replied in a dark hiss, "he *will* make you a dead body!"

The ache of simmering resentment in my muscles faded into a numbing tingle as my parents transformed from spoons to knives. I had never heard them argue before.

"His father would have never done this," Father said in a low voice. "Alastar the Wise would have never forced all those boys to—"

Father cut himself off as soon as our doormen opened the manor doors. Mother quickly tapped me on the back and I straightened my spine.

Shoulders back, eyes down, mouth shut. Stay frozen. Stay hidden.

The Duke's entourage of more than a dozen men flooded into the foyer, each one wearing the rich blue color of the House of Hyton. A small man hurried to the front of the crowd and his booming voice echoed off the dark wooden panels of the foyer. "Announcing His Excellency, Alastar XI, the Duke of Lycaster!"

Through the manor doors, I watched as a tall man with a round belly stepped out of a golden carriage that gleamed like starfire in the fading daylight. The man wore a flowing Hyton Blue cape trimmed with fur and the golden crown of Lycaster on top of his salt and pepper hair—Alastar Anders Hyton, the man who would take Ravenwood.

My mother had warned that he would also own *me* if I did not marry. The suffocating numbness in my body kept me from shuddering at the thought as the Duke stomped into the foyer.

The announcer's voice rang out like a bell again. "Announcing the heir to the House of Hyton and the Dukedom of Lycaster, Lord Alastar Derrick Pervale Hyton!"

I shocked myself out of the numbness. Mother clapped her hand over my wrist to keep me from jumping out of my skin. We did not know *he* would come to the manor!

I had spent my entire life imagining what the famed heir to Lycaster looked like. He would have just turned fifteen, but I still braced myself for the broad shoulders, sharp eyes, and cocky smile that was sure to swagger into my home.

Another figure emerged from the golden carriage and I finally laid eyes on the boy I needed to marry. I let a tiny breath pass my lips—he was thinner than I thought he would be.

Lord Hyton timidly followed behind his father into the manor with his white-gloved hands clasped in front of him. He walked with his chin dipped, like he wanted to disappear behind his dark curls that softly fell to his shoulders.

What his hair could not hide, even though he looked only at the floor, were the most beautiful blue eyes I could ever imagine—dark and dynamic, like the sea. I suddenly could not breathe.

Only Duke Hyton's brash voice could tear my eyes off his son. "Baron and Baroness Ravenwood, the House of Hyton offers our deepest condolences for your loss. *So* sorry we could not attend the funerals."

"We did not have funerals," Father clipped bitterly. "We had no bodies."

Duke Hyton's eyes narrowed and he lowered his voice. "Do not forget to whom you speak, *Frederick*. Besides, no one is angrier about the results of the battle than me."

My stomach dropped. If Duke Hyton had ordered every son of Ravenwood and Bloodstone provinces to fight the giants with no provocation, what would he do if someone actually made him angry?

Mother smiled and inched closer to Father—a silent plea to not provoke the Duke.

"Due to Ravenwood's *and* Bloodstone's failure on the mountain," Duke Hyton said with a low, pointed voice. "I had to do a little…damage control."

Duke Hyton snapped his fingers. His announcer unfurled a large scroll and proudly read: "The last sons of the House of Ravenwood valiantly led the mighty Ravenwood militia to fight alongside His Excellency's army on a righteous quest against the giants of Nordingaard mountain. Erik Frederick Ravenwood, twenty years of age, and Endre Kristofer Ravenwood, seventeen years of age, fell as heroes in battle. May they conquer in another life."

I clenched my fists together so tightly I thought my fingernails would pierce my palms. Valiant. Righteous. Heroes. Nothing in Duke Hyton's proclamation told the truth about the battle. There was no mighty Ravenwood militia—only the sons of herders and woodsmen forced into battle. Erik and Endre had unknowingly led thousands of knob-kneed and wide-eyed imitations of soldiers into a bloodbath. Not a single giant fell.

The numbness in my body grew until it threw me into the memory of cold fog at dawn. Endre stood in front of me with his dark green cape around his shoulders and his new sword against his hip. His freckled cheeks rose up to his mossy eyes that shone with valor. He gave me a nearly bone-crushing hug goodbye and his merry laugh tickled my ear. He smelled like mint and fresh smoke.

His cheek brushed against my hair and I could hear his signature bright smile in his voice. *"The first giant I kill is for you, Sera. I love you."*

I was so foolish to believe him. No one had ever killed a giant.

Father's curt voice snapped me back to the present. "How does spreading that scroll of lies around the Dukedom solve anything? Ravenwood lost *half* its boys. No one can work the land. My people will starve!"

Mother grabbed Father's wrist as quickly as the strike of a viper. I hated standing motionless with a frozen tongue and a shattered heart as my family crumbled before my eyes, but I had no power to change anything and I never would. I belonged to my father, with no money and no choices for my life, and then when I graduated from school and married at age twenty-one, I belonged to my husband.

All I could do for the rest of my life was what my mother had commanded—smile.

I clutched my hands even tighter as Duke Hyton chuckled low. "You requested my army to destroy the giants that plagued *your* lands and all I asked in return was that the Northern provinces send their sons up the mountain as well. Unless you want to hand full control of Ravenwood over to me now, I suggest you solve your own problems." His eyes flicked down to the sparkling gems on Father's chest. "Regardless of what your peasants produce at harvest without their sons, I think you will find a way to pay Ravenwood's taxes this year."

Father's jaw tightened but Mother cut in before the tension could grow. "We are delighted you traveled all the way from the capital city to stay with us, Your Excellency!" Her voice was bright as a meadowlark song with no sign of the strained growl from moments before. "While we are certainly not as grand as Hyton Palace, we will ensure you are just as *comfortable* for the next two weeks."

Duke Hyton's eyes wandered down my mother's body. He looked somehow…hungry. My stomach flipped as I fought the urge to run away.

As if he sensed my fear, Duke Hyton's blue eyes swept from my mother to me. He smiled in a way that did not seem friendly. "Adalia, is this charming young lady your daughter? How old is she?"

The question made my stomach turn over and I had no idea why. Mother took a step toward Duke Hyton, shielding part of my body with her shoulder. "She is fourteen, Your Excellency. She is set to start at the Ashmore Academy for Young Ladies in September."

Propriety forced me to keep my eyes on the Duke while I really wanted to shrink into my skirt and disappear. The last thing I wanted from His Excellency was his attention.

Duke Hyton clapped his hand on Lord Hyton's shoulder—who winced at the touch—and his voice was sickeningly sweet. "Why, that would make her in the same class as my son! How fortunate that they could meet before they left for the academies."

Mother responded with a coy smile that did not reach her eyes.

I did not know why everyone pretended it was a surprise that I was one of the three girls eligible to be Lord Hyton's bride. Anyone who knew I was only six months younger than the heir also knew Lord Hyton could choose me to be the next Duchess of Lycaster when we graduated from school.

Not that he had any reason to.

The numbness enveloped me again as Mother's and the Duke's voices faded into the background. Suddenly my fists were not clutching each other, but instead clinging to Erik's dark green cape as I silently begged him to stay.

Erik's permanently serious brow was sullen and his black eyes swam. I breathed in the scent of charcoal and tea leaves on his chest as he gently embraced me. He rested his chin on the top of my head one final time and his low voice surrounded me.

"The Duke's heir should marry you and take care of you. You will survive."

The memory of Erik faded back into the fog as Mother placed her hand on my back. The Duke left Lord Hyton in the foyer while he raided Father's wine stores and talked of Ravenwood's affairs.

Lord Hyton politely stepped toward us at Mother's behest. As soon as he was within arms reach of me, he inhaled and his eyes widened. My heart pounded against my ribs—he had smelled the rose oil on my chest. He threw his gaze back to the floor and I did the same, but Mother's hand imperiously pushed on my spine as she led us into the sitting room.

Her touch conveyed everything her smiling mouth of lies could not—*charm him.*

As I struggled through the mental fog to form a plan, Mother twittered at Lord Hyton about the upcoming school year, failing to coax him to speak. She sat Lord Hyton and I in wooden chairs across from each other and made up a flimsy excuse about procuring refreshments.

Charm him, what a joke. I was as charming as a nettle in a stocking. Mother, on the other hand, could sprinkle sugar onto a demand and serve it like dessert. I had neither her allure nor her beauty, and she somehow wanted me to charm the next Duke of Lycaster?

The fire popped in the stone fireplace and punctuated the heavy silence. I tugged at a loose thread on my sleeve as I tried to begin a flattering conversation, but Father's harsh words kept repeating in my head.

Ravenwood lost half its sons. Our heirs were gone. The province would starve.

And I could do nothing about it.

My heart jumped as Lord Hyton cleared his throat. He slowly took his eyes off his polished leather shoes and looked me in the face.

"I am…terribly sorry for your loss, Miss Ravenwood," he stuttered quietly. "I…I miss my sisters very much. I understand how you feel."

An earthquake in my chest rocked me out of the numbness and fury spiked through my throat. "No, you cannot understand!"

Lord Hyton froze. My chest went tight. My whole life of preparation to allure the heir was wasted with one burst of stupid emotion. Damn it all!

Lord Hyton's eyes darted to the wooden floor and his cheeks turned red. "My…my sincerest apologies."

I had to salvage the situation. I placed my hands delicately in my lap and leaned forward. "No, my Lord, I—"

"No, you are right," he interjected as he closed his eyes and shook his head slightly. "My elder sisters are about to be married in foreign kingdoms. That is not the same as…as being…"

"Dead," I finished. The word was heavy as a boulder as it left my lips.

He swallowed and looked back up at me. His freckled cheeks were still scarlet and he trembled like a leaf in autumn. I could not believe it, he was terrified of me.

I ran my thumb over the embroidery on the hem of my sleeve. Lord Hyton was everything and I was nothing, and yet he was scared of *me?*

"You need not apologize, my Lord," I said quietly, like I was trying not to startle a lark on a branch. "You have done nothing wrong."

Lord Hyton let out a relieved breath and slumped over to lean on his knees. He reminded me of how Erik used to stoop when he was deep in thought, but I shoved the memory away and locked it behind iron bars.

I could not think about my brothers—not with the heir in front of me and the fate of Ravenwood on my shoulders.

I added up everything I had learned about Lord Hyton—the flinch at his father's touch, his stutter, and his refusal to look anyone in the eye—and realized I had nothing to fear with him. The famed heir to Lycaster was not a miniature version of his bombastic father like I had imagined, but rather a big-eyed bunny rabbit, skittish and needing reassurance.

I bit my tongue as a thought sparkled in my mind like the first evening star—if someone could give the heir the reassurance he needed, what would he give her in return?

Lord Hyton would inherit Ravenwood when he became the Duke, could I use the Duchess's position to ensure Ravenwood had everything it needed? If I became the Duchess, Ravenwood could have food, security, safety from the giants…

Imaginary threads like puppet strings appeared around Lord Hyton's wrists. I pictured myself wearing the Duchess's crown and whispering into those dark curls, cajoling him to fulfill my every demand.

My heart pumped with a startling amount of strength. The numbing fog dissolved and a clear path to the crown appeared. My feet pressed into the wooden floor, my shoulders steadied, and I finally tasted a morsel of something I never had before…control.

And I craved more.

A cool smile spread across my lips. My heart pounded heavier and heavier, as if I were encasing it in granite. I would not simply bat my eyelashes and hope the heir would marry me, I would go for his throat to save Ravenwood. I had to be the best option—no, the only option—when he chose his bride in seven years.

I would make him need me, I would make him love me, and then the Dukedom would be *mine*.

I did not have a natural charm, but I had watched Mother sing her siren's song for years. All I had to do was imitate her, just for a little while, to get Lord Hyton in my grasp.

Just as I was about to make my first move, Lord Hyton worked up the courage to speak again. "I will be honest, Miss Ravenwood. I have never spoken to a girl who is not my sister. Noble sons and daughters have so many rules, and I am not even supposed to meet you until we graduate from the academies…"

He knew nothing of other girls? Interesting.

I coyly leaned on the armrest of my chair and made my voice as smooth as my mother's. "My Lord, I am nothing but a girl, you do not have to address me so formally. Call me by my given name."

He raised his eyebrows. "Your given name? Is that allowed?"

"You are the Duke's heir," I answered with a wry smile. "You can make your own rules."

Lord Hyton mirrored me, loosening his shoulders and leaning on his fist. My puppet began to dance. "All right," he said with a smile. "What is your given name?"

I demurely flicked my gaze to the floor and then back to Lord Hyton's smiling face, a trick straight out of Mother's book. "Serafina, my Lord."

"Serafina," he repeated like he savored the taste of my name. "Call me Derrick."

Derrick was clay in my hands for the rest of his stay at Ravenwood Manor. He told stories of his annoying twin sister while I pretended to hang on his every word. I smuggled his favorite treats from the kitchen for us to eat under the stars. We both quietly mocked his father, letting Derrick have a sip of the freedom he never had in Hyton.

I had all but stitched my name onto the back of his neck by the time his two-week stay had ended. Right before the Hyton carriage pulled away, Derrick stole me away to the shadows of the manor and made me a promise— he would write to me in secret.

"But boys and girls can only write if they are family," I said with a gentle smile, keeping my shocked astonishment bottled where he could not see.

"I am the Duke's heir, remember?" Derrick said with a wink. "I make my own rules."

Duke Hyton bellowed Derrick's full name from the front of the manor— our time together was over.

"Seven years is a long time, Serafina," Derrick said as he took a quick glance over his shoulder. "But I am counting down the days until I see you again."

Derrick took my right hand and kissed it. To my surprise, my cheeks turned hot and my breath stilled as his lips met my skin. Derrick's beautiful dark blue eyes flicked back up to me as he held my hand. I tried to think of something to hook him further, but I could not find my breath.

Fear flashed in Derrick's eyes as his father called for him again. He let go of my hand and dashed off to the carriage.

I rubbed the back of my hand and savored the lingering warmth from his lips as I watched him leave. The puppet strings slipped from my fingers and an airy warmth filled my stomach like sunlight on the first day of spring.

Maybe I took the charm too far. Derrick seemed nice, maybe I could abandon the plan to manipulate him. Maybe I could throw his first letter into the fire, go through school without breaking any rules, and hope he marries me the honest way.

My hand quivered in fear, but I threw it down in a huff. No, I had to stay in control.

The Serafina who read faerie stories and believed good girls got their happy endings had died with Erik and Endre on the mountain. The Serafina who would be the Duchess of Lycaster had to tell whatever lies Derrick needed to believe so he would need her, love her, and ultimately *choose her.*

Losing my brothers had turned my heart into stone, but at least it would never break again.

I was the last Ravenwood and I had to survive.

Seven years later

Chapter Two
The Midnight Letter

The moon shone brighter when an urgent letter came to Ashmore Academy for Young Ladies in the middle of the night, and the news was too important to wait for the sunrise.

The giants finally fell.

The entire school had crowded into the Junior dormitory to hear the news. I had staked my claim next to Brietta Elvar on her bed, but the other girls piled onto the other three beds, huddled into the available space in the corners of the dorm, and even sat on the floor to listen as Julietta Thornebow read her brother's letter.

I hugged my knees against my pounding heart as I sat on my best friend's bed. Brietta wrapped her arm around my shoulders and leaned her soft cheek against the top of my head.

I could not believe it was real. The giants had destroyed the Northern provinces for decades, ruined my family, killed my brothers, and they were just…gone?

"With the aid of my arrows," Julietta read, theatrically mimicking her brother's voice as she read his words, "His Excellency's army felled ten giants!"

The crowd of girls gasped and muttered to each other, but I was speechless. One giant could eat a herd of sheep, dozens of cattle, and a few families in a year. Killing just one spared countless lives in the Northern provinces, but ten?

I let out a disbelieving breath and Brietta smiled against my hair. Julietta was just a girl in the class below me, but for a moment she became my favorite person with her brother's tale of vengeance.

I hoped the giants had died as painfully as possible.

Suddenly, an irate voice shouted over the crowd. "What are you yelling about, Thornebow?"

The crowd of girls shuffled out of the way as Annalisa Hyton stomped through the door of the Junior dormitory. Annalisa was Derrick's twin sister, but they looked nothing alike aside from a matching pair of dark blue eyes. Annalisa had a body like an hourglass and a mouth like a fist. Her usually perfect blonde curls stuck out wildly around her head from a night of tossing and turning.

"Our Selection Night is in two days!" Annalisa yelled at Julietta. "I swear if you keep me from my beauty rest—!"

"This news is more important than your supposed beauty rest, Anna," I snapped.

Annalisa shot me an icy look. "Only to *you*. No one else is from the Northern provinces nor cares about those damn monsters."

Brietta's hand rubbed my shoulder, a silent "*I care.*"

Annalisa eyed the letter in Julietta's hand and sneered. "And why the hell would someone deliver a message in the middle of the night to *you?*"

Julietta looked down her nose at Annalisa as if she were a hairy spider. She flipped her ash-brown braid over her shoulder and steeled her voice. "According to the messenger, it was the Duke's direct order to relay any post from the victorious battlefront as soon as possible. And since my brother is one of the top cadets at your uncle's military academy and the best archer in the army, I get immediate correspondence…"

Julietta smiled like a cat drinking cream as she glanced around the room, "…that I get to share with all of you!"

All the girls in their nightgowns looked at Annalisa with big eyes, silently pleading for the Duke's daughter to leave us in peace to hear the rest of the letter.

The other two Seniors dutifully flanked Annalisa and groaned at Julietta.

"Do you have to yell about the battle *now?*" Dinah Pebblebrooke whined as she tugged at the roots of her chestnut hair.

Camille Meadowshyre's golden waves bounced as she stamped her foot. "Come on, Julietta, let us sleep!"

I rolled my eyes. Neither of those twits could handle the Duchess's crown.

My voice was calm yet pointed. "The faster we hear the rest of the message, the faster you three can go back to bed."

The crowd chattered quietly in agreement. No one else at Ashmore had a personal stake in the destruction of the giants, but we rarely saw any excitement while cloistered behind the academy's tall stone walls. Reading the letter from the battle had been the most interesting event in the whole school year.

Julietta quieted the crowd, relishing both the attention and Annalisa's frustration. She cleared her throat and imitated her brother's proud voice again. "I led the archers in shooting the monsters in the eyes. Once the giants were blinded, the Beast came up behind them and sliced off their heads!"

I quietly let out a breath. No one could decapitate a giant. I had to know who had achieved the impossible. "Who is the Beast?"

Julietta looked up at me with a twinkle in her eye. "You will never believe this, but there is a half-giant cadet the same age as my brother. Grigory told me that he is over nine feet tall and vicious—all the cadets call him the Beast!"

"A nine-foot-tall half-giant?" I scoffed. "That is impossible."

Camille shuddered. "No human would survive…*mating* with a giant, right?"

Annalisa gave a cruel laugh and glanced in our direction. "Of course it is possible. How else would you explain Brietta? The Beast could be her half-brother!"

Annalisa, Camille, and Dinah all laughed and the mattress shifted as Brietta shrank in on herself. Some of the younger girls laughed too, but they all quieted under my sharp glare. Brietta was well over six feet tall, making her the largest girl at Ashmore, but she was *not* a half-giant.

Before I could bite back at Annalisa, Brietta squeezed my arm. As much as I wanted to lay into the other three Seniors, the last thing I should do was break my nails or mar my hands with cuts right before we met the suitors.

"Anyway," Julietta said with a glare in Annalisa's direction, "Grigory writes 'We are coming back to Hyton immediately. His Excellency will host a victory celebration for his army in the center of the city the day after Selection Night. I look forward to seeing you once I am a married man!'"

"What?" Annalisa half-gasped. "A married man?"

Dinah's eyes widened with panic as she whispered to Camille. "His Excellency is allowing military cadets into Selection Night this year?"

Julietta's face contorted with indignation. "Excuse me?" She thrust Grigory's letter in Annalisa's direction. "My brother is a hero! Is that not good enough for you brats?"

Annalisa's initial shock smoothed into a sneer. "Your brother might be a little hero, Thornebow, but *my* brother is also in Selection Night." She glanced over to Camille and Dinah. "Why would anyone want your brother when they could be the future Duke's bride?"

Brietta chuckled so softly that only I could hear. My face was stone, revealing nothing.

Camille leaned toward Annalisa with her hands clasped in front of her button-nose in a plea. "You mentioned me in your last letter to your brother, right, Anna?"

"Yes, and me as well?" Dinah chimed in.

"Of course," Annalisa purred at Camille and Dinah's devotion. "I would do anything for my two best friends, even when I become a princess."

A wry smile flicked up my cheek. I could not keep silent. "How are you so sure that prince of yours is a suitor this year?"

Annalisa whirled around to face me. "Because, Sera, all six of my elder sisters married a foreign prince. Marrying royalty is a Hyton tradition!"

Julietta mumbled that being a pain in the ass was also a Hyton tradition.

"One of your sisters is even an empress now, right?" Dinah asked.

"Unfortunately," Annalisa answered with an eye-roll. "Anyway, it is only logical that the daughter of a man as powerful as my father marries a prince. Not that I expect those of *lower breeding* to understand," she finished with a sniff in Julietta's direction.

Her prince was not coming. In my secret correspondence with Derrick, he revealed that no foreign princes wanted to pay for a spot in our Selection

Night. Since only three suitors were in our class, Grigory Thornebow had earned his place as the fourth suitor.

Annalisa and her two stooges were too snobby to see a cadet worthy as a suitor, but anyone who felled ten giants more than earned the honor of an Ashmore bride.

Before I could defend the cadet-turned-suitor, Julietta's eyes narrowed at Annalisa. "Lower breeding? You are the granddaughter of a murdering *sorceress.* No one is of lower breeding than you Hyton dogs."

The air in the room went still aside from a few quiet gasps. Even I bit my tongue at the mention of Duchess Ilsa Hyton.

Even though we never spoke of her, Ilsa's infamy was ever-present in the backs of our minds. She had conspired with her lover, the Baron of Thornebow, to murder Alastar the Wise using sorcery. Ilsa died the same night as her husband, but her punishment for her treachery was not over. Duke Hyton had ensured the entire Dukedom banished his traitorous mother into the realm of the forgotten. Outside of the frightened whispers of warning from our mothers, Ilsa's name, her image, and even stories about her disappeared at the beginning of the Duke's reign. Mentioning her at all was illegal, but Annalisa had finally pushed Julietta too far to care.

Annalisa leapt for Julietta with her teeth bared and her curls flying out like a lion's mane. Dinah and Camille gripped her arms to keep her from tearing the smirking Julietta limb-from-limb.

"You Thornebow rat!" Annalisa spat as Dinah and Camille dragged her out of the room. "You are a House of fucking traitors! Your blood is sewage! If you so much as *look* at me again, I will ram my foot so far up your—!"

I reached over from Brietta's bed and closed the dormitory door before Annalisa could finish her threat. Her irate screaming echoed through the stone hallway as Dinah and Camille pulled her back into the Senior dormitory.

The rest of the girls quickly filed out of the dormitory to escape the tension. Julietta still stood proudly in the center of the room with her brother's letter in her hands and a satisfied smile on her lips.

"Jules," Brietta said in a breath, "I cannot believe you did that."

Julietta shrugged. "What is she going to do? Execute me like my grandfather?"

If Annalisa had inherited her swift wrath from anyone, it was her father. Duke Hyton had Baron Thornebow beheaded for high treason mere hours after his father's lifeless body was found. The executioner's axe was final, but the Thornebows' grudge against the Hytons was everlasting.

The House of Thornebow believed the Hytons slaughtered the innocent. The House of Hyton believed the Thornebows plotted to overthrow the Dukedom. Sitting between Julietta and Annalisa at mealtimes and in classes never failed to liven up a normal boring day.

I lingered on Brietta's bed and re-braided my hair while Julietta snuffed out her candle. Illuminated only by the nearly-full moon, Julietta and the other two Juniors crawled under their blankets and all was still.

"Thank you for not wringing Annalisa's neck," Brietta whispered as I finished tying off my braid. "I did not have the energy to pull you off her again."

Moonlight highlighted Brietta's soft features on her round face. She had just turned twenty at the beginning of May and youth sparkled in her big brown eyes. She was an unusually large girl with broad shoulders, but no one could actually believe the auburn-haired beauty resembled a grotesque giant.

"Just think," I whispered back, "two more days until you never have to listen to her bullshit again."

"I might not, but you will since her brother will marry you."

My eyes darted to the silhouettes of the sleeping girls, looking for any sign they had heard Brietta. No one stirred, so I unclenched my jaw.

No one knew about Derrick and I's letters other than Brietta. I trusted her as my best friend, even though she was from the obscenely wealthy House of Elvar.

Unlike every other girl who had arrived at Ashmore by carriage, Brietta came to Hyton in the House of Elvar's grandest ship bearing their emblem— the mighty sea serpent. She entered Ashmore like a goddess from the legends—robed in the richest purple fabrics and dripping with jewels as she towered over the other students. Even though Headmistress Blackiston forced every girl into the school uniform with no familial adornments allowed, Brietta had already made her mark as a rival to the riches of the House of Hyton. Annalisa was threatened by a rival of any kind, so she cut at Brietta's self-worth as soon as classes started.

Annalisa's jealous ire combined with Brietta's extremely large stature had made my best friend an instant target of unwanted attention. As the only person in my class who had the nerve to stand up to Annalisa, I had protected Brietta from her cruelty as often as I could.

In exchange, Brietta had helped me with my letters to Derrick. I had sharpened my charming skills to an art in our conversations, but my heart was still too damn stone-cold to return Derrick's warm and fuzzy prose. Brietta was a swooning romantic, so she whispered lines of her poems in my ear and fluffed up my words as I wrote.

I was too mean and jaded to be romantic and Brietta was too soft and timid to defend herself. We made a perfect pair.

Most importantly, Brietta kept my secret safe. If anyone found out about our forbidden letters, I would be expelled from Ashmore and immediately ineligible to marry under the Duke's law. My cunning and Brietta's tight lips were the only defenses preventing me from becoming the property of Duke Hyton if I were kicked out of school.

I had played a dangerous game for the last seven years, but I was still careful.

Derrick and I used code names in case anyone intercepted our messages, so he bared the depths of his heart unencumbered by his title. I pretended to do the same, keeping the ugliest parts of myself in an iron cage that he would never unlock.

I kept him as close to me as I could without seeing him. I did not get a single glimpse of him, or any other noble young man, since Derrick left Ravenwood Manor seven years ago.

Ashmore was both in theory and presentation an elite institution for the proper upbringing of future wives, but in practice, it was a prison. We were rarely allowed outside of the stone walls unless we were performing chores. If we earned a walk in the sunshine, matrons and guards flanked us with every step.

Derrick's school was not as strict. The boys of Heaston were even allowed to go home for a summer holiday, but the girls of Ashmore had no such privilege.

Mother had mentioned Ashmore used to not be so harsh, but must have cracked down some time after her graduation. Headmistress Blackiston had made clear when we first entered Ashmore, and then branded into our minds by the school matrons, that our chastity was our most valued asset and the Ashmore rules were put in place to keep us pure for our husbands.

The marriage on Selection Night that the men of Heaston and princes around the world paid fortunes for was a bond of magic, forged by Fraleigh, the Great Sorceress of Nordingaard. The magical bond joined the blood and hearts of a man and a woman together for life, keeping both parties free from disease and able to only produce children with one another. The magical blood bond was so strong that when one half of the marriage died, so did the other. The matrons had told us the bond was so special because both suitors and brides had to be chaste at the time of the bond, keeping their blood pure for the magic.

The answer to keeping both parties pure from intimate knowledge of each other, apparently, was placing only the women under lock-and-key for seven years.

Since the virginity prison we were housed in never allowed us to go home, our families visited us on select days. The three girls eligible to become the next Duchess waited anxiously for the entire royal family to visit Annalisa, but we had to stifle our disappointment when only the Duchess showed up each time. Derrick had told me his father forbade him from taking trips to Ashmore, but I foolishly got my hopes up whenever Annalisa mentioned a family visit.

Even though I had dreamed of those beautiful blue eyes for seven years, my stomach clenched at the thought of seeing him again. Derrick had made clear that he carried a deep affection for me in his letters, but he had not seen me since I had grown into a woman.

He would be disappointed that I had not grown any taller. Not only was I the smallest of all the Seniors, I was even shorter than the teenage first-years. Although I was the same size as a child, no one could mistake me for one— my cheekbones were sharp as a knife's edge, my nose was long and pointed, and my eyes were intimidating instead of pretty. I was not classically beautiful like Annalisa nor did I have a warm and gentle face like Brietta. I looked, as Annalisa had pointed out while we were embroidering, like a "tiny troll."

"Brie," I whispered, "what if he thinks I am ugly and chooses Dinah or Camille?"

Brietta scrunched up her nose. "Why would he think you are ugly?"

I clenched my fists. "What if he is expecting someone not as scrawny or small? What if he has been picturing a Serafina with rounder cheeks, a smaller nose, fuller lips, and larger—"

"Sera, stop!" Brietta interjected, placing both her hands on my shoulders. "Look, I understand why you are nervous. Even though the suitors get reports of our accomplishments and skill proficiencies, they really choose us based on how we look at the Suitors' Ball and the Presentation."

My mouth went dry. The Suitors' Ball was the next day—when suitors and brides were supposed to meet for the first time before Selection Night. I had practiced my dance steps for weeks to make sure my dance with Derrick would be perfect, but nothing could prepare me for the Presentation.

I picked at the sleeve of my nightgown as I pictured entering the Duke's ballroom, arm-in-arm with Father, and promenading in front of all the suitors and all the nobility of Lycaster. The Presentation was the grandest and most important two minutes of my life, but it was still just the opening of an auction. If Derrick did not select me after he saw me at the Presentation, the other three suitors would fight for what was left of my dignity.

Brietta's thumbs stroked my shoulders and she lowered her head so her big brown eyes met mine. "You should not worry about how you look. I have read Lord Hyton's words over the years. He is in love with you."

My heart thumped with a little triumph, but I was not convinced. Brietta was the one sprinkling romance in my letters like rose petals, maybe she was imagining a faerie tale that did not exist. "How can you tell?"

"Come on, Sera," she said with a smile. "He tells you that you are all he thinks about, he asks you about your studies, hell, he even mentioned you as the future Duchess a few times! When you hold a parchment with his words, you have his whole heart in your hands. The mere fact that he paid the school guards to deliver and receive letters in secret all these years is proof enough!"

Half of me wanted to believe that my plan had worked and Derrick was in love with me, but the other half remained cynical. He could very well pretend to show love in his letters because I had pretended with him all along. I had lied, but I had to become Duchess and secure Ravenwood. No matter what.

Brietta playfully shoved my arm. "Besides, you are too critical of your looks. Trust me, men want to marry a small woman they can pick up and twirl on the dance floor with ease. You have dainty hands, the sun's rays in your eyes, and sleek hair. You may be small, but you have such strong features that no one would ever think you were weak."

I looked down at my supposedly dainty hands and smiled softly. Brietta was much too kind for a place like Hyton where everyone only looked out for themselves.

Brietta smiled back. "Frankly, *he* should worry about seeing *you*. Do you remember what his father looks like? Lord Hyton could also have ruddy cheeks and a belly full of liquor for all you know."

I covered my mouth with my hand to stifle a laugh. "Good thing everyone else is asleep, or else you could face treason charges if anyone overheard that."

Brietta scoffed. "I tower over most of the Duke's guards. I would like to see them try arresting me."

Brietta's radiant optimism put a smile on my face. She would never even speak out against Annalisa, but pretending she would stand against the Duke himself was still fun to imagine.

I glanced out the window at the thin blue haze on the horizon—the dreaded morning was coming. Brietta squeezed my hand one more time and I crept out of the Junior dormitory to slip into my own bed.

The first moment of daybreak flowed through the dormitory windows and cast the other three sleeping girls in a soft glow. In mere hours, we would become adult women dancing the night away with the suitors of Lycaster.

I reached under my pillow and retrieved a small, folded-up piece of parchment. I looked over the room to ensure the other girls were fully asleep before unfolding the note and reading Derrick's words in the light of the fateful morning.

Dearest Birdie,

Next week, we will finally be reunited. The men participating in Selection Night this year are Sir Myles Amberfield, next-in-line to the Amberfield baronage, Sir Gerond Pebblebrooke, a minor noble, whoever the top cadet in my uncle's military academy is, and myself. As I am the "top student" of my class, I will select a bride first. The Duke's heir is always "top student" and no one, not even the richest foreign prince, chooses a bride before the heir to Lycaster.

I will select you, Birdie. Without hesitation. I cannot wait to see you. I cannot wait to touch you. I cannot wait to marry you.

—Midnight

I folded up the letter as small as I could and tucked it into my fist—holding Derrick's heart in my hand like Brietta had said. I smiled, letting myself trust in my seven-year-long plan, and closed my eyes. Derrick's assuring words played over and over in my head like harpsong until they lulled me into a short sleep.

I danced in a dream with the crown of Lycaster on my head and a Ravenwood free from giants, but a jolt of barbed truth forced my eyes open.

If I had lied to Derrick for seven years, Derrick could also lie to me.

Chapter Three
Five Brides

The Great Sorceress's purity examination was the last obstacle between me and the Suitors' Ball.

I held my knees together and shifted in my wooden chair as all four Seniors waited in the main lecture hall for the examination to begin. The Great Sorceress had sworn fealty to the House of Hyton centuries ago, so it was her honored duty to ensure Lycaster's brides were chaste before she attempted the magical marriage bond.

Every second we waited was agony. Annalisa's fingernails clicked as she picked at them under her desk, Dinah tapped her foot, and Camille twirled a strand of her golden hair.

I glanced up at Duke Hyton's portrait hanging at the front of the room—painted right after his coronation when he was thirty and still handsome. Instead of the dreamy hopefulness that used to fill my stomach while imagining Derrick in the portrait, a vortex of acid churned at the thought of seeing him at the Suitors' Ball.

My palms started sweating and I forced myself to calm down. I wrung my hands together to dry them out instead of wiping them on my skirt and staining my damn uniform. The Ashmore uniform was all white from neck to ankle except for a black thread trim around the wrists of our sleeves, the collar, and the hem of the skirt.

The all-white ensemble was a burden to keep clean, but the Ashmore founders wanted it that way. Not only did wearing white force us to have impeccable hygiene standards and table manners, it also deterred us from participating in un-ladylike activities such as sitting on the floor, running around, or rolling in the grass with a handsome school guard.

As if any of the guards would ever touch us. Allegedly, the Great Sorceress had placed a curse on each of the Duke's soldiers that guarded the school. If a guard's skin touched ours, his blood would boil until it roasted him to death from the inside.

I picked at the black trim on my sleeve and squeezed my thighs together even tighter. The Great Sorceress was only minutes away from entering the lecture hall to inspect us. If she had placed a deadly curse on simple guards at a girls' school, what would she do to someone who posed a real threat to the Dukedom? Like someone who had manipulated the heir for seven years?

I had nearly torn out the trim to ease my panic when Headmistress Blackiston entered the lecture hall.

Our unreasonably stern Headmistress kept her silver hair tied back in a tight bun and her hands neatly folded in front of her as she walked. Her shoulders were set back and her spine was as straight as a pin—modeling the perfect posture she expected each Ashmore student to carry herself with.

"Ladies," she said in a lofty voice, "please welcome our exalted guest, Fraleigh, the Great Sorceress of Nordingaard."

Her delicate footsteps echoed outside like powerful whispers. Everyone kneeled and looked down in reverence for the only sorceress in the Dukedom. Duke Hyton had outlawed all magic and attempts at sorcery after his mother's death, but the deathless and all-powerful Fraleigh was the sole exception.

Fraleigh's footsteps entered the lecture hall and only then did I dare lift my eyes. She looked exactly as I heard she would—tall, dressed in rich, blue robes, and her long black hair cascading to the floor. She wore a golden collar around her neck and rings on each of her sharp fingers. No one could mistake her for a mortal with her bright golden eyes and her pale skin shining with an iridescent glow that shifted from blue to green as she moved. Her cheekbones were even sharper than mine and her thin eyebrows arched up into points.

"Rise," she commanded in a voice like the croon of a dove.

We obeyed and adjusted so we stood shoulder-to-shoulder in a line facing the sorceress. Fraleigh eyed Annalisa, the first in line, who trembled under her piercing golden gaze.

"What are your accomplishments?" Fraleigh asked.

"Drawing and painting, your majesty," Annalisa said quickly. "I also have perfect pen—"

A loud knock on the door cut Annalisa off. Fraleigh looked over with mild annoyance at Headmistress Blackiston, who had a rare look of confusion on her face. Headmistress Blackiston quickly walked over to the door and opened it, revealing a man wearing a Hyton Blue coat—one of Duke Hyton's servants.

"Pardon me, Headmistress," he said softly, "His Excellency is here."

"Father?" Annalisa gasped with a hopeful look in her eyes.

Headmistress Blackiston furrowed her brow and looked over her shoulder at Fraleigh.

"Go on, Lenora," Fraleigh said calmly. "I certainly do not need your supervision."

Headmistress Blackiston nodded with a look of confusion in her black eyes and she quietly left with the servant. When the door closed, Fraleigh returned her attention to Annalisa and ordered her to continue.

"I also have perfect penmanship," Annalisa said softly as she eyed the closed door.

"Visual arts exude vitality," Fraleigh said. "You will be a satisfactory bride."

Annalisa let out a relieved breath. Fraleigh then turned to Dinah.

"Your majesty," Dinah said with more confidence in her voice than Annalisa had, "I am accomplished at the harp, the lyre, and the flute. I also sing."

"Music brings much happiness," Fraleigh said. "You will be a satisfactory bride."

I held my breath. Derrick could play both the harp and the violin. I had told Derrick that instruments were too complex for me to handle, hoping I would come off as demurely humble while bolstering his own musical accomplishments. I had not considered that he might want a Duchess who could play multiple instruments as well as he could. He could change his mind and choose Dinah once he learned of her talent.

Fraleigh turned her attention to Camille as my palms began to sweat again.

Camille smiled and kept her eyes to the floor. "Your majesty, I take joy in herbology. I cultivate roses and experiment with herbs in cooking and medicine."

"Delightful," Fraleigh crooned. "You will be a satisfactory bride."

Camille was sweet as a daisy with rosy cheeks and an air of natural grace. She might have been one of the dullest girls at Ashmore, but she was at least genuine. I had worked for years to charm and deceive while Camille had formed lasting connections with just a few blinks of her long eyelashes. Maybe Derrick would notice Camille's air-headed smile at the Presentation and decide that he would rather have a Duchess who was easy and would never argue.

Fraleigh's golden eyes flicked over to me. I had worried so much about my competition that I did not think of what my accomplishments even were. I enjoyed sewing and arithmetic, but servants did all the household sewing and arithmetic was solely for the man of the house to worry about. I quickly thought of something to impress Fraleigh.

"Your majesty," I said, "I am accomplished in the design of fine garments as well as the means of logic and practical thinking."

Fraleigh shot me a predatory look. "Those are not your accomplishments."

My heart stopped. Fraleigh stepped over until she was right in front of me. Her face was uncanny, like it was carved by magic and not from a natural life. I dared to flick my eyes to her golden collar long enough to read the words *Ipse Dixit* engraved on the gleaming metal.

Fraleigh looked down at me for a moment before she spoke in a chilling voice. "I see you, Serafina Ravenwood. Your accomplishments are nothing you have learned here."

She pointed her long finger at my forehead with her sharp fingernail barely touching my skin. A chill shot from my head to my toes and I stopped myself from quivering.

"You have a strong wit." She moved her finger down to my lips. "And a quick tongue."

She removed her finger from my lips and placed her hands behind her back.

"You are manipulative and an excellent liar."

My blood froze. I waited for her to tell me that I, too, would be a satisfactory bride. Without another word, Fraleigh's golden eyes were off me and she walked back to the front of the room.

My thoughts raced. I was not a satisfactory bride. She knew about my secret relationship with Derrick and that ruined my chastity. I was going to be the property of Duke Hyton.

I shuddered as I pictured Duke Hyton's wolfish eyes wandering down my body instead of my mother's, but Fraleigh spoke again. "You all passed the purity examination. Now you may know the secrets of Selection Night."

I let a tiny sigh of relief escape my lips. The plan to marry Derrick was still on.

"That was it?" Dinah asked. "Y-your majesty, I mean."

Fraleigh smirked. "Had you not been chaste, I would have smelled it on you. Sit."

We returned to our chairs as I tried not to think about what a lack of chastity smelled like.

Fraleigh glowered at us as she spoke. "Tomorrow, you will present yourselves before not only the five suitors, but to an audience of nobility who travel to Hyton to watch the Presentation."

Five suitors? No, that was not possible. Derrick's letter said our class had four suitors for the four brides. Having an equal number of suitors to brides was the only reason anyone from the military academy was allowed to participate in Selection Night at all.

Fraleigh shot me a look. Maybe she could even read my mind! I straightened my back and folded my hands on top of my desk to look as prim and innocent as possible.

Fraleigh's eyes moved from me to the rest of the Seniors as she spoke again. "After the Presentation, the suitors will adjourn to make their bride selections in secret. Once the selection is made, the brides are paired with their suitors in order of selection for the marriage ceremony. The blood bond takes effect immediately after the ceremony, but you and your new husband have until midnight of the next full moon to consummate your marriage or the bonding enchantment fails and your marriage annuls."

She paused for exactly three seconds, a planned part of her centuries-old speech, to let the weight of the devastating consequences of an annulment sink in. Shame. Exile from noble society. Living under the charity of your father and other male relatives until you relieve your family of the burden by dying.

"I can perform the marriage enchantment one time only," Fraleigh emphasized. "Should your marriage annul, you will never marry a noble son again. You have only one moon cycle to be sexually intimate with your husband. Do you ladies understand?"

"Yes, your majesty," we all responded in soft voices.

The red and gold sunset streamed through the windows as I walked alone back up to the dormitory. I had tried to practice my dance steps for the Suitors' Ball as I made my way through the sitting room, but a heavy weight sat in my mind ever since Fraleigh dismissed us from her lecture.

You are manipulative and an excellent liar.

Fraleigh had said cruel Annalisa was a satisfactory bride, but not me? Lies flew off my tongue like notes to a song and I could play the strings of someone's heart like a harp, but that did not mean I would not be a satisfactory bride. I was a Ravenwood—I had to use all that I had to survive.

Apparently all I had was a strong wit and a quick tongue.

Maybe Fraleigh was losing her mind after all those centuries. She did believe five suitors would be at Selection Night, after all.

The foyer steps creaked as I headed to the Senior dormitory to get into my ball gown. My fingertips gently traced the banister as I rehashed the rest of Fraleigh's speech in my head. She said we had to consummate our marriages to make our blood bonds permanent, meaning I could be…*intimate* with Derrick as soon as tomorrow.

My heartbeat quickened even though my footsteps slowed on the stairs. Headmistress Blackiston had given all the Seniors a stiff-lipped and prim-voiced lesson on sexual intimacy two weeks ago. With diagrams. She had grabbed the backs of our necks if we looked more than a few seconds at a man, but she forced us to study drawings of a naked man's body parts and listen to a grueling lecture on the functions of each one.

Camille's cheeks burned for hours after, Dinah could not stop talking about the *parts* she saw, Annalisa was finally quiet for an evening, and I could not reply to Derrick's letter for two days.

I placed my hand on my lower belly like I was bracing myself as I walked through the dormitory halls. Derrick was sweet, but intimacy just seemed so…ugly and gross. Headmistress Blackiston never said consummating our marriages had to be enjoyable—I could just close my eyes and think about the power of the crown while the blood bond sealed.

I bit my tongue and suddenly the sound of muffled sobbing reached my ears. I passed the dormitory doors and the crying got louder until I reached the Juniors' door.

I took in a breath as I recognized the voice underneath the sobs—Brietta.

I pushed open the door and quickly stepped inside the dormitory. Brietta kneeled on the floor and sobbed with her face on her bed. A woman with silver streaks in her curly brown hair and her Hyton Blue skirt pooled on the floor knelt beside Brietta and rubbed her back.

"Brie!" I cried as I kneeled beside her. "What happened?"

Brietta lifted her wet and splotchy face from her mattress and her voice hitched with her sobs as she spoke. "I am graduating. The Duke is forcing me into Selection Night tomorrow."

My stomach dropped. Fraleigh was not losing her mind—Brietta was the fifth bride for the fifth suitor.

Merri, the Duchess's personal maid, eased Brietta's shock about her graduation. After a long, reassuring talk, Merri patted Brietta's sticky cheeks and promised she and the other maids would make her sparkle like a diamond for the Presentation.

Lie. A lie she had to tell since no servant would deny the Duke's orders, but Merri had no time to get Brietta ready for Selection Night.

All Seniors had elaborate Presentation dresses ready at Hyton Palace. Each Presentation dress took months to design and construct, and Brietta did not even have a full day to have a dress made for her. Merri still assured Brietta she would find her a dress and she left to make arrangements.

I whisked Brietta away to the Senior dorm to keep her away from the other girls' gossip. We sat on my bed as she told me what happened while I went through Fraleigh's examination.

Brietta said she was reading one of her poems for the younger girls as an example of master wordsmithery when Headmistress Blackiston and Duke Hyton took her to the Headmistress's private quarters.

"I thought the Duke knew about the you-know-whats and was going to interrogate me," Brietta whispered. "Instead, the Duke said he was so impressed with my poetry and writing that Ashmore had nothing left to teach me and I was ready for Selection Night. Headmistress Blackiston tried to protest, but the Duke would not let her speak. He took his entourage, except Merri, and left as suddenly as he came."

Brietta ran her fingers back through her auburn hair and shook her head. "Graduating early…because of my poetry? None of this makes any sense. I am not…I am not ready!"

Brietta's voice broke into a sob. I pulled her into a hug and let her cry on my shoulder.

No one graduated from Ashmore early. The Ashmore founders made twenty-one the ideal age for marriage because women's bodies were finished developing. Previous councils of Barons had pressured the Duke's ancestors to lower the graduation age for a better chance at more heirs, but even that argument could not force Ashmore students into marriage before the supposed magic age of twenty-one.

Besides, Duke Hyton had no desire to visit Ashmore for the last seven years, but had come unannounced just for Brietta? Duke Hyton was a boar of a man, but he was intelligent enough to have ulterior motives.

Anger burned in my stomach as I pictured the Duke using Brietta as a pawn in one of his games, but I calmed myself and continued consoling Brietta as she cried louder.

Annalisa groaned from the other side of the room as she sat in her undergarments at her dressing table. "Could you at least sob quietly, half-giant? I am trying to concentrate!"

I glared at Annalisa. She rolled her eyes as she caught my reflection in her jeweled hand-mirror and applied a red wax mixture on her lips and cheeks.

"Dinah, get me soot from the fireplace," she commanded.

"Anna," Dinah protested, holding her skirt in both hands, "I already put on my gown!"

Each Senior wore a dress of white satin fabric that showed off some cleavage if a girl were blessed. The ball gown was adorned with black trim like the school uniforms, but each Senior had embroidered the trim on her own gown.

Our gowns were our only opportunity to show off both our embroidering talents and a little of our own personalities to the suitors. Dinah had embroidered her wrists and neckline to look like sheet music. Camille had stitched her sleeves with crawling vines. Annalisa never had the patience for needlework, but she had managed to sew simple flowers at the lowest part of her neckline to draw the suitors' attention to her ample bosom. As for my gown, I had to be sneaky.

I spent weeks embroidering the neckline and shoulders of my dress with hundreds of stars. Derrick would love the stars, but the two small ravens flying right over my heart were just for me—I wanted to remember home. Ashmore forbade House emblems in any form, but even the most eagle-eyed matron would not find the birds hiding in the night sky of my own creation.

The Suitors' Ball gown was another important garment Brietta lacked— she was just going to the ball in her normal uniform. She would look underdressed and childish standing next to the four of us in our custom gowns, but no one could help her.

While I cared for Brietta, I had to outshine Dinah and Camille at the ball to ensure Derrick would marry me. I needed to devote what little time I had left to ensure everything about my appearance was absolutely perfect.

I worked out a loose thread from a star on my shoulder as Annalisa glared at her two best friends for refusing her command to fetch her some soot. As much as I had hoped either Dinah or Camille would be stupid enough to bend over the fireplace and stain their hems with soot right before they met Derrick, even they were too afraid to ruin their perfect white gowns. Their normal obedience to Annalisa's ridiculous whims stopped when vying for the Duchess's crown.

"You two are worthless!" Annalisa roared. She rose from her table and marched to the fireplace. Just as I had wished she would shove the two of them into the cinders, she instead bent over the hearth herself. Annalisa picked up some soot with her index finger, licked her thumb, and rubbed the two fingers together until she created a small drop of black paste. She returned to her vanity, grabbed her mirror in her left hand, and applied the paste to her blonde eyelashes.

"You know Headmistress Blackiston does not allow makeup at the Suitors' Ball," I said as I watched her nearly poke her eye out with her fingernail.

"She will not allow *you* to wear makeup," she snapped as she tinted her eyelashes black. "I can make it so subtle she will never notice."

Annalisa cleaned her fingers with a rag and stood up from the vanity. "Tighten me!"

Camille and Dinah rushed over and tugged her corset strings. As soon as Annalisa was gasping for air at a rate that satisfied her, someone knocked on our door.

I furrowed my brow. Who would dare bother us when the ball was only minutes away? I got up from my bed and answered.

Julietta stood in the doorway with a large pile of white fabric folded up in her hands.

"This is for Brietta," she said as she handed me the fabric.

I unfolded the pile and the fabric came tumbling down. I raised my arms as high as they could reach to keep the fabric off the floor—it was a ball gown.

Brietta gasped and left my bed to take the dress from my hands.

"Since you will not be at Ashmore much longer," Julietta said, "we figured you would not miss your bed linens for one night."

Brietta's eyes watered as she held the dress. "Jules, you are the most wonderful—"

"All the Juniors stitched it together," Julietta cut in, blushing at the praise, "the fourth-years made most of the skirt, so do not dance too wildly tonight. I cannot guarantee the integrity of the construction."

I could guarantee the dress had no integrity. The sleeves and the hem of the skirt were uneven, the bodice would hang too loosely, the neckline was too straight, and the fabric was thin. Still, a gown of bedsheets was better than wearing the school uniform.

Brietta smiled for the first time in hours. "It is *perfect.*" Her smile dampened my cynicism over the linen frock and I walked over to help her into the dress.

"Have fun tonight," Julietta said as she left the room. Brietta was too enraptured by her dress to notice, but Julietta's smile dropped and I could not mistake the look on her face—pity.

I quickly dressed Brietta. The dress hid all her voluptuous curves, but I had no time to alter the dress and save her drowning silhouette. I carefully tightened Brietta's shoe-string laces on the back of the flimsy bodice as the other girls filed out to head to the ball.

If the dress made it four hours without falling apart, I would swear Julietta had become a sorceress. I gave Brietta a once-over and a false smile before taking her hand and leading her down to the academy foyer.

As soon as we took the first few steps into the stiff and grey foyer, I noticed Brietta's hem was too long. I helped pick up Brietta's skirt so she would not trip and we reached the bottom of the stairs.

The five of us waited shoulder-to-shoulder in a line. I wrung my clammy hands together as I thought of a plan for the ball. It was too late to lie about my musical talent, I could not fake wistful beauty, and even if I danced on my raised toes, I could not change my stature. I tried to think of a line from one of the poems Brietta had sent to Derrick, but my mind was spinning too quickly for me to remember.

I let out a cool breath. I had countless shortcomings I could not change, but my constant strength was that I knew how to play Derrick like no one else. I had charmed him for seven years, and I just had to keep telling him what he needed to hear for one more night.

Hopefully that would be enough.

I closed my hands into fists as the tall clock in the foyer ticked down the seconds.

Tick.

Derrick was waiting for me.

Tock.

He said he would marry me.

Tick.

But nothing is ever a guarantee.

Tock.

I had to keep the lies going. He *had* to be mine.

The clock chimed eight times. Time for the Suitors' Ball.

Chapter Four
The Suitors' Ball

We trembled as we waited in the Ashmore foyer to go to the Suitors' Ball.

As soon as I thought Headmistress Blackiston would be late for the first time in her life, she walked in from a dark hallway accompanied by two other matrons. She approached Brietta and her mouth tightened into a thin line as she inspected Brietta's hastily-made gown.

She would never show it for fear of appearing insubordinate to the Duke, but I knew Headmistress Blackiston hated breaking centuries of protocol to force Brietta to graduate early. She could not defy the Duke's order to put Brietta through Selection Night, but the Suitors' Ball was within her control as the head of Ashmore. She could easily determine Brietta was improperly dressed and exclude her from the ball to maintain order. Keeping Brietta from the ball might save her from potential embarrassment, but then she would marry someone she had never met or spoken to. I could not allow that to happen.

"Julietta created the dress, Headmistress," I said, interrupting her scrutiny of the gown.

Headmistress Blackiston turned her attention to me. "Is that so?"

I kept her on the hook and pulled her in. "Along with all the Juniors and the fourth-years. They worked for *hours* constructing the gown from Brietta's bed linens. Quite inventive, if I may say so."

Headmistress Blackiston smiled softly. Nothing kept us girls in order more than camaraderie and teamwork. Both the Juniors and the fourth-years would be ill-tempered for days if Headmistress Blackiston rejected Brietta's gown, and she knew it.

"How thoughtful," she crooned. "Nevermind that this dress is not of the approved fabric and lacks the required details," she plucked a loose strand of red hair on Brietta's bodice and tossed it away, "but men do not notice details anyway."

Headmistress Blackiston gave me a quick once-over and moved on.

After approving Dinah and Camille, Headmistress Blackiston faced Annalisa and held out her hand. One of the matrons placed a linen rag in her outstretched palm.

Annalisa whined as Headmistress Blackiston scrubbed the paint and soot from her face.

"Nice try, Lady Hyton," she scolded. "I am old, not blind."

She left Annalisa with a raw and red face. Annalisa pouted and refused to look Headmistress Blackiston in the eye. Brietta let a giggle escape.

Headmistress Blackiston re-arranged our order and led us to the Great Hall. Annalisa led the line as a member of the House of Hyton, but the rest of us followed behind her in order of last name. Brietta Elvar was right behind Annalisa, then Camille Meadowshyre, then Dinah Pebblebrooke, and finally me.

All the girls' differences in stature became glaringly obvious from my spot in the back of the line. Brietta was so tall and broad-shouldered that she completely obscured Annalisa. Camille was taller than Dinah, but only barely, and the top of Camille's head did not even reach Brietta's shoulder.

The order was not going to flatter me—the suitors would see classically beautiful Annalisa first, then gorgeous and tall Brietta, Dinah and Camille with respectable heights and pleasant faces would follow, and then they would have to see me, the tiny troll.

We reached the double-doors to the Great Hall. A school guard dressed in white held each door handle, ready to present the first bride. The suitors were already waiting for us like a pack of hungry wolves.

Headmistress Blackiston gave us a soft smile. "It is time, ladies. You will do well." She noticed Brietta's pallor and added "*All* of you will do well."

A loud male voice announced the first bride from the other side of the door. "Lady Annalisa Ilsa Hyton, youngest daughter of the Noble House of Hyton!"

The doors swung open into the Great Hall. Annalisa stepped forward and the doors shut behind her like a pair of jaws.

The announcer boomed Brietta's full name and she disappeared through the doors. Then Camille. Then Dinah.

My heart pounded and I fought a hard lump in my throat as I tried to swallow. Seven years of secret letters and a fabricated romance all came down to the moment I entered the ball.

Derrick had to love me.

"Miss Serafina Helia Ravenwood, last daughter of the House of Ravenwood!"

The doors opened and my footsteps clicked on the stone tile. Each year, the girls of Ashmore push away the dining tables and decorate the Great Hall for the Suitors' Ball while the Seniors dress. Because many of the girls were putting together a gown for Brietta, the hall was barely decorated.

Even though the walls and arched windows were bare, bouquets of pink and purple flowers from the school garden filled the hall with a sweet aroma. Stars twinkled through the windows. Flames danced from the iron chandeliers and candelabras.

I found the line of four suitors amid the swirl of fire and starlight. Three suitors wore the Heaston formal uniform—all black with white trim. One strong, blonde suitor wore the blue military uniform and could be none other than Julietta's brother, Grigory. Each suitor wore a cape of their House colors over their uniforms and only a single heartbeat passed before I found the man in the Hyton Blue cape.

Derrick's deep blue eyes met mine and my heart stopped. He had grown so much since I saw him last, making him taller than any of the other suitors. His freckles had faded and he was no longer lean and timid, but instead broad-shouldered with a strong stance. He was more handsome than I even imagined. I could not breathe.

I fought the temptation to stare at him and stood next to Dinah at the end of the line across from the suitors. I would raise suspicions if I regarded Derrick with any familiarity, so I kept an expression of polite awe on my face as the ball began.

The first suitor usually took the first bride in line for a dance, but Derrick and Annalisa were siblings and would not waste valuable time dancing together. Instead, Derrick escorted the next suitor in line, a man of medium-build with red hair who wore a yellow cape, to his twin.

Derrick bowed gracefully to Annalisa and she returned with a stiff curtsy. The red-haired man, who must have been Sir Myles Amberfield, bowed too low and almost lost his balance. Even seven years of gentleman training could not get rid of the awkward bumpkin nature of the House of Amberfield.

Derrick waved his arm to "give" Myles to his sister. Derrick shot Myles a sly glance as Annalisa took his hand and then he moved on to Brietta, the next in line.

Brietta wrung her hands together as Derrick bowed in front of her. I gave her a reassuring look from the corner of my eye and silently gave her my permission to dance with him.

A shorter, brown-haired man in a light blue cape—Sir Gerond Pebblebrooke—paired with Camille. Grigory, proudly wearing the stone grey cape of the House of Thornebow, walked with a slight limp to pair with Dinah.

Everyone paired to dance except for me, the last in line. I stood quietly on the edge of the dance floor next to Headmistress Blackiston as a few Ashmore girls played a slow melody on lyres and violins. While everyone else watched the Duke's heir effortlessly dance with a woman who was even taller than him, I scanned the room looking for the fifth suitor.

No fifth suitor, but I found Duke Hyton standing near the dance floor with a large goblet in his hand. The headmaster of Heaston attempted to chat with His Excellency, but the Duke was too busy keeping an eye on his heir to make conversation.

On the Duke's right-hand side stood the tallest man in the room. The towering figure had a square jaw, short white-blonde hair, and wore a military uniform adorned with brass medals—the Duke's younger brother, General Hyton. General Hyton joined his older brother in intently watching Derrick and Brietta dance, but his Hyton Blue eyes did not follow the heir. Instead, he tracked the shining auburn waves and swirling white skirt of the heir's partner.

General Hyton, despite being in his early forties, had never married and did not have any children as far as I knew. General Hyton could have attended the ball to represent his top cadet the same way the headmaster of Heaston sponsored his students, but the mystery of the missing fifth suitor hung in the air and the way he focused on Brietta raised my suspicions.

Brietta, though, took no notice of the leering General. She focused only on Derrick, who, *somehow,* made her laugh as they danced.

A tense breath hissed through my nose as Brietta's large bosom bounced with her laugh. I looked down at my chest—I did not have much to offer in comparison.

"You are lucky," Headmistress Blackiston said calmly, as if she sensed my discomfort. "You get a good view of everyone else before you are thrust into the fray."

She was right. I tore my eyes away from Brietta and Derrick and focused on the other pairs. Myles's eyes were wide with panic as he clumsily stepped on scowling Annalisa's toes. Camille and Gerond gently swirled on the dance floor. Grigory and Dinah carried on a loud, but happy conversation as they danced.

The music ended and the pairs bowed and curtsied to one another. Annalisa stormed out from the middle of the dance floor to take my place on the side.

"He stepped on my feet eight times!" she hissed. She settled next to Headmistress Blackiston, who patted her shoulder as she fumed. No handsome prince for Annalisa, the toe-mashing Baron's heir was the best she could get.

Grigory's tall boots clicked on the tiles of the Great Hall as he approached me. He flashed a charming smile and offered me his arm.

"I'm afraid I'm not much of a dancer," he said, his voice both bright and smooth. "I have an old battle injury in my left leg, but I'll do my best to give you a good time."

Grigory's wavy blonde hair was handsome, even though it was cut short in the military style. His steel House pin—a fox with its fluffy tail curled around its legs—gleamed in the candlelight as it secured his cape.

I took his strong arm and he led me to the dance floor. His calloused palm found my hand and a tiny shock went up my arm. Clinical sketches of nude men flashed through my mind until the music pulled me back into reality. Grigory found the beat and led me in the dance, but he faltered on his left leg a few times.

I peered around him to see who the new pairs were. Brietta danced with Myles, who was not adjusting well to a partner who towered over him, and Derrick had Camille. Camille desperately wanted to marry Derrick, but she kept her mouth shut—too shy to charm him with conversation.

Relief washed over me and I turned my attention back to Grigory. Might as well try to make an alliance outside of the House of Hyton while I had him in my hands.

My voice was as sweet and lush as the first bite of an apple. "I heard of your victory at Nordingaard. The House of Ravenwood is incredibly thankful for your feats of heroism."

"My most glorious victory yet," Grigory said with relish. "Now young Ravenwood ladies will feel safe going to bed at night again."

"Oh, I feel *much* safer thanks to you. What was the battle like?"

Grigory threw me into a faster spin than I expected. A belly-tickling laugh escaped my lips as the candlelight swirled around me. He caught me with a firm grip on my waist and gave me a flirtatious half-smile. He was showing off the strength in his arms, the only advantage he had over the other suitors. He did not need to impress me, but he still clearly wanted to.

Good. Prideful men were the easiest to flatter.

"Since I am from one of the Southern provinces," Grigory replied with a gleam in his dark brown eyes, "I had only heard tales of the giants of the North, but they were much larger and more ferocious than the stories."

"Really?" I asked, playing along like I knew nothing of the beasts who terrorized my province when the snow melted off Nordingaard each year. "Please, tell me more."

Grigory's face swelled with pride. "They were living chunks of the mountain with footsteps like thunder, but they weren't so strong once I shot out their eyes. When we took out ten of them, the last three retreated."

Flattery rolled off my lips as thick as syrup. "You must be very brave."

Grigory slung me into another spin, and when he grabbed my waist again, he dug his fingers into my back and pulled me close so my chest mashed into his. My cheeks burned—I had never been so close to a man before.

My heart thumped against my ribs. Did I like the closeness? Did I hate it? I kept my teeth tightly closed as I tried to decide.

Grigory's voice dropped as his warm breath skated across my forehead. "Ravenwood was beautiful. I could almost believe the rumors that magic flows around the trees. I can tell by the ravens on your gown that you also carry a deep affection for your province."

My stomach dropped. I thought men did not notice those details!

"How did you know the ravens were there?" I whispered.

Grigory flashed a small smile. "If my sight is sharp enough to land an arrow in the eye of a moving giant, I can certainly find the two ravens on your chest."

A chill ran through my body. I did not like this, not at all.

"What of the man you call 'the Beast?'" I asked, quickly changing the subject. "I heard from Julietta's letter that he killed the giants too."

Grigory's smile fell. "He is the Beast for a reason—he's a bloodthirsty monster. His family sent him to the military academy to try to tame him, but it didn't work. Even General Hyton couldn't break him, but he at least put him to good use—hurting those who deserve it for once."

I took a small sip of air, my chest pushing slightly against his in protest of how tightly he held me. My head started feeling light, but Grigory had piqued my curiosity and I needed to know more.

"Is he really a half-giant?" I asked quietly.

"He is," Grigory replied. "He's as tall as a house. He sleeps outside in a pile of hay because he can't fit into the barracks. But the reason I know for certain he's a half-giant?"

He leaned in close until his mouth brushed against my ear. He tightened his hold on my waist and locked me in place against his body.

"He has a beast's heart," he whispered. "He cannot feel or love, he can only destroy."

Before I could ask him what he meant, a loud ripping noise and a gasp echoed through the hall.

I looked around Grigory. Myles was frozen in place, his face as scarlet as his hair, and his foot on Brietta's skirt that pooled on the floor. The white skirt had completely torn from the bodice, leaving Brietta standing on the dance floor in her undergarments.

"Brie!" I gasped, pushing out of Grigory's hold and running to her. I picked up her skirt and held it up to her waist to cover her up.

Myles sputtered out apologies, but I ignored him and took Brietta out of the Great Hall and upstairs as quickly as I could. Once we were safely in the Senior dorm, Brietta broke down.

"They all saw me!" she cried. "Lord Hyton, the other suitors, even the Duke himself!"

"No," I lied, "everyone was too distracted with each other to notice."

I held back an angry breath as I thought of the leering General Hyton enjoying the view of Brietta in her undergarments. I dismissed the thought and continued comforting Brietta.

"Really?" Brietta sniffed through her tears.

"Of course," I replied, expanding on the lie. "In fact, Grigory and I were having such an engaging conversation that I did not notice anyone else in the room."

Brietta rolled her eyes. "Grigory can really go on. Especially about himself."

"He actually was not talking about himself," I said with a smile, happy to distract her. "He mentioned the Beast."

Brietta snorted out a small laugh. "You mean the alleged half-brother of mine?"

"Grigory said he was a violent half-giant with a beast's heart." I swallowed. My attempted distraction only opened up more questions. "He only had one short dance to talk to me, and he chose to talk about this…Beast character? Do you have any idea why?"

Brietta's brown eyes rolled around in thought as her tears dried. "A few weeks ago, Grigory sent a letter to Julietta asking about the girls in the Senior class. I think he knew he was in Selection Night and wanted information on the brides. I helped Julietta with the reply letter and we told him that you and I are friends, gave a quick description of Camille and Dinah, and then told him *everything* about Annalisa."

I furrowed my brow. "Was he just looking for a bride who hates the Beast as much as he does?"

"I can see that," Brietta replied. "Grigory *hates* him. We do not even know his name because Grigory only calls him 'the Beast' or 'that monster' in his letters."

Whatever obsession Grigory had with the Beast was no concern of mine. What did concern me was that I had new competition for the Duke's heir. As I looked at Brietta's flushed cheeks and auburn hair that shone like a warm glow around her gentle features, I could not help but wonder if she had the beautiful face Derrick preferred over mine.

"Brie, what did Derrick say to you to make you laugh?" I asked.

"You will not believe it," she replied with a smile. "He took me by the hand and said, 'So, you are the famous Brietta.' Anyone could have overheard, but he did not care. We talked through the whole dance as if we were old friends."

I silently cursed myself for mentioning Brietta so much in my letters. Of course, I could not have pretended that my best friend did not exist, especially since she was involved with my scheme to make Derrick fall in love with me.

I had been so stupid. I should have just learned how to write poetry.

Maybe all was not lost. Brietta had helped me with the most romantic parts of our correspondence, but I still wrote to Midnight as myself. I had stars in my belly any time a guard slipped me a new letter. I enjoyed reading about his life at school, news from the palace, and musings he had throughout the day. I knew him better than anyone else did.

A tiny bite of guilt tainted my confidence—I knew Derrick, but Derrick did not really know me. I was not a romantic like he was, I did not really think his lessons about wartime strategy were interesting, and I did not actually believe I was about to get my happily ever after like in a faerie story. I just needed to marry him so I could pull his strings and save Ravenwood.

Regardless of my silly feelings about Derrick, I needed to return to the ball and put the plan back in motion.

Before I could make an excuse to leave, the dormitory door flew open and Annalisa stormed in.

She pointed an accusatory finger at Brietta. "This is all your fault! The ball was canceled! I only got to dance with that brick-footed jackass, and now all the other suitors are gone because *you* could not keep your clothes on!"

Camille was right on Annalisa's tail and gently contradicted her. "That is not fair, Annalisa. Sir Two-left-feet stepped on her dress and destroyed it. You would think after seven years of training he would have learned how to dance!"

Dinah ran in after Camille with her fists on her hips. "You cannot blame him! It was a clear accident!"

As the four girls squabbled, someone banged on the door. The knock did not come from the small hands of any Ashmore student, but the knuckles of a grown man. I cautiously walked over to the door and cracked it open. On the other side stood two Ashmore guards.

"Miss Ravenwood," one of the guards said, "you must come with us immediately."

My heart stopped. I reluctantly filled in the gap the guards made between them and closed the dormitory door.

"Great!" Annalisa shouted from inside the dorm. "Now Sera is in trouble!"

They found out. Derrick was too careless with his words on the dance floor. Headmistress Blackiston was going to expel me immediately. The guards silently led me through the halls, but instead of taking me to the Headmistress's private quarters, they opened the glass doors to the garden.

The guards left me standing on the garden path at the bottom of the steps and shut the academy doors behind them. The faint aroma of pink roses hung in the evening mist. The scent briefly sent me back to the smell of rose oil on my chest when I saw Derrick for the first time at Ravenwood Manor. The near-full moon cast all the flowers in a gentle glow as I tried to find my breath.

Before I could finally inhale, a soft and deep voice made me freeze.

"Hello, Birdie."

Chapter Five

Midnight

My mind was playing tricks on me, I was sure of it. The voice I had heard in the night was too deep to be Derrick's…or was it?

No, I was just on edge. The suitors were all gone. I had no idea why the Ashmore guards had brought me into the garden, but surely it was not because—

> *"Of all the places I could be,*
> *Over the moon or across the sea…"*

There it was again, the voice. I took a tentative step on the garden path and slowly scanned the rows of flowers.

> *"Between the clouds or under skies of blue…"*

I followed the voice until it practically whispered in my ear.

> *"I only want to be next to you."*

I whipped my head to the right. Derrick was right next to me in the shadows, his black Heaston uniform making him nearly invisible. He had his arms casually folded across his chest and his broad shoulders against the stone wall of the academy.

He looked down on me with a soft smile spread across his face, but my heart thumped with fear. He was even taller than he looked in the Great Hall.

"I always loved that one," Derrick said. I finally matched the voice to his face.

I kept my face schooled as my mind spun. What was he talking about?

Derrick gently pushed off the wall and took a silent step toward me. His smile did not falter. "You wrote that poem three years ago, but I still think about it all the time. Technically not your best one, but it was too cute to forget."

I smiled back. The poem, *right*. Brietta's mind behind my pen had been fruitful. I needed to pretend that I had humbly forgotten that I had written it.

I tried to craft the lie, but my hands trembled as he towered over me. My eyes fell to the cobblestones and my cheeks burned. Hopefully he would see me as being demurely bashful, but I felt so tiny and insignificant in front of him that I was too scared to speak.

What was I doing? I could not just stand in the open alone with a suitor, regardless if he were the heir. If anyone found us, I would be expelled!

"We could get into serious trouble." My eyes flicked up to his face for a brief moment. "You know seeing each other like this is against the rules."

A sly smile crept up his lips. "I thought you said the Duke's heir could make his own rules?"

He remembered Ravenwood Manor. That was a good sign, at least.

"How did you get the guards to bring me here?" I asked.

"They may guard Ashmore, but they are still my soldiers," he replied. "I snuck away from the Great Hall and ordered a couple of them to help me out. They could not refuse an order from a Hyton."

"Oh, so you are in charge now?" I laughed softly. "I hope your father does not hear you say that."

"No one will hear us say or do anything out here."

My heart fluttered and my breath disappeared again. He took my hands and gently pulled me further into the shadows of the academy's walls. I immediately noticed the tiny calluses on his fingertips—proof that he actually had played the harp and violin for years.

Good thing I did not invent my own musical talent, my soft hands would have given me away. As long as Derrick did not ask me to recite any poetry, I was in the clear for the rest of the night.

Derrick did not quiz me about my romantic notions nor did he test my poetic finesse. Instead, he placed his finger under my chin and raised my face to meet his Hyton Blue eyes.

"You are more beautiful than I imagined," he whispered. "I waited seven years for this…"

He leaned down and his lips pressed against mine.

Oh…*yes.*

I closed my eyes and melted into the moment. Suddenly I remembered Ashmore's warnings about temptation and pulled away like he had sent lightning through his lips.

"Derrick!" I whispered. "What about my chastity? We could ruin everything!"

"Do not worry," he said smoothly. "I know exactly when to stop."

I looked up at his shadowed face. My chest heaved even though my breath was shallow. He was handsome, his body was warm against mine, and his full lips were soft and inviting.

I may not have loved him, but I *wanted* him.

Almost as if he read my mind, he wrapped his arm around my waist and pulled me close. He slid his fingers through my hair to cradle the back of my head and bent down.

"I cannot wait one more day," Derrick whispered. He leaned in again and my lips opened to meet his.

He tasted as sweet as rich wine. He smelled like oak and vanilla. I wrapped my arms around his neck as he weaved his fingers deeper into my hair. I raised up on my toes so he did not have to bend over as much and he rewarded my kindness with more passion.

Derrick bit my lower lip and I gasped, not because he hurt me, but because I *liked it.* I dug my fingernails into his shoulders and pressed my body against his. He lightly bit the left side of my jaw and kissed it, then his lips grazed my skin before stopping at my neck. He held my waist stronger and tighter as his teeth sank into the side of my neck.

A soft moan escaped my mouth as his lips and teeth took me to the stars. I grabbed his soft black curls in one of my fists. His hot breath on my neck sent tingles all the way down to my toes. I did not know how far he was going to go, but I did not want him to stop.

He kissed me on the lips again and I smoldered hotter and hotter as we held each other. I slid my hands down to his chest, hoping he would move his hands lower on my body too.

Derrick suddenly pulled away and I gasped like he took my breath with him.

"We have to stop now," he panted.

"What? No!" I pleaded. "Surely there is more—"

"There is," he interjected, grabbing both my hands. "We could do *so* much more without breaking any rules. This is just where *I* have to stop or else I will ruin you."

I nodded and tried to slow my racing heart. Derrick held the back of my head again and brought his lips to my forehead for a sweet kiss.

"One more day," he whispered into my skin. "We just have to wait one more day."

He held me tightly in his arms. His heart pounded against my cheek as he stroked my hair. My eyes fluttered closed and I let myself smile.

Derrick took in a slow breath. "I love you, Serafina."

Victory bells rang in my head.

"You are everything I ever wanted," I said softly. I needed to take it one step further to seal the deal. The lie formed on my tongue and then left my flushed lips like another kiss. "I love you too."

Derrick let out a breath and kissed the top of my head as a reply. His heartbeat slowed to a gentle thump against my cheek as we held each other for a few more moments in the shadows. He pulled away and then kissed the back of my right hand.

"I have to go," he said with a note of regret, "but tomorrow everything will change."

I wished I could hold onto him for the rest of the night. "Sleep well, Midnight."

"Sleep well, Birdie," Derrick replied with a soft smile.

Derrick disappeared into the shadows but I lingered behind for a moment.

He said he loved me. I should have felt triumphant, but worry shredded my fledgling happiness.

Those three little words did not give me the crown. They did not make me Duchess. They did not save Ravenwood from poverty. Was his professed love a good sign? Of course, but I would not exhale until the marriage was sealed and I was dressed in Hyton Blue.

I had heard enough stories of tearful girls and angry fathers to know only one thing was certain—nothing was a guarantee on Selection Night.

I snuck back up to the Senior dormitory like a phantom, running my hands against the walls to guide my way in the darkness. I opened the dormitory door without so much as a creak and found everyone asleep. Brietta was passed out in my bed. I would not wake her after the day she had, especially since she did not have any linens on her own bed.

My eyes sleepily flitted from girl to girl, watching them sleep peacefully after the chaos I had left them in. A silent sigh escaped my lips. Being pitted against each other for the honor of being "First-selected," or even just the stress of being chosen by the right man, had brought out the worst in all of us. I had never seen everyone so hostile to each other—especially Annalisa.

I turned to Annalisa's bed and listened to her soft breath. Her blonde curls were splayed on her pillow and her cheeks were marked with dried tears. I could not help but pity the only Hyton daughter without a prince. She might have been mean, but she still deserved a man who did not step on her.

I quietly lit a candle and left the girls in peace. I crept downstairs to the sitting room to curl up on one of the plush couches. I placed a small decorative pillow under my head and hugged another one to my chest.

In the dark, all alone, I thought only about Derrick.

For once, I did not think about Derrick in terms of strategy, but instead as a *man*. I…liked him. I liked the sound of his voice, the feel of his hands, and the taste of his lips.

As soon as I imagined his lips on mine again, a seismic shift rocked my chest.

I furrowed my brow and squeezed the pillow tighter against my breast. Through the cracks in my granite heart, a tiny red ember danced, alive and flickering where everything was once cold. My belly was warm, my hands trembled, and all I could smell was oak and vanilla. I had always planned to make Derrick fall desperately in love with me, but I did not expect to feel *anything* for him.

I let out a breath and tossed the pillow to the floor before rolling over to my side. I folded my arms over my breasts and did not let my thumbs stroke the threads of the stars on my sleeves.

Whatever the red ember was, it was not love—not when I had sworn off that weakness long ago. What danced inside me with a low burn was just the temptation Fraleigh mentioned, the dirtiness of desire Headmistress Blackiston had warned us about, and what I was taught was only the body's response when a woman gets too close to a man.

The tiny ember continued to burn in my chest as I squeezed my eyes shut and shook my head in the darkness.

Nothing was a guarantee on Selection Night. Nothing.

Especially since we still did not know who the fifth suitor was.

Chapter Six
His Choice

The earliest rays of gentle dawn stretched through the tall windows of the sitting room. The day I married Derrick had finally arrived.

I successfully evaded matrons and guards as I crept up to the Senior dormitory. I silently pushed open the door and my stomach dropped when I met sharp ocean eyes. Annalisa sat up in her bed and faced the door with a hard scowl on her face.

"Where were you last night?" she hissed.

I bit my tongue and started spinning lies in my head before I answered. "Out in the garden. I needed to clear my head after meeting with Headmistress Blackiston."

Annalisa stalked out of her bed and stood in front of me with her arms crossed. "How odd. She *never* sends the guards up to the dormitories."

Damn it. Annalisa was mean, but she was not stupid.

"The guards came because the House of Hyton got involved." A little truth would throw her off.

Annalisa reached over and brushed my hair off my neck. "What happened here?"

I turned from her and grabbed my silver hand mirror from the dressing table nearby. I looked at my reflection and forced every muscle in my face still. The left side of my neck was covered in red marks, some of them clear impressions of teeth. Damn you, Derrick!

"I was stung by a bee," I lied.

"Really? What a special bee to sting you so many times."

"It only stung me once, Anna. I am just allergic to them, so I have a rash."

Annalisa grabbed my jaw. She firmly held my face in her sharp fingers as she examined my neck. I did not move out of fear she would suspect me more.

"That bee must have been quite a bother," she replied. "I have been dealing with that issue my entire life. Luckily for you, I can help."

She let go of my face and silently walked to her corner of the dormitory. She picked up a few pots of paint and a brush out of her box of art supplies. My eyes darted to the other girls, who were still sound asleep, as Annalisa walked back to me.

Annalisa and I stared at each other in silence for a heartbeat. Annalisa and Derrick had identical blue eyes, but you could leisurely swim in Derrick's and drown in Annalisa's.

Her deadly eyes flicked down to her paints. She dipped her brush into a pot of pale green and patted the cold paint onto my neck. She blew on the thin layer of wet paint before mixing pink, yellow, and white on the back of her hand until she created a color that matched our skin. She brushed the flesh-colored paint on top of the green and then put her brush down.

"Just try not to sweat too much and you should be fine," Annalisa said quietly. She gently brushed my hair back over my neck and said nothing more.

I half-expected the paint to burn my skin or force me to break out into a *real* rash, but the cover remained firm. Sheets stirred and the rest of the girls yawned and stretched out of their beds before I could wonder why cruel Annalisa had bothered to help me.

After preparing for the day, the five brides went downstairs wearing flowing linen dresses. We ate a hearty breakfast in the Great Hall, boarded a golden House of Hyton carriage, and headed to the palace.

Annalisa stayed sullen and silent as we rode through the streets of Hyton while Dinah and Camille twittered with excitement. I kept out of their chatter and held Brietta's hand as her face turned from white to green during the ride. Right as I feared Brietta would lose her breakfast, the carriage stopped.

The sprawling Hyton Palace had multiple towers reaching to the sky like they competed with each other to be the tallest. The palace overlooked the Western Sea on the edge of a steep cliffside that separated it from the rest of the city. Banners of Hyton Blue streamed proudly down the stone walls, each bearing the House emblem of a rearing black bull with golden horns and hooves.

A sea of servants in blue coats and dresses trickled out of the palace doors to greet us. We were whisked inside in a flash of blue fabric and smiling faces. Our footsteps clicked softly on the polished stone floors as the servants led us into the first preparation room.

Five maids, including Merri, waited to attend us in the small room with multiple doors and opulent portraits of maidens from centuries past.

"Merri!" Annalisa cried—her first sign of happiness in days. She ran to Merri and threw her arms around her.

Merri smiled and patted Annalisa's curls as she held her. "I've missed you, Lady Hyton."

"I am so glad you are preparing me today," Annalisa said with a wide smile.

"Actually," Merri replied in a strained, but still cheerful voice, "your father instructed me to prepare Miss Elvar today."

"What?" Annalisa snapped. "Brietta?"

I gritted my teeth behind my lips. There was the Annalisa I expected.

Merri let go of a bewildered Annalisa and walked to Brietta. Merri gently patted Brietta's large hands. "Forget about yesterday. We took care of everything."

Merri took Brietta through a door to tend to her. Meanwhile, Annalisa threw a small fit when she paired with a maid who was *not* her favorite. I paired with a stout, older woman and she took me through a different door than the one Brietta went through.

In the tiny wood-paneled room filled with bouquets of white flowers was a porcelain tub filled with steaming water. I undressed and slipped in the tub, careful to not let the water touch my neck. Normally I was terrified of water, especially if I was in a tub big enough to feel the floating sensation, but I forced myself to not panic.

The maid scrubbed me from my collarbone to my toes. She sprinkled red rose petals in the water that floated around in the swirling bath, gently caressing my collarbone and the tops of my breasts. I played with one of the petals and hung my head back over the edge of the tub as the maid washed and combed my hair in a separate bowl of water.

Wisps of fear fluttered around my chest as I tried to relax. Yes, Derrick had professed his love for me. Yes, he was choosing a bride first. Yes, he said he would choose me. No matter how many times I heard my imaginary Derrick say "yes" in my head, my pragmatic brain could not stop repeating that nothing was a guarantee on Selection Night.

I hugged my knees in the bathwater. I needed to stop being so cynical and have faith in my plan. I put in the work, I wrote the letters and told the lies, and it was all about to pay off.

The maid worked an oil in my hair that smelled like wildflowers. As I stepped out of the tub, she applied the oil to the rest of my body. I smelled like I had stepped out of a faerie story. Once the maid finished fussing over my too-thin calves, I slipped my linen undergarments over my silken skin and entered the main dressing room.

The large dressing room had multiple dressing tables and plush pink and blue loungers. The furnishings were worn from use, a reminder of decades of brides before us. At first I thought the room was huge, but then I realized it was just an illusion from the wall of mirrors that stretched end-to-end on the other side of the room.

I looked at my own reflection in the wall of mirrors as I stood in the doorway. My face and chest were pleasantly flush from the hot water of the bath, my skin was luminous, and my dark hair had formed shining waves that fell down my back. I was almost beautiful.

I pried my eyes away from my reflection and searched for the most important garment of my life to complete the picture of beauty that Derrick would see.

I scanned the room—finding dark blue, light blue, and pink dresses on mannequins—until my eyes stopped on the smallest dress that had to be mine.

The velvet dress was the beautiful dark green of the House of Ravenwood with long sleeves and a train. Gold ribbon with pearls sewn in wrapped around the wrists and the tightly cinched waist. The neckline would slice across my shoulders and end at a point above my heart. The green skirt split down the middle, revealing an underskirt made of rich black satin.

Just when I thought the outfit could not get more luxurious, I looked down and found a pair of white gloves, a pair of matching green slippers with a high block heel, and—to my extreme relief—a thick black choker adorned with more pearls.

I touched a velvet sleeve and guilt robbed me of the joy of luxury. Father had used the last of our wealth buying food staples to keep the peasants of Ravenwood from starving. I did not want to know what he had to sell to buy my Presentation dress.

Not wanting to give the finances of my dress more thought, I sat down at one of the dressing tables to let the maid comb and braid my hair as the other girls filtered into the room. Dinah and Camille were still all chatter, but Annalisa and Brietta were silent as their maids styled their hair.

Most of my hair fell loose, but my maid braided a thin band over the crown of my head to attach the family diadem to. The golden diadem was in the shape of a raven and its wings stretched down my temples to my ears. The Ravenwood diadem was one of the few family jewels Mother did not sell.

I caught the reflection of me wearing the diadem in a mirror—I was the last remnant of Ravenwood dignity.

I walked over to the mirror wall and inspected every detail of my body. My hair was shining and the Ravenwood diadem gleamed in the sunlight from the windows. My face was clean, but the flush from the hot bath had disappeared. Mother had sent her own wax and berry mixture, so I opened the familiar round pot and applied the scarlet balm to my cheeks and lips. I licked my lips and tasted the faint sweetness of the berries—perfection.

Annalisa was a few mirrors down, hastily applying her own makeup. She smeared red pigment to her cheeks and lips so heavily she looked like she had just finished running for her life. She used brown wax to define her eyebrows, line her eyes, and darken her eyelashes. Her blonde curls were swept up on her head and held by a sparkling diamond tiara. Between the jewels and her painted face, Annalisa would have no trouble being noticed.

Brietta stood in her undergarments and watched my maid help me into my dress. She wrung her hands faster as the seconds ticked by, so Merri tried to reassure her. "Don't worry, Miss Elvar. Your dress should be on its way."

Annalisa fussed as her maid laced up her deep blue dress with a flowing skirt. "I hope my father does not step on my skirt when he escorts me. He always hits the spirits before the Presentation and we all know how clumsy he gets."

"Actually," Merri said with a wince, "His Excellency will escort Miss Elvar today."

Annalisa's nostrils flared and her painted cheeks turned even more scarlet. "What?"

"Lady Hyton, you see," Merri said, clearly choosing her words carefully. "His Excellency said since Miss Elvar's father could not be here due to the, uh, short notice of her graduation, he did not want her escort to be a man she had never met. Good news, though! Your uncle, Baron Amberfield, will escort you! I know how much you like him!"

"Uncle Thorin?" Annalisa roared. "He chews grass like a cow!"

I kept my head down and used all my willpower not to roll my eyes. Only a few more hours before Selection Night began and I would get a reprieve from Annalisa's bad attitude.

Before Merri could calm the dragon in the Hyton Blue dress, someone knocked gently on the door. Annalisa's maid, happy to escape the proximity of the Duke's fuming daughter, rushed to the door. On the other side were a pair of sweating maids who held a large bundle of silvery fabric between them.

Merri sighed with relief and quickly beckoned the maids over to Brietta. In a flash, they began to dress her in the silver fabric.

"What is this?" Brietta asked as she stepped into the skirt of the dress.

"It is an old dress that belonged to...a former Duchess," Merri said, tying the skirt tightly around Brietta's waist. "She was also, uh, a woman of significant stature."

She tried to be subtle, but I knew exactly who she alluded to. Duchess Ilsa was rumored to be a half-giant since she came from the most northern part of Ravenwood. She had white hair, violet eyes, and skin so pale she looked as if she were chiseled from ice and brought to life with magic. All of Lycaster had called her the Diamond of the North.

Ilsa's shimmering gown was at best a bad omen and at worst a warning of what would come. Dinah and Camille's eyes were wide in fear as Brietta dressed in the clothing of the murdering sorceress, but Annalisa was incensed.

"How dare you break into the vault for her?" Annalisa spat, close to breathing fire and incinerating us all. "That was *her* Presentation dress. No one else should even touch it!"

Even though it was tainted by a dark history, Ilsa's stunning gown was absolutely fit for a Duchess—a timeless square neck paired with swirls of white embroidery decorating the bodice. The silvery blue fabric moved with the light of the room and complemented Brietta's auburn hair and brown eyes spectacularly.

The maids slipped Brietta's arms through the sleeves of the bodice and Merri went around to fasten it closed. The bodice did not fasten with laces or clasps like the rest of our gowns, but instead had a column of twelve silver buttons on the back of the dress. Merri tried to bring the two sides of the bodice together at Brietta's back, but Brietta's breasts were so large that the dress would not fasten.

"Hold your breath, Miss Elvar," Merri grunted, tugging at the sides of the bodice with all her might but failing to join them. Brietta's eyes welled up with tears as she sucked in her chest and made herself as small as she could.

No. No more tears. I walked over to look at the back of the dress myself. The two sides of the bodice were nearly a forearm's length apart. I eyed the buttons and had an idea.

"Take the buttons off," I said to Merri. "We can thread laces through the button holes."

"No!" Annalisa roared as she stormed over to us. "You will *not* destroy my grandmother's dress!"

"Anna," I hissed in a low voice so Brietta could not hear, "this is the only way the dress will fasten and we have no time to find another—"

"Of course the dress is not going to fasten!" Annalisa shouted. "None of the Hyton dresses would ever fit Brietta's huge body!"

I gritted my teeth even harder as Brietta started to sob.

Annalisa's wrathful eyes turned to Brietta. "It does not matter how much money your family has, or how good you think your poetry is, you do not belong in the Selection Night that *we earned!*"

Annalisa yanked at the shimmering blue bodice. Rage crashed behind my eyes like lightning and lit up my hands like fire.

"Get out!" Annalisa screamed. "You presumptuous, annoying, half-gia—!"

Slap.

Annalisa fell to the ground. Everyone gasped. No one moved, not even me, with my right arm still raised after making contact with Annalisa's cheek.

"Brietta is *not* a half-giant." My words were pointed as knives and my eyes burned. "And she does belong here. You will never, *ever* speak to her that way again."

Annalisa's maid helped her up. Annalisa did not answer me, or even look in my direction as she slowly rose from the floor. Neither Camille nor Dinah offered Annalisa any help. Annalisa could not influence Derrick through her letters any longer, so their friendship had apparently dissolved.

All the power in the room lay with the future Duchess, who was certainly not the brat being scraped off the floor by obliging maids.

My white glove was stained red from the paint on Annalisa's cheek. Shit! Oh well, no time to fix it. I tossed both gloves aside before pointing to Camille and Dinah. "Help me take off these buttons."

I directed Merri to get me a needle, thread, and scissors. Brietta stood still but quietly choked on her sobs. I ran around to her and reached up, taking her face into my hands. "I will fix this, but you have to stop crying."

"All…all right," Brietta said, wiping tears from her eyes with the back of her hand.

I patted her cheeks and went around to the back of the dress. I whispered an apology to the spirit of the Diamond of the North and tore the first silver button off, leaving a small hole in its place. Camille, Dinah, and I all ripped off the rest of the buttons in a flurry of hands.

We needed to make a lace and a back-panel, but nowhere to get extra fabric.

Soon, Merri re-appeared with the sewing supplies. I ordered her to cut off the train of my dress along with a portion of my black underskirt. She asked if I was sure I wanted to mutilate my own dress, and I assured her I was. She knelt down and cut the train off and then disappeared under the green overskirt to cut off a piece of black fabric.

The maids quickly cut and tore the fabric from the train of my dress into tiny strips and braided them into a long lace. I threaded the lace through the twelve buttonholes on either side of the dress and pulled it tight.

"It fits, Brie!" I cried. I slid the black fabric behind the laces, covering up Brietta's skin and chemise. "Now just hold still."

My fingers quickly sewed the black panel securely into the dress. I stepped back to inspect the work, but I was not satisfied. The black and dark green securing the back of the bodice looked out of place amongst the rest of the silvery blue dress. I tied pretty ribbons of green fabric above her elbows and around her waist to try to help with the clashing colors. The extra dark green helped with the balance, but the outfit still needed more black.

I reached up to take my black choker off, but I stopped. I knew my cover-up had worn off underneath the choker. All of the Barons of Lycaster were outside for the Presentation and none of them would believe I was stung by a bee.

But I had a man who said he loved me waiting for me. I did not need to look perfect to marry the man I needed. Brietta, though, needed a fighting chance at the Presentation. She deserved to look like she belonged with the rest of us.

I untied my choker and handed it to Brietta. "This will make it perfect."

Brietta lowered herself to my eye level and I tied the choker around her neck. Merri placed an emerald tiara on Brietta's head before she rose to her full height.

Brietta gave me a thankful hug, careful not to mash my face into her chest, and we turned to the mirrors to admire our work. The emerald tiara coordinated with the green ribbons on the dress and my black choker was the perfect final touch. The hem of Ilsa's gown only made it to Brietta's ankles, but her breasts were bursting out of the top of her tight bodice so much that none of the suitors would notice her feet.

I was underdressed and small while standing next to Brietta in all her silver splendor. My elegant train was gone, my neck was covered in red marks, my hands were bare, and other than the pearls sewn into my dress and my old family diadem, I did not have any jewelry. I was the perfect embodiment of the House of Ravenwood—torn, bruised, and stripped of riches.

"How can I ever repay you, Sera?" Brietta asked in awe as she looked at herself.

I could not help but smile, even as ragged as I looked. "Just remember me after you marry your handsome suitor, okay?"

As soon as the words left my lips, it was time for the Presentation. Father waited for me in the hall outside the ballroom where the Presentation would take place. The hardship of leading Ravenwood through poverty had worn on him—his hair was fully silver and his face crinkled with deep lines as he smiled when he saw me.

Father's arms twitched like he wanted to hug me, but his warmth was contained to his voice. "You look so beautiful, Serafina."

Either Father was a man who truly did not notice details like Headmistress Blackiston said or being an excellent liar was a Ravenwood family trait.

"I cannot believe you ordered this dress," I said, hoping he would not notice the alterations I made. "How did you afford it?"

Father's eyes twinkled. "Miss Elvar's father sold me the pearls at a discount. Worth every last coin we had. My future Duchess needed to shine, after all."

Trumpets blared inside the ballroom and my body went numb. My vision turned fuzzy and I held onto Father's arm to keep my balance.

The Presentation began exactly like the Suitors' Ball. Annalisa, escorted by old and balding Baron Amberfield, entered the ballroom first and promenaded in front of the suitors. Then Brietta entered with Duke Hyton, who was too drunk to notice she wore his mother's gown.

Camille left with her father. Dinah and her father followed.

I stared at another pair of wooden doors. My heart pounding in my ears drowned out the sound of my announcement and I startled myself as the doors swung open.

I tried to will myself into calmness as I walked into the ballroom. My skirt's ragged hem glided along the polished tile floor as the eyes of nearly every noble man and woman in Lycaster examined me. My heart drummed even harder, my palms were sticky with sweat, and my head spun amongst all the colorful clothes, hissing whispers, and strong perfumes.

The world slowed down as soon as I found Derrick. He stood amongst the audience of suitors, wearing a coronet of gold that marked him as the heir on top of his shining dark curls. His brilliant Hyton Blue cape draped across his broad shoulders and he carried a bejeweled sword on his hip. His regal outfit and strong stance announced loud and clear that the heir of the House of Hyton was ready to take his bride.

I loosened my grip on Father's arm as I found my footing again. I could have looked into those beautiful blue eyes forever. Derrick smiled at me and I dared to let myself smile back.

Before Father and I exited the ballroom, I noticed a tower of blue that was not Derrick amongst the suitors—General Hyton.

Before I could investigate any further, the ballroom doors creaked shut.

We waited inside a small sitting room under the agonizing ticking clock as the suitors made their bride selections.

Father and I sat on a velvet couch as I caught up with my breath. I dared to glance at Annalisa, who sat alone and looked at her shoes while Baron Amberfield chatted with Dinah's father. The two men talked of the promising harvest in the Middle provinces and ignored glassy-eyed Annalisa.

Her own father did not pay her any attention, either. Duke Hyton still had Brietta on his arm and offered her drinks from his flask to calm her nerves. Brietta politely declined until Duke Hyton finally shrugged and tipped the flask into his mouth.

Even though I had imagined the worst-case scenario each time I worried about the Presentation, I never thought it would be so…unpleasant. Nothing seemed right or fair, but when had *anything* in my life been fair?

Still, just because life was unfair did not mean we all had to be miserable. Just as I was about to get up to extend an olive branch to Annalisa, my ears burned as Dinah and Camille whispered to each other.

"How many suitors did you count?" Dinah asked Camille. "I only saw four!"

"Same here," Camille whispered. "The same four from the Suitors' Ball!"

"Who is the fifth suitor?" Dinah hissed. "There has to be a fifth suitor!"

"Did you see your mother in there?" Father said, breaking my attention away from Dinah and Camille. "She was tearing up."

"No," I replied. I ran my sweating palms along the velvet seat. "I was distracted."

"Of course," Father said with a small smile as his voice hitched. Father looked at the wallpaper and then back down at me with tears welling up in his brown eyes. "You know, you used to be my Little Ember. You had fire in your sun-spotted eyes and a vibrant spirit…but when your brothers died, you went cold and it was like I lost you too."

My chest shuddered as I started to crumble. I closed my eyes to shut out tears, but I could not shut out Father's shaking voice. "But just now, when you looked at Lord Hyton, I saw your fire return. Erik and Endre would be so proud of you."

Memories of my brothers slipped out from behind my stone walls. I pictured Erik's eternally serious face and Endre's mirthful smile. The tip of my nose burned like I was about to cry for the first time in years, but a banging noise shocked me out of my sorrow.

One knock. Two knocks. Three knocks.

The selections were complete. He had made his choice.

Chapter Seven
The Blood Bond

The world spun as soon as the final knock reached my ears.

I held onto Father's hand to keep my balance as he led me back into the ballroom for the reading of the names.

We waited with the other brides and their escorts in front of the audience of nobility. The suitors had all left the ballroom to make their choices, but all the other nobles examined us.

I was no more than a butterfly with my wings pinned to a board.

Seven gorgeous women all dressed in rich, colorful gowns and adorned with more gems than I had ever seen whispered to each other off to the side. The women had hair from blonde, to brown, to black, but their identical blue eyes were all on Annalisa. They could be no one else but the women of the House of Hyton. Derrick's six elder sisters had returned to Lycaster and stood around their mother, Duchess Freya Hyton.

Duchess Hyton was classically beautiful just like Annalisa—blonde curly hair, heart-shaped face and lips, and stunning blue eyes with long and heavy eyelashes. I looked from the elegant Duchess to the ragged hem of my skirt and choked on my own insignificance.

Before I could let myself drown any more, my eyes found Mother's in the crowd. She was easy to spot with her dark hair and dark green dress amongst a rainbow of bright colors. A confident smile spread across her painted lips.

I kept my eyes locked on hers and nodded, silently assuring her that I did my best. I charmed him. Everything that I could control, I did.

I just hoped it would be enough.

"I remember when I saw your mother at her Presentation," Father whispered as he stroked the sleeve of my gown. "Light-colored dresses were the fashion back then. A few girls paraded out in pastel frocks but then your mother entered the ballroom wearing a dress in the darkest purple you could imagine—oh, how her green eyes sparkled. Good thing I had the first selection as a Baron's heir, otherwise I would have caused some damage to any suitor who dared speak her name during the selection."

"Do the suitors really fight back there?" I asked softly, keeping my eye on a door on the other side of the room.

"No," Father chuckled. "No one can interfere once the bride's name is said aloud and claimed. You may want to kill the bastard who stole your dream girl, but you have to keep your mouth shut with Fraleigh there."

A man in a blue tunic appeared out of the door on the other side of the ballroom. He held up a paper list with a flourish. The low chatter of the room hushed as soon as the candlelight illuminated the list that spelled out both the fate of each bride and of Lycaster's lineage. The first name read was the next Duchess of Lycaster.

"The selection is complete!" the announcer boomed in a grand voice. Trumpets blared. Women clapped and cheered. Men whistled and stomped their feet.

My heart crashed into my ribs. I wrung my hands that were slick with sweat and held my breath.

"First selected, Serafina Helia Ravenwood!"

I let out my breath. Father squeezed my hand in triumph. The audience cheered and I finally let myself smile.

I did it. I really pulled it off.

My eyes raised toward the sound of approaching footsteps and my stomach plummeted. Instead of Derrick, someone else had entered the ballroom to claim me.

General Hyton.

The audience murmured. My eyes darted from the approaching General to Brietta. Her brown eyes were wide with panic.

Father gripped me closer to him and glared at the General in front of us. "What are you doing here?"

Before the General could answer, the announcer shouted: "Second selected, Brietta Alyce Elvar!"

Derrick appeared through the door and the audience dropped their scandalized whispers and erupted into cheers. The crowd chanted the Hyton name, but Derrick's face bore no trace of celebration. Those beautiful blue eyes rimmed with red did not look in my direction once, but instead fixed on Brietta as he walked toward her. His jeweled sword was missing.

No. None of it could be real, my mind was just playing tricks on me again.

Brietta glanced at me with tears shining in her eyes and I could no longer deny what was happening. My heart fell through my body and crashed through the ballroom floor as the Duke proudly handed Brietta over to his son. Derrick glared at his father, but took Brietta away without saying a word.

I gritted my teeth and pulled my heart back up by its frayed strings. I should have been smarter than to get my hopes up, but Derrick's soft lips and wandering hands had melted my mind and turned me into a fool. The House of Hyton would have never let a Ravenwood be Duchess again—not when Ilsa Ravenwood had nearly destroyed them.

I clenched my fists so tightly my fingernails drew blood from my palms.

General Hyton's voice was a gentle rumble amongst the cheering crowd of nobles. "Do not worry, Miss Ravenwood, I am not a suitor—just a representative for the real one."

General Hyton offered his arm, but Father did not release me. He gripped my arm like a vise as he refused to let his last living child go.

He stared General Hyton down and his voice was low. "I do not care what you are, Ragnar, you will *not* take my daughter too."

"Suit yourself, Frederick," General Hyton said with a wry smile. General Hyton turned and walked out of the ballroom through the same door Derrick had left through.

Father still held onto me tightly, but I swallowed in fear. Who was the General a representative for? Why would he not show his face? And why did he get to choose first?

During the tension, Myles selected Dinah and Gerond selected Camille. The room muttered with scandal as soon as Camille's name was read aloud, making the Duke's own daughter "Last-selected." Annalisa straightened her back and tried to keep a proud face, even though shame hung around her like a raincloud.

Grigory Thornebow strode into the ballroom to collect the Duke's daughter as if she were a prize instead of last-picking. Annalisa obligingly accepted his arm with a defeated look in her eyes.

Some clapped politely for the Last-selected, but most whispered to each other with their eyes filled with scandal and salacious gossip on their lips. A Thornebow was going to wed a Hyton. Either the marriage would end in disaster like the ill-fated relationship between Baron Thornebow and Ilsa or it was the beginning of mending relations between the two Houses after the traitorous conspiracy.

The rest of the Hytons clearly did not want to use the marriage to build a bridge. Duke Hyton's six other daughters took one look at Grigory's grey cape and could not hide the shock and disgust on their faces. They did not cheer at all.

As soon as the door shut behind Grigory and Annalisa, Father and I stood in the center of the ballroom and all eyes were on us. The audience murmured like clucking birds. The fifth suitor had chosen me, and if he was not General Hyton, the rest of the nobility made their guesses on who he was.

The door opened again, and just as I expected to see the mysterious fifth suitor, two palace guards cautiously walked in.

"Miss Ravenwood," one of the guards said in a shaky voice, "the Great Sorceress of Nordingaard requests your audience."

The murmurs of the audience erupted into frightened gossip. Father squeezed my arm as we carefully followed the palace guards out of the ballroom. Father was brave enough to disobey the general of His Excellency's army, but not Fraleigh.

"Stay close to me, Serafina," he whispered.

We walked through the door together and followed the guards down a long hallway. The guards turned and opened a door leading to the outside of the palace.

Father stepped into the night first, hiding me behind him as much as he could. All I could see over my father's back and shoulders was the full moon amongst the stars. Father stepped out onto the stone patio and froze, gripping my hand with all his strength. I stepped around him. Flickering torchlight cast shadows on my father's stiff jaw and harrowed eyes that looked up and not forward. I followed his eyes as I turned my head.

Where I should have seen the face of the fifth suitor, I instead saw an enormous chest dressed in a military uniform and bathed in pulsing shadows. I held my breath as my eyes moved up higher, seeing wide shoulders draped in a crimson cape that flowed down like blood, a muscular neck as thick as my thigh, and a strong, square jaw. I had to tilt my head all the way back to see his face—strong brow and nose, light hair, and blue-grey eyes that looked down on me with an intensity that sent a chill up my spine.

The Beast was the fifth suitor.

My hands trembled but my throat stayed frozen. If I had any bravery at all, I would have forced the word out of my mouth and into the night as loudly as I could—no.

No, it was a mistake. No, Derrick was supposed to choose me. No, I could not marry a half-giant.

I screamed "no," in my head over and over, but Father's voice was dangerously quiet. "This *monster* will not have my daughter."

The Beast did not take his eyes off me. Grigory had said he was nine feet tall, but he was so huge he could have even been ten feet. My heart pounded like it was trying to escape, but I could not stop staring at the Beast, trying to find any clue on his stony face of why he had chosen me. I did not even notice Duke Hyton was with us until he spoke up.

"Frederick," Duke Hyton's tongue was thick, but his voice low and tense, "you put your daughter into Selection Night knowing you had no say in who selects her."

"You say as if I had a choice, as if *any* of us have a choice," Father said, his grip on me growing tighter and his voice growing louder. "You force us to sell off our daughters."

Duke Hyton quirked his chin up. "This is how it has always been. You certainly did not complain when *you* got to pick first."

Father ignored him and looked up at the Beast again. "You could have had any bride and you chose the smallest one, you cruel fucking bastard!"

The Beast finally took his eyes off me and glared at Father. I wanted to speak out, argue, or fight, but whatever I could say froze in my throat.

"He selected her!" Duke Hyton roared. "Let her go, Frederick!"

Father jerked me into his chest and wrapped his arms tightly around me. His chest shook with outrage against my back. "Never! Damn you, Anders, what else will you take away from me? You took my boys, my home, my…"

His voice broke, but he found strength I had never seen him show. "…but you will *not* take Serafina!"

Duke Hyton gave his guards a pointed look and they approached us to seize Father. Father let go of me and ran toward the first guard. He punched the guard in the jaw with a crack and sent him to the ground.

I gasped and clutched my arms as my father turned his gentle hands into weapons. I should have grabbed him by the cape and pulled him back, but I was too scared to move.

Father's eyes blazed with animalistic fury as he turned to Duke Hyton. His knuckles were white as he held onto seven years of sorrow and outrage, but each fist was about to satisfy his vengeance for the two lives Duke Hyton had stolen.

"No one else should suffer as I have!" Father shouted. He charged toward Duke Hyton. "Your reign must end!"

General Hyton drew his sword, but did not step forward. More soldiers ran from the palace and they outnumbered and overpowered Father before he could take another step toward the Duke. My chest shook with a dry sob as the guards forced Father to the ground.

"Take him away!" Duke Hyton spat. "Baron Ravenwood is charged with high treason!"

High treason. A sure death sentence.

My stomach fell through my body. The torchlight and moonlight swirled around me until I fell to my knees. I squeezed my eyes shut. My face hit the rough stone pavement. My breath escaped my chest in sharp, jagged heaves.

My mouth watered, and just as I thought I was about to be sick, a pair of strong hands wrapped around my arms.

"Miss Ravenwood," General Hyton said gently. "Miss Ravenwood, please rise."

My body trembled as I gasped into the stone. No tears fell from my eyes. No words came from my mouth. My muscles would not move. I would die on the stone. I would rather face the axe than the wrath of a beast's heart.

The tiny Serafina in my mind who had screamed "no" until she was blue in the face cried out for help one last time, and an unexpected voice answered.

"Rise, Serafina."

The blood in my veins ran cold and my muscles shook and bent until I rose to my feet. Fraleigh had entered my mind and enchanted me to stand. My chest calmed and my stomach eased. I looked up into Fraleigh's golden eyes as serenity washed over me.

Fraleigh was dressed in splendid black and white robes and a bejeweled gold circlet adorned her head. She had gold rings on each finger, two jeweled collars on either side of the main golden collar on her neck, and a long belt made of a gold chain around her waist. Fraleigh could wear the most precious, purest gold in the Dukedom, but no metal could compare to the intense golden heat in her eyes.

I see you, Serafina Ravenwood.

"Serafina Helia Ravenwood," Fraleigh said in a low imperium. "First-selected. You will join us for the marriage ceremony."

Fraleigh's lips did not move, but I heard her voice again in the back of my mind.

You will not die here, Serafina.

A wave of calm rolled from my head to my toes. I slowly blinked, still not taking my eyes off the sorceress. Serenity floated in my head like a cloud as I nodded to Fraleigh. She nodded back and then turned to walk down the gravel path into the Duke's garden.

General Hyton still held on to me in case I fell again. The tiny Serafina in my head danced around with loose limbs like she was drunk, singing words of reassurance over and over.

He did not need to hold me, I was fine. Everything was just fine. Just fine. Just fine.

I gently patted General Hyton's hands and he released me. My feet were firmly on the ground, but my spirit levitated in the night air.

Just fine. Just fine.

General Hyton cleared his throat and brought me back down to earth. He gestured up to the Beast. "Miss Ravenwood, may I formally introduce you to Sir Bloodstone, the Hero of Lycaster."

Hmm, Bloodstone. I should have recognized the crimson cape. Despite being our neighbors in the Northern provinces, the mysterious Bloodstones had not communicated with us at all since the crushing defeat against the giants seven years ago. They lived in a secluded fortress on Nordingaard mountain, hiding generations of secrets.

The half-giant was their best-kept one.

I examined the half-giant giant slayer who chose me. His hair was the color of honey and cut short like all military cadets. The Bloodstones were known for their grey eyes, but Sir Bloodstone's eyes were more blue than grey.

Just fine. Everything was just fine.

Sir Bloodstone leaned down and extended a hand the size of a dinner plate. I calmly placed my hand in his calloused palm. His fingers curled over mine and completely enveloped my hand. His arm, which was almost the length of my entire body, was fully extended down to hold my hand. The top of my head only came up to the height of his hip as I stood next to him.

I was half his size. Half.

Good thing I was *just fine.*

After a few careful steps down the patio stairs, he led me through the Duke's garden. The crunch of pebbles on the garden path beneath each of Sir Bloodstone's massive footsteps was all that disturbed the evening air as we walked into a maze of tall hedges. We turned left and right through dizzying walls of foliage as I tried to think of an escape, but Fraleigh's waning enchantment had put all my cunning to sleep.

Just fine. Just—

No, I was not fine. The serene fog in my mind was fading, revealing the heightened panic underneath. I glanced at Sir Bloodstone's hand gripping mine and quickly looked away. The green hedges of the maze seemed to grow taller and taller.

Suddenly, the maze opened up to reveal a large stone pavilion covered in lichen.

Beyond the pavilion was the steep drop off the cliffside. We looked out over the Western Sea to the left and the river flowing out of Odeneye lake to the right.

Even if Sir Bloodstone released me, I had nowhere to escape. I was trapped. Completely powerless. Frozen.

Inside the pavilion stood Fraleigh, Duke Hyton, and the four other pairs. Sir Bloodstone released my hand and stooped as low as he could to duck under the stone roof of the pavilion. Once inside, he kneeled next to the others who stood in a half-circle. Even on his knees, he was still taller than all the other suitors.

Derrick stood next to Brietta at the opposite end of the line. He looked at me with shining bloodshot eyes and my heart ached. If I had a choice, I would have run to him and begged him to fix what was about to happen.

But I never had a choice. No noble woman in Lycaster had a choice for hundreds of years.

Sir Bloodstone extended his hand to help me up the pavilion steps. I gulped—I had nowhere to go but forward. I reluctantly wrapped my hand around his thumb and climbed the steps to stand at his right side.

Fraleigh turned to Duke Hyton and lowered herself into a graceful bow. Her black and white robes rippled as she dipped so low the tip of her nose touched the stone floor. Duke Hyton barely regarded her as he wobbled from drunkenness. Fraleigh turned back to us.

"Midnight approaches!" Fraleigh said in a cool yet commanding voice. She produced a glass vial from her robe that contained glittering water. Duke Hyton handed her an old silver chalice. With a flourish, Fraleigh poured the water into the chalice. She held the chalice out in front of her, fixing her eyes on the ancient cup, and spoke:

"He triumphed over trials, his bride is won,
Day has died and a new era begun,
This night two hearts will transform into one,
When his heart stops beating, her life is done,"

The water in the chalice glowed white. Fraleigh continued the enchantment, speaking louder and with more deliberation.

"Give them virility, give them their health,
Give them their legacy, give them their wealth,"

Fraleigh walked to Derrick and offered the cup from her hands, the water inside still glowing white. Derrick refused and I let in a hopeful breath.

The hope was fleeting. Under his father's wrathful glare, Derrick finally accepted a drink. He winced as the drink passed his lips. Brietta was next, her eyes widening as she took the drink.

Fraleigh went to each couple, each person obediently drinking from the chalice and then grimacing afterward. Sir Bloodstone took a small drink, the chalice looking tiny compared to his large lips, but he did not flinch.

Fraleigh offered me the last of the glowing water. I placed my lips on the silver and Fraleigh tipped the contents into my mouth. The water burned all the way down my throat and into my stomach.

Fraleigh returned to the center of the pavilion while Duke Hyton commanded the men to hold out their right palms and the women their left. We all obeyed and Duke Hyton took a small knife from a sheath on his belt. He quickly cut a small gash in the palms of each couple and joined their hands.

He clumsily sliced Sir Bloodstones' palm and blood that nearly gleamed in the low light rushed down his hand. Even though the cut was longer than one of my fingers, Sir Bloodstone did not flinch. Duke Hyton jerked his knife over my hand but left an almost dainty cut with only a few beads of blood rising to the surface of my skin. It barely even hurt.

He smashed my hand on top of Sir Bloodstone's open palm, leaving a cloud of spirits from his breath as he walked away.

Fraleigh's voice boomed as she finished the spell.

"Man of the Mountain, hear my own command!
Bind these hearts by the torn flesh of their hand!"

My stomach burned with the intensity of the sun and I nearly doubled over from the pain. Sir Bloodstone held my hand so tightly the strength of his grip nearly crushed my fingers. The pain like needles crawled through my veins from my chest, then my arms, then my left hand. The others cried out as the enchantment ravaged their bodies.

The bond blazed and I let out a gasp of pain. I fell to my knees again and hung from Sir Bloodstone's arm, unable to break free from his grip. My heart raced as it burned, beating so quickly I was sure it was going to explode.

I glanced up at Sir Bloodstone. Even though he was still kneeling and he was surrounded by nine suffering people, his face showed no grimace, no tears, nothing.

Grigory's words came back to taunt me. *He has a beast's heart. He cannot feel or love, he can only destroy.*

A beast's heart—the same heart I was binding to as I suffered under Fraleigh's enchantment. Golden fire raged through my entire body until it was white-hot underneath my skin.

My entire body, even my thoughts, were nothing but pain. I thought of Father being led to the execution scaffold, Mother slipping away once his blood wet the chopping block, giants tearing through my brothers as they screamed, homes in Ravenwood crumbling and skeletal bodies grappling at empty bellies, and facing everything without Derrick's arms around me.

My body could not take the pain any longer. I was going to die.

Just as I slipped into unconsciousness, the pain stopped. I gasped from the instant relief. My sweating face was plastered on the smooth and mossy floor of the pavilion. I had somehow escaped Sir Bloodstone's grip as both my palms were pressed against the stone. I raised myself up and I noticed my left arm was soaked with crimson from Sir Bloodstone's cut hand.

All the others were also gasping and slowly rising from the floor except Sir Bloodstone, who remained still and stoic. I looked up—a hole in the roof of the pavilion revealed a full moon high in the sky. Midnight.

"This stage of the binding enchantment is complete," Fraleigh said. "You should feel the effects of the spell presently. However, you must consummate your union before midnight of the next full moon, or else the enchantment fails and your marriage is annulled."

Consummate the union. I looked over at Sir Bloodstone, who had left the pavilion already and offered his non-bloodied hand to help me down the steps. Sir Bloodstone was twice my height and twice as broad as me. None of the intimacy lessons at Ashmore had prepared me for a body like his.

Grigory had made a point to warn me about Sir Bloodstone. He had to have a reason. Maybe Sir Bloodstone knew me because of my family and had told Grigory he wanted me. Maybe Grigory wanted to give me a fighting chance.

My chest tightened as I looked at Sir Bloodstone's outstretched arm. The half-giant could have planned to ravage me or even eat me. My mind raced as I thought of how I would survive the night when a calm voice echoed in the back of my mind.

You are manipulative and an excellent liar.

Fraleigh's words played like a triumphant song in my head. She was right, I was not a satisfactory bride. I was a Ravenwood. I was a survivor.

Sir Bloodstone may have been a killer, but I would outplay him, outsmart him, and come out of the next twenty-eight days unbroken.

My shoulders were heavy and my chest was weak, but I used my last bit of strength to grab Sir Bloodstone's hand.

My salvation would not come from Derrick. I had to keep my wit sharp and my tongue quick. No one would save me but myself.

I had to survive. No matter what the Beast had planned.

Part Two

Parchment and Wine

Chapter Eight
A Bigger Puppet

Sir Bloodstone and I followed the other newlyweds to the palace. The blood bond enchantment had left me sore and weak, so I gripped his thumb for support. Even though he held me upright, I refused to look at him, instead keeping my eyes fixed on the line of other couples in front of us.

Each couple trudged up the patio steps to enter the fray of the ballroom. Silhouettes of nobles danced and laughed through the ballroom windows on the other side of the garden.

I rolled my eyes. Glad everyone else was having a good time while I was figuring out how to keep my half-giant husband from breaking me into pieces.

Derrick and Brietta entered the palace first. Within a few moments, thunderous applause from the ballroom echoed through the stone walls and glass windows. A moment later, Annalisa and Grigory received noticeably less celebration when they entered the ballroom.

Dinah and Myles had just walked into the palace when General Hyton stepped in front of our path.

Sir Bloodstone halted so quickly that I nearly tripped over my own feet.

"Bloodstone," General Hyton barked. He was the tallest human man I had ever seen and even he had to crane his neck to look up at his soldier. "No one can see you before tomorrow."

His Hyton Blue eyes flicked down to Sir Bloodstone's crimson-stained right sleeve and the matching stains on the entire left side of my dress. "Especially while looking like this," he added with a note of disapproval. "You will retire to your quarters at once."

"Yes, General," Sir Bloodstone replied. His voice was powerful and low— like the darkest depths of the rolling sea.

Duke Hyton appeared next to his brother and clapped him on the back. General Hyton wrinkled his nose at the stinging cloud of spirits that had suddenly enveloped the three of us.

"All right, Ragnar," Duke Hyton said with a thick tongue. "I will take it from here. Now get that son of mine good and drunk for me, would you? I do not want him running around the palace looking for me tonight."

General Hyton gave his brother a small bow. "Yes, Your Excellency." He turned back to the palace, but not before looking up over his shoulder and shooting Sir Bloodstone an imperious glare.

Duke Hyton gestured for us to follow him. I bit my tongue, preferring to curl up and hide in a nearby rose bush than go anywhere with that horrible man. I glanced up at Sir Bloodstone's hand wrapped securely around mine— maybe marrying the notorious Beast had an unexpected benefit. Even while drunker than a sailor on payday, Duke Hyton would not so much as *look* at me with a monster at my side.

My chest relaxed a little as I let Sir Bloodstone guide me to follow the Duke.

Duke Hyton led us through a hidden door on the northern side of the palace. Just like the maze of hedges outside, the Duke's palace was made of endless twisting hallways and rooms that would make anyone lost. After what seemed like an eternity of walking around in circles, Duke Hyton opened a door to reveal a large conservatory with tall glass windows that looked out onto the Western Sea.

No one had lit any candles, so I blinked as my eyes adjusted to the dim light from the windows. Blue strips of moonlight glistened on the leaves of lush plants that grew in a small garden below the huge windows. A few freestanding bookshelves stretched upward near two sets of spiral staircases on either end of the room. A large, flat square laid in the center of the room and I blinked some more as it came into focus.

My stomach dropped—it was a mattress. If Sir Bloodstone did not have such a firm hold on my hand, I would have turned on my heels and sprinted through the door.

The Duke pointed at the two of us. "Stay here until someone fetches you in the morning. And, since you ruined your dress Miss Ravenwood, erm, Madame Bloodstone—whatever your name is!—someone will bring you a new one tomorrow. We need you both looking well for the victory celebration."

The Duke walked away, grumbling about needing another drink, and slammed the wooden door to the conservatory shut behind them.

The lock clicked. I was trapped with the Beast.

My eyes flitted around the room, looking for means of escape. The two sets of wrought iron staircases on either end of the conservatory were my only way out. I dared to turn my head back toward the mattress and noticed two couches on either side, one with a white nightgown draped across the back. A small round table next to that couch supported a silver platter with a large loaf of bread, grapes, and a bottle of wine with two brass goblets next to it.

I looked around a few seconds more and waited for a maid to get me out of my ruined dress.

Sir Bloodstone stepped over to the mattress and sat down on it, the stuffing of the mattress heaving under his great weight. He leaned down and began unlacing his boots. As soon as his massive fingers untied the laces, I realized no maids would come—*he* was supposed to undress me.

No. Absolutely not.

A quiet hiss cut through the air. I softly stepped over to the couch on the left side of the mattress, following whatever the noise was. I had just picked up the soft white nightgown off the couch when I heard the hiss again.

"Sera!" whispered a small voice from the bookshelves.

I glanced over to Sir Bloodstone, who was still busy unlacing his boots, and snuck over to the bookshelf. Behind it was a woman hiding in the shadows—Mother!

"Sera!" she whispered again. She yanked me behind the bookshelf with her. She let go of my wrist and her emerald eyes swam as she examined my disheveled appearance.

"How did you find me?" I asked.

"I know the palace well," she replied, dragging her eyes from the trail of blood on my skirt back up to my face. "I heard who selected you and this room is the only place large enough to put him."

"H-how could you know?" I asked, panic filling my chest. "No one else was around when—"

"Serafina, you cannot panic," she said, grabbing my hand and pressing her thumb into the center of my right palm. "Someone heard your father in the garden and word circulated."

I had forgotten about Father's certain fate. My lower lip trembled only once before Mother squeezed my palm again.

"Do not worry about your father." Her once glimmering emerald eyes swirled like two pools of poison. She spoke low and seriously, but without a trace of fear. "Anders will *not* execute another Baron. Villagers from Ravenwood and Bloodstone will be in Hyton square for the celebration tomorrow, many of them soldiers in the first siege against the giants. Anders will not lay a finger on your father anywhere near that celebration—not with a crowd of emotional peasants from the Northern provinces near the palace."

I furrowed my brow. "Then why did he charge him with high treason?"

"Oh, Andie has to put on a show in front of the others," she replied with a lightness to her voice I did not expect. "Especially his brother. He and Ragnar have had…some struggles in the past. But your father is safe, at least for now."

Andie. My throat tightened, but I needed answers. "How are you sure?"

Mother's mouth briefly formed a fine line. "I have my ways. Speaking of which, I need to be off."

She snuck off to the staircase. The sick feeling of helplessness tugged on my wrist like a ribbon and I reached for my mother for the first time in years.

"Wait, Mother!" I whispered. "Could you please undress me?"

Mother turned and looked at my bloody dress with a wry smile. "Looks like Andie spent too much time in the wine barrel before the ceremony. What a clumsy cut! Oh well, I told your father this dress was a waste of money. The Presentation dress is usually torn off anyway."

My stomach turned as Mother quickly loosened my laces. "What?"

"Oh, surely they told you at Ashmore," she teased. She slid the ruined bodice off my body and then helped me with my corset. "These men waited at least twenty-one years for tonight. Do you really think they have the patience to unlace a dress?"

My cheeks burned hot but my blood ran cold. "Um, Mother, do you think that he will, um…"

"Maybe," she answered as she helped me out of my skirt. "Some men are intimidated by a bride, others just go for it."

I could not imagine anyone earning the name "the Beast" and being intimidated by a little bride. If he just "went for it," like Mother suggested, he would flatten me as thin as parchment.

I swallowed a hard lump in my throat. "Do you think I would survive? If he…"

"Serafina," she interjected with a chuckle, spinning me around to face her, "think about it, someone had to survive a union with a giant to create him, right?"

Dying *underneath* him was not my only concern. Which side of him was stronger—the human half or the bloodthirsty giant half? Did he lust after flesh in a different way than most men?

I took off my chemise and slipped my nightgown over my breasts. "Since he is a half-giant, you do not suppose he would…eat me, do you?"

"Not if he has half a mind," she replied with a smirk. "The enchantment works both ways—if you die, so does he. He will not hurt you without risking his own death."

Mother may have had a point, but I doubted the Beast was intelligent enough to weigh out the risks of his own mortality when it came to his primal instincts. I tucked a strand of hair behind my ear and touched the band of the gold Ravenwood diadem. I took out the pins securing it to my head and handed the last family heirloom to Mother.

"I am not a Ravenwood anymore." A millstone dropped in my stomach as I spoke. "No sense in keeping this."

The diadem passed from the hands of the last Ravenwood to its last Baroness. Mother ran her thumb over the raven's beak and smiled softly at me.

"You may have a different name, Serafina, but you are always a Ravenwood. You will survive this."

She gave my palm an almost affectionate squeeze and then slipped up the stairs and out the door high above me.

I took a deep breath. Leaving my tattered clothes in a pile on the floor, I peered around the bookshelf to spy on my new husband. The moonlight streaming through the windows illuminated Sir Bloodstone as he sat on the mattress and looked out onto the sea…while naked.

I shut my eyes and slammed my back into the leather spines of the books. No, not yet. *Not yet.* I raised up on my toes, ready to sprint up the stairs regardless of what the Duke had ordered.

Although, was he really naked? I never actually saw his…maybe I needed to look again. I wrapped my fingers around the corner of the bookcase and took a peek.

No, he was not naked. He had some sort of pants on, but nothing else. He had taken off his boots and his blood-stained uniform and placed them both neatly on a chair near the mattress. I had seen multiple diagrams of nude men at Ashmore, but none of them had as much muscle as Sir Bloodstone. Moonlight crested the contours of his massive arms and the grooves around his stomach.

I gulped, weighing my odds of getting through the night without having to be underneath all that muscle. I looked closer—he rested his face on his left hand as his drooping eyes looked out the window. Hopefully he was too tired to undertake any more activities for the evening.

I stifled a yawn. The excruciating marriage enchantment had sapped the last remnants of my energy. I eyed the couch by the mattress and decided to stake my claim there for the night. My bare feet softly padded across the cold tile floor back to the center of the room.

Only when I sat on the couch did Sir Bloodstone even realize I was there.

"Good, you came back," he said. "I'm starving."

My heart skipped a beat. Just as I was about to make a run for the stairs, Sir Bloodstone held up the large loaf of bread in his right hand. He tore the loaf in half and offered me a portion.

He might have just intended to fatten me up to eat me later, but I was so hungry that I did not care.

I took the piece of bread that was almost the size of my chest and nibbled on it. Sir Bloodstone finished his half in five bites and popped some of the grapes into his mouth. I expected him to say something, but he was too distracted by the food to pay me any attention. I savored the bites of bread in my mouth—my momentary salvation from conversation.

After I had eaten about half of my portion, I put the rest of the loaf down on the platter and poured myself a goblet of wine. The small sip I took tasted incredible, especially after that horrible potion Fraleigh made us drink.

Maybe an offering of my own would keep him in a friendly mood. I had nothing else to work with, so it was worth a shot.

I put down my goblet and handed the rest of the bottle to Sir Bloodstone. He took the bottle in his fingers and eyed it with a smirk. "It will take a lot more than that to get me drunk, Ravenwood."

I furrowed my brow. "Get you drunk? I just…the wine will wash out the taste of that magical water, or whatever it was."

Were those really the first words I said to him? I sounded like I was fourteen again and awkwardly fumbling through my first conversation with Derrick.

Well, if I was still able to charm the heir to Lycaster after my initial ineptitude, surely I could do the same with the half-giant hero. Maybe I could even charm him into not harming me.

I rolled my shoulders back and smiled—time to start all over again with a bigger puppet.

I put on a quizzical face and sweetly curled up on the couch. "You called me Ravenwood. Should I not be a Bloodstone now?"

"You are," he replied flatly, not taking his eyes off the wine bottle. "I just know you because of your family."

I took another drink out of my goblet and cocked my head to feign curiosity. "Incredible, we were in neighboring provinces all our lives but never met."

Sir Bloodstone took a swig from the wine bottle, downing half the contents in one gulp. He pulled the bottle from his lips and stared at the floor. "Can't imagine why. What father wouldn't trip over himself to introduce his young daughter to someone like me?"

He was at least self-aware, but I needed to learn more about him to outplay him.

"Are you Baron Bloodstone's son?" I asked.

"Grandson," he replied. "My mother is his daughter. I suppose I'm his heir."

No mention of a father. I was tempted to ask, but decided it was unwise. I tactfully changed the subject.

"No need to use our family names now that we are…*you know.*" I took another drink of wine from my goblet and batted my eyelashes up at him.

"Married."

"Yes," I said as I choked on another gulp of wine, "exactly."

He was not one to mince words—noted.

I tipped the goblet back and emptied it into my mouth. Sir Bloodstone did the same with his bottle and drained it.

He was not much for conversation and he certainly was not responding to my wiles like Derrick had. Maybe I needed change tactics, but I needed more information before I knew what would work best. Did he want to be flattered? Entertained? Reassured?

As long as he did not expect to be seduced, I could manage.

My head buzzed and my eyelids drooped as sleepiness punched me in the eyes. I laid my head on the couch and the soft cushions against my face felt even sweeter than the wine.

But I could not sleep—not without knowing more.

"You know my name," I said softly in an exhale. "But I know nothing of you other than your family name. It…does not seem fair, does it?"

A yawn forced its way out of my mouth. My eyes crashed shut. I drifted into slumber on the tides of my new husband's deep voice as he spoke.

"I have been in General Hyton's academy since I was nine."

I let out a breath through my nose. I inhaled his words as he spoke again.

"I killed ten giants nearly two weeks ago."

Right before sleep enveloped me in its embrace, the voice like satin caressed my ears and entered my mind one final time.

"My name is Riyan."

Chapter Nine

Faerie Princess

Sunlight slapped me in the face. I threw my arm over my closed eyes to block the rays, but I was already awake.

I groaned and forced myself to sit up on the couch. My head hurt, my body ached, and my stomach growled in fury. A soft knitted blanket covered my legs that I did not remember using the night before.

The rumble of low and slow breaths echoed around the room. I turned toward the noise. Riyan Bloodstone was sound asleep face-down on the mattress with a blanket barely covering his legs.

The reality of what had happened the night before crashed down on me all at once. Derrick married Brietta. I was magically bound to a half-giant. I had less than a month to somehow consummate my marriage with him or else Duke Hyton would own me.

My heart raced, but I pressed my hand against the center of my chest and shut my eyes. I could not panic. No one was going to save me, so I had to keep a clear head.

At least I had survived the first night.

Someone gasped above us and I looked up at the spiral staircase across from my couch. Two young maids leaned over the iron railing at the top of the steps and looked down at Riyan. Their eyebrows almost disappeared into their hairlines as their mouths hung open. I made an obvious stretch accompanied with a wide yawn to let them know I was awake and they immediately scurried down the steps.

They ran past the mattress and around to the back of the couch where I sat, putting as many obstacles between them and Riyan as possible. They bowed and told me they were going to prepare me for the celebration that afternoon. I left the couch and followed them in my nightgown and bare feet to the opposite staircase.

When we reached the top of the tall staircase, I took a quick glance at the sleeping half-giant. If I ignored all the normal-sized furniture around him, he looked almost like a regular man as I stood a story above him. He was almost handsome too.

I did not dwell on him any longer and made my escape with the maids. They led me through another maze of hallways and doors until I reached a ladies' dressing room. Squishy pink and purple lounging couches and dainty white chairs stood in the center of the room and against the wall. Multiple wardrobes and dressing tables lined the walls, fit for a dozen women to dress all at once. Gilded mirrors hung all over the walls of the room, but none as magnificent as the mirrors in the dressing room before the Presentation.

The maids led me to a purple lounger and then picked through a wardrobe in the corner of the room. I noticed a trunk bearing the House of Ravenwood crest near the wardrobe—Mother must have sent a trunk with all the outfits I would need for the post-Selection Night festivities.

My ears perked up as the maids gossiped with each other.

"Do you think she…*you know?*" one of them whispered.

"No way," the other replied in an even softer whisper. "She can walk, can't she?"

I swallowed a scowl and pretended to not hear.

The door opened and a familiar mop of red hair ran into the room— Brietta! I stood up from the couch as Brietta ran to me. She flung her arms around me and squished my face against her bosom.

"You are all right!" she cried as she squeezed me tighter and almost crushed my ribs. "Thank goodness he did not hurt you. I was so worried I would never see you again!"

"I cannot breathe!" I protested, my voice muffled by her chest. "You might kill me before he does!"

She gasped and released me. I tried to regain my breath as she continued to explain. "He wanted you. He wanted you the whole time, Sera."

"What happened, Brie?" I asked.

Brietta ran her fingers through the roots of her hair. "Right as the suitors were about to make their selections, General Hyton announced that the Beast was going to choose first. The Beast chose you without a moment's hesitation. Lord Hyton was outraged and tried to stop him, but General Hyton and the other palace guards got in the way."

None of that made any sense. Why would Riyan choose me if he had never seen me before? More importantly, Derrick was the heir to Lycaster and not even a prince with a mountain of gold could bribe his way to choose a bride before the heir. How could Selection Night have gone so wrong?

"Why did Riyan choose first? Derrick was always supposed to pick first!"

"Wait what was his name?" Brietta asked. "*Kee-an?*"

"No, *Riy-an,*" I responded with a scoff. "Sounds like a scream."

Brietta's eyes rolled upward and her full lips mimicked the way "Riyan" would sound before she answered my question. "Duke Hyton apparently decided that the B…uh, Riyan, would get the first selection, but no one knows why. Lord Hyton has not talked to his father since before the Presentation."

My stomach knotted. Had Riyan threatened the Duke to give him the first selection?

Brietta reached into her nightgown and pulled out a folded piece of parchment that she thrust into my hands. "He wanted me to give you this."

Another note from Midnight. Before I could undo a single fold of the parchment, a door at the far end of the dressing room opened. The maids all bowed and so did Brietta as Duchess Hyton slunk in.

Whatever marks were still visible on my neck burned with guilt. I moved all my hair to the left side to cover the damning evidence and I bowed deeply.

Duchess Hyton was also in her nightclothes, but she wore a lush pink robe that covered her nightgown. Her perfect face from the night before was only a memory—she was tired and pale. Her blonde curls streaked with white stuck out in every direction from her head.

I suppressed a laugh—she looked exactly as Annalisa did in the morning.

A large brown cat that was more fluff than substance sauntered around the Duchess's feet. Merri appeared in the doorway behind the Duchess, avoided the lump of fur with legs, and handed Duchess Hyton a golden goblet.

Duchess Hyton immediately took a few sips as Merri spoke to her. "Shall I fetch your daughter, Your Excellency?"

"No," Duchess Hyton groaned. "Let her enjoy the throes of marital bliss a little longer. Just make sure she is presentable before we have to leave."

I almost rolled my eyes. Of course Annalisa was allowed to sleep in. She was not even a Hyton any longer but she still received special treatment.

Duchess Hyton took another sip from her goblet and dragged herself over to us.

"So," she said sluggishly as she eyed Brietta, "you are the next Duchess, are you?"

An invisible spear plunged through my chest. *I* was supposed to be the next Duchess.

"I…I suppose so, Your Excellency," Brietta said with her eyes low to the ground. Brietta did a quick bow as she finished, but Duchess Hyton waved her hand dismissively.

"Do not bow," Duchess Hyton said with a small amount of exasperation in her voice. "Not in here. There is no pretense in my dressing room. No one to impress."

No one to impress? Easy for the Duchess herself to say.

Duchess Hyton swirled her goblet in her hand and clicked her thick tongue. "Just call me Freya. And you are…"

"B-Brietta," Brietta choked out as she wrung her hands together in front of her. She hunched her shoulders forward, bowing slightly even though she did not mean to.

"I remember your name," Duchess Hyton snapped. "What I was saying was you are *not ready to be Duchess.*"

Brietta glanced at me. I bit my tongue, but agreed with the mean old drunk who needled Brietta. Unlike me, she did not spend a lifetime preparing for the role because she was never in the consideration for Derrick's bride.

Duchess Hyton's fatigued but sharp eyes examined Brietta for a moment, then she snorted out a laugh and shook her head.

"Stop me if I am wrong, and I never am," Duchess Hyton said with a smile that I could not tell was cruel or kind. "You are a hopeless romantic who dreamed Selection Night was just like the end of a bedtime story. All you ever wanted was your happily ever after, right?"

She could not read Brietta any better than if her entire history were written on her forehead. Brietta would lie on her belly and read faerie tales and love stories with stars in her eyes and a sigh on her lips, but she had no stacks of books to hide behind as Duchess Hyton reached into her soul and chewed on her spirit.

I grabbed my wrist, hiding Derrick's folded message inside my palm, and kept as still as possible. Duchess Hyton kept her ire on Brietta and I hoped she would forget I was there.

"You also never thought the Duke's heir would choose you, but here you are." Duchess Hyton's smile turned feline as she stepped toward Brietta. "Sorry to disappoint, but your happily ever after is not coming. You make heirs for your Duke and then you are thrown away. You are no faerie princess, you are just *meat*."

I gritted my teeth and gripped my wrist harder as Duchess Hyton stalked over to Brietta, who was so scared she did not even look the Duchess in the face.

"Good thing you have these big birthing hips!" Duchess Hyton shrieked as she smacked Brietta on her ass.

Brietta's face turned scarlet and she blinked back tears. My throat burned from the sharp words clawing to escape. I did not care what title that woman had, she was *not* going to bully Brietta like her daughter did.

I threw my fist to the side, keeping the note locked tightly in my grip. "Leave her alone."

The maids around us sucked in air and froze. Duchess Hyton turned to me with blue eyes like blades. My chest tightened as I hoped she would not look closely enough to find the marks on my neck or her son's note in my hand.

"You are Adalia's daughter, right?" she asked with an amused smile.

I bit my tongue and did not answer. Duchess Hyton raked over me with her vicious eyes but I did not flinch. She chuckled and took another sip from her goblet.

"First-selected, *lucky you*," she said with an edge of poison in her voice. "I was First-selected too. As were all of my daughters…well, all but one."

She took a big gulp of her wine, completely unbothered as I stared her down. She turned to face Brietta again and gestured to me with her goblet. "Are you going to wait for her to defend you for the rest of your life? After today, she is headed to Bloodstone Fortress to live with that monster. No one in the House of Hyton will fight your battles for you, so you need to *toughen up*."

Brietta's lip quivered and she sniffed back her tears. I glared at Duchess Hyton and fought the urge to give her a taste of the back of my hand.

"You have a lot to learn." Duchess Hyton licked her lips and her eyes softened. "My predecessor let me believe I was a faerie princess for far too long. I will *not* make the same mistake with you."

I held my breath and glanced around at the maids who were still as wide-eyed statues. Even the Duchess could not mention Ilsa without invoking the wrath of the Duke. We all made a silent agreement to forget what she had just said, lest the Duke's ire fall on all of us.

Duchess Hyton lowered her empty goblet and turned from Brietta. Brietta hugged her arms and stared at the rug beneath her feet, but I kept my eyes on the Duchess as she walked over to her dressing table and untied the belt of her robe.

Derrick had never mentioned that his mother was so…odd.

The tinkle of a tiny bell at my feet made me look down. The cat rolled onto its back near my toes and looked up at me with round green eyes, begging me to pat its fluffy white belly.

As cute as the cat was, I needed to keep my focus on the insane Duchess. I glanced up and nearly choked on my tongue.

Duchess Hyton wore nothing but a smirk as she returned my stare.

I quickly looked back down to the cat, but still caught a glimpse of a body ravaged by child-bearing.

My cheeks burned as the cat's tail swished the hem of my dress. The Duchess's intense stare burned into me, but I felt no malice from…whatever she was doing.

After a few thudding heartbeats, I started to understand the madness. Duchess Hyton's tired frame bore the marks and folds of seven pregnancies that led to eight children. Even though she had already fulfilled her only job to give Duke Hyton an heir, she still gave her wisdom to the new generation of Lycaster brides, as harsh as it was.

She gave the world five princesses, an empress, and a future Duke, but someone had made her believe she was nothing but meat.

The little bell tinkled again as the cat rolled onto its wide feet and prowled over to Brietta. Brietta moved her eyes from the rug to the cat rubbing its cheek on her calves.

Brietta bent down and ruffled the cat's fluff with a tiny smile on her face. Any anger I had left melted into a stale, grey sadness. The gilt of the furnishings around us betrayed how…desolate the Duchess's life seemed.

As odd as it was, I had to give the mad Duchess some credit. She had shown us her most vulnerable form—naked, wounded, and honest.

Duchess Freya Hyton gave us the gift of an ugly truth in a world of beautiful lies.

I dared to look back at Duchess Hyton and met her sharp but kinder eyes as she looked over her bare shoulder at us.

"We are all trapped in the hourglass, little kittens," Duchess Hyton chimed in a sing-song voice. She cut Brietta a look and flashed a smile a wolf might give a lamb. "Welcome to hell, *meat.*"

Chapter Ten

A Hero's Triumph

Brietta and I exchanged embarrassed glances across the splendid dressing room as Duchess Hyton guzzled down more wine and told us in excruciating detail how she sealed her blood bond with Duke Hyton.

"I used to be the fastest runner at Ashmore," Duchess Hyton slurred as Merri laced up her dress. "But I could only outrun *that man* for a week before he got me. I should have just sprinted out of that damn pavilion on Selection Night and jumped off the cliff."

I stared at the pink rug beneath my feet as the maids put me in a linen dress perfect for a sunny afternoon. The dress was a gentle plum color with tiny blue and white flowers that I had stitched on the bust and waist—simple, but pretty enough that no one would suspect the House of Ravenwood had no money for finer clothes. My hair fell to the left side of my head and completely covered Derrick's marks.

Brietta was in a similar outfit. The borrowed pale blue dress had another too-short hem and mashed her breasts, but at least it laced up without any intervention.

Even after two bottles of wine, Duchess Hyton had completely transformed into the version of herself I recognized from the Presentation.

With the help of a few dabs of paint placed with the precision of a master artist, her previously tired and pallid face was flush with vitality. She was stunningly elegant, wearing a flowing Hyton Blue dress and sparkling amethyst jewels.

Duchess Hyton adjusted her breasts in her corset and then signaled for us to follow her. She was drunk as a woodsman in winter, but she still guided us through the winding hallways as if she could escape the palace even in her sleep. We walked a respectful distance behind her as she stumbled down to the front of the palace where two Hyton coaches waited for us outside.

Lines of soldiers in their best brass flanked the sides of each carriage, but Riyan was nowhere to be seen. Maybe he was busy terrorizing some of General Hyton's other cadets like Grigory had mentioned.

Duchess Hyton instructed Brietta to enter the second coach and said I would stay behind to ride with her and General Hyton. The carriage designated for us was the grandest I had ever seen—white with golden accents and blue and white banners streaming off the sides and the top.

As long as it was *just* the Duchess and the General joining me in the splendid carriage, the ride to the city might be bearable.

Brietta left Duchess Hyton and I to enter the second carriage. She took the footman's hand as she ascended the steps, but her slipper got caught on the hem of her skirt and she tripped. An arm reached out from inside the carriage and caught her—Derrick. Brietta's cheeks flushed pink and she smiled softly as Derrick helped her inside the carriage.

Creeping green thorns curled around my ribs, but I swallowed my feelings and stood beside the Duchess like a painted statue. I needed to calm down—whatever was in Derrick's letter would reveal what I needed to do next. No sense burning over silly feelings.

The noon sun blazed down on us. My chest fluttered in short and shallow breaths, but not from the heat of the sunny day. I had hidden Derrick's message between my breasts and the parchment burned my skin like a hot iron as I stood next to his mother. I kept myself from trembling next to the Duchess as she fanned herself in the heat and mumbled about everything being pointless and how she did not have time to waste.

General Hyton's boots clicked on the palace's stone steps and my heart skipped a beat when his brother followed behind him. Duke Hyton was as sober as I had ever seen him—his brow hard and his eyes sharper than arrowheads. Absolutely terrifying.

I stared at the hem of my skirt, hoping the Duke would not notice me. Duchess Hyton ignored her husband and clumsily walked up the steps of the first carriage with the aid of the footman, who guided her wobbling frame inside without so much as a surprised blink. I climbed the carriage steps and my shoulders dipped inward as I shrank away from the Duke's glare.

"Damn it, Freya, you drunk old fool," Duke Hyton growled. "You know how important today is for us!"

I sat next to Duchess Hyton on the luxurious blue velvet cushion. The stench of wine filled the carriage over the scent of her perfume.

"Oh, what are you going to do?" Duchess Hyton slurred with an eye-roll. "Charge me with high treason too?"

I wanted to sink through the velvet cushion and disappear.

I glanced out of the open door of the carriage just as Annalisa ran through the palace doors. She was barely dressed, wearing a long-sleeved gown and slippers only—no trace of makeup or jewelry other than a lace collar around her neck. Grigory was right behind her, wearing his military uniform and grey cape along with his bow and a quiver of arrows on his back. Both Annalisa and Grigory rushed to the second carriage.

The back of Annalisa's bodice was loose and the laces flew behind her like a pair of plucked wings as she ran. Duchess Hyton scoffed at the sight of her daughter and shifted on the cushion.

"Annalisa!" Duchess Hyton roared, her voice ringing in my right ear. "Fix your dress!"

The Duke and General Hyton ducked inside, the carriage rocking with their weight, and the door closed. With a crack of a whip, we were off to the city square.

"Looks like your youngest had a grand time with the rat last night," Duke Hyton groaned.

"No doubt," Duchess Hyton said, her voice heavy with sarcasm. "You should throw her a ball for her greatest accomplishment as a woman: letting some untitled worm from the House of Thornebow crawl all over her."

"I just might," Duke Hyton snapped. "If only just to punish you. I cannot believe you pulled this shit today of all days."

Duchess Hyton responded to her husband with a raised middle finger and Duke Hyton's ruddy face turned scarlet.

I threw my gaze down. I imagined a hole opening up in the carriage floor that I could slip through to escape the Duke's building rage.

"He is my best archer, you know," General Hyton interjected, breaking the tension. I gathered some quick courage to glance up at the General. He looked back at me with a gleam in his eyes and a soft smile before turning his attention back to the drunk Duchess. "He shot multiple giants in the eye. The worm at least has some *finesse.*"

"Ragnar, women do not enjoy being shot in the eye," Duchess Hyton replied. "But my damn husband would not know that."

Bile rose up in my throat. Maybe if I forced myself to vomit on the General's boots, they would kick me out of the carriage and let me walk back to the palace.

Duke Hyton lurched forward and pawed Duchess Hyton's legs underneath her skirt. I gripped the cushion and froze, but Duchess Hyton laughed at her husband until he threw himself back to his side of the carriage.

"At least you did not sneak in a flask," Duke Hyton said with a dangerously quiet anger. "Although I regret not bringing mine now that I have to stand next to a sloppy, drunk *bitch* for the ceremony."

"Eat a horse's cock, Anders," Duchess Hyton spat.

My heart stopped. General Hyton looked over at his brother with a strange mixture of fear and amusement in his eyes. Duke Hyton's glare at his wife made my stomach turn over.

"I swear," Duke Hyton growled, his face contorted with rage, "when we get back to the palace, you are going to regret every drunken word—"

"You cannot scare me anymore," Duchess Hyton laughed. She smacked me on the shoulder with the back of her hand. "But you are about to make Adalia's daughter piss herself!"

I eyed the carriage door and fought the urge to fling it open and throw myself into the street. The back of my mind burned and I could not help but glance over at Duke Hyton, whose furious blue eyes were on me as his mouth turned up into an evil smile.

I was still as a deer in an open meadow as he stared. Duchess Hyton was impervious to the Duke's rage, but he could redirect his ire to the smallest person in the carriage.

I could not even breathe as I faced the wrath that had already killed my brothers.

"I am not the one the girl should be scared of," Duke Hyton said in a low voice that made my insides clench. He glanced sideways at his brother. "Ragnar, how about you tell her about the perfect killer you made?"

Damn it all, please leave me alone. *Please.*

I turned my eyes to the General, but only out of politeness. I wanted to slam my eyelids shut and pretend I was anywhere else until the carriage stopped.

General Hyton's jaw tightened, but he answered his brother. "He was born *powerful,* and with power comes…challenges."

He softly glanced at me and then turned to face the Duke. His face glowed with pride. "When beating the pitch out of the other boys was not enough to satisfy his outrage, I gave him a more productive way to use that power. I had the Hyton blacksmith make the largest two-handed broadsword possible and taught him how to use it. He was the perfect executioner on the battlefield— one clean cut was all it took."

The words "Bloodstone," "power," "killer," and "executioner," spiraled in my head at a dizzying rate. I gripped the cushion to try to keep steady.

Duke Hyton faced his younger, taller brother and puffed out his chest. "You know, were I sent off to the military academy like you, the broadsword would have been *my* weapon of choice."

"*You* sent me to the military academy, Anders," General Hyton replied with a scowl. "We could have traded places any time you liked."

"You could have never lifted a broadsword," Duchess Hyton scoffed at her husband. "You old, delusional piece of—"

The carriage came to a halt. I let out a relieved breath, but then gripped my skirt as a crowd roared outside. Just how many people could fit in the center of the city?

The carriage door opened and Duke Hyton got up and squeezed himself out of the carriage first, jostling the whole carriage with the momentum.

Duchess Hyton groaned, and with the help of the footman, clumsily stepped out of the carriage herself.

General Hyton left the carriage with more grace than I expected from a man his size. Once he was on the cobblestone street, he winked at me and held out his hand.

Maybe the General was only taking pity on me because I had married his infamous soldier, but I needed an ally for the day. Hopefully I could get the Duke's not-so-little brother to stand between me and the Duke's rage. My stomach was still queasy, but I forced a smile on my lips and placed my hand in his palm as he helped me out of the carriage.

Instantly I hit a wall of noise. I snapped my head toward a sea of people cheering in the square. Young men and women hung out of the windows of the buildings around the square and waved the blue-and-white striped Lycaster flags. Children banged cooking pots in celebration. Smiling mouths chanted the Hyton name.

The capital city of Lycaster had no worry of giant invasions, or any regard for the Northern provinces whatsoever, but at least a thousand people crowded the square. Maybe the peasants of Hyton were just as starved for entertainment as we were in Ashmore.

I peeled my eyes from the crowd as General Hyton led me up the steps of a tall scaffold. Duke and Duchess Hyton sat on thrones in the center of the scaffold and faced the crowd with beaming smiles. Duchess Hyton's spine was straight as a board. Duke Hyton looked to his wife with soft, affectionate eyes before turning his attention back to the city square.

Damn. I was a good liar, but the Hytons had me outclassed. They had put on the mask of a happily married couple within seconds of being at each other's throats—almost as if they had transformed into different people.

My heart leapt into my throat as soon as I spotted dark curls and sad eyes. Derrick sat at his father's right-hand side, wearing the golden coronet of the heir and a brocade of rearing bulls on his blue doublet. Brietta sat beside him, her eyes wide and her hands wringing in her lap. Annalisa sat straight-backed beside her mother with an empty chair next to her.

Instead of sitting with his new wife, Grigory held his bow in front of him with an arrow notched. His dark eyes proudly examined the adoring crowd before him. I could not ignore the weight of a moment—the last time a Thornebow was on the Hyton scaffold, he kneeled before the chopping block.

Grigory smirked and held his bow with tight arms. The last thing he was about to do was kneel.

General Hyton led me to a seat separate from the royal family. I forced myself to not look at Derrick as I walked past him. I already had his teeth marks on my neck and his secret message over my heart—I could not risk even a single glance at him with the entire House of Hyton surrounding me.

The Hytons could see their sole heir's devotion to a woman he did not marry as a threat to their stability at best and a threat to the crown at worst. With my father already charged with high treason, the Hytons were already poised to see me as a troublemaker by association.

I needed to stay quiet to avoid suspicion—whether it was justified or not.

General Hyton helped me into my chair and then stood next to me like a guard. I was an island on the scaffold, distinctly separated from the House of Hyton. The raucous crowd somehow got even louder and I wanted to shrink into my chair. Too many pairs of eyes on me. I was *seen*.

Then I spotted a green banner bearing a raven in the crowd—the House of Ravenwood emblem. I examined the group of people under the Ravenwood banner and saw old men, lots of women with small children, and only a few young men amongst them. Many of the young men under the Ravenwood banner were missing arms, legs, and even eyes—boys from the first battle with the giants.

Each peasant under the banner had sulked through the Ravenwood hamlets for seven years and continuously turned up to the lakeside markets with empty stalls waiting for them. As they stood in front of me, though, their weather-beaten faces lit up with joy, their hungry mouths screamed in triumph, and their withered frames leaped amongst the crowd to see not the Duke, nor the beautiful Duchess, but to see *me,* a daughter of the House of Ravenwood, in a place of honor. I stood with the royal family unbound by the poverty of my homeland, untainted by the prejudice against the Northern provinces, and tasting the sweet elixir of victory with the rest of the crowd.

My heart swelled with pride. I had never been important before, nor powerful or adored. Instead of cowering under the watchful eye of thousands, the fear in my veins turned to exhilaration at the praise. The crowd's exaltation was more intoxicating than wine and more filling than bread.

Before I could drink in any more cheering, Duke Hyton moved to the front of the scaffold and addressed the crowd.

"People of Lycaster!" he roared with triumph. "The giants of Nordingaard are defeated!"

The crowd exploded into thunderous applause and spectacular clamor. Duke Hyton gestured to the crowd and boomed: "I give you Sir Bloodstone, the magnificent giant-slayer, the Hero of Lycaster!"

A small crowd beneath a crimson banner with a white bear—the emblem of the House of Bloodstone—jumped and yelled in celebration as their mysterious province was honored for the first time in generations.

War drums pounded over the roars of the people. The far end of the crowd parted like water and the half-giant appeared. Riyan marched through the adoring crowd with a face of stone and his eyes fixed forward to the scaffold.

My heart pounded like another war drum as my half-giant husband approached. He wore a humongous sword slung across his back and the right sleeve of his blue uniform was still stained with red from the night before. Just looking at him made my blood run cold, but the peasants ate up the drama. Behind him, two Lycaster soldiers escorted a horse-drawn cart with a canvas covering its contents.

Riyan stood in front of the scaffold and faced the crowd. He stood ten paces from me and his head was still even higher than mine as I sat on the tall platform.

Duke Hyton gestured to Grigory, who held his bow with a flaming arrow ready to fire. "Under the lead of Sir Thornebow, my archers blinded the monsters with their arrows!"

Grigory drew back his bow. His arrowhead smoldered with a small red flame like a beating heart. Like a flash of lightning, Grigory shot the flaming arrow high above the gaping crowd.

The heads of the crowd whipped around as the arrow hit its seemingly impossible target, a small ball of cloth hanging above the square that erupted into a magnificent blue flame. The peasants gasped. The tongues of mystical blue fire spread to a previously invisible cable that lit up more balls of cloth hanging all around the square until the fire surrounded us.

I let out a breath as the Hyton Blue flames danced above me. Fraleigh's sorcery had to have created the spectacle, but she must have kept herself hidden from the crowd. The beautiful flames were a statement of not only the House of Hyton's dominion over Lycaster, but as the master of all its magic.

"Then," Duke Hyton bellowed, "Bloodstone took his great sword, smithed here in Hyton to do what *none* have done before—kill a giant!"

Riyan unsheathed his sword and held the gleaming blade up to the cheering throng of people. The sword was longer than even Derrick was tall. He plunged the blade into the ground like he was trying to kill the very earth.

The two soldiers removed the canvas on the cart and the triumphant cheers soured into horrified gasps. I leaned forward to see, but Riyan's massive shoulders blocked my view.

The drums pounded faster and the blue inferno raged around the captivated crowd as Duke Hyton built up to the climax of the ceremony. "Bloodstone sliced off the heads of not one, not two, but TEN giants of Nordingaard!"

Riyan reached into the cart and held up what looked like a large, grey boulder. He gripped the stringy black moss on top of the boulder and dangled it in front of the screaming peasants.

Only when I spotted the arrow lodged deep within the grey mass did I realize it was not a boulder at all—but a giant's rotten head.

My stomach churned and my chest seized. The crowd roared louder than ever before, but the powerful exhilaration in my blood disappeared. Was that the giant that killed Endre? Or Erik? Or both? Did its crooked teeth crunch through their bones? Was the last thing they smelled its foul breath? Did those lumpy ears hear their screams?

My hands shook as I gripped the arms of the chair. No, stop, I had to calm down. Too many people. Too many eyes.

I forced the thoughts away and focused on Riyan's face. Unlike Grigory, who lit up with a prideful smile at his own triumph, Riyan stood before the crowd stone-faced, his eyes blank as he held the head aloft.

Riyan broke his stony countenance for a moment as he looked back to a bare spot on the scaffold. With one jump, he leaped onto the scaffold and the shockwave from his jump sent me flying backward off the edge of the platform.

I crashed on the cobblestones and my chair clattered next to me. Every muscle screamed at me to run. My arms shook as I forced myself from the ground and scrambled underneath the scaffold to hide from the crowd. My body ached from hitting the stones and my heart raced as I panted. I peered through the supports of the scaffold to see the soldiers handing Riyan the giant heads one by one, the crowd erupting in cheers each time Riyan showed off a new head.

Even though I could not see Grigory, I heard him again in the recesses of my mind: *He has a beast's heart. He cannot feel or love, he can only destroy.*

I pressed my hand to my heart and tried to catch my breath. Riyan had killed ten giants and hoisted their rotten heads without a trace of emotion. He threw me off the scaffold with the force of a casual jump. He was the perfect executioner, a killer, and a beast. Was I just next on his list of prey? Would all my charm and manipulation not be enough to subvert his killing instincts?

The note from Derrick crinkled against my heaving chest. I did not know whether the note contained his reassurance, an explanation, or even a final goodbye and a declaration of love for Brietta, but I did not care, I just needed my Derrick. I made sure no one was watching and pulled out the note.

Serafina,

I do not know how, I do not know why, but you were stolen from me. Do not fret, this is not the end. I will not lose you to that monster.

Annul your marriage, Serafina. Do not give yourself to Bloodstone. Damn my father's laws, we will have a peasant marriage if that is what it takes for us to be together. I promise to take care of you. No man, magic, or monster can stop us.

I could not choose you on Selection Night, but I will choose you today, tomorrow, and every day for the rest of our lives.

Eternally yours,
Derrick

Derrick had abandoned the secret names—he was done hiding.

My heart swelled and I held the letter to my chest. I still had a way out of this marriage with Riyan and a path to becoming the Duchess, being more to the people under the Ravenwood banner than a Baron's daughter in a pretty dress, and making everything as it should be.

Heavy footsteps thumped above me on the scaffold, then on the steps. I hurriedly stuffed the letter back into my corset.

"Madame Bloodstone!" General Hyton called as he spotted me in the shadows. "Are you all right?"

I quickly dusted off my skirt, forcing myself to smile through my aching muscles. "I am."

"My sincerest apologies, Madame," he said, taking me by the hand again. "Everyone was so distracted by the spectacle we did not see you fall."

General Hyton helped me up the scaffold steps again. Riyan held up what was, hopefully, the final giant head. When we reached the top of the steps, General Hyton leaned down so his face was near my ear.

"My brother wants you to stand next to his hero," he whispered. "Pretend to be happy."

My stomach churned—I was *seen* again. Could everyone tell how miserable I was? No, if a crowd of hundreds did not see that I fell off the scaffold, no one had paid enough attention to know I was unhappy. If Duke and Duchess Hyton had barely noticed my presence in their carriage, there was no way I had revealed the true nature of my mind to anyone in the House of Hyton.

Although, General Hyton was at the Suitors' Ball and in the ballroom during the Presentation. He may not know about Derrick and I's secret relationship, but might have noticed how we looked at each other. General Hyton also saw me collapse when I saw Riyan, was with me in the carriage when I nearly vomited at the mention of his "perfect executioner," and he was by my side through the entire grotesque spectacle celebrating Riyan's bloodthirst.

Or maybe General Hyton paid me no mind at all. Maybe anyone could see how wrong Riyan was for choosing the smallest woman possible to wed and bed, or even how wrong he was to show up to Selection Night *at all* knowing what he was. Hero or not, he was not a gentleman. He was not even fully human—he was a beast.

Regardless of what my husband was, I could not disobey the Duke's orders in front of the whole city. I tentatively crossed the scaffold to Riyan when I caught Derrick's gaze. Derrick's golden coronet gleamed in the sunlight, but the hopeful look on his face as blue eyes met hazel was more splendid than his attire.

My stomach lurched as Riyan grabbed my left hand and thrust it as high as he could get my arm to extend. I stood on the tips of my toes as he all but dangled me in the air in front of the crowd.

"As a reward for his valiant acts of heroism," Duke Hyton shouted, "I granted Sir Bloodstone the first selection last night, ahead of my own heir. Now, the Northern provinces will have springs and summers free from giant invasions, bountiful herds, and many SONS!"

The Bloodstone camp roared. The Ravenwood camp cheered. The rest of the crowd applauded, but I trembled as I hung from Riyan's arm in front of the crowd like another giant's head—just another prize for winning the battle.

I looked over my left shoulder into Derrick's hopeful and beautiful blue eyes. With an unspoken promise on my lips, I nodded. Derrick smiled softly, paying no regard to his bride next to him, and nodded in return.

Relief washed over me. The new plan to annul our marriages was in motion. I was not going to be bound to the half-giant for much longer.

The crown was still mine.

Chapter Eleven
An Unyielding Bull

After the victory celebration was over, I boarded the Hyton carriage again with the Duke, the Duchess, and the General. Unfortunately, the ride back to the palace was worse than the ride to the city.

Even though Duchess Hyton had hidden her drunkenness well during the celebration, Duke Hyton was still unsatisfied with her performance. He berated her the entire ride and accused her of undermining his control. I stared at the blue damask fabric lining the walls and wished I could disappear as the heat from the Duke's rage fumed around me like I was trapped in an oven.

As soon as the carriage stopped, Duchess Hyton flew out of the door without accepting any help from the footman. Duke Hyton chased after her with his teeth bared and continued to yell at her. None of the servants outside so much as flinched as their Duke screamed past them.

I held my breath and did not relax my chest until I was sure the Duke was gone. General Hyton quietly stepped out of the carriage and waited for me outside with an extended hand. I took his hand, but his help did not come without a price.

He bent at the waist until his cheek grazed the side of my hair. "Forgive my brother for his lack of manners," he whispered, his breath skating across the shell of my ear, "he locked you up last night before we could have a proper conversation. Shall we remedy that?"

I swallowed and silently nodded. I had no idea what General Hyton wanted out of me, but I would have rather gone anywhere with him than be near Duke Hyton again.

General Hyton led me into the palace and took me into a room with portraits of Dukes and Duchesses from centuries past lining each of the walls. As I avoided General Hyton's eyes, I noticed an empty spot on the wall where Duchess Ilsa's portrait must have hung years ago.

General Hyton cleared his throat. I turned to find him looking up at a portrait above the warm glow of the crackling fireplace.

"My father, Alastar Derrick Pervale Hyton," General Hyton said proudly. "Tenth Duke of Lycaster, known to history as Alastar the Wise."

The portrait of the murdered Duke looked down like he was still wise enough to see through us. Alastar the Wise had the same blue eyes and dark curls as Derrick but a square jaw identical to the General's.

I kept my hands from picking at my skirt, but still waited with baited breath for the General to make his point. He would not pull me aside for a mere history lesson.

"His wisdom was great, obviously," General Hyton said with a smile, turning his eyes to me. "His greatest lesson to me was that when your plan fails, simply change the plan. The rest will sort itself out."

Of course it would always sort itself out. The Hytons had the entire Dukedom in their hands, able to change the course of lives at a whim.

"I know yesterday's events went against your plan, Madame Bloodstone."

Shit. He knew about Derrick and I.

"I do not know what you mean," I lied, keeping calm despite my rising panic.

The firelight danced around the contours of General Hyton's chiseled face as he smirked and raised an eyebrow. His voice dropped to a wicked tone I had never heard a gentleman use. "Come on, Ravenwood. Your kind always has a plan."

He was pushing me. Instead of pushing back, my hand fluttered up to my chest in an evasive maneuver.

"General Hyton," I said in mock surprise, "I was merely a schoolgirl two nights ago, and you suspect me of plotting something? I only had a plan to marry!"

The fire lit his Hyton Blue eyes and made them sparkle like diamonds. "But that is not good enough for you, is it? Do not lie to me, Ravenwood, I know you better than you think. You had higher ambitions than just simply marrying."

Even though my chest froze, I did not even blink as General Hyton saw right through me. I mirrored him, matching his quiet calm with my own.

"I wanted to marry an heir, and now I have." Fine, I would admit to being a little ambitious, but just to throw him off. No one else in the House of Hyton could know of Derrick and I's plan to annul our marriages. "You make many assumptions, but you are mistaken about the nature of the House of Ravenwood. We do not plot or strive for great achievement. We merely *survive*."

General Hyton responded with a smile that made me uneasy. "I may not know the House of Ravenwood, then, but I do know the House of Hyton. For more than four centuries, the House of Hyton has survived famines, wars, and every conflict imaginable. Do you know why?"

I sensed an incoming threat, but kept a cool composure. "We did study Lycaster's history in school, but please illuminate me."

General Hyton glanced up at the portrait of his father, but his quiet smile did not falter. "The House of Hyton embodies our emblem—the rearing bull. Like the bull, we are powerful, we fixate on problems, and we do not yield until we get what we want."

Posturing. All I needed to do was sound impressed and he would back off. "How interesting, General. I trust the House of Hyton can handle *any* challenge."

"Madame Bloodstone," he said in a hard voice, not letting me off his hook, "you need to understand that the House of Hyton and its lineage now rests on the success of *one* marriage. You have unwittingly stepped into a delicate situation."

He squared his shoulders to me and only then did I realize his broad frame stood between me and the only door to the room. Between his tight jaw and his soft eyes, I could not tell if he was blocking my exit or shielding me from whatever was outside the portrait room.

General Hyton took a single step toward me and I sucked in a breath. He gently brushed my hair off the left side of my neck and his eyes gleamed when he revealed the marks Derrick had left. I kept still and looked as innocent as I could even though my knees were weak.

His voice was low as an incoming tide. "My nephew was named after his grandfather, but he did not inherit his wisdom."

General Hyton looked away from my neck and back up to my face. My throat twitched, desperate to choke out anything to fix the situation, but my strong wit and quick tongue failed me. He lowered his hand from my hair and locked both hands behind his back.

"You do not want to play the games of the House of Hyton, Madame Bloodstone," General Hyton said with concern in his eyes. "Just go to Bloodstone and save yourself. Ravenwoods do survive, after all."

The meddling General thought this was all a game? A needle of flame flicked up my throat and I straightened my back and crossed my arms.

I dropped the pretense and faced the bull head-on. "Survive? I saw today what Riyan Bloodstone can do to giants. Are you really going to stand there and tell me with a straight face that I can survive a moon cycle with '*the Beast?*'"

General Hyton put on a half-smile, clearly familiar with his soldier's infamous moniker. "As General of His Excellency's army, I can guarantee that you are safer with him than in this palace." He chuckled and his voice lightened. "You know, all that boy has ever wanted is for someone like you to just give him a chance. Maybe consider that before *you* make assumptions."

His words sat on top of my chest like boulders. Give him a chance? How did he expect me to give the Beast a chance?

Before I could ask, a furious voice echoed in the hallway outside.

"Father!"

Derrick.

"Damn it, boy!" Duke Hyton's bellow responded. "Let me get a drink in before you confront me!"

"No, you cannot run from me any longer," Derrick yelled. "How could you?"

"Boy, *not here!*"

General Hyton's half-smile turned into a full smirk. "Don't believe me? Stick around to see the current state of the noble House of Hyton on full display." He glanced at the windows on the far side of the room that were dressed in long blue drapes. "Your small stature is more of a boon than you think, you can hide pretty much *anywhere.*"

Angry footsteps pattered closer. General Hyton turned his head to face the door. "But you had better hurry."

Without having time to weigh my options, I ran to the window and hid behind the curtains. The curtain was fastened far enough away from the wall that I concealed myself completely behind it, even my feet.

Two pairs of footsteps entered the room.

"Get out, Ragnar," Duke Hyton snarled.

"Gladly," General Hyton replied. The heavy wooden door clicked shut as he left the room.

My heart thumped in my chest twice before Derrick's roar filled the portrait room. "You gave Bloodstone the first selection just for winning a battle?"

"Calm the hell down," Duke Hyton snapped. He slurped something that likely was not water before speaking again. "That Elvar girl you married comes from a powerful family. She is not bad to look at and she smells pretty nice too. She will make fine heirs for the House of Hyton."

"Oh, *now* you care for the House of Hyton?" Derrick snapped. "You made us look weak! The House of Hyton always has the first selection—we get the best brides, the strongest unions, and the best lineage. We yield to no man, but you just showed all of Lycaster that we will yield to *Uncle Ragnar's monster!*"

Did General Hyton just want me to witness Derrick without his charming veneer, thinking it would disillusion me enough to want nothing to do with him? The General had underestimated my constitution—it would take much more than some righteous anger to scare me away.

If anything, Derrick's fierceness awoke little butterflies in my belly. Nice to hear he was more than just the starry-eyed and suave Midnight.

"Are you just upset because the Elvar girl is taller than you?" Duke Hyton teased. "Come on, son, women are always smaller when they are lying down."

The crunch of a fist against muscle and metal clattering on the stone floor echoed in the room. I clamped down my teeth to hold back a gasp. Had Derrick lost his mind?

The Duke returned the punch, then another. Leather shoes scuffled on the wooden floor as the two men exchanged blows.

"You…miserable…drunk!" Derrick shouted between breaths. "I love Serafina!"

My head shook over and over. Stop, Derrick, *stop!*

A fist cracked into a jaw. "And you gave her to *him!*" Derrick spat. "She is going to die!"

I stared at the blue curtain as my blood turned to ice. He did not say I was going to get hurt, or that I would be miserable, no, Derrick thought Riyan was going to kill me.

The fight raged until a body slammed into something hard with a grunt. Even though I was paralyzed with fear, I had to see what was happening. I gently gripped the blue fabric and barely pulled it aside to get a peek of the room.

Horror spiked through my bones when I saw blood on the floor. Duke Hyton held Derrick up against the side of the marble fireplace and gripped both sides of his doublet in tight fists. The Duke's rings were stained red and thin ribbons of crimson streamed from Derrick's cheeks and lips. Derrick's golden coronet glowed orange from the raging firelight, but his eyes were white-hot from his outrage.

Duke Hyton's strong arms trembled and he panted as he held his son back, but Derrick still would not yield. The two men were in a deadlock, eye-to-eye, underneath the fierce portrait of their ancestor.

The Duke spat blood onto the floor. "You think you are grown enough to take on your father? You think you can stand against *your Duke?*"

"I will not stand by while you send the woman I love to her death," Derrick said with a snap of his red-stained teeth. "You will not take her away from me."

Stop, Derrick. Stop telling Duke Hyton about us!

"Listen to me, you fucking moron!" Duke Hyton yelled as he threw Derrick down.

Derrick's body hit the floor with a crack. My hand flew to my mouth to cover my lips. I wanted to scream, or scrape Derrick up off the floor, but I had to stay hidden. If even Derrick could not handle his wrathful father, I did not stand a chance if he discovered me spying on them.

Derrick's arms shook as he struggled to rise from the floor while his father lumbered to a nearby cabinet to retrieve a bottle of spirits. Duke Hyton uncorked the bottle with his teeth and took a quick swig before padding over and pushing Derrick's face back to the floor with his foot.

"You know what makes us look weak?" Duke Hyton growled. "When two of our provinces lose half their sons in battle and everyone in the Dukedom feels it."

Derrick was smart enough to stay down, but he still glared up at his towering father.

"What are you talking about?" Derrick asked indignantly as he pushed himself up a little. Duke Hyton scowled and kicked his son back down again.

"Have you not noticed nothing is being built in the Dukedom?" Duke Hyton said after taking another gulp from his bottle. "We get most of our timber from Ravenwood and our masonry from Bloodstone. You know what you need to fell trees and break up rocks?"

Duke Hyton leaned down and poked Derrick in his bloodied cheek to punctuate his point. "Young. Healthy. *Sons.*"

The loss of thousands of boys was not just a splinter in the hearts of everyone in Ravenwood, but a real problem for the whole Dukedom? Good. The rest of Lycaster could suffer with us.

Duke Hyton backed off and paced in a circle around his son, swirling his bottle in his hand as he spoke. "And then there is Baron Frederick Ravenwood—another symptom of the problem. I have him locked up as damage control, but he is just a reflection of how his peasants regard the House of Hyton. Bloodstone is the same—they did not lose their heir, but they lost sons too. They hate us."

I gritted my teeth. For once, I agreed with him. He took my brothers from me, my father from me, and since he gave Riyan the first selection, he took Derrick away from me too. I hated Duke Hyton more than anyone else alive.

"And your solution to this problem," Derrick said darkly as he rose to his elbows, "was to sacrifice my innocent Serafina to make the peasants of Bloodstone happy?"

"Shut up about Serafina!" Duke Hyton shouted. "Think beyond your own selfish heart, boy! All eight Barons are angry at us for sending the Ravenwood and Bloodstone heirs to fight. And if they think their heirs could be next? What is to stop them from banding together and sending militias of their own to Hyton? Baron Elvar could siege the palace from the Western Sea with half a dozen of his boats! They could overtake us all!"

I could not believe it—Duke Hyton was…insecure. Maybe the crown was not as powerful as I had thought.

"So you made Bloodstone your hero," Derrick said quietly, now sitting up and still glaring at his father, "let him select a bride before anyone else, and then everyone is supposed to respect you again?"

"I *reframed* the situation," Duke Hyton said as he stopped in his tracks to fully face his son. "Remember, the peasants' reality is whatever we say it is. I made it look like we only paused that first battle, not lost, and came back years later to finish the job. I elevated that beast, made him a glorious hero, and gave those simple peasants in the North something to be proud of again. They needed a reason to keep working, make more sons, and not take up arms against the House of Hyton. The other six Barons should calm down too."

So that was it. I was the final pawn in the Duke's plan—giving me to the Bloodstone heir in front of a crowd of emotional peasants from the Northern provinces was supposed to secure peace in the Dukedom. A Bloodstone hero and a Ravenwood bride unified through the sheer grace of the House of Hyton.

I pretended to look at the victory celebration through the eyes of the peasants—what a flattering portrait it made of Duke Hyton, even though he had never washed the blood of thousands of boys off his hands.

Impressive, but gut-wrenchingly disgusting.

Derrick rose to his feet with his fists at his sides. "I could have managed all this with Serafina as my Duchess. None of this had to happen."

"The monster was not supposed to choose her," Duke Hyton said in a low voice as the fire popped behind him. "I specifically put someone close to his size in Selection Night for him to chew on and he ruined everything by going back on our agreement."

I held my breath. Riyan was supposed to choose Brietta. She was a logical bride for a half-giant—she could at least put up a fight if Riyan attacked her.

I leaned back against the wall and closed my eyes as my heart pounded in my ears. Riyan did not see me at the Suitors' Ball or the Presentation and he had never met me before. Why would he break the Duke's agreement and choose me over Brietta?

"Regardless of what that monster did," Duke Hyton reached into his doublet and pulled out a handkerchief, "we adapt. We always do."

He quickly wiped his hands clean and then tossed Derrick the handkerchief. "Clean yourself up and get out. Since I am in no position to execute another Baron, I have to decide what to do with our treasonous Frederick and I have no time to deal with your tantrum."

My heart raced, but I grounded myself in Mother's assurance that Duke Hyton would not hurt Father. He could not harm another Baron, not while he was standing on parchment-thin ice with the rest of the Dukedom.

Derrick gripped the white handkerchief, staining it with the trickling blood from his split knuckles. "What about *her?*"

Duke Hyton's cheeks flushed with anger. "What about her? Keep annoying me and I will make Frederick's punishment that I bend his daughter over in the middle of the ballroom once her marriage annuls."

My knees buckled but I caught myself. I let go of the curtain and took shelter in the darkness of my hiding place. I would lawfully be Duke Hyton's property the moment my marriage annulled. He would not hurt Father, but he could hurt me.

"You would not dare—"

"Oh, I would." Duke Hyton's voice was the growl of a lion, each word the slash of a claw across my stomach. "Let this be a lesson to you, boy. There is *nothing* I will not do to show this Dukedom who is in charge. And unless you want another example of what I am capable of, get out of my face."

I squeezed my eyes shut and silently begged Derrick to stand down.

Derrick choked on his next words. Footsteps grew quieter. My Derrick retreated.

The Duke and I were alone.

My hands pressed tightly over my trembling lips, but I did not dare move. Duke Hyton sighed and took three more long, agonizing gulps of his spirits. My breath seized in my chest when his lips pulled off the bottle. All was still.

I waited for him to rush over and fling back the curtain, but his footsteps grew quieter and quieter as he left the portrait room.

I counted to thirty before daring to emerge from behind the curtain. I walked to the center of the room, avoiding the spots of blood and the spilled goblet of wine on the floor, and settled on a couch before the fireplace. I grabbed a small pillow and crushed it against my chest as my heart pounded in my ears.

I focused on the one beacon of light to keep the suffocating numbness at bay—Derrick was truly in love with me.

But his love could not protect me from his father…or Riyan.

Riyan. The half-giant. The killer. The soldier who went back on his promises. The Duke's hero. The pawn used to mollify the people of the Northern provinces and some cantankerous Barons. The beast who was going to kill me.

And dying was better than bending over the Duke's knee to punish my father.

Duke Hyton had not declared he would direct his ire on me, but he did not swear off it either. The uncertainty gripped me so tightly I could barely breathe.

The bulls had locked horns to decide whether to save me or ruin me, and all I could do was stand behind a curtain and watch.

I squeezed the pillow tighter as my head got lighter and lighter. I hoped Derrick had a plan to run away with me the moment the moon was in the center of the sky on the twenty-eighth night. My marriage might annul, but Duke Hyton would not put a hand on me if I were the next Duchess, even if I married Derrick in a peasant ceremony.

My heart pounded harder as my chest shook. At least Father would keep his head. Although, maybe death would be preferable to whatever punishment Duke Hyton came up with.

My throat hitched with a sob. The corners of my eyes burned with tears.

No. Do not cry. Do *not* be weak!

My fingernails dug deep into the pillow and snapped some of the threads. I threw the pillow aside with a scream behind my teeth and goosefeathers spilled out of the open seams. I counted to ten over and over, forcing myself to calm down.

As I breathed through the cold fog in my lungs, I glanced over to the spots of blood smeared across the floor like a macabre portrait of the Hyton legacy. *That* was what General Hyton had wanted me to see. *That* was his warning.

Leave with Riyan and survive or remain with Derrick and bleed.

The tiny white feathers floated to the floor, some staining red as they landed in the blood and the wine. The tangible evidence of the Hyton chaos was plain as day, but I still was not sure who or what to trust.

One feather like a dandelion tuft swirled down into the center of a spot of blood. As the crimson swallowed the white fluff, an oddly comforting thought finally made my breath still.

Even the Duke bleeds.

Footsteps tapped outside the door and I straightened up. A maid entered and took a quick glance of the blood and feathers. Even though it looked like she had just caught me in the aftermath of slaughtering a chicken, the maid sweetly told me Lady Hyton requested my presence.

Good, a distraction—even if it was Annalisa.

I weakly followed the maid until we reached what had to be the private chambers of the royal family. The maid opened an opulently carved and painted wooden door and I stepped into the chamber.

Inside, I found auburn waves instead of blonde curls. Annalisa was no longer Lady Hyton—Brietta held the title instead. Brietta sat on a lounger near a massive wooden bed that could belong to no one else but Derrick. The icy fear lingering in my veins melted into thorns of envy.

Brietta gestured to a spot on the lounger next to her. "I thought we should talk, really talk."

I joined her on the seat. Any words I wanted to say tasted sour, so I kept my mouth shut.

Brietta folded her hands in her lap. "I know about the plan. I agreed to annul my marriage, Sera."

The millstone I had carried around in my stomach since midnight lifted. "You did?"

Brietta nodded. "Annalisa was right, I do not belong here. I certainly do not wish to be the Duchess, not after everything we heard this morning! If that means I go back to Elvar and live with my brothers for the rest of my life, so be it."

I could not believe Brietta was willingly turning down the crown, but I was not going to argue her way out of it. The annulment was my only salvation.

Brietta shook her head slightly as she stared at the floor. "I…I cannot do it. I cannot be drunk just to get through the day. Or married to someone who does not love me. I cannot end up like Freya."

The harsh words in the carriage screamed in the back of my mind. I swallowed. "Derrick will never turn into his father. He would never…treat a woman the way his father does."

"He is not ugly like his father either," Brietta said with a smirk.

Jealousy flared in my chest again, but Brietta laughed and held my hand. "It is just the magic of the blood bond, Sera! I felt nothing for him at the Suitors' Ball, but now I feel, well, *something*. Fraleigh did say the spell would have an effect…"

I looked up at her and doubt laced my words. "Then why do I feel nothing for Riyan?"

"Probably because you are terrified of him!" Brietta said with a hint of pity in her voice. "As any of us would be if we were in your position."

I almost told her that my fate was almost hers. Making Brietta feel even more guilty about the situation would have made nothing better for me, though, so I kept quiet.

"Regardless of whatever I feel for Derrick," Brietta said as she took my other hand in hers, "I am loyal to you. You rescued me so many times over the years. I will gladly annul my marriage to the Duke's heir if it means you get to be with your love."

I bit my tongue. It was better for me, better for *everyone,* for Brietta to believe that I was really in love with Derrick. The glass house of my fabricated romance was my only shelter amongst the warring Hyton bulls and Bloodstone bears. Brietta agreeing to sacrifice her marriage for the cause of true love could keep me from being a bloodstain on the palace floor or a pile of broken bones underneath a half-giant.

I leaned into Brietta's shoulder as she wrapped her arms around me. I could not look her in the eye as I made the lie as wistful as possible. "Thank you for making my dreams come true, Brie. I finally get to be with the one my soul loves."

Brietta sighed. "Of course, Sera. And do not worry, he slept on this couch last night. He has not touched me once."

Brietta laughed but I kept my smile quiet. Brietta was far too kind for the House of Hyton. Derrick and I at least gave her the mercy of an escape on the next full moon so she would never have to see the bulls go head-to-head like I did.

I just hoped that whatever Duke Hyton had planned after his fight with Derrick, he kept Brietta out of it.

Chapter Twelve

Falling

Duke Hyton had decided to throw a ball celebrating his daughter's deflowering after all.

As disgusting as it was, at least he found a way to occupy himself without involving me or Derrick. Besides, a ball would provide a merry distraction from my father's high treason charges. Hopefully the Duke's wrath toward my father was quieting into embers that a good party would stomp out.

After we received the message that our attendance at Annalisa's ball was not optional, Brietta went to meet with Duchess Hyton, leaving me to get ready alone.

Since my Presentation dress was ruined and whisked away somewhere unknown, I had to find another dress fit for a ball. The days after Selection Night were full of parties since all the Barons were together, so Mother had sent multiple dresses to the palace for me.

The maids laid out all my dresses across the couches in Duchess Hyton's dressing room. I frowned as I realized my ambitious parents had sent multiple Hyton Blue dresses and few others.

House colors were like a uniform in Hyton—noblemen wore their colors to show where they hailed from and noblewomen wore their colors to show who they belonged to. Showing up to Annalisa's ball in the House of Hyton color might as well tip off the entire Dukedom about my plan to eventually marry Derrick—or worse brand me as the property of Duke Hyton. I tried not to gag at the thought and picked through the dresses, looking for anything that might even resemble red.

No crimson dresses since no one knew someone from the House of Bloodstone was a suitor, but I did find a deep wine-colored dress that could work. I had spent last summer stitching yellow and white floral filigrees along the short sleeves and all over the bodice—elevating the day-dress into something elegant enough for a Duchess.

Even though I had given the burgundy dress an ornate flair, the dress was dark enough and the design was simple enough that I could disappear into the crowd. Hopefully I would blend in so well that my half-giant husband would not find me.

The maids quickly dressed me. Mother had sent the last of the family jewels—an amethyst pendant on a silver chain and a black choker inlaid with a large onyx. Grateful for another choker, I tied it around my neck to hide the purple marks still on my skin.

I glanced at my reflection in a mirror and my face fell. All the work I had put into the dress still did not give me the elegant, noble glow I had ached to achieve. I might have wanted to look plain, but I did not want to *feel* plain. Disappointment seeped down my body like a disease.

The maids led me from the dressing room through the labyrinthine palace to a grand dining room where Annalisa sat at the head of the table.

Annalisa looked down her nose at me, but I cooly brushed her off. Her invitation to dinner with the rest of the girls in our class was a silent agreement to never speak of our scuffle before the Presentation, and I was happy to oblige.

Annalisa wore a long-sleeved silver dress—the closest color to Thornebow grey she could possibly bear—the same sparkling diamond tiara she wore to the Presentation, and a thick bejeweled choker. I suppressed a smile as soon as I saw the choker, knowing Annalisa was likely hiding a "bee sting" just like I was.

Dinah in Amberfield yellow and Camille in Pebblebrooke sky blue sat on either side of her, each wearing glittering headpieces and bracelets.

Annalisa examined my simple outfit with a scowl as I sat down next to sparkling Camille. Her disapproval was cutting, but a good sign. If Annalisa thought I was plain as a peasant, I was unremarkable enough to hide in the crowd.

Brietta entered the dining room. Her loose auburn waves glowed in the candlelight. She wore a simple but elegant sapphire tiara in her hair and a matching pendant necklace that rested on top of her large, half-exposed bosom. Her rich, deep blue dress signaled she was indeed a Hyton, at least for the next few weeks.

"Stand up when Lady Hyton enters the room!" Annalisa ordered as she rose from the table. The rest of us followed. "I swear, had I not gone to school with all of you, I would think you had no etiquette training!"

Brietta crossed her arms in front of her chest. "I do not want you to stand for me."

Annalisa rolled her eyes and took her seat. "It is not about *you,* it is about respect for the House of Hyton."

Brietta took her seat next to Dinah, sitting across the table from me. The servants entered the room and filled our goblets with wine and served us plates of steaming beef.

"So we all know I had a successful first night," Annalisa said smugly before taking a sip from her goblet. "What about you Camille?"

"Oh," Camille said, looking down at her plate, "I did not have the courage to be, um, *intimate* last night. Sir Pebblebrooke went to sleep, but I stayed awake until very early this morning because I was so nervous."

"Too bad," Annalisa said, her voice dripping with wicked pride. "What about you, Dinah?"

Dinah swallowed her gulp of wine. "I would have been fine with intimacy, it was poor Sir Amberfield who had trouble. He started crying as soon as he unlaced my bodice and did not stop for an hour!"

"Oh my," Annalisa said in a mock-caring voice. "I guess he was too afraid to perform. He was so clumsy at the Suitors' Ball, I could not imagine how inept he is in the bedroom."

"Well, he had better figure it out," Dinah grumbled. She took another sip of wine. "I am not bearing the shame of an annulment just because he is nervous around women!"

Brietta and I glanced at each other. The beef was drier than normal in my throat as I tried to swallow, but Brietta gave me a reassuring look. What a shame that she would never marry again after her annulment. I suddenly lost my appetite at the thought. I hated that Riyan selected me and ruined Brietta's life.

Annalisa leaned onto her folded hands and flashed a feline smile. "We know nothing happened between you and my brother, Brietta. I am sure we will never hear the end of it when it does happen, but I must thank you for sparing me at least one day of that disgusting drivel."

Brietta narrowed her brown eyes at the Duke's daughter. "You are quite welcome."

Annalisa turned to me. "And, Sera, I am certainly glad you avoided the clutches of the half-giant, at least for now. I hope he does not end up breaking you in half."

"Thank you, Anna," I said dryly. I rolled my eyes and tipped back my wine goblet, finishing up the contents of the cup.

After she finished interrogating the table about our lack of sex, Annalisa went into detail about her first night. I lost myself in the metallic world of my goblet as she spun her tale. The words "passionate" and "could not help himself" hit my ears, but I focused on putting as much wine past my lips as I could. The only silver lining to my chaotic day was that I could have all the wine I wanted now that I was out of Ashmore.

Maybe the wine would flush out the memory of bloody Derrick on the floor and the Duke's cruel threats.

As the wine disappeared down my throat, my shoulders eased and my throat unclenched. Annalisa prattled on as I floated on my fluffy cloud of bliss, getting a taste of peace at last.

We all sat on blue and purple couches in the same sitting room we were held in after the Presentation as we waited for our husbands to arrive. We raised our empty goblets to servants who dutifully ensured we never thirsted for more than a second.

I lazily traced the rim of my goblet as I sat half-melted next to Brietta on a couch. Dinah and Camille chatted brightly about their new husbands as they drank. Annalisa interjected into their conversation over and over, asserting that her new husband was the best catch of all.

Brietta rolled her eyes as soon as Annalisa began regaling her own version of her war-hero husband's victorious battle. She swirled her goblet and made a small vortex inside the deep red wine. "You know, I have never had a full goblet of wine before tonight, and now I am on my third and starting to feel a little brave. I have half a mind to go over there and smack Annalisa myself if she does not shut up about Grigory."

My head buzzed from the wine, so I only nodded in response. Brietta downed the rest of her wine in a big gulp, probably a trick she learned from Duchess Hyton. A servant appeared next to Brietta with a glass bottle in his hands.

"Lady Hyton, His Excellency offers a gift," the servant said, gesturing with the bottle. "The finest wine from the Duke's private stores."

Well, it certainly did not take long for Brietta to receive special treatment as a Hyton. Brietta gave the servant a half-smile and offered up her cup, which the servant dutifully filled with an oddly purple wine. Brietta took a big sip and her eyebrows raised in pleasant surprise.

"Mmm!" she hummed, her brown eyes shining with delight. Her face then contorted into a grimace and she stuck out her tongue as she tried to banish a foul taste from her mouth. "The Duke has, uh, an interesting taste in wine." She carefully took another sip out of politeness.

Brietta had worked her way through Duke Hyton's gift when the door opened. Grigory entered the sitting room with his limp slightly more prominent than usual. Myles, Gerond, and Derrick dragged in after him with red cheeks and snickering smiles.

I could not keep my eyes off of Derrick's face—he only had a few tiny cuts on his cheeks and his lower lip after his fight with his father. Either Fraleigh had healed him or the Hytons kept a secret store of the strongest medicinal potions imaginable.

I let out a small breath of relief. At least he was all right.

Grigory stumbled toward Annalisa and her eyes widened with panic. "What is the matter with you?"

"Your father brought out the good stuff from his private stores," Grigory said as he leaned toward Annalisa and almost bashed his forehead into hers. "He, uh, was *very* generous with us…but especially Derrick."

Derrick's cheeks flushed and he crossed his arms to hold back a laugh.

"We have to perform the first dance!" Annalisa whispered with her eyebrows knitted in fear. "Everyone is going to be watching and what if you trip—"

"Relax, Annalisa," Grigory slurred, grabbing Annalisa by the right wrist. "Don't be so dramatic!"

I waited for Riyan to duck into the room after the others, but to both my relief and surprising disappointment, my own husband was nowhere to be found.

I scoffed. "Just be thankful you have an escort, Anna. Mine is missing."

Gerond chuckled. "Oh, he is not missing." He pointed to the door that led to the ballroom. "Take a look!"

Gerond and Myles snickered to each other while Derrick angrily rolled his eyes. I threw my shoulders back and walked over to the ballroom door to peer outside.

Riyan sat on the floor on the far end of the ballroom, holding a small barrel of wine in his hands as if it were a large cup. Duke Hyton and a small crowd of Barons and other nobles gathered around him with amused smiles. The Duke amongst the nobles was not the same cruel and scheming Duke from earlier, but instead a jovial and lively man. He was the life of the party— yet another mask he could wear.

"Did you all really think I was going to let the boy go through all my best wine?" Duke Hyton said in a roaring laugh. "I bet he can empty the barrel in two minutes!"

"I bet one minute!" shouted another man.

"I bet thirty seconds!" laughed another.

Duke Hyton turned to Riyan. "You heard them, boy, drink!"

Riyan tipped the barrel into his mouth and gulped down the wine while the crowd cheered wildly around him. Riyan was once again a happy stooge for the Duke's plan to charm the Barons. I huffed and slammed the door closed.

"Wow, he is really going for it!" Myles laughed as he awkwardly stumbled on his feet.

Derrick sneered and wobbled slightly as he stood. "That damn brute. I would take you myself, Serafina, if I had any choice."

I clenched my fists. Father had once told me that some men were happy drunks, some sad, some flew into a rage, and some became rakishly handsy the moment a drop of wine entered their bodies. I was not about to stick around to find out which kind of drunk Riyan turned into, nor any of the other men.

"I do not need an escort!" I snapped. "Especially not a drunk one!"

I flung open the door and stormed into the ballroom. Everyone was too busy watching Riyan drain the barrel down his gullet to notice me enter unaccompanied.

My head was swimming after my own three goblets of wine, but I found the only person in dark green standing near the wall. Mother wore the Ravenwood diadem on her head, the gold clashing slightly with the silver streaks in her hair, and held her own goblet as she watched the crowd cheer around Riyan. She stood in the shadows, not speaking with anyone. An ideal place to be.

"No escort, Serafina?" Mother said with a wry smile as I walked over to stand beside her.

"I cannot believe him," I scoffed as Riyan held the empty barrel upside-down to the applause of the crowd. Gold coins flashed in the candlelight as they changed hands between the old noblemen. "He is enough of a spectacle by just existing, why does he have to play Duke Hyton's games?"

"When the Duke is happy, everyone gets to exhale," Mother said before taking a sip of her wine. "Your husband is certainly providing some good entertainment tonight."

A servant rolled out another small barrel and pried the top off with an iron bar. The crowd shouted out more wagers on how quickly Riyan could drain the second barrel.

I took the goblet out of Mother's hand and took a drink myself. "The last thing I want tonight is to be part of any entertainment. I am trying to blend in."

Mother laughed and took her wine back from me. "Being a grump is not the way to blend in with this crowd. Also, be careful with that wine.

You cannot handle as much as you think you can and you do not want the drunkenness to hit you all at once. Wine does make the lips loose, after all."

Riyan gasped as he finished the second barrel and the crowd cheered. I rolled my eyes. A third barrel was on the way when Duke Hyton laughed and held up his hands.

"Hold on!" Duke Hyton said to the crowd. "I think I need to actually start this damn ball before we thoroughly inebriate the boy."

Duke Hyton staggered to the back wall of the ballroom and bounded up on the small dais that held two thrones. Duchess Hyton sat on her throne in her regal splendor but scowling like her husband really was punishing her. Duke Hyton sat on his throne and barked at a servant to go fetch his daughter.

As the servant ran off, I noticed an arc of dark red marks on Mother's shoulder peeking out from underneath her hair. "Mother, what is that?"

Mother did not look at me, but instead kept her eyes on the mingling crowd and smiled. "Oh, Andie likes to have fun. He is just punishing your father for his…outburst with a little humiliation. That is all."

I looked away from her body as my stomach turned. The Duke's plan to punish Father for high treason was to bite his Baroness? That could not be enough, but…she was surely not…

"You are not…" I looked around to see if anyone would overhear and lowered my voice to a whisper. "…you are not *sleeping with* Duke Hyton are you?"

"Oh, yes," Mother said nonchalantly. "I have for years."

I blinked, thinking I may have misheard, but Mother's refusal to look me in the eye confirmed her affair.

My hand flew to my mouth in shock, but Mother's soft, unbothered smile made me crunch my hand into a fist. How could she?

"Does Father know?" I hissed.

"Of course he does," Mother answered. "He does not like it, but he agrees that I need to be the Duke's mistress. Anders sends Ravenwood money to keep the markets stocked with food, among other favors. He likes to tell people he supports us because he is generous, but I can say from experience that he is anything *but* generous."

I thought I was going to throw up. Mother had pushed me to marry Derrick since I was a toddler, but she was crawling into bed with his father? The same man who sent Erik and Endre to die? She betrayed Father over and over just for some food?

"How could you?" I cried. "You…you are married!"

Mother pointed to the crowd. "So are all of them."

I looked out into the ballroom. I did not know the other nobility very well, but I still noticed mismatched House colors flirting with one another. A man in a purple cape, who had to be Baron Elvar, grabbed the backside of a man in Amberfield yellow. A Meadowshyre woman in pink kissed a man in Thornebow grey. A Mydina man in light green snuck out of the ballroom with another man in Pebblebrooke sky blue. I even spotted Brietta's parents in the arms of other people.

Mother leaned close and kept her voice low. "When everyone has a magical enchantment in their blood that keeps you free from disease and ensures you only have children with your spouse, no one has consequences for sleeping around. Well, except for the lack of heirs since all the men are too busy sticking their peckers into everything but the person they bonded to."

I watched a light green cape tangle with a yellow dress. "The Ashmore matrons all told us our hearts and souls were bound to our husbands. Do people not get hurt from all this?"

Mother laughed. "The matrons lie, marriage in Lycaster is just for heir-making. Welcome to the adult world, Serafina. No happily-ever-afters here."

She sounded just like Duchess Hyton. I was never a romantic person, but watching the throngs of the crowd twist up in each other opened up a pit in my chest. We stayed chaste for twenty-one years for the promise of a special entwining of souls once we were married…and that was all a lie?

I tried to swallow but my throat was too dry. Almost as if she could read my mind, Mother handed me her goblet and I took another sip.

"Do not worry about Freya either," Mother said. "Eight babies in nine years destroyed her body to the point she can never be intimate with a man again, not that she would want to. She is quite grateful someone else can… *handle* her husband for her."

My sip of wine crawled down my shaking throat as I pictured my mother "handling" Duke Hyton. I shoved the thought away, but a sickening realization took its place—if the Duke still had not decided on a punishment for Father's treason, his threat to Derrick could still be in consideration.

The hair on my exposed arms stood up as I pictured myself in a skin-tight blue dress with Duke Hyton's liquor-soaked breath on my ear. His hand pushed on the small of my back as he bent me over in the middle of the ballroom like he had said…

I closed my mouth to keep my wine from coming back up when an announcement boomed throughout the ballroom.

"Announcing newlyweds Sir Grigory and Annalisa Thornebow!"

The crowd whispered, swapping gossip about their predictions of the fate of the Thornebow and Hyton marriage as Grigory and Annalisa stepped into the ballroom. Annalisa showed off her dazzling Hyton smile and Grigory put on the same showman's swagger he had at the victory celebration, even though he could barely walk from his drunkenness. A chill ran up my spine—they reminded me too much of Duke and Duchess Hyton, waving to the peasants in the city in a masquerade of contentment.

Before I could worry about Annalisa's fate, Derrick and Brietta entered next, looking like a beautiful pair in their matching blue clothes. I clenched my fists again as I watched them promenade into the ballroom. I did not care if everyone agreed to annul our marriages, they looked too comfortable on each other's arms.

I scowled and crossed my arms. Brietta's time as a Hyton was running out, she should be careful not to get *too* comfortable.

The three other pairs waited on the side of the dance floor while Grigory and Annalisa danced to slow, dreamlike music. Grigory stumbled on his bad leg a few times, but Annalisa kept her smile on.

Watching Grigory and Annalisa swirl on the dance floor was making me dizzy. I glanced at one of the ballroom doors—I had made my mandatory appearance, maybe I could sneak out.

Applause thundered in my ears and I looked back at the dance floor. Annalisa and Grigory had finished their dance and the whole ballroom cheered—except for the cluster of Annalisa's beautifully adorned sisters. They stood near their father's throne, sneering and muttering to each other. Grigory was clad in white, silver, and grey—as conspicuously "Thornebow" as possible. All six pairs of Hyton Blue eyes glared at him.

"Now I want all the newlyweds to have the next dance!" Duke Hyton said with a flourish of his goblet, sloshing some wine onto Duchess Hyton's dress. Duchess Hyton cut him a look and pulled her stained skirt away.

I hid behind Mother as the pairs matched up on the dance floor, hoping everyone would forget I existed.

Riyan walked onto the dance floor and looked for me over the heads of everyone else in the crowd. He was also allowed out of his military uniform for the ball and wore a simple white shirt, black pants, and boots. He also wore his bright crimson cape over his ensemble which, combined with his massive size, made him impossible to miss in the crowd. I could not pretend I did not see him, but I could only hope that he could not find me.

"Where is Madame Bloodstone?" Duke Hyton called. He left his throne and walked onto the dance floor, making a big show out of looking for me.

Mother pulled me out from behind her. "Go. You do not want to make Anders find you."

Her voice was gentle, but the underlying threat in her tone was so cold I nearly shivered.

I took a breath and started walking. I kept my eyes down as I walked out to the middle of the dance floor that was decorated with black and white tile like a game board. My hands shook as I approached Riyan.

Amused whispers pricked my ears as the crowd wondered how the half-giant was going to dance with the girl the size of a thimble.

As soon as I saw the toes of Riyan's boots on top of the black and white tile, I dared to tilt my head all the way up to look at him. Riyan neither smiled nor snarled, but looked down on me with an expression that I could only read as reserved caution.

The whispers turned more serpentine and some were bold enough to openly laugh at us. My face was on the same level as his hips. His knees were just below my waist. Dancing would be impossible—this was all a cruel joke.

The music started up and I held my breath. Riyan leaned down, bending at his knees, and took my hands in his. I closed my eyes as he awkwardly swayed my arms. My cheeks burned as the laughter around us grew louder.

"Come on, boy, you look ridiculous!" Duke Hyton shouted. A fist thumped into muscle. "Pick her up!"

My eyes popped open and I gasped as my feet left the ground, but then all the air was forced out of me as he shoved me into his muscled chest. Riyan had scooped me up in his left arm, supporting my backside with his forearm and his hand around my thigh.

I was so scared, I could not even blush at him touching me where I had never been touched before. All I could see were his big blue eyes. I could not breathe. I was too high, *too high.*

Riyan took my trembling left hand and held it between his forefingers and thumb. I squeezed my fist around his thumb and dug the fingernails of my right hand into his shoulder muscle as he awkwardly danced the steps himself. He dodged one of the iron chandeliers as he danced, narrowly avoiding lighting his hair on fire.

The stench of wine fuming off his breath was nauseating. I looked down to keep him from breathing in my face but immediately regretted it. I could only see the tops of every head in the room. The light and colors of the ballroom started to spin and I let out a frightened whimper into Riyan's chest.

Riyan's chin tilted down against my temple but I did not dare look up at him.

"I am not going to drop you," Riyan said softly. "I promise."

Maybe the low rumble of his promise against my cheek made my heart slow down or maybe it was just the wine, but I let out my breath and the world stopped spinning.

I watched the other couples dance below us. Gerond danced sweetly with Camille. Myles awkwardly stepped around Dinah, who led *him* in the dance, but he had a relaxed smile on his face as he let Dinah take charge. My stomach tightened as Derrick and Brietta swirled around the dance floor in drunken bliss. They talked and laughed through wide smiles and I even caught Derrick glancing down at Brietta's chest a couple of times.

I looked away, but my stomach still knotted and jealousy burned behind my eyes. Whatever attraction they had was from Fraleigh's enchantment, that was all. I needed to calm down.

Although, was I only jealous because Brietta and Derrick shared an attraction, or was it also because I felt nothing for Riyan? The matrons might have lied about the sanctity of our marriages, but the blood bond was too painful for the magic to not be real.

I glanced down at the smiling couples on the dance floor for only a moment—the alleged magic attraction seemed real enough for them. Was I just too mean and cold-hearted for the magic to work on me? Is that why Fraleigh did not tell me I would be a satisfactory bride?

I pursed my lips. Give Riyan a chance, General Hyton had told me. Fine. I could put the annulment plan on hold for a few minutes just to see if any magic could crack my granite heart. Nothing more.

I looked up at Riyan's face. His head was not as large as a giant's, nor was it ugly and malformed like one. His honey-colored hair was cut short and combed back, but one strand of hair fell in his face and curled at his forehead. His eyes were as beautiful as a twilight sky.

My breath fluttered like butterfly wings, and maybe it was the wine, but I could no longer deny that Riyan was handsome.

Riyan caught me looking at him. Even though he held me close to his chest, I wanted to shrink away from him. He then held me a little tighter, a little stronger, and my breasts pressed into the hard wall of muscle on his chest. His alleged beast's heart pounded strongly, yet slowly, against me. A golden light like a tiny sun glowed with warmth in the center of my chest.

Time melted around us. The only ticking clock was the slow, rhythmic thump of the heart that was bound to my own.

My lips parted. I looked at him as if I could say a thousand words in complete silence. Was the magic…actually working?

Riyan smiled at me, revealing a dimple on the right side of his face. He took in a breath and his voice rumbled low as he spoke. "You are—"

His body jerked before he could finish. He stumbled and lost his balance. The nobles screamed and scrambled out of the way as Riyan and I fell to the floor.

Riyan squeezed me into his chest. *Crack!* He hit the floor. My face was pressed into his chest as we both lay in the middle of the dance floor.

The music stopped. I shoved myself out of his grip and put my feet on the floor. I gripped my arms and tried to ignore the horrified thrumming of the crowd. My head ached as my vision swam.

Of course Riyan had dropped me, he had a record of breaking promises. Stupid, drunk, *liar!*

Riyan slowly started to sit up as he rubbed the back of his head. Some nobles gasped and pointed at the floor—the black and white tile had a large crack like a bolt of lightning from the impact of Riyan's skull.

I squeezed my arms tighter and looked over at the other newlyweds as embarrassment burned my cheeks. Annalisa's hands covered her gaping mouth. Grigory's face contorted with rage as he stared at Riyan.

"You can't go six hours without ruining something, can you?" Grigory snapped. He turned from Annalisa and stormed through the glass doors into the Duke's garden.

Riyan heaved himself off the floor with his eyes narrowed at Grigory as he walked away. He followed Grigory into the garden as the rest of the crowd scrambled out of his path.

I gripped my arms tighter—Grigory had invoked the Beast's wrath.

Annalisa ignored Riyan and threw her fists to her sides. "Great! My ball is ruined!"

"Quit being so dramatic, Anna!" Dinah said as she held Myles close to her. "Just have another drink and keep dancing!"

The music started up again and people began to dance and throw their goblets to their lips as if nothing had happened. Dinah and Camille danced away with their husbands and I was trapped standing next to fuming Annalisa.

Great.

"With whom?" Annalisa replied with a growl, not accepting that her former best friends were ignoring her. "My husband ran off!"

"Get over yourself and just find someone else to dance with," said a woman with curly brown hair who wore a large, glittering crown—Sapphira, Annalisa's sister. Two more of Annalisa's sisters stood behind Sapphira— midnight-haired Rubia and milk-haired Pearl. "None of our husbands are even in Lycaster and *we* are having a great time."

"Definitely a better time than if they were here," Rubia chimed in wryly. "Maybe you should be thankful that the traitor's grandson left so the rest of us can enjoy the ball in peace. Better hope he does not come back, or else you might get strangled in your bed too."

Pearl giggled at Rubia's side. I had forgotten how awful Annalisa's sisters were, but becoming princesses and empresses had somehow made them worse.

Annalisa snarled and pointed at Rubia. "*Your* husband is a damn troll. Just because he is a prince does not mean he is handsome."

Annalisa then pointed at Pearl, who flinched. "I can tell by your dowdy frock that *your* husband cannot fill the kingdom treasury."

Annalisa turned to Sapphira, who glowered at her baby sister with her arms crossed. "And *your* husband, Empress Sapphira, cannot get control of the civil war in his own empire. That lineage of yours is going to end under an axe because of your dear Emperor's weakness."

I smiled and folded my arms across my chest. The ball suddenly became much more entertaining.

Annalisa's older sisters fumed at her, but she spat venom like an adder. "The three of you can tell Emeralda, Garnet, and Amethyst too. If you are going to talk down to me because I was not the First-selected like you, or a princess like you, you can go fuck yourselves all the way back to your weak little kingdoms. Enjoy my damn party."

I let a hiccuping giggle escape. Annalisa glanced back at me with the familiar wickedness in her eyes but a friendly smile on her lips. Usually her viciousness was unjustified, but Annalisa had used her tongue like a sword to put her snotty sisters in their rightful places. It was *her* ball, after all.

I looked around to see if Derrick had witnessed his twin sister in her shining moment, but I could not find him. Nor Brietta.

What I did see through the windows, however, was Grigory and Riyan having a tense conversation in the garden. Curiosity pulled me over to the windows and I pressed my hands against the glass to get a better look.

Riyan and Grigory talked in the shadows of the palace. Grigory smirked and said something. Suddenly, Riyan picked him up and slammed his back against the palace wall.

I gasped. Riyan held Grigory up high so their eyes were at the same level. Grigory's eyes were wide with terror and Riyan's face darkened with rage as he snarled at him.

The urge to go out in the garden pulled on my chest, but I did not move. If Riyan was an angry drunk and thirsting for blood, it was better for him to unleash his wrath on Grigory than me. I just wanted to survive, not be a hero.

I took a single step back from the window and hugged my arms as I witnessed Riyan's rage—all the more reason to annul my marriage.

A loud cheer cracked through the ballroom like lightning. "He has done it!"

I whipped my head around. Duke Hyton was on the other side of the ballroom, grinning madly and holding up Derrick's arm. They were standing just outside the open doors to the sitting room we had waited in mere minutes ago. Derrick's face was scarlet and he was frantically trying to put his breeches back over his hips. Brietta was nowhere to be found.

"The marriage is consummated! Duke Hyton announced. "The House of Hyton shall have a new heir!"

My stomach dropped like I fell through an endless black hole. Derrick slept with Brietta. In the middle of the ball. Their union was sealed for eternity. I fell further and further into the blackness as my thoughts continued to race.

They went back on their agreement. They ruined our plan. I would never be his Duchess.

My Derrick was gone.

Chapter Thirteen
Nothing

"Now this is a real party!" Duke Hyton cheered. "A real reason to throw a ball! Bring out the good stuff! The House of Hyton is strong!"

The crowd chanted the Hyton name. Derrick was still locked in his father's grip with horror and confusion burning on his blanched face. Duke Hyton shot Derrick a look out of the side of his eyes—he really would do anything to keep everyone under his control, especially his rebellious heir.

Derrick and I were no match for Alastar Anders Hyton. We were all mere puppets under his hands, playing our silly games until he decided he did not want to play anymore.

I held my hands by my sides in tight fists as the cheering pierced my ears. Had Derrick said nothing to his father about us, Duke Hyton would not have gotten Derrick so drunk that he would slip up and ruin the plan. That stubborn and arrogant Derrick thought he was doing me a favor by standing toe-to-toe against his father when my situation was so delicate? Damn him straight to the high halls of hell!

My throat hitched as I fought back a sob. I hugged my arms as my eyes burned. I had planned and schemed and lied for seven fucking years to become the Duchess of Lycaster and it was all for *nothing*.

I spotted General Hyton standing next to Mother against the far wall in the shadows. He was also out of his military uniform and wearing his Hyton Blue cape to match his brother. Mother handed him a goblet of wine, which he accepted with a smile and a long sip. General Hyton's eyes met mine from across the ballroom before he turned and walked out of the room, his work apparently done.

I hissed out a breath. Of course General Hyton was involved! He and his brother must have planned the whole spectacle to secure the Hyton lineage and get me out of the way.

"What is going on?" Grigory asked behind me.

Apparently he had survived his encounter with Riyan. Fucking good for him. Hopefully I would be so lucky now that I was stuck with the giant, raging asshole.

Annalisa's voice cracked as she answered. "He ruined my ball. Derrick could not let me have *one thing* for myself."

"Annalisa," Grigory said quietly, but not gently, "did you really think your father would throw an entire ball just for you? Don't be such a brat."

I whipped around. Annalisa was a brat, but she was *our* brat, damn it. As soon as I opened my lips to match Riyan's wrath with my words, Annalisa turned from Grigory and ran to the garden.

Riyan leaned against the wall near the garden doors as Annalisa cried past him. His eyes scanned the crowd after Annalisa left, but then they locked on me.

I wobbled on my feet as the wine hit me like a fist, but my eyes were still as I stared across the room at the half-giant. I forced myself not to scowl at him, the piece of shit who chose me and ruined my life.

Riyan's throat bobbed and he swallowed. He lifted his massive shoulders off the wall and took his first step toward me when the third barrel of wine appeared at his feet.

"Bloodstone!" cried Baron Amberfield. He and a small group of nobility crowded around Riyan. "I just bet Lance Pebblebrooke fifty marks that you cannot finish this barrel faster than I can unlace his wife's bodice!"

An older woman next to Baron Amberfield cackled and smacked his arm playfully. Riyan took the barrel in his hands and started drinking again.

Disgusting. I scoffed and looked away, but the frenzy of House colors in the crowd made my head spin. Purple. Yellow. Grey. Pink.

But no crimson.

Surely Baron and Baroness Bloodstone had to be present at Selection Night every year just like the other Barons. If I was stuck with Riyan forever, I needed to form a new alliance with the Bloodstones. I sucked up my anger and shoved it behind iron bars as I scanned the room for more crimson.

"So, Madame Bloodstone," said a voice as smooth as ink.

I turned around. The voice belonged to Rubia who stood with a snickering Pearl.

"Could you be a dear and let us know when you have had your first night with him?" Rubia asked coyly. "We want a go at him too."

"A half-giant would be fun," added Pearl. "I would die happy underneath that man."

I stormed away as they cackled. I clenched my fists so tightly my fingernails pierced my palms again. I hated those damn nobles and their disgusting games. I hated the smell of wine everywhere. I hated my stupid, drunkard husband. I hated Derrick. I hated him for making me yearn for him, forming a plan to be together, and then pulling the rug out from under me in front of everyone.

In my rage, I spotted Duke Hyton dragging Derrick around the ballroom in a sort of drunken parade. Every noble that passed him gave Derrick a clap on the back or offered him more wine to celebrate his glorious achievement.

I nearly spun on my heels and left the ballroom, but his beautiful yet sad eyes found mine through the crowd. Any hatred I had for him instantly slipped away. He looked back at me like he wanted to jump into the black pit with me and stay there for eternity.

I could not hate Derrick, that would be unfair. Someone else shared the blame for my life shredding to bits in an instant.

Brietta. My supposed best friend. The person who agreed to an annulment because she had brothers to care for her while I had nothing. Brietta did not care that I had nothing, she was from the House of Elvar. Her spoiled, over-privileged ass never knew what *nothing* was like.

My rage ignited into a burning fury—I would give her a taste of what *nothing* could really do.

My eyes darted to the open door of the small waiting room and my outrage pushed me through the crowd. Inside I found Brietta, sitting on the very same couch we had just relaxed on together.

Her tiara sat askew on top of her mussed hair. She did not even give me the decency of looking at me. She just sat there, hands folded on top of her wrinkled skirt, and stared at the gold wallpaper with her brown eyes as wide as tea saucers.

That fucking bitch.

I slammed the sitting room door closed behind me. "How could you? You ruined everything!"

"It was the magic, Sera!" Brietta pleaded, her eyes welling up with tears. "We did not mean to…it all happened so quickly! One minute we were dancing, and the next—"

She was an idiot if she thought I was going to dry her tears again. "Do you realize what you have done? You doomed me to a life with that monster! You doomed Ravenwood! You betrayed me, Brietta!"

Brietta dipped her head so low her tiara nearly fell off. "I am sorry, it was not my fault. I did not want to—"

"Oh, it was all just the *magic?*" My teeth ached from fury. She thought I was stupid. She thought I was less than nothing. "Tell me then why the magic has not worked that way on Dinah? Or Camille? Or me? Stop making excuses, admit that you chose to fuck my Derrick!"

"*Your* Derrick?" Brietta snapped, rising from the couch. She towered over me and her eyes lit up with anger. "Serafina, you lie to everyone, even to yourself, but you cannot fool me. I know you do not love him!"

I took a step back. "You do not know anything."

Brietta folded her arms across her breasts. "I was the one who helped you write all those letters, remember? You are as sincere as a serpent and could not have charmed him without using me. I played along because I felt like I owed you for your kindness, but I have had *enough*. You were going to have me annul my marriage and live the rest of my life in shame!"

"You should not even be here, Brietta!" My hoarse voice crashed through my sore throat. "Duke Hyton only brought you into our Selection Night for Riyan. He was supposed to pick *you!* I am the one who is supposed to be in

Hyton Blue, wearing the family tiara, and standing arm-in-arm with the man who loves *me*, not you!"

Brietta's voice hissed out from her lips like a frost. "And if Riyan did marry me, you would have never even considered annulling your marriage to the heir to save me."

My chest heaved. How dare she try to compare our situations? It was obvious to anyone with at least one functioning eye and half a mind that I was in danger, all thanks to my supposed best friend.

"He is going to kill me." My voice was strained as I glared up at Brietta. "He is a monster."

Brietta's lower lip trembled. "Just because he is big does not mean he is a monster. I thought you knew better than that."

"And I thought *you* knew better than to take things that were not yours." I threaded my words and shoved the needle where I knew she would bleed. "Derrick will *never* love you."

Brietta's chest shuddered, but I could not taste the sweet milk of vengeance. My head spun and my stomach lurched. The wine had hit me harder than I thought, just like Mother had warned. I needed air, fresh air, before I threw up.

I slammed my hand over my lips and left. I ran across the ballroom, dodging more drunk nobles as I fought to keep my churning stomach still, until my hands found the handles to the garden doors.

The breeze from the Western Sea filled my lungs and gave my face a refreshing kiss as I stepped out into the evening air. It was not the same area of the palace garden where we had entered the hedge maze, but a much more peaceful place with yellow and red roses growing all around. Right in front of me was a large statue of a rearing bull, its golden horns pointed straight up to the night sky.

Annalisa sat on a stone bench underneath the bull, doubled over and sobbing into her arms.

My head buzzed and my legs wobbled as I stood. Even sitting next to a wailing Annalisa would be less agonizing than being anywhere near the revelry of the ballroom. I groaned as I walked down the steps into the garden and sat beside Annalisa on the bench.

"Ruined," Annalisa choked out between sobs, "everything is ruined."

"Worse things can happen to you than your ball getting ruined, Anna," I snapped.

Annalisa sat up and faced me. Her eyes were red and her makeup stained her cheeks with black tears. She bared her teeth between trembling lips. "After everything I did for you, why are you still so *mean* to me?"

I crossed my arms and shifted my shoulders away from her. "What are you talking about?"

"I knew," she hiccuped. "I knew about your letters, Sera."

I played cool as I tried to hide how tight my throat was. "What letters?"

Annalisa glared at me. "Stop lying. You know I mean the letters between you and my brother. I found one years ago and I noticed the guards slipping you messages ever since."

I blinked as the red roses danced in my vision. "How? I was so careful."

"*He* was not careful," Annalisa scoffed. "Midnight? Really? The only way his dramatic ass could have been more obvious is if he signed off as 'obnoxious pile of bullshit.'"

I gripped my skirt as my stomach lurched. "And you did not tell anyone?" That was not the Annalisa I knew. She did not do favors for people. "Why?"

She sighed softly and looked back up at me with whirlpools of sorrow in her blue eyes. "I wanted him to choose you. If the choices were Camille, Dinah, or you, it was obvious who should have been the next Duchess."

Annalisa sniffed and wiped away her tears with the heels of her palms, streaking black makeup all over her cheeks. "Plus, I like you, Sera. I am sorry I called you a tiny troll—I did not mean it! I was just mad because your Suitors' Ball gown looked so much better than mine. I just wanted to stand out at the ball…but I guess that would not have mattered."

Annalisa let out another shuddering breath. I focused on the yellow roses in front of us as both my mind and my stomach settled into a still sadness. Annalisa would never scrub away the stain of being Last-selected as the Duke's own daughter. The only worse shame was an annulment.

Annalisa lolled her head back. "Besides, if anyone was going to calm down my obnoxious twin, it was going to be you. You would have been good for him."

Waves crashed against the distant cliffside as I pieced Annalisa's confession together. "Were you writing to him about me?"

Annalisa nodded and hiccuped, stifling another sob. "I just wanted him to make the right choice."

I gripped the edge of the stone bench and stared down at the cobblestone garden path as the truth sunk in—Annalisa was actually my friend. She wrote to Derrick for me. She helped me cover up the marks Derrick left on my neck. Annalisa was rough around the edges, sure, but she was a caring friend…and I struck her in front of everyone. Guilt swirled with the wine in my stomach.

I took her cold hands and looked her in the eyes. "Anna, I am sorry for… what happened in the dressing room. You were a better friend to me than I realized."

Annalisa smiled softly and squeezed my hands.

"A–and," I hiccupped. "You are too damn pretty to have been picked last. I call bullshit."

She snorted a laugh. "The real bullshit is Brietta getting her first fuck in the middle of my ball. I never understood why you liked her so much, with her always doing anything for attention."

I rubbed my arm across my cheek. "Because I thought she could protect me."

Annalisa raised a blonde eyebrow. "You thought *she* could protect *you?*"

Brietta would never throw a punch for me, nor would she ever dress someone down for looking down their nose at me, but she was still a person of *substance*. She was tall and wealthy, her parents were influential, and she had a magical way with her words. She was more powerful than I had ever let her believe she was, and I had foolishly thought her proximity kept me safe.

And now she was going to be the Duchess, and I was still just a weak little *nothing*.

Despite the bruises on my spirit, I gave Annalisa a half-smile. "Life is a lot harder when you are small, Anna."

An angry voice bellowed through the night air. "Get away from my wife!"

Annalisa and I looked behind us. My stomach dropped and Annalisa's sharp hand clapped over mine.

Riyan towered over us, having walked out into the garden without us hearing. Grigory glared at him from the palace steps like he regretted not bringing his bow and quiver to the ball, but Riyan did not even notice him.

Riyan's shining blue eyes looked only at me.

Chapter Fourteen
A Mirror's Edge

Just as I had worked up the nerve to tell Riyan to get lost, Annalisa stood up from our bench and marched over to him. Her teeth were bared in a snarl and her face was stained with black streaks. Riyan swayed as he stood but widened his glassy eyes and raised his eyebrows as she approached him.

"I do not care whose hero you are!" Annalisa cried as she pointed up at his chest. "If you hurt Serafina again, I will kill you! I will shove a knife in your chest and carve out your beast's heart with my bare hands!"

I gripped the edge of the stone bench as Annalisa valiantly defended me. The wine had turned her into a lioness, but my heart thudded as she challenged the Beast. Riyan could have swatted her away like a fly, but instead he merely looked down at her with knitted eyebrows.

Annalisa's voice dropped to a quiet growl, but her threat did not dampen. "How could you do this to her? You *monster.*"

A muscle feathered in Riyan's cheek, but he did not move.

Grigory bounded down the steps as fast as he could and put a protective arm around Annalisa. Her Hyton Blue eyes shot threats like invisible arrows at Riyan, even as her husband led her back into the ballroom.

I should have shoved myself off the bench and followed them, but Riyan stood between me and the ballroom door. I crossed my arms and turned away from him. Maybe if I gave him the cold shoulder, he would get the hint and leave me the hell alone.

His footsteps were uneven on the cobblestones as he lumbered over to me. "Serafina," he slurred.

I clenched my teeth as he said my name, further solidifying that I was his.

I kept my eyes on the roses and squeezed my arms. "Get away from me."

Riyan ignored me and plopped down on the ground in front of the bench. I wrinkled my nose as the burning stench of wine followed him.

The blood in my arms boiled. I snapped my head toward the colossal drunk slumped in front of me. "For a soldier, you are shit at following orders. Go away!"

Riyan scrubbed his face with his meaty hand. "Look, I know you are upset—"

"Upset?" I screamed, launching up from the bench. Finally my head was higher than his. "Of course I am upset! You ruined my life!"

Riyan blinked and his shoulders dipped forward. "I…I know."

Fire danced on my tongue. He knew. He knew he had doomed me and he had no remorse.

I gritted my teeth and flung my arm back toward the light of the ballroom. "Derrick loves me. I was supposed to be his Duchess and you took it all away!"

Riyan said nothing. He just sat there, watching my life fall apart. Was my misery just his entertainment?

I stomped closer to him so he could see just how much he had hurt me. He deserved to feel every slice of pain I had endured and more. "I hate you."

That was not enough. I screamed so loud the words echoed off the stars. "I hate you! If I could do it without dooming myself, I would *kill you.* I would kill you before you could hurt me any more!"

My throat was sore. My body trembled and my chest rattled with dry sobs. Riyan just looked at me, blinking his watery eyes for a few infuriating seconds before he swallowed.

His voice was a tiny rumble in the evening air. "You would really kill me?"

I crossed my arms and suppressed a hiccup. I pictured stabbing him in the eyes and holding *his* head up in front of an adoring crowd. The fire of my rage cooled to steel, and the word that left my tongue cut through the air like a blade. "Yes."

Riyan ran his hand through his hair, letting a few strands fall in his face as he looked down at the cobblestones. His voice was heavy. "I don't blame you." He finally looked me in the eye. "I'm sorry."

Despite how tightly I held my arms against my chest, my body kept shaking. My cold, steely anger disappeared, leaving behind something…wet and mushy that I could not contain. I opened my lips and what came out was more of a plea than a question. "Then *why?* Why me?"

Riyan sighed. "I…I had to. I could not marry Brietta Elvar after I saw you."

"What are you talking about?" I cried. I threw down my arms in frustration. "You never saw me before the marriage ceremony! Why are you lying to me?"

Riyan furrowed his eyebrows and raised his voice slightly. "I would never lie to you! Look, I saw you stand up to the Duke's daughter. You were so commanding and…and strong! I just…I knew I had to be with you after I saw that."

I gripped my arms again and backed away. "How could you know about that? That happened in our dressing room!"

Riyan clumsily slapped his palm to his face and cursed under his breath.

"You were spying on us?" I cried. "You disgusting piece of—!"

"We all were!" Riyan snapped. His low voice echoed around the stone. "All the suitors, even your precious Lord Hyton. We all saw it happen."

My head swam as I scanned the stones, looking for an explanation. Even Riyan was not tall enough to have looked in the windows of the dressing room. No one else was around when the altercation happened, either.

Then it hit me—the wall of mirrors. Duke Hyton was wealthy beyond my comprehension, but not even his own Duchess's dressing room had mirrors that large or numerous.

My breath skated over my lips in near disbelief. "Those mirrors, they were magic!"

"I, uh…will neither confirm nor deny."

"Were they? Tell the truth!"

Riyan threw up his hands. "They were cursed! Duke Hyton said if we ever told a woman about them, a…uh, great misfortune would befall each of us."

I shook my head. "What misfortune?"

Riyan's eyes fell to the ground. "I will not say, but you'd better hope I didn't activate the curse, for your sake."

A scream crashed out of my throat. I was sick and tired of playing games when it came to my own life. I wanted a damn answer already!

He shrank back as I bared my teeth. "You broke your agreement with Duke Hyton because you saw me smack Annalisa? What, did you just want a wife as violent as you are? Did you want me to be the perfect killer too?"

Riyan hunched forward and his blue eyes were as big as moons. "No."

I crossed my arms and grounded my feet in the cobblestones. "Then tell me. I…I at least deserve the truth."

Riyan nodded with a guilty look on his face. He shook his head like he was trying to swim through his own drunkenness. "You…you stood up for Brietta. You were so kind to her. And…and you said she was not a half-giant."

Riyan's voice became slower and more thoughtful. "As soon as I heard that, I don't know, it's hard to explain. You had never even met me, but I felt like… you already knew me. I felt *seen*—and it was the most wonderful feeling, Serafina. I could not give that up."

I knew what he was saying about feeling seen, but I had never felt the same way about it. I had always felt vulnerable, like I was trapped behind glass as someone examined my true intentions.

But that was not the only part of Riyan's confession that did not make sense. "Why would you feel seen? Why would you care if Brietta is a half-giant?"

His watery blue eyes looked into mine and his mouth turned up in a tiny smile. "Because, Serafina, *I* am not a half-giant."

My drunken haze fogged my vision. I squeezed my eyes shut and then opened them again, expecting Riyan to shrink to the size of a normal man when I looked back at him. "You…are not a half-giant? Then what are you?"

"A curse," Riyan groaned. "Long story short, my blood is full of magic and…it made me bigger than I should be."

Riyan ran his hand through his hair and looked down to the dirt. "My mother came home for a summer holiday after her third year at Ashmore. She went on a walk to the top of Nordingaard alone and came back down with me. I'm a child of magic, Serafina. I don't have a father."

Even in the wildest faerie stories I grew up reading, I had never heard of a child of magic. "How can you not have a father? Everyone has to have a father."

Riyan shrugged. "My grandfather told me the day she went up the mountain she was completely normal. Then they found her on the ground outside of our fortress, screaming for help. I was born right then. I came out the size of a one-year-old…I destroyed my mother."

Riyan sniffed and clumsily wiped a tear off his cheek. "She had to leave school. She can't even walk because I…was too big. She went mad at the first sight of me and can't talk anymore either. I completely ruined her life."

He looked at me with glassy red eyes and took a shuddering breath. "And I ruined yours too."

I gripped the fabric of my skirt. I tried to swallow my guilt down my sore throat. I should not have yelled at him, or told him I hated him and wanted to kill him. Riyan was not wrathful or cruel like I thought. He was just…sad.

Riyan was as tall as a house. He was the perfect killer and the Duke's valiant hero. And yet, sitting before me in the garden, he looked so small and vulnerable. Against my better senses, I started to reach for him.

My voice fluttered out softer than I expected. "Riyan, I—"

Riyan closed his eyes and laughed sharply. I drew my hand back, but he kept laughing. "You know, when the Duke's son was all outraged when I made my selection, I thought it was just his stupid pride. He even drew his sword on me and those little palace guards had to hold him back."

I sucked in a breath. If I had not witnessed Derrick's wrath earlier that day, I would not have believed him.

Riyan's laughter quieted into a smirk. "He kept shouting 'you cannot take her,' over and over but all that did was make me want you more. My selection was the one thing the Hytons couldn't control and I took advantage of it."

He sighed and looked down. The smirk disappeared. "Then I saw what that little prick did to your neck and it all made sense. You two were a couple and I broke you up."

My hand flew to the left side of my neck, covering up anything the satin ribbon of the choker did not. "How did you…how did you know it was him?"

"Only a Hyton would be bold enough to mark up a girl right before Selection Night," Riyan said with a low laugh. "You know, for someone who was so worried that I would eat her, you sure do like biting."

My hand dropped from my neck and crunched into a fist at my side. "Oh, so this is funny to you?"

Riyan looked to the side and dipped his chin. "No. It's not."

He slumped to the ground, lying on his side on the garden path. He stared at the hooves of the bull statue in front of him and shook his head slightly. "The Hytons can't own you."

I walked over to where he rested his head on the path and looked down at him with my arms crossed. "You do not know the law, then. If our marriage annuls, Duke Hyton *does* own me. He will own all of Ravenwood when my father dies too."

Riyan's face twisted up in confusion. He was a Baron's heir—he had not known the law because it would never apply to him or anyone he loved.

"Who would make a law like that?" Riyan asked with a hint of disgust in his voice. "Hyton is kind of a sick bastard, isn't he?"

My nails dug into my arms. "I hope you are referring to Duke Hyton and not his son. Derrick was going to help me *and* Ravenwood. Once I was his Duchess, I was going to influence how Ravenwood was run."

"I get it," Riyan said quietly, keeping his glassy eyes at the hem of my skirt. "Anyone outside of the Northern provinces would run Ravenwood into the ground. Us from the North deal with a lot of magic, so we know what to do when things get weird."

"That was why my marriage to Derrick was so important," I stressed, cringing at saying "was." My chest shook as I started to sob. "We had a secret relationship for seven years. I had everything planned out. And then you…"

Overcome by sadness, and maybe also by the wine, I knelt down on the cobblestones beside him as I struggled to catch my breath. No tears fell, but Riyan reached over and placed his hand on my back like a warm, heavy blanket.

"I'm sorry—for everything." His voice was so sweet that I heard him even over the pounding in my ears. "I'm sorry I dropped you on the dance floor.

I'm sorry I knocked you off the scaffold this morning. I'm sorry that…that I broke your heart. All I have ever done in my life is hurt people. I really am a monster, aren't I?"

Riyan's eyes swam with a mixture of drunkenness and sorrow. I caught my breath as I looked at him and my heartbeat slowed down. I did not know if I could ever forgive him for choosing me, but I could not hate him.

My chest shook. Maybe it was Fraleigh's enchantment in my blood or maybe it was just the wine compelling me to touch him, but I reached over to brush the stray blonde hairs off Riyan's forehead. His eyes brightened as my fingertip gently swept across his warm skin and his mouth turned up into a smile that revealed his dimple.

"You are not a monster." The words rolled off my tongue like a string of pearls. "A monster could not feel what you are feeling right now."

Riyan closed his eyes and groaned. "Maybe I do want to be a monster, then. This feels like hell."

I took my hand from the top of his hairline and gently pressed it against the side of his head. "By the way, is your head all right? You cracked the dance floor when you fell."

"Really?" He leaned his heavy head into my hand as he looked up at me. "My head is fine. I heal very fast thanks to all the magic in my blood. The stars are starting to spin, though, but I think that's from the third barrel of wine."

Against my better senses, I smiled. "Why did you drink three entire barrels?"

His smile grew even bigger. "One of those crusty old Barons told me I couldn't do it. I had to prove him wrong."

Laughter and clanging goblets rang through the night air above us. I looked up. Duke Hyton stood on his balcony, four stories above us and the massive bull statue, with a group of others.

"Go for it, boy!" Duke Hyton called down, leaning dangerously over the edge of the balcony's stone rails. "We all want to see the show!"

"Twenty marks says he does not shatter her pelvis!" cried a man in light green.

"One hundred marks says he does!" cried another man in purple.

The blood drained from my face and I backed away from Riyan. I was not about to be part of any show.

Riyan pressed his palms into the cobblestones and lifted his body off the ground. "Leave her alone!" He winced at the volume of his own voice and plopped back down on the stone path.

"Too much wine, boy?" Duke Hyton laughed above us.

Riyan looked at me with puppy eyes as his strands of hair fell back into his face. "I don't think I can get up. I'll just sleep here tonight. Get inside and go to bed before they can harass you some more."

"Outside? All alone?" I said in slight protest.

He smiled, showing off that little dimple again. "I'm used to it." He looked me in the face for a few more seconds and his voice became slower and more thoughtful. "You look just like them."

Before I could ask what he meant, someone yelled "Tear her skirt off!" and I ran to the palace. The crowd of nobles on the balcony jeered and hissed at me as I made my escape. I dared to look up at the balcony again and my stomach dropped. Mother was amongst the other vile nobles with Duke Hyton's arm around her waist. She smiled wickedly on Duke Hyton's arm as the men continued to wager on my body.

Bitterness coated my tongue and I fought the urge to spit it out. Mother was an even better liar than me. She could act like the Baroness, but she was nothing more than the Duke's willing whore.

I swallowed and retreated into the ballroom. I did not want to be around anyone for the rest of the night.

The ballroom was empty but trashed with discarded goblets and empty glass bottles. The candles in the room were either dimming or snuffing themselves out, so most of the light came from the moon outside.

I looked back out the windows at Riyan. He laid on his side, fast asleep already, in front of the bull statue. From where I stood, the rearing bull looked like it was stomping on Riyan or about to gore him. An hour earlier, I would not have minded if a bull really did gore him, but I looked at him with new eyes as he slept in the moonlight.

He was not a monster. He did not seem to have a beast's heart. He certainly also had feelings other than rage.

The tiny sun in my chest blinked to life again and warmed my blood. I shut my eyes, leaning into the strange warmth around my heart that pumped new feelings through my body that I named with each heartbeat.

Pity. Empathy. Understanding. Hope.

I let out a breath and turned away from the windows, ignoring the tiny tingling sensation in my fingertips and toes. Was the blood bond enchantment finally working? Was I just really drunk? Why else would I feel…*anything* for Riyan?

But did it matter? I only had two choices: seal my blood bond and risk shattering my pelvis like the nobles had wagered or let my marriage annul and live under the iron fist of Duke Hyton for the rest of my days. None of my stupid feelings played any role in the matter of my future.

But not hating Riyan at least gave me something to work with.

A maid appeared and offered to escort me back to the conservatory. I took one last look at Riyan and guilt crept through me for leaving him out in the garden alone.

We entered the conservatory and the maid helped me change into my nightgown. I tied my hair into a braid as I sat in the middle of the gargantuan mattress like I was drowning in a sea of blankets and pillows.

I tied off my braid as I weighed my two options: Riyan or Duke Hyton. I pressed the heel of my palm against my throbbing temple and laid down, pulling a blanket over my shoulders like a shield. My body was shutting down—rest would have to come before a new plan.

I admired the plants near the mattress as I breathed through my headache. Above me were wide, heart-shaped leaves, tiny black flowers in the shape of fangs, and tall, jagged leaves that pointed up to the sky.

As I started to drift off to sleep, the scent of the mattress tickled my nose. The scent was slightly masculine, probably what Riyan smelled like without the stench of wine. I took in a few breaths before I pinpointed the smell— nectar and wheat. As I was deciding if I liked the way Riyan smelled or not, a soft voice echoed in the darkness.

"Serafina?"

I rolled over toward the voice. There, nearly glowing in the moonlight, stood Derrick.

Chapter Fifteen
A Bronze Promise

I sat up on the mattress and covered myself with a blanket. Derrick stood next to my bed with a rectangular black case in his left hand. He had discarded his cape and coronet and wore a simple linen shirt and trousers. His dark curls fell in his face without the coronet to hold them back. His face was pale white in the moonlight with beads of cold sweat shining on his temples.

"You have a lot of gall to come here," I said with a snap of my teeth. "My husband could be back any minute! And after what happened at the ball—!"

"I know, Serafina," Derrick said softly with a wince. He put the black case down on a small table near the mattress. "But do not worry about that drunk brute, he is passed out cold in the garden. This was just my last chance to help you and I have a lot to explain."

"Do you?" I dropped the blanket and folded my arms across my chest. "Everyone in Lycaster knows what happened by now."

"You are right," Derrick sighed. He ran both his hands through his hair, stared up at the ceiling, and took in a deep breath. "And it happened in front of all those eyes."

To my surprise, my heart ached. My fists fell into the blanket as I searched for an explanation. "Then why? I thought you loved me!"

"I do!" Derrick cried softly. He quickly sat down on the bed and grabbed my hands. "Serafina, you are more precious than gold. You are the song in my heart, the air in my lungs—!"

I yanked my hands out of his grip. "You did not answer my question."

"I do not know how it happened, Serafina," Derrick pleaded. "I was dancing with Brietta like I was obligated to and then suddenly I was possessed with an overwhelming urge to…" His throat bobbed as he choked. His lip trembled only once. "I…I had no control over my own body."

I leaned away from him. "Did you and Brietta get together and make sure your stories matched? I did not believe the enchantment excuse with her and I am certainly not about to believe it from you!"

Derrick gripped his knees. "I swear, Serafina. She confessed she had a strong attraction to me while we were dancing and we were worried how that attraction could ruin the plan. Then the brute fell and ruined my ballroom. Once I was sure you were all right, Brietta and I ducked into the sitting room to address the problem before it got worse. But then…the problem got worse. Before I even fully realized what was happening, my father burst into the room and dragged me out in front of everyone."

His timeline added up from what I could remember, but I kept my arms tightly folded. "And that was it?"

"That was it," Derrick replied desperately. "I…I know you deserve a better explanation. I wish I could…I wish I had…but everything was a blur."

I looked down at the blankets. He had no reason to lie to me. He had looked so sad and confused as his father yanked him around the ballroom after the *incident*—just as he appeared as he sat on my mattress.

Blame floated through the air like a raven's feather—not knowing on whose shoulder to land and whose actions to condemn—but I knew for certain my Midnight would have never hurt me.

I met his shining blue eyes again. "I believe you, Derrick. Brietta did say that it happened very fast."

Derrick furrowed his brow. "It was not *that* fast, was it? I cannot remember…any of it."

The question burst out of me before I could process what he had said. "Do you love her?"

He did not hesitate for a moment. "No."

I dropped my arms. My voice broke and revealed how disgustingly weak and vulnerable I was. "Why did you choose her, then?"

Derrick absent-mindedly gripped the blanket underneath him. "My world crumbled when Bloodstone selected you. I tried to kill him, but a man's selection is sacred—no one has the power to change a selection after it is made. Not even me."

His knuckles turned white as he tightened his grip. He let out a shaking breath. "Regardless, I had to make a choice. Brietta is your best friend, so I married her knowing she would annul the marriage if it meant helping you."

Brietta and I had stood before the magic mirrors when she asked how she could repay me for helping her into her dress. Derrick must have heard every word.

I picked at a loose thread on the blanket in my lap. "You also knew she owed me. After what happened with your sister and your grandmother's dress."

Derrick's eyes widened and he quickly looked away from me.

I let out a short laugh, cutting the suffocating tension. "The mirrors are enchanted, Derrick. I know you saw everything."

Derrick shook his head in response, still refusing to meet my eye. I still did not know what the alleged curse was, but it had to be bad if even Derrick was afraid. "I also know the mirrors are cursed, so you cannot speak of them."

Derrick looked back at me with a look of disgusted surprise. "Bloodstone is an even bigger fool than I thought. I cannot believe he told you."

I smiled with what little pride I had left. "He did not tell me, I figured it out."

"Well, congratulations," he said flatly. "You are the first woman in the Dukedom to ever know about them. They are a *very* well-guarded secret, for obvious reasons."

"Oh, please," I scoffed. "I do not think any woman would be surprised to learn the suitors all wanted to see the brides in their undergarments."

Derrick's brow furrowed. "That is not the reason. You girls come out into the Presentation with all this makeup and jewelry and big hair that we cannot even really see who you are. The *you-know-whats* let us see your true selves before we make the biggest choice of our lives. It is just to keep things fair."

"I do not think you want to hear my opinion of what 'fair' is."

"Look, I know you are angry with me." He looked at me again and suddenly I was trapped in the deep sea of his shining eyes. "And you have every right to be. Whether I was in full control of my actions or not, I…I betrayed you."

Derrick's head dropped into his hands, his hair falling around him like a curtain. "I cannot believe I did this. A thousand apologies would not be enough. You must hate me."

As I looked at Derrick—hunched over in shame and vulnerable—, the tiny ember in my heart sparked again. I placed my small hand on his back as I leaned closer and tried to peer beneath the shield of his dark hair. My eyes danced along the small red cuts that marred his face, but I caught a peek of his curled eyelashes and smiled. "I could never hate you, Midnight."

Derrick's head rose and he looked at me with watery eyes. He took a breath and his despair hardened into determination. "I promised to take care of you, Serafina, and I will not go back on that promise."

"What do you mean?" I asked.

He turned his shoulders toward me. "I did not come here to sulk. I made another plan, but I need you to trust me."

My stomach knotted, but I had nothing else to lose.

"All right," I said in an exhale. "Tell me. I trust you."

Derrick's eyes shone as he spoke. "Fraleigh developed the blood bond centuries ago under the first Duke of Lycaster. Since then, each Duke and heir of Lycaster has memorized every rule, loophole, and requirement of this very old magic."

He took my hand in his. "You can still end your marriage with Bloodstone and go through Selection Night again."

I furrowed my brow. Fraleigh made clear she could perform a blood bond only once. How could any loopholes exist when *she* was in control of her own magic?

Derrick leaned in closer. "Brietta's brother will have his Selection Night next year. I will offer him a fortune large enough to even tempt an Elvar if he marries you…"

He looked to the side and swallowed. "…and since he is not in line for any titles…the House of Hyton will also make him the Governor of Ravenwood after your Father dies. You will not be Baroness of Ravenwood like your mother, but the House of Hyton will support you for the rest of your life."

Governess of Ravenwood. Derrick would let me marry again *and* invent a title for me? It was too good to be true. "How? I thought…I thought you could only marry once?"

Derrick kept his voice low as if he were afraid of being overheard. "The Dukes and heirs of the House of Hyton all know the way out of a less-than-desirable match without an annulment, but we only consider it in a situation like yours. Bloodstone has to die."

My hand flew to my chest and pressed on my heart. "Die? Would…would that not kill me?"

"Not if you do not consummate the marriage." Derrick's voice was serious, but he still attempted to be comforting. "Consummating seals the blood bond, attaching your hearts together forever. If you are not…*intimate* and one of the partners is killed before the next full moon, the bond does not fail, but is merely severed. Fraleigh can then re-attach the bond to another person at the next Selection Night."

I blinked. I was taught my whole life brides only had two options after marriage: consummation or the shame of an annulment. There was never a third option.

"How does no one know about this…this third option?" I asked.

Darkness flashed across Derrick's eyes. "The House of Hyton has kept it a secret for the last four hundred years. Alastar the Terrible killed seven of his wives, one after the other, trying to find the perfect one. My ancestors were so disgusted that they never wanted anyone to use the abhorrent practice again… unless we were desperate."

I swallowed. That was not the Alastar the Terrible we had learned about in history lessons at Ashmore. He was named "the Terrible" because he was a great war lord…not that he murdered seven innocent women.

Murder. Was Derrick actually suggesting that someone murder Riyan? A chill ran up my arms.

"Would he really have to die for the plan to work?" I cringed as my question left my lips like a plea.

Derrick nodded and the darkness did not leave his eyes. He reached over to the black rectangular case that he brought with him and placed it in his lap.

"Tomorrow, you and that beast leave the palace to travel to Bloodstone Fortress." Derrick flipped the latches of the case with twin clicks. "The Bloodstones are secretive, calculating, and cold-hearted, so very few have been inside that fortress. I could not send a man inside to kill him myself, much less without being detected by the rest of the Bloodstones. That is where you come in."

Derrick opened the lid of the case. Inside was a dagger the size of my forearm sitting on blue velvet.

He carefully removed the dagger from the case and presented it to me. The steel of the blade gleamed in the moonlight. The hilt was made of bronze and was forged into the shape of a bull's head with horns that pointed down to the blade.

"You have to kill him, Serafina," Derrick said.

I caught my scream before it could escape my throat. I was stuck between the dagger and my desperation as my pounding heart echoed in my ears.

How could he expect me to kill Riyan? I could not...I *would* not, kill him. I had manipulated, I had lied, but I was no murderer.

I pressed my palms into the mattress and leaned back, putting as much distance between me and the dagger as possible. "No...no! I cannot do it."

Derrick's voice hardened. "There is no other way. Baron Bloodstone has not allowed anyone from the outside into his fortress for decades. You are the only one who can end him."

My fingers clutched the knitted blanket underneath me. "Even if I could—the House of Bloodstone would know it was me. They would have me killed!"

"No, they will not," Derrick said calmly. "I certainly will not send our guard out to investigate his death, and, frankly, that beast has made enough enemies that no one would suspect you. You would be surprised how many people want the legendary half-giant dead."

My heart thudded against my ribs. "He is not a half-giant—just a child of magic. He only has magic in his blood, he is not a monster—"

"Makes no difference." Derrick's brow hardened. "How many times has he hurt you just today? On the very first day of your marriage?"

He was right—between the fall in the city square and being dropped on the middle of the dance floor, I was lucky I was not seriously injured. My mouth suddenly went dry.

"He did not mean to," I answered meekly. "They were just accidents, Derrick."

"That did not stop it from happening, did it?" Derrick said with a harshness I never expected coming from his lips. "How many more of these 'accidents' is he going to have? Or, more importantly, what is going to happen when he gets *impatient?*"

The last word hissed out of his mouth like it burned his tongue.

"Bloodstone is the last of his family line and he is desperate for an heir." His voice was dark as smoke. "If he forces himself on you, he will not just hurt you, he will *break* you."

Gold coins clinked when men wagered how hard my body would shatter. Women saw Riyan as a man worth dying under. Riyan had already broken his mother, was I next? A hard lump formed in my throat as I looked down at the massive mattress.

If I got into bed with Riyan, would I ever get up again?

My hands trembled. Derrick gently wrapped his warm hands around mine and held them as I went still. "I hate scaring you, but I heard so many stories about what…what he can do. You have no idea how much danger—"

"I know," I whispered. I looked back up at Derrick's colorless and serious face. "But *please* do not force me to kill him."

"I will not force you to do anything," he replied in a softer voice. "I just want you to understand that you do not have to suffer a horrible fate at his hands."

A cold, shaking breath escaped my lips. I squeezed my eyes shut and counted to ten. In the darkness, I took shelter in Derrick's promise—I would not suffer.

As I repeated his words in my head, Derrick slowly unfolded my right hand and turned it so my palm faced up. He placed the hilt of the dagger in my hand and guided my fingers to wrap around it. My eyes popped open as the cold bronze hilt stung my sweating palm.

"Just promise me you will keep it with you." The plea was cloud-soft as I gripped the dagger. "When you realize you are in danger, just sneak up on him when he is asleep…"

Derrick drew a line across his throat with his thumb. "One cut right here. That is all it takes."

My lower lip and shoulders trembled as my heart raced. "I am not a killer, Derrick."

Derrick placed his hands on my shoulders and held me steady. His jaw ticked but then he let out a slow breath and shook his head. "No, you are not. I cannot ask that of you. All I ask is that if you have to choose between your life and his, you will choose yourself. Promise me you will choose yourself."

I slowly flipped the dagger and held it inward so the blade rested against my forearm. I carefully folded my arm down and laid the dagger in my lap, hidden underneath my right arm.

Guilt consumed me like an inferno as I accepted the dagger, but what choice did I have? Derrick was right, I was in danger. Riyan was not a half-giant, but that did not mean he would not hurt me, accidentally or not.

The reality of it all was colder than ice-kissed steel yet plain as day—I would not survive if Riyan broke me.

Iron hands shoved my guilt into a shadowed abyss. Instead of tripping over emotions, I had to look at my situation logically. Before Derrick entered the conservatory, I had two options—consummate my marriage with Riyan before the next full moon or sit at the feet of Duke Hyton in the shade of his cruelty for the rest of my life. Each option all but promised suffering, injury, or even death. Derrick's promise of a new marriage and the title of Governess of Ravenwood was a beacon of light in the dark forest of my circumstances.

Besides, I did not *have to* kill Riyan. The blade beneath my arm was not a weapon thirsting for blood, but a mere lifeline. Nothing wicked.

Just a promise from a man who loved me that I would not suffer.

I took a deep breath and set my jaw with a silent vow—no more weakness, no more confessing feelings under starlight, and no more leaving myself open and vulnerable. I had to stay strong.

Even in the strength of my vow, the dancing red ember remained. The warmth from Derrick's hand still holding mine fanned the tiny fire in my heart. I flicked my eyes up to Derrick's serious face.

"You really would do all of that for me?" I asked. "A second Selection Night, bribing Brietta's brother, and making me Governess?"

Derrick took my face in his hands. "Of course I would." His thumbs stroked my cheeks as he leaned in to make his own vow. "I will do everything in my power to protect you. I promise."

His words sent warmth down my body and seeped into my bones like honey. Derrick was a good man. He took on his father for me. He crafted plan after plan to keep me safe. Even after the…*incident,* he still refused to leave me in a freefall.

My chest swelled and my lips flushed. Riyan was Lycaster's hero, but Derrick was mine.

My eyes fell to Derrick's lips but then flicked up to his moonlit eyes. "You also said you would annul your marriage to Brietta. How can I take you at your word?"

Derrick flashed me a half-smile and leaned in closer. His whisper skated across my lips. "How about I seal this promise and make it binding?"

I gave him a little nod and he pressed his lips onto mine.

I kissed him back and wrapped my arms around his neck. Oak and vanilla filled my nose. Lingering mint on his lips spiked my tongue. I melted into his arms—grateful for a distraction from the chaos.

Derrick grabbed me by the waist and pulled me against his chest. He took a deep breath and kissed me as if my lips were not enough. He wanted my breath. My soul. My spirit. He softly bit my lower lip and I quickly pulled away.

"Be careful with that!" I pointed to the left side of my neck. "Everyone saw what you did last time!"

Smugness gleamed in Derrick's eyes as he glanced down at my neck. "Fine, I will show some restraint." He moved to the spot where my jaw met my left ear. I whimpered as his warm lips touched my skin and his breath tickled my earlobe.

Derrick pulled me into his lap, but I felt a small prick and jolted away.

"Ouch!" I forgot the dagger was still in my lap and it pricked me in the belly. I ran a hand along my stomach—no blood, but the dagger tore a small hole in my nightgown.

Derrick took the dagger out of my lap and held it in front of me. "Careful, the last thing I want is for you to get hurt."

The dagger glinted in the moonlight and the reflection of my eyes flashed in the sharp edge of the blade. The dagger shifted and I pictured Riyan's watery blue eyes in the blade instead—facing the steel right before it kissed his throat.

My blood ran cold and my chest softened. I had just told him he was not a monster and yet I had a plan to kill him.

I took the dagger out of Derrick's hand and set it blade-down on the mattress between us.

I cringed—the bull-headed dagger looked so menacing on the soft mattress. "Am I supposed to have this thing even when I am sleeping?"

"*Especially* when you are sleeping," Derrick replied. "Just keep it securely under your pillow so you do not stab your eye out."

Derrick took the dagger and placed it beneath a pillow near me. "There, just like that."

I laid on the pillow and frowned. The bronze bull's head was lumpy even through the stuffing. "This is not comfortable at all."

"Just think of it as a constant reminder of my love and protection," Derrick said with a smile. He kissed the back of my right hand and then held it against his cheek.

I bit my tongue, even as I savored his touch. "Am I really unsafe in my sleep?"

Derrick exhaled with his mouth closed tightly. He was both serious and somber, but he let himself smile after a heartbeat. "Not tonight, at least."

He laid down next to me and pulled me close, letting my head rest on his right arm. "I will guard you until he takes you away."

I looked up at him and smirked. "Your wife is not going to mind that you are abandoning her tonight?"

"She is probably grateful for a night of peace after…you know," Derrick replied.

I was still angry with Brietta for sleeping with Derrick, but I could not help but think I came out ahead in the events of the night. By ruining the annulment plan, Brietta got what she had always feared—stuck with a husband who did not love her.

I kicked traitorous Brietta out of my mind and took a deep breath as I snuggled against Derrick. His chest warmed my cheek and the flame in my heart danced to the rhythm of Derrick's heartbeat.

A few hours ago, I had nearly retched at the wandering hands and smeared lip paint as House colors mixed, but I was too quick to judge. I may have been tangled up with a man who was not my husband, but that was not our fault. Just because the stars did not smile on the Duke's heir and I on Selection Night did not mean we had to be apart.

Derrick kissed my forehead. My hands gripped his linen shirt around his belly and the ember in my heart ignited into a blazing flame, hungry for another…distraction.

My lips ran up the linen until they found skin. I closed my eyes and kissed Derrick on his collarbone. He let out a shuddering breath onto my temple that stoked the flame to burn brighter, making me arch my back and press my chest into his.

The heat inside me intensified as if it were picking up where Derrick and I had left off in the shadows of Ashmore. I kissed him again and his neck muscles tensed under my lips. Derrick had said he knew how far we could go without breaking any rules of the blood bond enchantment and I wanted to see just how far my Midnight would take me.

I arced my aching hips against his—an invitation. He sucked in a breath.

"Darling, I…," Derrick said, his chest tight underneath my hands, "I…cannot. Not after what I…not after what happened tonight."

I tilted my head up to look at him as he held me. His face was tight but his eyes drooped with sadness. My fire cooled down instantly.

"I am so sorry," Derrick whispered. "I wish I could do more for you."

I smiled up at him. "Just keep me safe. That is all I ask."

Derrick cupped the right side of my face with his left hand and looked into my eyes for a few slow heartbeats before he spoke again. "Until my last breath. Brietta will be the Duchess one day, but I am *yours.*"

Derrick raised my face up to his and kissed me goodnight one last time. "And you are *mine.*"

I buried my head into his chest and fell asleep to the lullaby of his heartbeat as he stroked my hair. He locked his arms tightly around me, shielding me from the debauchery of Hyton, from the wrath of his father, and even the harm from my own husband.

I was warm, I was calm, but most importantly, I was under the protection of the stubborn Hyton bull.

Even if that bull was made of bronze and steel.

Part Three

Sugar

and

Steel

Chapter Sixteen
The Bet

Derrick's arms had locked around me all night, shielding me even from the cruel dawn. I opened my eyes to see his chest in the golden light of the morning.

I looked up at him as he peacefully slept and gently brushed a few strands of soft dark curls out of his face. The faded remnants of his freckles still dotted his cheeks and forehead. I traced his jawline with the back of my finger and moved down to his strong, dimpled chin.

He might have married Brietta, but the handsome man under my hands was still mine.

Derrick's eyes fluttered open at my touch and he gave me a sleepy smile. He groaned and shifted his shoulder blades in an attempt at a stretch. "Good morning, Serafina."

I tilted my chin up, bringing my lips closer to his. "Looks like I survived the second night. Thank you for keeping me safe."

I kissed him once and then lightly bit his lower lip. When I pulled away, Derrick's sleepy eyes fogged with confusion.

"Oh no," he groaned, "my bad habits are rubbing off."

I propped my head up on my arm. "So are you not worried what Riyan would think if he found us together?"

Derrick pulled me into another snuggle. "You assume that beast is capable of thinking. Regardless, he is probably still knocked out in the garden. I will have the servants dump a bucket of cold water on his head in about an hour. I am in no rush to leave you."

Delicate footsteps echoed throughout the room and we both looked up. The same maids from the day before stood at the top of the spiral staircase again and looked down at us. With an eye-roll, I plopped back down on the mattress. I had given the servants enough gossip over the past three days to sate their appetite for scandal for the rest of the year.

After Derrick failed to shoo the maids away to give us more time together, he turned to me and cupped my face in his left hand. His voice grew serious. "Remember what we talked about last night, Serafina. Stay away from him as much as you can. Do not let him even try…"

He could not say it, but I knew what he meant. I squeezed my knees together in silent assent to his plea—I would not let Riyan hurt me.

Derrick pulled me in for one last gentle and passionate kiss, gripping my face and hair underneath his fingertips as if he could hold onto me until the last star blinked out of the sky. He pulled away but lingered for a moment to look at me.

"My eyes will stay north until you return," Derrick gently whispered. "Please stay safe, Serafina. Please stay alive."

Derrick reluctantly left me with the maids, his eyes shining as he walked away. The maids quickly dressed me in a simple, but unseasonably warm, crimson wool dress paired with wool stockings. As soon as the maids disappeared, I reached under my pillow and retrieved the bull-headed Hyton dagger. Remembering my promise to keep it on me at all times, I wrapped the ribbon of my garter around the bull's horns to keep it secure.

The door to the conservatory creaked open just as I let down my skirt to cover the dagger. To my surprise, Mother walked in. Her hair was still tousled from whatever she had done with Duke Hyton and his friends the night before and the bite mark on her shoulder had turned purple.

I looked at a nearby bookshelf instead of the evidence of her shame. "I suppose you had fun last night."

"I would not say that anything I am doing is fun," Mother replied cooly. "Besides, it seems you have followed in my footsteps when it comes to associating with Hyton men."

How dare she. We were nothing alike.

I glared at her. "I do not need an escort. I can manage my way out of the palace just fine."

Mother knitted her eyebrows and pouted her lips. "Oh, I just wanted one last walk with my only living child before she leaves me forever," she whined. "Is that really too much to ask?"

I groaned, but followed my wretchedly manipulative mother out of the conservatory. I walked behind her in the hallway for a few paces before she suddenly stopped and turned to a large tapestry on her right. Her eyes darted around the deserted hallway before she pulled the thick tapestry back, revealing a small door.

"What are you—?" I whispered.

Before I could finish, Mother took me by the wrist and pulled me through the door. She led me through a narrow hallway lit only by dim sconces.

"I heard you got yourself tangled in a few webs, Serafina," she said as she pulled me along. "I thought you were smarter than that."

"You heard wrong," I grunted, pulling out of her grip. "I am not tangled up in anything."

Mother whipped around, her face partially hidden by shadows but still illuminated from the dying light of the embers on the walls. Her eyes flashed with danger when she spoke. "Lord Hyton thinks he can outplay those senior to him but he cannot, he is just too young to see it. Whatever new plan you have with him, forget it."

My hands balled into fists. "What do you have against Derrick?"

"I have nothing against that sweet boy." She snatched my wrist and led me further down the hallway. "The House of Hyton is unstable and desperate to find steady ground. Anders pulled off a very calculated stunt in front of all the other Barons last night—stifling the rumors that the Hyton line was failing *and* putting his son under his foot with one move. You will not involve yourself with the Hytons any more—your only salvation is consummating your marriage with Sir Bloodstone."

She was wrong. I could still marry again, become Governess of Ravenwood, and take everything Derrick had promised me, but I did not owe her an explanation. She had the nerve to lecture me when she was the one *tangled up* with Duke Hyton. Mother, Baroness, whore—she had just as many masks as Duke Hyton himself.

Mother stopped so abruptly in front of another door that I nearly slammed my face into her back. She placed her palm on the door, but paused just before she pushed it open. She turned back to face me with much softer eyes. "Are you afraid of Riyan?"

What kind of question was that? Everyone was afraid of Riyan!

"What do you think?" I snapped.

To my surprise, Mother smiled gently. "Fear and love are just two sides of the same blade, dear."

She placed her finger on my temple and gave me a gentle tap. "The more you fear someone, the more they are on your mind—in every thought, every heartbeat—until they have completely consumed you, like everything you are belongs to them. But the more you love someone…"

Mother's hand fell from my head to my chin, holding my face. "…the more you fear losing them."

I wrenched my jaw out of her grip. "Are you drunk?"

Derrick had once told me the palace had wines that could expand one's imagination—you would think you were dancing on pink clouds and singing to birds when in reality you were barefoot in the middle of the ballroom and croaking like a toad. Maybe Mother had continued her party past the sunrise, because nothing she said made any sense.

Mother dropped her eyes to the floor and opened the door a crack. She looked back up at me and whispered, "Just…do what feels right."

Mother slipped out and I rolled my eyes. Any respect I had for her was ashes in the wind after Annalisa's ball. She could keep her advice to herself, I certainly was not going to take it.

I shoved the small door open with my shoulder, emerged behind another tapestry, and suddenly stood in the grand entrance of the palace. Servants and soldiers buzzed around like bees as the Duke and General Hyton barked orders near the front doors.

I stayed three paces behind my mother as we walked to the palace doors to find a large black carriage waiting outside. At first glance I mistook it for a funeral carriage, but then I noticed the carriage was draped in bright crimson banners and had a snarling white bear with a raised claw painted on the door.

I swallowed my sadness—time to face the world as a Bloodstone.

The faint roar of a crowd outside the palace gates grew louder as we walked nearer to the open doors, but General Hyton approached us before we could leave the palace.

"Stay here, Adalia," General Hyton ordered. "Bloodstone and your daughter will exit the palace together. If the plan is going to work, the crowd needs to immediately believe their marriage is strong and that means Mother Dearest cannot hover."

"Anything you say, Ragnar," Mother replied with a glimmer in her emerald eyes. I wanted to gag.

Heavy footsteps boomed in the foyer behind me and I turned around. Riyan slogged his way toward the door in the clothes he wore the night before with his sword slung clumsily across his back. He had dark circles under his eyes and his head was sopping wet—Derrick had been serious about that bucket of water.

"Bloodstone!" bellowed General Hyton as he stomped over to him.

Riyan snapped into attention. General Hyton grabbed his soldier by his sleeve and dragged him off to the side. They were unseen, but anything but discreet.

"Are you still drunk, Bloodstone?"

"Uh, maybe?"

"Damn you, boy!" General Hyton hissed with rage. "You better not make a mess of this, everyone will be watching you. And you need to impress that girl if you have any hope of making this work! You are doing a piss-poor job at wooing her!"

The understatement of the decade.

"What am I supposed to do, General? You know I don't know how to—"

"First, stop throwing her on the fucking ground. Second, *charm her* or you will reap the consequences of your actions. Third, lay off the damn wine, you are as bad as my brother!"

General Hyton's angry footsteps grew closer and I kept my eyes forward, pretending I had heard nothing. General Hyton fumed over to his brother.

"Get this over with, the boy is a complete mess," he growled to the Duke. Duke Hyton smiled wryly and motioned for me to take Riyan's hand again. My eyes flitted to the steps, preferring to stare at the bricks over meeting the Duke's eye.

Then, Mother did something she had not done in years—she hugged me. She grabbed me and crushed me to her chest so suddenly that I did not know what to think.

So I did not think. I just breathed.

My heart slowly thudded as I closed my eyes and leaned into the warmth of her skin and the smell of herbs in her hair. I was a little girl again—so small but still so safe. My only responsibility was to mind my nursemaid. Erik and Endre were ready to play all day.

But just as quickly as the hug came, Mother unlocked her arms and moved out of the way as Riyan appeared on my left side.

And then I could not pretend I was safe any longer.

"Good morning…Madame," Riyan slurred. He clumsily grabbed my left hand in his right, the fresh scars on our palms meeting again. "You look, uh, ravishing?"

I took everything in me not to roll my eyes at him. He was not a monster, but he was still an annoying drunk.

Trumpets blared and the crowd cheered. As Riyan and I stood on the palace steps, I could see the crowd outside the palace gates waving Bloodstone and Ravenwood banners. Many of them were the same peasants from yesterday.

Riyan was supposed to lead me down the steps, but he was too lost in his drunken stupor. I gently tugged on his massive arm to get him down each step but still smiled at the crowd, pretending everything was normal.

I looked to my right and found Derrick, dressed again in his coronet and spectacular blue cape, standing next to Grigory and Annalisa. Brietta and Duchess Hyton were nowhere to be found. Derrick could not keep his eyes off me as I led Riyan down the steps. I leaned down and subtly patted where the dagger rested on my leg and he gave me a soft smile in response.

Riyan and I miraculously reached the bottom of the steps without a fall. Duke Hyton approached us and faced the crowd at the gate. "Join me in saying farewell to Sir Bloodstone, Hero of Lycaster, as he takes his bride home!"

The crowd cheered. I picked up my skirt and made it into the carriage by myself, only pretending to use Riyan's hand to guide me in. I looked out the carriage window back at Derrick one last time. His beautiful blue eyes glistened as he mouthed, "I love you."

Regardless if I were a Bloodstone or not, Derrick was still mine. Making sure no one from the crowd could see me, I subtly blew him a kiss in response.

Derrick gave me a forlorn smile while Grigory fumed next to him and glared at the crimson crowd. Grigory huffed and wrapped his arm around Annalisa, who had her hands clasped in front of her and looked at me with watery eyes.

I waved to Annalisa through the window. "Write to me, Anna! I will miss you!"

Annalisa's face perked up and she waved back to me. "I will! I promise!"

A whip cracked through the mid-morning air and the carriage lurched forward. Derrick kept his eyes on the carriage for a few heartbeats before turning to Grigory.

Then the carriage passed through the palace gates and Derrick was gone.

We rode through the city and the carriage shook from the cobblestone path. I stuck my head out of the window and looked up at the people cheering and waving down at me from their tall houses. I timidly waved back, but I soon realized they were not waving at me, but at what was behind me.

I looked back. Riyan walked behind the carriage with heavy footsteps, effortlessly keeping pace with the horses. The decorated Lycaster cavalry flanked him on either side, guarding him as he paraded through the city. Riyan did not wave at the crowd. He kept his expression steeled and his tired eyes bolted forward, not that I expected much more from him.

As we rode on, the city faded into a town, the town faded into a village, and then the village faded into the countryside. I jumped up in my seat as the carriage bumped onto a stone bridge.

"We are entering Bloodstone, Madame," the coachman called. I looked out the window to see the shining river that separated the cliffs of Hyton from the foothills of Bloodstone.

The carriage jolted as we finished crossing the bridge and traveled on the dirt road again. After a few seconds, Riyan grumbled "Stop the carriage, I need a break."

The carriage pulled off to the side and the footman eventually came to help me down the steps. Might as well stretch my legs, too. As soon as I put my shoe in the grass, I heard a rustling noise, bounding footsteps, and a loud splash. I walked around to the other side of the carriage to investigate.

First, I spotted Riyan's crimson cape lying in the grass, then his shirt, then his boots, then his trousers until my eyes met the rippling shoreline of the vast Odeneye lake. The water was deep and dark, even in the afternoon sun, but I carefully walked over to the shoreline.

Riyan came up from under the surface and rubbed the water out of his eyes.

"Much better," Riyan sighed as he sank back into the water.

I stepped onto a small grassy ledge over the water, careful not to stand too closely to the lake. "What do you think you are doing? We are supposed to be going home!"

Riyan raised an eyebrow and cracked a wry smile. "Eager to go home? Well, things will be much better for you if I wash all the wine off first."

He disappeared into the water as my cheeks burned. When did he become so…*forward?*

"That is not what I meant!" I shouted at the rippling water. I waited for Riyan to resurface before I spoke again. "What I meant was that we have a limited time to get to Bloodstone Fortress before nightfall. We need to stick to the plan!"

"We won't make it before nightfall," Riyan said lazily as he stretched back in the water. More of his chiseled body appeared from under the dark water, so I looked north and focused on some trees as he spoke. "You don't know this about me yet, but I don't stick to plans."

"You are a soldier," I argued, staring at the foggy peak of Nordingaard in the distance. "You have to follow battle plans!"

"All the more reason to hate restrictive planning. Plans can't fail if you never follow them in the first place."

Another splash and then silence. I dared glance back over to the rippling surface of the water that glimmered in the sunlight as Riyan swam in its depths.

I had no idea how to handle the situation. Riyan was a stone-faced monster in the city, a weepy drunk at the palace, and now a lackadaisical twit? How was I supposed to outmaneuver him if I had no idea which Riyan to expect from one moment to the next?

I bit my tongue as his last words stung the back of my mind. If he thought I did not know his disregard for planning, he must not remember that he had confessed abandoning the Duke's plan to marry Brietta. Of course, after three barrels of wine, he probably could not remember much of anything.

Maybe he even forgot he was sorry for hurting me.

"Riyan?" I called, hoping he could hear me under the water.

Riyan resurfaced, raising his body over the ledge and anchoring himself on the grass near my feet. He rested his head on top of his folded arms and looked up at me.

My eyes followed a drop of water running down the muscles on his arm. Then my gaze hopped over to watch more droplets racing through the reddish-blonde hair on his chest and trailing all the way down to…

I gulped. Thankfully, the dark lake concealed the lower half of his body.

His big blue eyes gleamed in the sunlight as he looked up at me. "Yes?"

"What do you remember from last night?" I asked, trying my best to not let my eyes wander along his massive arms. "After you drank that third barrel of wine, I mean."

He hummed thoughtfully. "I remember seeing you were upset, so I came out to the garden to make sure you were all right. Thornebow's wife yelled at me. We talked. You brushed hair out of my face. We kissed—"

"We did *not* kiss."

Riyan looked off to the side and frowned. "I must have just dreamed that, then."

I picked at the tiny tulips embroidered on my bodice. "So you have no idea what we talked about?"

"No," Riyan answered suspiciously. He groaned and buried his face in his folded arms. "Did I say something embarrassing?"

"You did not," I lied.

Riyan looked up at me with a raised eyebrow and a smirk. "*You* said something embarrassing, didn't you?"

"No!" I snapped. I might have had too many goblets of wine, but *I* at least knew how to keep my mouth shut.

He pressed his arms into the grass and leaned closer to me. "Sounds like someone needs to get in the water. Maybe then you'll feel better about whatever you said last night."

My heart skipped a beat and I fearfully glanced down into the lake. I pursed my lips and crossed my arms across my chest. "I cannot swim."

Riyan raised his eyebrows. "You can't? How could you never learn how to swim? What do girls do all day? Sit around and sew?"

I gripped my arms and set my jaw. "Sometimes. Embroidery is quite relaxing!"

He raised his eyebrow and grabbed the hem of my skirt. "How about I teach you how to swim?" He tugged me toward the water. "Come on, it'll be fun."

My stomach jumped. "Stop!" I pulled my skirt out of his grip and kicked his hand away. I was suddenly very aware of the dagger's blade against my leg, ready and at-hand.

"Fine, I guess I do need to dry off anyway," Riyan groaned.

Riyan pressed his palms against the earth and started to pull himself out of the lake. I quickly turned away and headed back to the carriage before I had to see any more of that man's body.

I stomped up the carriage steps and slammed the door behind me. I sat for a few minutes but the carriage did not move. I stuck my head out the window to ask why we were still waiting when I saw Riyan lying out on the grass…completely naked.

My heart stopped. He looked nothing like the diagrams at Ashmore. He was…*big*.

I gasped and raised my hands to shield my eyes from everything below Riyan's waist. My ears burned as the coachman and footman snickered outside the carriage.

"What are you doing?" I shouted. "People can see you!"

Riyan rolled his head back on the grass to look back at me, his arms folded under his head. "How else do you expect me to dry off? I can't imagine there is a faster way than letting the sun do its job."

I hissed a breath out of my nose. Drunk, lazy, infuriating—Riyan's list of unpleasant qualities was just growing longer. One of the white horses flicked its tail out of the corner of my eye and gave me an idea.

I leaned out the carriage window and kept my eyes on Riyan's face. "You were in the military academy for close to twelve years, right?"

Riyan smiled. "Yes."

"Sounds like you had a lot of training—*physical* training."

Riyan rolled over onto his stomach and propped himself up on his elbows. He flexed the muscles in his arms in a way he must have thought was subtle. "More training than you can imagine."

I examined my fingernails, keeping my voice cool and aloof. "With your size and the amount of time you trained, you must be the strongest and fastest soldier in the whole Dukedom."

"Definitely."

"Maybe even the entire world?"

"Absolutely."

I nodded toward the horses. "But I bet you cannot outrun the carriage."

"What would you bet me?" he responded, his eyes glistening with pride. "A kiss?"

"No."

"I'll do it anyway." He pushed himself up from the grass. "Just to prove you wrong."

I ducked my head back inside the carriage and sat down. I folded my arms across my chest and tried to settle my pounding heart as I relived the first time I saw a naked man over and over in my head.

Heat spread from my cheeks down to my hips. How could he possibly be that...*big?* No wonder the odds of my survival were low when the nobles started making bets.

I forced myself to calm down as I listened to Riyan put his clothes back on and chat with the coachman about the bet. A flash of red shot in through the window like a huge blanket.

"Hold this," Riyan said. "I don't want it to drag me down."

His cape fell on my lap, filling the carriage with the stench of stale wine. I scoffed and shoved the cape off my legs.

The coachman cracked the whip and the carriage lurched forward, sending me back into the seat cushion. Trees and bushes flew out of my vision through the window. My heart raced. I had never gone that fast before. I gripped the cushion with both hands to try to keep steady.

Through the window, I spotted a sprinting Riyan. In mere seconds, he passed the carriage and caught up to the horses. I carefully scooted over to the window and stuck my head out to get a better look. Riyan kept up with the team of four horses at full gallop. Then, with a burst of energy, he outpaced them.

I should have been intimidated and taken the show of power as a warning. Instead, my belly filled with mirth at the ridiculousness of the situation and I laughed. He made me laugh harder than I had in years—I was as weightless as daylight.

Riyan turned around as he ran, his blonde hair glowing like a halo in the afternoon sun. He shot me a wide smile and then faced forward and kept running.

The horses snorted and the carriage slowed down. Riyan, however, did not. He kept running along the road until he was out of sight.

I kept laughing long after he disappeared. I never thought I would be so delighted to lose a bet.

Chapter Seventeen
A Vanishing Sweetness

My teeth kept falling out.

Derrick was on the other side of an invisible wall, his palms pressed against the barrier as if it were just a window. His eyebrows were knitted, his mouth moving as he desperately tried to communicate with me, but no sound came out.

I wanted so badly to press my body against the glass wall to see if it would give, but my legs were stuck to the floor. I wanted to cry out to him, but every time I moved my lips to speak, another tooth fell out.

I just kneeled behind the wall, hands cupped under my chin to catch each of my crumbling teeth, and stared at his terrified blue eyes as my heart screamed.

My eyes popped open to a light tapping sound. I stared at the burgundy cushion in front of me. Dandelion yellow sunlight filtered in through the curtain. My fists gripped wool and were balled up in front of my mouth. Warmth surrounded me.

I was just in the carriage, not trapped behind a wall.

My memory came back in pieces as I blinked, but the scent of nectar and wheat mixed with wine filled my nose and made everything clear. I had cocooned myself in Riyan's cape to keep warm and the rhythmic jostling of the carriage had put me to sleep.

My stomach growled like a bear cub. I had no idea how much time had passed.

Tap tap tap. Someone knocked on the carriage door.

I rubbed my eyes and sat up, keeping the cape wrapped tightly around me. I opened the carriage door and blinked in the blinding afternoon sunlight to see Riyan holding a juicy red apple in his hand.

He smiled a little. "Hungry?"

I groggily nodded and he handed me the apple. I took the apple in one hand and kept the cape closed at my throat with the other. My teeth pierced the skin of the apple and sweet juice exploded on my tongue.

My first taste of Bloodstone was sweeter than I had feared.

I took another bite, letting the juice from the apple drip down my chin. In almost a minute, I had devoured more than half the fruit.

Riyan's eyes brightened as I ate. "Do you want some more?"

I nodded again. I took in a sharp breath as he picked me up in his left arm. My fingernails punctured the apple as my other hand gripped his bicep.

Riyan put his free hand on my shoulder. "Don't worry, I've got you."

His word was no good since he had already dropped me, but his hold was so steady I unclenched. He carried me a short distance to a small grove of apple trees next to the carriage. Golden sunlight dappled through the dark green leaves of the trees. Riyan ducked to avoid a low-hanging branch with apples hanging off it like drops of blood.

He gave me another soft smile before picking another apple high up in the tree above us.

I looked around from my vantage point at Riyan's side. The coachman and footman ate apples near the carriage. The horses were off their reins and munching on fallen apples in the grass. I spied a pile of apple cores tall enough to reach my knee near the base of the tree where Riyan stood.

"Looks like you have been here a while," I said as I eyed the pile.

I tossed my own apple core into the pile and Riyan handed me a second apple. He reached up and plucked a third apple from the tree.

"You work up a big appetite when you're the fastest man in the world," Riyan said with a proud smile. "So you lost the bet. Now you owe me."

I took another bite of the apple. "I already said I was not going to kiss you."

"That's not what I want."

Before I could ask what he meant, he sat down on the ground. He set me on his right leg and my stomach flipped when I realized I was dangerously close to what was hiding beneath his pants. His face was hard as he looked down at me. Fear filled my belly along with the apples.

Riyan let out a soft breath. "I want you to tell me what we talked about last night. It's only fair."

He was right. If I had drunkenly spilled the deepest parts of my heart, I would want to know exactly what I had said.

Placing the pieces of our hazy garden conversation together like a puzzle, I planned out what I would tell him. I would keep it simple, leave out the teeth-gnashing and the weeping, but I would emphasize one point that might help me.

I ran my fingers along the deep crimson skin of the apple in my hands. "You told me that you were not a half-giant. You said you were made of magic and did not have a father."

Riyan nodded his head. "That's true."

"You also told me what you saw through the magic mirrors."

Riyan's eyes grew wide in panic and he cursed under his breath.

"You did not actually *tell me* about them!" I quickly corrected. "I do not think whatever the curse is will affect you."

Riyan sighed in relief and shook his head. "I sure hope not. What else?"

I deliberately avoided his eyes and made my voice soft as kitten fur. "You told me you were sorry."

His voice hitched with worry. "Sorry? For what?"

I donned a forlorn mask and sighed. I lifted my gaze to his face. "Taking me from Derrick Hyton."

"What?" Riyan asked indignantly. "I would never apologize for that. Hyton is a spoiled, pampered brat who thinks he can take anything he wan—"

"You said you were sorry for breaking my heart."

Riyan's face fell and he looked away from me. For a few heavy moments, all we could hear were the horses happily eating their apples.

"Did I really break your heart?" Riyan asked softly, almost in disbelief.

I looked at the grass. Truthfully, my heart was a smoky enigma surrounded by tall granite walls. My heart may have ached, its stony shields may have cracked, but it would *never* break.

But Riyan did not know that.

I might not have known exactly how to play Riyan, but I knew he could feel pain. His tears in the Duke's garden showed me he was capable of deep remorse, even if he did not remember any of it. The scourge of guilt on his back for breaking my heart might keep him from acting reckless and breaking my body.

Was it wrong? Maybe, but I had few options to keep myself safe. Telling a lie now was kinder than plunging a dagger into his throat later.

I waited another heartbeat before going in for the kill. I slowly raised my eyes as I knitted my brows and pouted my lips slightly—looking as tragically heartbroken that could be believable.

Riyan took a deep breath, taking my pathetic face as confirmation, and his face turned to stone. He started to rise and I scrambled off his leg.

He towered over me as he looked north. "Fine, Serafina. We will get what needs to happen between you and I over with, then you can go back to your precious Lord Hyton."

Without giving me another glance, Riyan solemnly headed north on his own and left the rest of us behind. As I watched him disappear up the road, a chill pricked my skin. I wrapped the crimson cape tighter around me to try to warm up again.

The heartbreak lie had worked better than I planned—Riyan had just given me the best outcome for this marriage possible.

I could continue my relationship with Derrick and influence the governance of Ravenwood that way—not ideal, but I could make it work. I could have the safety of a blood bond with Riyan, Derrick's affection, and a hand in running Ravenwood all at the same time. I could have everything I ever wanted—I should have been celebrating.

But I could not celebrate. I could not even smile. As I stood alone under the apple trees, holding Riyan's cape around me with one hand and the half-eaten apple in the other, all I could feel was a strange and empty sadness.

My fist loosened and my apple fell in the dirt with a thud. All the sweetness left on my tongue had vanished.

Chapter Eighteen

Fortress of the Mountain

The sun had disappeared behind the tall pine trees and the sky bled purple and blue as we ascended Nordingaard mountain.

Riyan had said we would not make it to the fortress before nightfall, but my palms started to sweat as we traveled alone in the dark without Riyan to guard us.

What a prick, leaving us undefended just because he had a bad temper.

I pulled Riyan's cape up around my head and held it under my chin, giving myself a small refuge. The smell of nectar and wheat surrounded my face underneath the burning stench of wine.

I searched my mind to figure out why I was unhappy with Riyan's new agreement. He would make our blood bond permanent, but would also let me return to Derrick. Once back in Hyton, I could form a plan to get Ravenwood the help it needed without having to slit any throats and spend as many nights as I wanted in Derrick's arms. I would just need to produce some Bloodstone heirs after a while to fulfill my duty as Baroness, easy enough.

In my head, the agreement all made perfect, logical sense. In my chest, however, a prevailing gloominess stopped me from being satisfied with the arrangement. Maybe that rain cloud inside me was what Brietta meant when she had blamed the marriage enchantment for having feelings she did not want.

I hummed in the silence of the lonely carriage. What would Brietta say if she were with me? Although, did I really even know Brietta anymore? The Brietta I knew before the night of Annalisa's ball would have told me to be careful, listen to my feelings, but to ultimately run to Derrick as fast as I could. But the new Brietta, the future Duchess Hyton, who fucked Derrick and yelled at me? Who knew what the new Brietta would say if I asked her about my stupid emotions.

Well, instead of Brietta, what if Annalisa had joined me on the trip to Bloodstone Fortress? I cracked a smile—Annalisa would have stormed after Riyan through the apple grove and yelled at him for throwing a tantrum like a toddler.

Weathered knuckles rapped on the front of the carriage and interrupted my thoughts.

"We're here, Madame Bloodstone," the coachman said. "Welcome home."

Home. I pulled back the burgundy curtains and looked through the glass. All I could see was a stone wall topped with battlements and lit up with torches. I slid back the glass window and stuck my head outside to get a better look.

I squeezed my shoulders out of the window and pulled myself up, craning my neck to see the top of the wall. I met the eyes of a few men who talked on top of the wall, each one wearing a red military uniform.

The first secret of the fortress revealed itself before I even passed through its walls—Bloodstone had its own army.

A province having its own army was treason. Either the Duke did not know about the red-chested army of the mountain or he had made a special exception for Bloodstone somehow.

We rode up to the only entrance into the fortress, a large iron gate. Riyan leaned on the wall next to the gate, seemingly waiting for us. He gave the gate guards a signal and chains clinked as the gate slowly started to rise. Riyan ducked to cross under the gate and went inside, not even bothering for the gate to rise all the way.

As the carriage crossed through the gate, the massive fortress keep grew closer and closer. The keep was huge, built from chiseled mountain stone, with large square towers on each of its corners. A giant crimson flag bearing the snarling white bear hung above arched double-doors into the keep.

My throat shook as I tried not to picture the iron gate slamming shut behind me.

"March on!" commanded an unseen soldier.

The horses slowed down. Soldiers with swords on their hips marched in lines flanking the carriage and outpaced us as we approached the keep.

The carriage rolled to a stop and my stomach twisted with anticipation. I pulled myself back into the carriage and sat down as the door swung open. I expected to see Riyan's hand lowered toward the door to help me out, but my heart sank a little when the raised hand of the footman appeared instead.

I accepted the footman's aid and Riyan's cape dragged behind me as I stepped to the ground. I spotted Riyan's large shadow out of the corner of my eye and looked around to find him standing behind the carriage.

Riyan had his arms crossed and his eyes on the arched doors at the top of the tall stone steps into the keep. Gravel crunched beneath my feet as I walked over to stand beside him. He did not even glance in my direction.

Bloodstone soldiers flanked either side of the tall stone steps with their right hands on the hilts of their swords.

"Salute the heir and Madame Bloodstone!" cried the same soldier from earlier, a lean man with a large scar across his face.

The two lines of soldiers on either side of the steps raised their swords aloft in a salute. I smiled a little at the impressive display. Riyan scoffed and rolled his eyes.

The two soldiers at the top of the steps tugged open the keep's doors wide enough that a carriage could pass through. I picked up my skirt with one hand and raised the other to Riyan so he could help me up the steps. He ignored me and stomped toward the keep. My hand fell like a wilting flower as Riyan walked up the steps, taking them two at a time, and leaving me to climb alone.

Asshole.

The scar-faced soldier appeared at my side and quickly wrapped my hand around his forearm.

"Here, hang on to me." The soldier started to lead me up the steps. He was relatively young, maybe late twenties, with a jagged scar that cut between his yellow eyes and stretched down to the left side of his jaw. "Forgive him, he forgets his manners sometimes."

I raised my eyebrows and smiled tightly in response. Of course, Riyan's brutish notoriety had preceded him.

We trudged to the top of the steps and the soldier escorted me inside. The entrance of the keep had a high ceiling and the stone walls were decorated with rusted shields, white bear skins, tapestries of beasts and monsters, and scarlet banners bearing the Bloodstone crest.

The keep was dark. Not dark like Ravenwood Manor—with blackthorn trim lining the walls and deep green and black fabrics draping the walls and covering the furniture—but dark as in foreboding.

I bit my tongue but the smell of cooked mutton made my mouth water. I peered through the open arched doors in front of us to find a large dining table piled high with steaming food. My stomach growled at the promised feast, and suddenly I did not have much of an opinion on the keep's decor.

"Riyan!" a cheerful voice cried.

A round, old woman with snow white hair and bright pink cheeks ran out of the arched doorway from the dining room. Her wide smile fell when her grey eyes raised up to her grandson's face. An old man with a withered face like an eagle's stepped in behind her, his face hardening at the sight of Riyan.

"You grew," the old man said with a sharp tongue.

"A boy tends to grow over seven years, Grandfather," Riyan replied flatly. "Don't see why you're surprised."

Baron Bloodstone's thin lips tightened and his eyes narrowed at Riyan before they looked over in my direction. "Thank you, Captain. Glad to see someone remembers how to treat a lady around here. You are dismissed."

The captain of the Bloodstone army let go of my hand and turned to walk out of the keep, but not before shooting Riyan a glare from his yellow eyes.

The old woman, who could have been no one else but Baroness Bloodstone, stepped forward into the keep's entrance. Her smile returned and her eyes sparkled as she looked up at her grandson.

"We prepared a feast for you!" Baroness Bloodstone said proudly, gesturing behind her into the dining room. "You must be starving after such a long journey."

"I lost my appetite," Riyan said. He turned away and walked into a dark stairwell in the corner of the room. He ducked under the archway and disappeared up the stairs. His thudding footsteps faded as Baron and Baroness Bloodstone looked at each other in stunned silence.

"I prepared all day, Nikkolas," Baroness Bloodstone whispered to her husband. "I fed Astrid and sent her to bed early so we could all enjoy a meal together!"

"That damn boy," Baron Bloodstone scowled as he looked down at his wife. "The marriage was supposed to fix him!"

On the mention of "marriage," Baron and Baroness Bloodstone both looked in my direction. I tugged the cape tightly around my shoulders as both sets of grey eyes examined their heir's wife. Baroness Bloodstone gasped and ran over to me.

"Oh, my dear girl," she exclaimed, placing my face in her soft hands. "You are skin and bones! You need to eat right away!"

She placed her warm hand around mine and led me through the arched doorway. I admired the needlework of red roses and amber wheat stalks on her bodice—beautiful, but much plainer than I expected of a Baroness.

The dining room was cavernous. A huge chandelier hung above us, wrought with iron claws gripping flickering candles. The dining table was not like the one at Ravenwood Manor with individual chairs all around, but was instead long enough to seat at least two dozen people with long benches on either side. The only chair was at the head of the table with a bear's head carved into the back.

I swung my legs over the bench and sat at the right-hand of the luxurious chair. Baroness Bloodstone giddily plopped down on the bench across from me while Baron Bloodstone slowly walked over and sat on the ursine throne.

I expected servants to come around to serve us the meal, but Baron Bloodstone picked up the carving knife and fork and sawed away at the roasted mutton on a silver platter in front of him. He speared a large slice of meat and plopped it on my plate.

"What is your name, dear?" Baroness Bloodstone sweetly asked me, her face slightly obscured by the steam drifting up from the mutton. "We know absolutely nothing about you!"

"My name is Serafina Ravenwood, Baroness," I replied, picking up my knife and fork and cutting a piece off the thick slice of mutton.

Baron Bloodstone dropped another slice of mutton on Baroness Bloodstone's plate and then carved himself a helping. He muttered something about Ravenwoods under his breath but Baroness Bloodstone piped up before I could figure out what he had said.

"Oh, please do not use titles here, Serafina," she said with a wave of her hand. "Just call me Hilda."

As Hilda spoke, Baron Bloodstone started attacking his meat with his cutlery like it was going to fight back.

"I know it may take some getting used to," Hilda said, completely unbothered by her husband's war with his dinner, "but Bloodstone is not part of normal Lycaster society. We are very…oh, what is the word I am looking for, Nikkolas? Instant? Inbred?"

"Not inbred!" Nikkolas spat, choking on his bite of mutton. "You mean *insulated*."

"Yes!" Hilda said with a smile. "Insulated. Why, we have not been to Hyton in decades!"

I put all my focus on grabbing a soft roll in the bread basket so I would not laugh. "I was surprised when I did not see you in the Duke's palace. I was looking forward to meeting you since all the Barons have to be in Hyton for Selection Night."

Nikkolas chuckled with a soft smile as he took a sip out of his silver goblet.

Hilda cut her husband a look, but her smile stayed sweet. "Duke Hyton gives us special permission to skip Selection Night. Our daughter, Astrid, cannot travel. We both stay here to take care of her."

Astrid. The woman Riyan broke.

"Sir Bloodstone and I had a lovely time during the festivities," I lied. "The House of Hyton were wonderful hosts."

Nikkolas glanced at me with an amused smirk on his face. "I am surprised my grandson has not scared you off yet. General Hyton wrote that he gets quite ferocious."

I tried to swallow the bite of my roll, but my throat suddenly went dry. How much more ferocious could Riyan get? Hilda pursed her lips and her eyes went wide.

"Do not say that to her!" Hilda smacked Nikkolas on the arm. "What Nikkolas means is that our Riyan is a spirited young man."

"No, I meant ferocious," Nikkolas said pointedly, stabbing his fork in the air for emphasis. "Savage. Bellicose. Sadistic. Pick one! Any word would fit!"

I had never heard the word "bellicose" before, but between the words "savage" and "sadistic," it painted an even more macabre portrait of my new husband than I had feared.

If I did not already have the Hyton dagger tied to my garter, I would have stolen a knife from the table before going to bed.

"So you were selected first, my dear?" Baroness Bloodstone asked dreamily, deliberately changing the subject. "I was the third selected—which was pretty good! Many more people were eligible for Selection Night back then, you see."

"I remember." Nikkolas's gruff face turned up in a soft half-smile. "I was sweating during our selections because Alastar the Wise and Baron Thornebow got to pick before me. Good thing they were both too stupid to choose the best bride."

Hilda's round cheeks flushed. "Stop," she cooed, "everyone just wanted the Diamond of the North."

I stopped chewing at the mention of Duchess Ilsa. No one would dare speak of Ilsa without fear of severe punishment in Hyton, but in Bloodstone we could casually talk about her over dinner as if she were an old friend.

"Bah, I never saw the appeal," Nikkolas scoffed. "If I had wanted to wake up to a mean, cold face every morning I would have slept with a mirror." He gave his mutton a forceful stab. "She always had the strangest eyes too. Not just because they were purple, but so rigid and unfeeling."

Hilda's voice dropped to a whisper. "Well, that was because she could not—"

"Anyway, I am glad everything worked out," Nikkolas interjected as he sliced his knife across his meat. "Well, except for my two former classmates who are now underground. You know, Richard Thornebow was as bright as the bottom of a well. No surprise he got tangled up with Ilsa Ravenwood and the Hytons."

"I liked Ilsa," Hilda remarked with a smile. "Regardless of what everyone said."

"Of course you did, darling," Nikkolas said brightly as he cut up his meat. "You do not dislike anyone."

Nikkolas gave me a wink. "Hilda is the only person in Lycaster who likes me. I have to be the luckiest man alive. Everyone fought over the Diamond, but I made off with the real jewel on our Selection Night."

Hilda's cheeks turned bright pink and she cooed in delight. I could not help but smile.

"Oh, but you were so grumpy at first!" Hilda giggled. "I was so worried you thought I was a foolish woman and hated me."

"Never," Nikkolas said with a small laugh.

Nikkolas and Hilda continued reminiscing about their first few days of marriage while I ate. A twinge of jealousy crept down my neck as I spread spiced honey butter onto my roll. I was supposed to have a nice marriage like them, but I was stuck with a drunk with an attitude problem. I shifted my right leg and the blade of the Hyton dagger caught the inside of my wool skirt.

I ignored the dagger and took a bite of the warm, buttered roll. I did not want to think about my options or plans, I just wanted to eat.

Hilda blushed. "We went into the third week of our marriage before we… you know. Remember, dear, it is all right to take your time."

"But not too much time," Nikkolas added with a pointed glance in my direction. "You only have, what, twenty-seven more days left after tonight? You know, Hilda, perhaps that is why my heir is still so cantankerous even after the marriage enchantment! He is all frustrated and bothered because they have not—"

"Shh!" Hilda hissed, whacking her husband's arm again. "You are the one who is going to scare her off, not Riyan!"

I needed to escape the conversation before they also started wagering how my husband would tear through my virginity.

I rose from the table. "Thank you for the delicious meal, Nikkolas and Hilda. The journey was long and tiring, so I need to be off to bed."

"Well, listen to her," Nikkolas said to his wife, jerking his thumb toward me. "Why are you so worried about me scaring her? She is just as eager to get to bed as any Ravenwood girl."

My eyes fell to the birchwood floor and my cheeks blazed. I half-ran
to a stairwell in the corner of the dining room and tried to ignore the
embarrassment plunging through my stomach as Hilda chided her husband
for his impropriety. I had no idea if that staircase led to the bedrooms—I
did not even care if it led to a dungeon just so long as I did not have to look
Nikkolas Bloodstone in the eye for the rest of the night.

I climbed the spiraling steps to the top story. Red runners on the wood
floor pointed the way to a dark hallway decorated with tapestries and small
portraits rather than weaponry—a good sign that I had found the family's
private quarters.

Might as well see if my bedroom was nearby. I walked up to the first
wooden door on my right and cautiously pushed my way inside.

I found a bedroom, at least. The bedroom had a tall, vaulted ceiling and a
huge square bed on a tall wooden frame. No one but Riyan would have a bed
that large. I held my breath as I scanned the room looking for my trunk, not
daring to take a single step inside.

I silently let out my breath with a smile when my trunk was nowhere in
sight. As crass as Nikkolas was, he had at least blessed me with a separate
bedroom. I turned around and tried the door on the opposite side of
the hallway.

A much smaller bedroom waited for me on the other side of the door. The
bedroom could only fit a small bed, a wardrobe, and a writing desk inside. I
looked closer into the room and spotted my trunk squeezed in between the
wardrobe and the writing desk. The room was tiny, probably by design so
Riyan would not fit comfortably inside.

I silently thanked Nikkolas for my little refuge from the brute as I
undressed. After a good five minutes of struggling to unlace my bodice
without maids to help, I finally wriggled out of my dress and slipped on a
nightgown from my trunk. I untied the Hyton dagger from my garter ribbon
and quickly shoved it under my pillow like it would catch fire if exposed to
the air for more than a second. I put all my clothes back into my trunk and
closed it with a pat on the Ravenwood crest.

I sat on the soft mattress and tied my hair into a braid as I looked out the
small window with diamond glass panes. Soldiers patrolled the top of the
fortress wall while others led the white horses through the courtyard, over

a small stream, and into stables near the wall. The waning moon glowed as ribbons of green light danced across the inky sky.

The celestial lights cast a soft green glow on the blankets. As much as I resented that I was on a glorified cot in a fortress instead of a four-poster bed in the palace, the lights brought a smile to my face. The lights never stretched down to Hyton, so I was finally far enough north to feel like I was home again.

Warm quilts and knitted blankets kept the mountain air out and I snuggled into my pillow, feeling the hilt of the dagger against my cheek. I took the small discomfort as a reminder of Derrick's love and protection, just like he had wanted.

Just a promise that I would not let Riyan hurt me.

The door creaked open and flickering candlelight crept in. I looked up from my pillow as shirtless Riyan ducked under the doorway into my bedroom. The wooden floor groaned underneath his bare feet and he bowed his head to avoid hitting the ceiling. His eyes were dark underneath the shadows of his brow. The dim firelight danced along the contours of his bare muscles as he approached my bed.

I squeezed my knees together and held my breath. He thought I was heartbroken and he still wanted to attempt sex? What a prick.

I knew it would happen eventually, but I wanted to acclimate to a new province before he got under my skirt. Nikkolas had given Hilda three weeks—Duke Hyton had even given his Duchess a week—but the infamously savage Riyan could not even give me *one night* of peace.

But I could not tell him no, Ashmore had made it clear brides never had that right.

Maybe I could fend him off by making him think I was dead tired. My right hand slowly slid under the pillow and wrapped around the hilt of the dagger, keeping a tight hold on my lifeline just in case he turned…bellicose.

"Where did you go?" I asked sleepily, pretending he had just woken me up. I put on a yawn like a mew of an exhausted kitten and nuzzled my head into my pillow.

"None of your concern." His short snap was like a cudgel in the air. "Doesn't matter, anyway. I'm here now."

He moved closer to the bed. My sweet yawn and heavy eyelashes did not throw him off his hunt. I glanced up at his pants and caught the hard outline of his…oh, *shit*. It was the size of my forearm. Sweat beaded on my palm around the bronze handle of the dagger.

The sleepy plan had failed. Time to distract him with thoughts of his kindly old grandmother.

"Your grandmother set out a wonderful dinner," I said with a false smile. "I cannot believe you left us."

"I wasn't hungry then," he replied in a low voice.

As soon as he shifted his weight to take another step closer, a coil in the back of my mind that had wound tighter every year I had been alive sprung loose and rancid resentment spread through my body.

A lifetime without choices or control all led to this—the moment where I had been trained to not say no. To always give in. To seal that precious blood bond no matter what.

And I was *so tired* of not getting a choice. I could not choose who I married. I could not choose my home. I could not choose when I became a mother.

But if I was not going to be given a choice, I would *take* my choice. I chose a night of peace, and if Riyan put a single hand on me, I would spill blood.

As I glared up at Riyan, I faced something larger than him, larger than even a real giant—but like a beast of the ocean depths, I did not even know what it was.

But I was going to fight it anyway.

"She planned out a whole feast for you, Riyan!" Fury burned the edges of my voice. "And you just stormed off! Just like you stormed off from the carriage. And you stormed off after Grigory at the ball. Is there *anything* that you do not ruin with your temper?"

"I don't follow plans." Riyan's deep voice was rough, filling the tiny room with the threat of his force. "Never have, and don't expect me to start just because you're particular."

How lucky for him—being so big and strong he could do whatever he wanted while others had to survive as serpents in the shadows.

I nearly bit off the tip of my tongue with how hard I snapped my teeth. "And you called Derrick Hyton spoiled?"

"What?"

"You heard me."

Riyan stared down at me for a moment with intense eyes set deep into his strong brow. Tallow dripped down the candle in his hand as the failing flame withered. My heart throbbed in my throat as I glared back up at him. I waited for him to tear me out of the blankets and carry me out of the room, or throw me against the wall, or reach down to try to take me.

The man who towered over me with shadows across his face was not the same man who playfully ran around the Bloodstone countryside and fed me apples or who spilled fat tears of regret in the Duke's garden. He was just as Derrick warned, *impatient.*

Riyan's hissing breath sliced through the tension like a sword.

"Are you still in love with him?" He spat out the question like it tasted bitter.

I gritted my teeth. What I truly felt for Derrick was locked up safely in the dungeon of my mind. Riyan might take my chastity, but he would never get that secret out of me.

I lifted my chin. "None of your concern."

Riyan's jaw clenched at my answer. "Is this really how you want this to be, Ravenwood? I thought you wanted to get this over with."

He pinched the flame of his candle and enveloped us in darkness. My right arm trembled with the tightness of my grip around the dagger.

My eyes adjusted to the dim glow of the waning moon and the familiar green lights of the night. The thin bands of light whipped across Riyan's back as he turned away. His head bowed low and his shoulders slumped forward as he walked with heavy footsteps out of my room. He closed the door shut behind him with a sharp thud.

My body unclenched and I let out a long, shaking breath.

I released my grip on the dagger and wiped the sweat off my right palm. I rolled over onto my back and listened to my heart pound as my thoughts raced.

Twenty-seven nights were left. "Getting it over with" had seemed like a simple task mere hours earlier—just one last hurdle before I could go back to pulling Derrick's strings—, but *nothing* was simple with Riyan.

I had spent the day tip-toeing on a blade's edge, not knowing whether the man who could snap my bones in half would be sweet or cruel. Silly or stoic. Ridiculous or ravenous.

I hissed out a breath through my nose. The longer I watched the waning moon slowly dip through the night sky like sand falling through the hourglass, the less probable consummating my marriage seemed.

But why should I keep walking on the blade when I could wield it instead?

I pressed my face into the pillow, letting the tiny horns from the dagger's hilt poke me in the cheek despite the stuffing. I would not annul the marriage and be at the mercy of Duke Hyton. I would not shatter under the hands of my brutish husband.

I might have lived in Bloodstone, but I was still a Ravenwood. I would survive.

I closed my eyes and remembered Derrick's words as I fell asleep.

One cut. That is all it takes.

Chapter Nineteen

Splintered

Morning sunlight peeked behind puffy clouds and lit up my bedroom as I opened my wardrobe. The Bloodstones had left a few garments in the oak wardrobe, most of them shades of red, but some in gentle forest tones. I picked through the clothes and found a grey wool skirt and a light green linen blouse. Annalisa would sniff and call them peasant clothes, but I called them comfortable.

I took the lack of maids barging into my room as a sign I was supposed to dress myself. After three days of servants interrupting my private moments in Hyton, I relished in my impenetrable bubble of privacy.

I secured the Hyton dagger to my garter just after I dressed. I had laced the leather waist cincher as tightly as I could to hold the baggy linen blouse in, but the sleeves still hung past my wrists. The skirt completely covered my leather shoes and swept the wooden floor. The Bloodstones had clearly expected Riyan to choose a bride of a respectable size.

My heart jumped when a loud boom rattled the glass panes of the window. I ran over to the window to see if a giant had stomped down the mountain's peak to attack the fortress.

Thankfully, no giants in sight, only Riyan storming away from a large tree trunk that he had dragged through the grass and slammed onto the ground. He crossed the courtyard to a rack of shining battle axes and grabbed one. In a blink, he growled and hurled the axe at the tree trunk. The blade splintered the bark and stuck into the wood. Riyan threw another axe, but missed the trunk and sent the spinning blade toward the eastern wall. Riyan had thrown the axe with so much strength that the blade sliced off a chunk of the stone wall before ricocheting toward a fleeing group of soldiers.

I scoffed and turned away from the window. Was he raging because I rejected him last night? Although knowing Riyan, he could just as well be angry because he found a fly in his porridge or because one of the soldiers looked at him wrong.

Before I could think about it any more, my stomach growled louder than Riyan had. Wanting to ignore my husband's tantrum and hoping a large breakfast would help fill out my clothes, I headed toward the smell of another feast. Once I reached the bottom of the flight of stairs, I peered from the stairwell archway into the cavernous dining room.

Hilda sat at the dining table and picked at a bowl of porridge. Nikkolas stood in front of the eastern window with his arms clasped tightly behind his back. I almost left the stairwell to join them when Nikkolas scoffed in disgust. I hung back in the shadows to listen in, hungrier for information than breakfast.

"He is worse than when we sent him off to General Hyton," Nikkolas said bitterly. "Look at him, he is destroying the courtyard."

Hilda met her husband's distain with calmness. "Riyan is just anxious."

"Are you blind? He is not anxious, he is in another rage!"

"You have not given him a chance since he arrived, Nikkolas."

"Arrived bathed in the stench of wine, you mean?" Nikkolas snapped. "Or has your nose gone as blind as your eyes? He is a disgrace!"

I swallowed. Of all the terms I could use to describe Riyan, "a disgrace" would not have been one of them. No one who felled ten giants could *ever* be a disgrace.

"Nikkolas, he is a war hero!" Hilda cried in a high-pitched voice. "You know boys always come back a little different after a big battle. Why, even just yesterday some of our soldiers got into a little tussle."

"I never asked him to galavant around the mountain and lop off giant heads!" Nikkolas shouted, turning around to face his wife. "All he had to do was get married and sire an heir. He had the damn first selection! And who did he pick? That tiny Ravenwood girl! Idiot!"

Hilda slammed her spoon on the table. "He is not an idiot!"

"What do you think is going to happen when that moron tries to have sex with her?" Nikkolas spat. "He is going to break her legs or snap her spine, or worse! He will crush her to death!"

I bit my tongue as an icy spider of fear climbed up my back.

"He is not that cruel!" Hilda cried.

"Her dying is not even the worst that could happen." Nikkolas slowly walked to the table, punctuating the tense silence with every footstep. "What if he hurts her so horribly she loses her mind? Do you want to care for another Astrid? Do you want to leave *two* broken women with him when we die?"

My head swam, but I planted my feet on the floor and grounded myself. My bones were unbroken, my mind was intact—I was fine. Just fine.

"Quiet, Nikkolas!" Hilda hissed quietly as she rose from the table. "She will hear you!"

"Maybe she should!" Nikkolas replied, not bothering to keep his voice low. "Ravenwoods are smart. Maybe she has already run away!"

I leaned up against the stone wall of the stairwell and took a deep breath. Father had seen the danger I was in, as did Derrick, and even Riyan's own family argued about when and how I would die. I reached down and patted the dagger through my thick skirt, needing the reminder of my lifeline.

I was a Ravenwood. I was a survivor. He could not break me.

The stone wall shook as another boom thundered through the keep. I clenched my teeth and pushed against the wall, propelling myself out of the stairwell and toward the keep's doors. I was sick of Riyan's damn temper. Someone needed to put a boot in his ass before he hurt something.

Apparently, the tiny Ravenwood girl was the only person in the damn fortress brave enough to stand up to him.

I stood at the top of the steps outside of the open doors as Riyan hurled another battle axe. A trio of soldiers, including the captain, stood on top of the wall above the tree trunk. Those cowards said nothing and merely looked down at Riyan with a mixture of fear and amusement on their faces.

Riyan had flipped the tree trunk over so he could whack at new bark. He stood twenty paces from the tree trunk and threw another axe. The axe splintered off some bark as it bounced off, the shining steel blade whirling through the air before thudding into the grass off to the side.

"You are going to take someone's head off!" I shouted.

Riyan glanced up at me as I stood at the top of the steps. Sweat dotted his temples and wet the hair on his forehead. His chest heaved with his breath as he panted.

Riyan took his eyes off me and focused on the tree again as he grabbed another axe off the rack next to him. "I don't know if you've heard, but that *is* my specialty."

He threw the axe with an angry grunt. The axe hit the tree and ricocheted into a nearby pen of hairy white and brown goats. The goats bleated in a panic and ran around the pen, but none of them were hit.

I gestured to the terrified goats. "Calm down before you kill something!"

"What do you think I am doing?" Riyan snarled, picking up an axe from the rack next to him. "I did this at the academy all the time. Just go away!"

He threw the axe with an angry hiss through his teeth. Luckily for the goats, that one stuck to the tree.

I picked up my skirt in my fists and stomped down the stairs. I did not care what titles he was born with or earned, he would *not* dismiss me like I was nothing.

I marched through the grass over to the tree trunk as the soldiers on the wall gasped and whispered to each other. Just as Riyan was about to hurl another axe, I stood in front of the axes sticking out of the bark and stared him down with my hands planted firmly on my hips.

"Move, Serafina!" Riyan shouted.

"Put the damn axe down!" I shouted back.

Riyan glared down at me, his shoulders rising and falling with the outrage hissing out of his breath. I glared back up at him and grounded myself in my unmoving stance.

Not breaking his furious gaze, Riyan slowly lowered his arm and finally dropped the axe on the ground. He had a large tear in his right sleeve, probably from grabbing at the axes like a barbarian. He only had one shirt as far as I knew and someone needed to fix it before he tore the entire sleeve off. I could mend it in fifteen minutes.

"Get over here," I said in a calmer and cooler voice.

Riyan blinked in confusion, but stomped over to where I stood. I folded my arms and tilted my head back to look up at him as he glowered down at me.

"What?" he growled.

"You tore your shirt."

"So?"

I held out my hands. "Hand it over."

"Why?"

"If I cannot stop you from acting like a beast, I can at least stop you from looking like one. You are scaring people."

"That's what I do—I scare people! I've scared people since I was a child! You don't think I'm not used to it by now?"

"You want me to be afraid of you?" My voice was softer and incredulous, like I would not believe him if he said yes.

Riyan's face softened and his shoulders drooped a little. He melted back into the Riyan I had met in the Duke's garden. "Well, no. Serafina, why are you—?"

"Damn you, boy!" Nikkolas yelled, standing outside the keep's doors at the top of the steps. "Get out! Go destroy something else!"

Riyan growled, but he quickly took off his shirt and threw it down to me before stomping toward the gate.

I caught the shirt in my arms—it absolutely reeked. I groaned as I quickly folded it up and stuffed it under my arm to get it as far away from my nose as possible. I eyed a small stream by the wall that sparkled in the morning sunlight and promised myself I would wash the putrid shirt after I mended it.

Maybe a clean, mended shirt would put Riyan in a nicer mood and make him easier to deal with.

I climbed the steps into the keep like I was on a mission. I had already stepped toward the stairwell to my bedroom when I caught sight of Hilda at the dining table with her head in her hands.

I let out a breath. I did not want to get involved in the family tension, but Hilda was too sweet for me to not repay her kindness. I walked over to the table and sat a respectful distance from her on the bench.

"Good morning, Hilda," I said softly, placing Riyan's folded shirt in my lap.

Hilda lifted her face from her hands and her tired eyes lit up when she saw me.

"Oh, my dear!" she said breathily. "I am so sorry for all the chaos. Riyan has not been home in so long and I am afraid he is not adjusting well."

Clearly.

"Do you know why he was in such a temper?" I asked.

Hilda sighed and looked down at the wooden table. "Has he told you about his mother?"

I could not look her in the face as I answered. "A little. He told me she cannot walk or speak."

Hilda nodded, still keeping her grey eyes on the table. "Astrid has been, well, *afflicted* ever since Riyan was born. She may have survived the birth, but we lost our daughter."

She looked up at me and smiled softly. "Little by little, though, parts of her have come back to us." She took my hand as it rested on top of Riyan's shirt. "Come, I would love to show you."

I did not know what to expect, but I followed the warmth of Hilda's hand and rose from the table with her. Hilda took one glance at my loose-fitting blouse and reached into a wicker basket on the table. She pulled out an iced bun and popped it into my mouth without so much as a word.

I chewed through the sweet icing and bread and held the rest of the bun in my hand as she led me to the stairwell on the opposite end of the room. We climbed another spiral staircase to a similar dark hallway with red runners.

We stopped in front of a door with a rainbow of painted flowers on the wood and Hilda pushed the door open. Inside was a large bedroom with paintings on parchment tacked to the wall. The paintings were smeared in smudges and dots like they had been finger-painted.

I noticed a painting of domineering and dark figures. Then a painting of a large pool surrounded by tall rocks and snow. Then a painting of Bloodstone Fortress.

"The magic of Nordingaard is not just giants and destruction," Hilda said as she looked at all the paintings. "Now that you are in the House of Bloodstone, you get to know our secrets."

Hilda's sweet words sent a warm hug around my heart as I ate the rest of the bun. My blood bond with Riyan was not even sealed, but Hilda still considered me her family. The dagger burned on my leg as I swallowed my bitter guilt along with the icing.

I had always wondered what having grandparents would be like. Hilda was so kind and Nikkolas…at least cared enough about me to be concerned for my fate. I had seen the mysterious Baron and Baroness of Bloodstone as potential allies, but they saw me as their family—for better or worse.

Would life at Bloodstone Fortress be an endless cycle of Nikkolas giving me hard advice and Hilda soothing me with warm pats to the hand and a sweet treat? Would Hilda teach me new embroidery techniques? Would Nikkolas show me how he commanded his army? Would we sit next to the hearth at winter solstice, sipping hot milk as they told me old mountain legends?

My stomach fluttered. I was…excited to be a Bloodstone.

Hilda looked at me with a smile and a twinkle in her pewter eyes, like she noticed.

She gestured to the paintings. "We know of a magical healing spring near Nordingaard's peak. Ever since Riyan's birth, we have taken Astrid to the spring as often as we can and let her bathe in it. Each time, she comes back with something to tell us."

She placed her hand on a painting of a woman with light brown hair holding a little blonde girl. "As soon as she comes back from bathing in the spring, we give her a parchment and paint and she recreates a memory—a picture from what is left of her mind."

Hilda lovingly stroked the painting, running her fingers gently over the little blonde girl's face. "This one is my favorite. A few years ago, she came back from the spring and painted her and I together. My precious daughter has only spoken five words since Riyan's birth, but she can still tell us she loves us in her own special way."

She crossed the room to Astrid's bed, where someone had tacked a dozen paintings of a blonde baby and a blonde child. Hilda pointed to a portrait of the yellow-haired child with blue thumbprints for eyes.

"This is how she remembers Riyan," she said in a wistful voice. "I do not think she even knew he was her son, but she enjoyed being around him for the most part. He would sit in her lap and she would stroke his hair. He brought her flowers nearly every evening and told her she was the most beautiful lady in the world. She could not understand him, but he still tried every day, hoping one day she would answer back."

I hugged my arms. I had only pictured splintered bones and a shattered mind when I thought of Astrid, not the little boy on the other side who just wanted his mother. Riyan went his entire life with a ghost of a mother, hoping every day a flower or a smile could bring her back to life.

But it never did.

Hilda's face fell as she sighed. "Then, Riyan started growing. Riyan was always big, but he started having these fits of rage when he was six. Every time he would have a big outburst, he would grow again. By the time he was nine, he was bigger than most grown men. Astrid got so scared of him because of his size and that only made Riyan's fits worse. He loved her so much and… and he never understood why she was so afraid of him."

Riyan's words in the courtyard were a hammer against my granite heart. *"That's what I do, I scare people! I've scared people since I was a child!"*

Fat tears rolled down Hilda's face. "Nikkolas made a deal with General Hyton to send him to the academy to try to fix him." She mopped up her tears with the edge of her sleeve. "He might have been as big as a man, but he was still only a boy, *our* boy, and we had to send him away…"

I could not bear to see Hilda cry alone—not when she was my new grandmother. I released my arms and gently placed my hand on her shoulder.

"He…he got to see us right before the first Nordingaard battle," she said through her tears. "He was fifteen and passed for just a very tall man. He could have had a normal life…but he got even bigger. General Hyton wrote that Riyan's rage had not stopped—and it has not! We all saw it today! But I know it is not all just rage, he is just scared."

I could not imagine Riyan being scared of anything. "What would a man like him be scared of?"

"Astrid is at the healing spring today," she answered. "As the Baron of Bloodstone, Nikkolas knows of a secret pass to get up and down the mountain quickly and safely, and we send a party of our best soldiers with Astrid just in case, but we always worry when one of our own goes up the mountain."

Hilda looked at a picture of a small boy holding purple flowers. "Riyan has not seen his mother since he went to the military academy. He must know that she will come back from the spring safely, but I know he is terrified of what she will do when she sees him at his size."

I stared at the smudged images of child-like Riyan. Astrid had made enough portraits of him that she at least had a fascination with the blonde boy who lived in the fortress, but she had no idea who he was. I hated my mother for her disgusting *affiliation* with Duke Hyton, but at least she knew me. At least she could understand me. Riyan did not even have that.

Hilda pulled me into a hug. I squeezed my arms around her soft body as she wept.

"I am so glad Riyan chose you," she whispered. "He just needs someone who is not afraid of him."

I bit my tongue. Anyone with sense would fear someone Riyan's size who had seemingly limitless strength and a high capacity for bloodshed…but I did not think I could fear him any longer. All I could see when I thought of him was a sad child holding wilting flowers in his hand.

Someone needed to not be afraid of the little child of magic, even if he had grown up.

I looked over Hilda's shoulder, still snuggled in her warm embrace. Amongst the portraits I could recognize as the Bloodstone family, I noticed a painting of a strange red creature. The creature had horns like a goat and cloven hooves for feet, but the chest, arms, and face of a man. My eyes darted around the room and found painting after painting of the creature.

"Hilda," I said quietly, my eyes fixed on one of the smudges of red that formed pointed horns. "Are *all* of these pictures from Astrid's memories?"

Hilda released me from the embrace as she sniffed away her tears. "Oh, did you find the monster?"

She was too calm. "Is the red creature the monster?"

"Yes," she replied with a brightness in her voice that I was not expecting. "He was there when Riyan was born. Nikkolas and I found him standing over Astrid outside the fortress with newly-born Riyan in his hands. The monster cut him out of her."

Questions spun in my head but shock held my mouth closed. My eyes darted from Hilda to the picture of the monster and back. Hilda took note and laughed softly.

"Giants are not the only monsters hiding in Nordingaard, Serafina," she said sweetly. "Bloodstone is curious and wonderful…but we do have tall walls for a reason. Please just promise me you will be careful."

I nodded and shifted my weight so my blade scraped against my stocking again.

Maybe the Hyton dagger would taste the flesh of a monster after all.

Chapter Twenty
Mending

The world was at peace when my needle was in my hand.

The bright rays of noon sunlight kissed my bare shoulders. I sat at my writing desk in my undergarments, shortening the sleeves of my blouse to the proper length. I moved on to my skirt, humming a few tunes as I hemmed my skirt to skate around my calves. The sun had barely dipped in the sky when I had finished and re-dressed.

I rolled my silver needle on the pads of my fingers, itching to sew more. I grabbed Riyan's shirt from the top of my trunk and started stitching the torn edges of his sleeve together. His shirt sleeve was longer than my leg, but the tear only took me minutes to mend.

Hilda had created a pitiful portrait of Riyan after breakfast—a sad and lonely boy who was cast aside by his terrified mother and sent away by his cold-eyed grandfather.

Riyan had mentioned on our first night together that he was sent to General Hyton's military academy when he was only nine years old. Until I saw Astrid's paintings of him, I had not even realized how young that really was.

The guards at Ashmore were disciplined enough to keep quiet around us, but I still picked up bits of information they dropped under their breath in the hallways. They always shuddered when they remembered their time under General Hyton.

And Riyan was only nine when he had endured it all.

My scissors snipped the thread when I finished. I ran my finger down the long white stitch—the bond was strong, but somehow felt incomplete.

Maybe…I could do something nice. Maybe I could show the little blonde boy that he had at least one person who was not afraid of him.

I retrieved my embroidering hoop from my trunk and set up the sleeve to add extra detail. I pulled the first stitch of white thread through the linen, imagining one of the painted flowers on Astrid's door.

My hands weaved my silver needle faster and with more precision than my silver tongue could weave lies. General Hyton had told me to give Riyan a chance, Mother had told me to surrender my body to him, and Derrick had told me to slit his throat. All of them whispered in the back of my mind, but as I pulled the needle and finished the first flower, their commands quieted into silence.

My granite heart bore cracks, but still held strong. I was not so weak that I was falling for Riyan, but I at least pitied the scared and lonely child of magic. Besides, if I could get him to soften up like I did earlier in the courtyard, the next twenty-five nights might go more smoothly.

The needle gleamed in the sunlight as it poked through the linen. I pictured a bouquet of spring blossoms in a large hand with the smooth knuckles of a young boy as I created the second flower. Riyan had given years and years of flowers with no response. Maybe once you tire of flower stems to pick, you pick up the wooden handle of an axe instead.

I sighed as I started the third and final flower. Riyan Bloodstone was a drunk with a bad temper, but he was still no monster. He at least deserved a response to his flowers.

And I was finally giving him one.

The light of the golden afternoon filtered through my window as I finished the three flowers that completely covered the mended stitch. White thread on white linen made a subtle design to the eye, but a beautiful texture under my fingertips.

I looked down at Riyan's cape on the floor, which still reeked of wine. I gathered both the cape and Riyan's mended shirt in my arms and walked down to the stream near the western wall.

The stream was shallow enough that my stomach did not tumble with fear as I leaned over the water and washed the cape. Once in a while, Headmistress Blackiston would take all the Ashmore students to one of the streams in Hyton to wash our uniforms. She said it kept us "meek and humble." Annalisa and most of the other girls had whined about laundry being servants' chores, but I never minded. I could think of no greater satisfaction than fixing something and making it clean and new again.

Any of the other girls from Ashmore would laugh if they saw me bent over the stream. I was First-selected—by a Baron's heir, no less—and still breaking a sweat on chores. Regardless of what anyone else in Lycaster would have thought of me dressing and acting like a mere peasant, I enjoyed the peace and solitude that came with the work.

As I worked the cape into the rocks on the side of the stream, I listened to the bleating of the goats, the lowing of the four cows, the whinny of horses in the stables, and the footsteps and low chatter of the guards on top of the wall. I heard no angry heirs throwing weapons or frustrated Barons yelling—just the peaceful sounds of a working courtyard.

I finished washing the cape and hung it on a clothesline to dry. Riyan's shirt was much easier to wash since it was a thinner fabric, so I finished it quickly. The sky was a burning orange as I hung the shirt on the line and a jovial cry rang through the courtyard.

"Raise the gate! Miss Bloodstone has returned!"

I looked south to the gate and a parade of red-chested soldiers walked into the courtyard. I left the clothes on the line and walked over to meet Astrid Bloodstone for the first time.

Hilda ran out of the keep toward the party. Nikkolas stood in the middle of the courtyard, keeping guard over a large easel with parchment and paint ready.

The largest soldier in the party carried the woman who had to be Astrid in his arms. She was a frail woman with wispy hair the color of honey and wore a simple linen dress, very similar to a nightgown. She had no light in her grey eyes, but wore a crown of purple and white flowers on her head as if she were a faerie princess.

"Beautiful girl, how are you feeling?" Hilda asked as she stood in front of her daughter.

Astrid whimpered and her arm trembled as she pointed to the easel.

Hilda clapped her hands and smiled. "She is ready!"

The soldier carrying Astrid carefully jogged over to the easel and rested Astrid on her knees in a limp sitting position. Without hesitation, Astrid dove her hands in the pots of paint on the ground next to the easel and smeared her fingers all over the parchment.

I stood next to Hilda and watched in awe as Astrid's hands flew between the parchment and paint, her grey eyes sparking like thunderclouds as they fixed on the painting.

"I swear, if she paints *that thing* again," Nikkolas grumbled.

Hilda hissed at him to be quiet. Everyone watched in silence as Astrid finished the painting.

She had not painted the red monster, but a human man. The man had long blonde hair with a square jaw and dots of blue paint for his eyes.

Astrid touched the sides of the parchment with her pigment-stained fingers and looked at her mother. Her eyes were pleading and almost shaking with energy.

"She painted Riyan," Hilda whispered in amazement. "She wants Riyan."

"You do not know what she wants, Hilda," Nikkolas said sternly yet gently. "You do not even know if she really painted the boy."

Hilda turned to her husband and her voice grew serious and determined. "It is time, Nikkolas. We cannot keep them apart forever. Astrid *will* see her son as soon as possible."

Chapter Twenty One

A Breaking Dawn

Astrid ran her fingers on the edge of the parchment and looked up at her parents with glassy eyes. One of the maids tried to clean Astrid's hands off with a rag, but Astrid violently fought off her help as she whimpered.

I never thought a woman so frail could swing her arms with so much force, but both the maid and Hilda were unbothered by Astrid's strength.

An excited smile spread across Hilda's face as she rushed over and knelt next to her daughter. "Do you want to see him?"

Astrid responded with more pleading eyes, pulling her right hand out of the maid's grip to point at the man she had painted.

Hilda cheered and held her daughter in her arms. "You will see him soon, dearest. We just need to let you rest after a long day."

I smiled. Riyan would finally see his mother for the first time in twelve years.

"Madame Bloodstone," said a gravelly voice behind me.

I turned at the mention of my new name. A young Bloodstone soldier carrying a courier's bag stood with two letters in his hands.

"These just arrived for you, Madame," the soldier said as he handed me the letters. Both letters were sealed with the crest of the House of Hyton stamped on blue wax. My name on the first letter was scribed in perfect, straight lettering—Annalisa's writing. The other bore my name in a familiar slanted and swooping script. Brietta.

The letters nearly burned the skin on my hands. Hilda was distracted with Astrid, so I bade goodnight to Nikkolas and rushed back up to my bedroom.

I sat at my writing desk and laid the two letters in front of me. After the long day, I needed whatever amusing anecdote or witty complaint was in Annalisa's letter. However, my mind burned from whatever Brietta could to say to me after what had happened at the ball.

I grabbed Brietta's letter, curiosity overcoming any other reasoning, and tore the Hyton seal off the envelope. I unfolded the letter and read Brietta's beautiful handwriting on the page.

Sera,

I must begin with an apology. The Brietta you knew drowned to her death in wine at the ball, but I recognize that I unwittingly placed you in a precarious position of which I do not envy and could never understand. For that, I am deeply and truly sorry.

Brietta Elvar was a weed among roses and a weeping sapling caught in storm after storm—unable to stand on her own. For years, you were my support, my safety net, and then a hindering crutch. Do not mistake me, I am eternally grateful for you and what you sacrificed to keep me content in times of strife. Brietta Elvar needed you. Brietta Hyton, however, will stand on her own. Brietta Hyton shall face any storm wearing the Duchess's crown like the rays of a breaking dawn.

I apologize for how Brietta Hyton came to be, but I will not apologize for stepping out of your shadow. I refuse to be meat.

By the way, I am not so foolish to think our one entanglement erased the years-long bond you have with my husband. I expect to see you at the palace soon, and I hope to see you again as my friend.

Sincerely,
Brie

I threw the parchment back down on the writing desk in a huff. Apparently Brietta had adopted the Hyton arrogance after only a few days in the palace. At least she recognized Derrick did not love her, but nothing she said made my situation any better. I sat at the writing desk and stared at the flickering candle as I debated burning Brietta's letter.

Before I gave into my destructive urge, I opened Annalisa's letter, hoping she had something more pleasant to say.

Dearest Sera,

I hope you are not freezing to death on the mountain. I hate thinking about the First-selected being trapped in that snowy wasteland for all eternity. Speaking of wasteland, I only have a few days left before Grigory comes back from his army mission and I am shipped off to Thornebow forever. I hope Father lets me stay in the palace longer, but honestly being home is not all I hoped it would be.

If Mama is not with my sisters, she is with Brietta. In fact, Mama and Brietta are together so often that I have barely seen her at all.

Since I am spending so much time by myself, I looked all over the palace for the paintings I sent Father while we were in school. Do you remember the painting of the three pink roses I made? It was the best painting in the whole school—and we were only fourth-years! I had sent it to Father as a birthday gift. Well, Sera, I could not find the painting anywhere. Nor any of the others I sent him.

By the way, I need to hear from you immediately so I know you are all right. If Bloodstone has hurt you, I will ride up to the mountain and stab him.

Do not give yourself to him, Birdie. I love you.

Best regards,
Annalisa

I read the last line of the letter over again. The entire letter was in Annalisa's perfect handwriting, so I had no doubt she wrote it. Derrick must have stood over his twin's shoulder and told her what to write. If tensions between the Barons and the House of Hyton were high, no one could know the Duke's heir had commanded a future Baroness to annul her marriage.

I bit my tongue and hissed out a breath. Derrick had wanted me to protect myself if Riyan became too ferocious, but he also wanted me to not consummate my marriage at all? Even though he knew his father would own me otherwise? Was he really so jealous that he would rather risk his father's fingerprints on my skin than let me have security with Riyan?

My mind spun like gears inside a clock. Yes, he would—my sweet Midnight was still a Hyton. Once his father died, not only would Derrick inherit the crown and Ravenwood, he would inherit *me* if my marriage annulled.

Derrick's whispered words sunk their claws in the base of my mind and seared themselves into my consciousness like a brand. *"And you are mine."*

I clapped my hand over my neck where the ghosts of his bites still lingered. I had worked for years to make the heir mine, but I somehow had let my control slip.

Derrick was not mine. *I* was *his*.

Lightning crashed from my chest to my hands as I yanked up the hem of my skirt. I untied the Hyton dagger from my garter and threw it onto my bed with a tight-lipped scream.

Love and protection, my ass. That dagger was a symbol of Derrick's *ownership*.

I hissed out short breaths as I shoved my clothes off my body. I threw my nightgown over my head and let the soft fabric flutter over my skin like a calming breath.

I let out another slow breath. I was not going to let emotions overtake me. My fingertips ran over the bumps of the white thread at the edge of my sleeve, imagining that I was sewing again.

Like a needle through linen, I was focused, deliberate, and calm.

The floorboards sighed softly as I walked to my bed and gently slid the dagger under my pillow. As much as I hated what that dagger symbolized, I was not stupid enough to sleep without a weapon—especially when Riyan's mood was so unpredictable.

I sat at the writing desk again and brought out a piece of parchment to reply to Annalisa. Even though Derrick could shove his sneaky little demand up his ass, I would not ignore his innocent twin's letter.

Anna,

I am alive and unharmed. The mountain was chilly at first, but I grew used to it. Bloodstone is truly different. You would not believe it—I was doing laundry myself!

I think whatever your mother is doing with Brietta is turning her into a true Hyton. Maybe you could talk to her.

Your rose painting was magnificent, but those without an eye for true beauty could never see that. I would love to see more of what you can create.

And do not worry. I am not afraid of Riyan.

—Sera

I folded the parchment into an envelope and thought about what I would reply to Brietta.

Regardless of the tightness in my chest as I thought of Brietta wearing the crown that was supposed to be mine, I had to give her some credit. Brietta saw the truth of everything and was brave enough to speak out, something I was never able to do.

Frankly, I envied her. I envied her not just because of her stature, her beauty, her family's money, the fact that she was going to be Duchess, or even that she married Derrick, but that she could be *honest.*

Probably because she never needed to lie to get what she wanted. How fortunate for her.

I crumpled Brietta's letter and shoved it into the top drawer of the writing desk. Brietta could sit in the dark for all I cared.

I addressed my reply to Annalisa and then sealed the envelope with red wax and the stamp of the snarling Bloodstone bear.

As soon as I finished sealing the letter, the bedroom door creaked open. Riyan stood in the doorway, candle in-hand and shirtless, just like the night before.

Riyan softly walked over to the writing desk and bowed his head to avoid one of the beams in the ceiling. I shrunk in my chair, my chest teeming with guilt as Derrick's secret message sat on the writing desk between us.

"You mended my shirt," he said.

I stared at the wooden top of the desk. "I told you I would."

"No, I mean you did something else to it."

Riyan plopped the shirt on top of Annalisa's letter. He grabbed the sleeve I had mended and turned it so the embroidered flowers faced me.

"What's this?" he asked.

"I embroidered it," I replied. My eyes fell to my hands in my lap. He did not like it.

"Why?"

I swallowed and my palms began to sweat. "I thought you would like it."

"I do like it—very much, actually. But why did you do it?"

I chewed on my tongue, not wanting to answer him, but then I released my fists in my lap and sighed. If Brietta was brave enough to be honest, I could try to be.

"I wanted to make you happy," I admitted. "Maybe if you were happy seeing the flowers on your sleeve, you would not lose your temper again."

Riyan did not respond. The only sounds in the room were the flames fluttering on our two candles. I stared at the shirt on the table, too bashful at my confession to look up at him.

"You need to comb your hair," he said.

My hands flew to the ends of my hair, which were horribly tangled after a day's work. My cheeks burned and embarrassment crinkled in my chest like balled-up parchment.

"I must look awful," I mumbled. I stared at the floor as I walked over to my trunk. I opened the lid and dug through my clothes for my comb.

I cried out as one of the tines of the comb pricked my finger. I ignored the bead of blood on my fingertip and raked through the tangles, pretending Riyan was not even there.

"I can do that for you," Riyan said.

I looked up from my tangles. Riyan's eyes were soft in the candlelight and the corners of his mouth flicked up in a tiny smile.

"You would comb my hair?" I asked.

"You mended my shirt, didn't you?" he replied.

Riyan gestured to the chair at the writing desk. I hesitated at first, but sat in the chair. I had nothing to be afraid of.

He snuffed out his candle and I tentatively placed my comb in his outstretched hand. The floorboards groaned behind me as he sat down.

He started with the ends of my hair. A chill crept up my spine as the tines of the comb gently grazed my back.

My voice came out shakier than I wanted. "For someone who does not have a lot of hair, you can comb quite well."

"I used to comb Mother's hair when I was a boy." His warm breath caressed my shoulders and my hands curled into fists in my lap.

I let out a breath and released my grip. "D-did you hear you are going to see her?"

"I did."

His breath warmed me again. I swallowed as my heart pounded. "Are you excited? Your grandmother told me you have not seen her in twelve years."

"That's not true."

I blinked. Before I could ask, Riyan spoke again. "I went to see her last night. She was asleep, but I still got to see her. She has gotten so much smaller."

"Is she really smaller?" I asked. "Or are you just bigger?"

Riyan did not respond. Maybe that was the wrong thing to say—my silver tongue was losing its shine.

Maybe I could mend things. I rested my hands against my belly and let out a breath. "I am not afraid of you, Riyan."

He kept combing. "I knew you wouldn't be."

His voice might have been even, but he still sounded relieved.

The tines of the comb traveled up to the back of my neck and sent tingles down my spine again. He gently ran his palm down my hair to smooth it. I held my breath as my stomach fluttered.

His low voice rumbled through the stillness. "Do you still hate me?"

My heart skipped a beat. "You—you remembered that?"

He hummed in assent as he smoothed my hair again. "Bad memories always come back to haunt me. I can't forget things, despite how much I want to sometimes."

I swallowed my guilt. "No, Riyan. I do not hate you."

Riyan reached with both hands on either side of my neck, pulling the front strands of my hair back so he could give them attention. I sucked in a breath as his fingertips grazed my skin.

A wisp of his breath kissed the left side of my neck before he started combing again. "The marks from Hyton are almost gone. I still don't understand why he did that—marking you like he owns you."

I clenched my teeth, but forced my jaw to release. "He does *not* own me."

I stared at the candle on the desk—the flame faltered as tallow spilled down the side. The candle was lopsided, uneven, and shrinking as the seconds thumped away. The flame disappeared for a blink as Riyan took a long breath.

"Do you still love him?"

The flame flickered again and then snuffed itself out. The dim moonlight and Riyan's breath were the only signs of life in the room. I closed my eyes and savored the touch of his gentle hands as they smoothed my hair. His hands fell and I betrayed my sense by wishing he would keep going.

As if he heard my foolish plea, his touch returned. I took in a shuddering breath as his fingertips grazed my temples, my cheekbones, my jaw, my neck, and finally my collarbone. The cracks in my granite heart grew bigger and a warm light glowed out of the seams.

Time stopped again. Riyan and I were alone in the darkness. No one else in the world existed. I could be honest. I let out my fear with my breath as his hands left my body, ready to give him the answer he had waited for since yesterday evening.

"No," I replied. "I never did."

Riyan exhaled and his breath warmed my shoulders to match the warmth of my chest. I twisted in the chair to face him and we finally looked each other in the eye at the same height. Riyan's eyebrows were slightly knitted and his lower lip trembled. His mouth was silent, but his chest rose and fell as the moonlight glowed in his eyes.

He did not say it, but I still understood—he realized that he never broke my heart.

My breath stilled, waiting for the fallout from my dishonesty, but Riyan's face softened. He was not angry with me for lying, he was…relieved.

All he wanted from me was honesty.

The warm glow around my heart burned brighter, but my stomach knotted in fear of what could come out of my mouth next. I was freeing my secrets like finches from an iron cage and I did not know what else I was holding in.

Riyan broke the silence before any more truths could escape my heart.

"I…I want to make you happy, Serafina," he said breathlessly. "I wanted to send you back to Hyton as quickly as I could, but if you want to be with…if you want to stay here…"

Before I knew it, I was on my feet and out of the chair, the light in my chest glowing brighter and warmer. My head was higher than his. Riyan did not speak, but he did not need to—his glistening eyes spoke for him.

My heart pressed into my ribs toward Riyan. The drops of magic in my blood sang out for me to touch him. I began to reach for him, but then stopped myself and drew my hand back.

No—it was too much, too fast. Damn the magic of the blood bond, I could not just…

But like the rays of sun from a breaking dawn, the golden warmth flowed through my veins to my fingertips and won over my fear. I reached over with bravery and hope pulsing through my blood and gently brushed the stray hair out of the middle of Riyan's forehead.

Riyan held his breath as I let my fingertips linger on his temple for a heartbeat. He was so damn warm. I needed more.

I lowered my hand and gently traced his cheekbone. I caressed the hard lines of his face like I was charting a new world. Riyan let me explore, his eyelashes only fluttering down a few times—as if he did not want to take his eyes off me for a single blink.

I had already surrendered to the fact that he was handsome, but I suddenly had a deeper appreciation for him that I could not quite grasp.

His soft breath on the inside of my wrist nearly made me jump as I realized why I was having such a strong connection with him. I was not seeing him as the Beast, the monster, the hero, the pitiful child of magic, or just as my husband—I was finally seeing him as a person.

I let my fingertips rest on his strong jaw. As if my touch had given him the bravery he needed, Riyan let out a whisper. "I want to make our marriage work, I just don't know how."

My breath was so heavy, but I needed to answer. "Me neither." I let my hand drop from his face. "You are not alone."

Riyan caught my hand with his own. The skin on his palms was rough but his touch was soft. My cheeks burned as his heat traveled through his hand into mine.

"You know…a gentleman is supposed to kiss a lady's hand," I said.

"Really? Why?" Riyan asked with a chuckle.

"I…well, no one ever explained why," I replied. "I suppose gentlemen do it to show affection and respect."

Riyan's eyes twinkled. He brought my hand up to his massive lips and gave it a soft kiss. The light in my veins sparked even brighter. Sunspots danced in my head as heat surged up my arm.

"This is what you want?" Riyan asked with a half-smile and a raised eyebrow, the heat of his breath kissing my hand as he spoke. "You want me to pretend to be a gentleman?"

Good question. What *did* I actually want?

"A gentleman is better than a brute who throws blades." I gave him a smile as I tried to tame the restless energy beneath my ribs.

"Well, you're going to have to teach me, because I am no gentleman. I'm the biggest brute there is."

I pried my eyes away from his dimple and stared at the back of my hand. "As long as you do not get drunk and throw me on the ground again, you are off to a good start."

Riyan closed his eyes and groaned. "I feel horrible for that. I ruined your big moment in front of everyone. You weren't hurt, were you?"

"No, but the Duke's ballroom floor sure was."

He stroked the back of my hand with his thumb. "Eh, I don't feel bad about that."

I wanted to laugh, but I was too afraid of the heat glowing in my body to let myself. Instead, I gently bit my tongue and smiled. "What am I going to do with you?"

Riyan looked at me with a fire in his eyes that matched the ball of light in my chest. "Anything you want, Serafina."

I let out a little breath and the powerful heat pacified into a comforting warmth. He was letting me have control.

All right. I was not foolish enough to raze my defenses, but I would meet Riyan on the battleground to fight for our survival. If he would try to be a gentleman for me, I could at least try to be honest for him.

Against all logic and sense, I would give Riyan Bloodstone a chance.

Chapter Twenty Two
Flowers for the Sun

Damn, I needed to eat.

I tugged the laces of my waist cincher tightly against my empty stomach as I finished dressing for a new day. I placed my foot on my chair, lifted up my skirt, and tightened my garter strings around my thin legs.

My leg felt so much lighter without the Hyton dagger weighing me down.

I had promised Derrick I would keep the dagger with me, but the tiny light still shining inside my chest whispered to me to break that promise. The thought of Riyan's gentle touch and his dimpled half-smile made me throw my skirt back over my leg with a decisive flick of my wrist.

If Riyan was going to attempt to be a gentleman, I was not going to attempt to be an assassin.

I braided a strand of hair around the crown of my head to keep my hair out of my face. I grabbed my hand mirror to make sure the braid was even when I caught the reflection of my neck—the marks from Derrick were indeed almost gone. I gently touched the skin of my neck, remembering his lips, his breath, the way he had made me burn inside…but I stopped.

I took a deep breath and let it go. I had to stop thinking about Derrick and what *he* wanted for me and discover what I really wanted for myself.

Nikkolas and Hilda were my new family, was I ready to consider Riyan my family also? Did I want to don a crimson cloak and fully submit to my fate?

Or did I want something that no one in the House of Bloodstone could give me?

Whatever I truly wanted, I had to let out the prisoner inside my granite heart. I had to find out who I really was.

I followed the sweet smell of breakfast to the dining room. To my delight, I found a spread of bread and butter, cured meats, and chicken eggs waiting on the table. Nikkolas and Hilda were already eating, but Riyan was nowhere to be found.

"Oh, good morning, Serafina!" Hilda said in a chipper voice as I joined them at the table. "Eat up, dear. You have a big day ahead of you!"

"I am looking forward to it," I said as I spread some butter on a thick and warm slice of bread. "When is Astrid going to see Riyan?"

Nikkolas scoffed, but Hilda paid him no mind.

"Astrid was still tired from yesterday and she was…well, in a bad mood this morning," Hilda said, still not losing the happy lift in her voice.

"She does not remember her own name, but she sure remembers what today is," Nikkolas grumbled.

Hilda pursed her lips and glared at her husband for only a moment before she was back to her chipper self. "Anyway, everything must be perfect for the reunion to go smoothly, so we will try tomorrow. But! Riyan rose early this morning and made special plans for a *special* day!"

"Is he going somewhere?" I asked between mouthfuls of bread.

Hilda shot a quick glance at Nikkolas, who did not look up from his plate. Hilda looked back at me with a giddy smile, hiding a secret behind her rosy cheeks.

"You will see," she said with a tiny giggle. "Just make sure you get your fill of food."

I gladly spread more apple butter on my bread slice.

Nikkolas gestured to me with his fork. "Eat more, girl. I could cut parchment on your cheekbones. You have to be more robust if you are going to give me an heir."

"Nikkolas, really?" Hilda cried.

"I am not going to apologize for telling the truth, Hilda," Nikkolas said before chomping on some cured meat.

I glared at Nikkolas and took a bite of my bread as defiantly as I could. After eating my fill, Hilda handed me a wicker basket filled with treats for our "special journey." The basket was heavier than it looked, but I sweetly accepted it and walked through the keep's doors to see Riyan waiting for me at the bottom of the steps.

"Since I will not see Mother today," Riyan said, "I thought you might like a tour of your new ho…of Bloodstone province."

I had only heard stories of Bloodstone—our cold, unfeeling, and mysterious neighbors to the west. Of course, those stories were really only rumors of the Bloodstone family and tales of the beasts that lurk on the mountain. My stomach fluttered with a little excitement as I tugged on the handle of the basket.

He walked up the steps—stopping halfway up so his head was just below mine—and offered his hand to me. He stumbled on the steps as he attempted to bow, but I had to give him credit for trying.

His mouth turned up into the dimpled half-smile that made my stomach jump. "Is this what a gentleman would do?"

I smiled back. "Close enough."

I held onto the basket with one hand and placed the other in his palm. Riyan held my hand and awkwardly twisted his body back around so he could walk with me down the stairs. Our feet touched the grass and my hand was raised almost to the level of my eye as he held it.

"Now what am I supposed to do?" Riyan asked.

"When a gentleman walks with a lady," I responded, "he leads her, but does not walk too quickly. Usually, a lady holds onto the arm of a gentleman while walking, but—"

"But I am a big, ugly brute," he interjected. "You couldn't hold my arm even if you stood on your toes."

"Holding hands is fine," I reassured. "Also, if we are on a path, the gentleman always walks on the side closest to any perceived danger."

"Gentlemen have to be told that?" Riyan scoffed. "None of those pompous bastards have any morals."

"When I say 'danger,' I mean whatever would be in the road if we were walking through the capital city," I added. "Gentlemen normally do not promenade around the mountain."

"For good reason too." Riyan's eyes gleamed with mischief. "I feel bad for them, having to learn all those bullshit society rules and yet nothing about how to actually fucking survive."

"Gentlemen are not supposed to swear either," I added with a smirk.

He groaned. "This is going to be a lot harder than I thought."

Riyan walked with heavy footsteps, his boots making imprints in the grass and dirt as we made our way into the rocky hills outside the fortress. I tugged on the heavy basket and gripped onto Riyan's hand as I nearly ran beside him to keep up with his pace. Riyan tried to slow down to adjust, but he tripped over his heel and caught himself just before falling.

"Riyan, hold on," I panted as I tried to catch my breath. "I cannot keep up with you."

Riyan lowered himself onto one knee to look me in the face. "Would you hate it if I carried you?"

I bit my tongue and glanced away. He had already dropped me once, but he did carry me just fine when we were in the apple grove. After a few moments of deliberation, I decided to just trust him.

Riyan scooped me up in his left arm again and cradled me against his chest. He took the basket from me while chastising me for carrying anything heavy with him around. I wrapped my arms so tightly around his neck I thought I was going to choke him. My face was up by his and I caught the scent of nectar and wheat as he held me. As we walked, my body swaying in time with his, I let myself loosen my grip.

Big, puffy clouds lazily traveled through the bright June sky, occasionally rolling in front of the sun and giving us moments of shade. We passed pine trees, singing birds, and chattering squirrels, all in the shadow of the great snow-capped mountain's peak.

"Are we going up the mountain?" I asked.

"No, I wouldn't take you up there," Riyan replied, his voice rumbling in his neck near my ear. "The peak of Nordingaard is dangerous—filled with horrors none of your soft little gentlemen could even imagine."

"What is up there?" I asked, remembering the pictures of the red monster that Astrid had painted. "I know of the giants, and that red goat-man, or whatever it is, but what else?"

Riyan shrugged. "I don't even know myself. Most of the people of Bloodstone avoid going too far up the mountain, mainly because of the giants…and their queen."

Ganora, the infamous Queen of the Giants. Tall statues of her image carved from tree trunks stood in every Ravenwood village. Villagers offered scraps of meat at the wooden feet of her statue, painted images of her on their doors to deter the giants from bashing their roofs in, and held wild bacchanalias in her honor on the first day of spring, hoping their revelry would stay her wrath during the warmer months. Ganora was a monster, a legend, and to many, a goddess.

Father never allowed totems of Ganora in Ravenwood Manor and rolled his eyes at her shrines in the villages. He said the fanatic reverence of Ganora was all bullshit.

"Do people worship Ganora in Bloodstone like they do in Ravenwood?" I asked.

"Some do, but it's more common the farther north you go," Riyan replied. "The worship is useless, though. You can't just offer meat outside the village gates or shake your ass around a bonfire on a full moon to get rid of the giants. General Hyton sent scouts up Nordingaard for years, and the few that came back gave us all the information we needed to defeat Ganora."

I blinked. The idea of defeating something as mythical as Ganora seemed impossible.

"Giants are beasts," Riyan explained as he trudged on through the woods, "but not like wolves in a pack or lions in a den. They are like bees in a hive— completely controlled by their queen. Ganora makes them from dirt and magic and sends them down the mountain to hunt humans. She hoards all the magical power of the mountain for herself and doesn't care who or what she destroys to maintain that."

Magical power of the mountain? What power was there? Before I could ask, Riyan scoffed. "I wish I saw her at the last battle so I could have her head too. I hate that Duke Hyton tells everyone we defeated the giants when

Ganora still breathes. It's all a lie—the giants are just going to come back next spring."

"Well," I said with a rare optimistic lift in my voice, "at least you will be here to kill them all again. Maybe you will even face the legend herself."

"You make it sound so fucking easy," Riyan chuckled.

"Gentlemen do not swear, Riyan!" I teased. "You promised!"

"And I'm beginning to regret that promise," Riyan groaned. "Swearing is like breathing to me!"

We passed more trees, a small gurgling waterfall that Riyan stepped over with ease, and weaved through small gaps in the craggy rocks of the mountainside.

I pressed against Riyan's chest as he shimmied through another gap between two rocks. "Since this is clearly a long walk, we should get to know each other better."

"You already know me," Riyan said with a small grunt as he nearly lost his balance coming out of the gap. "Giant-slayer. Massive brute. Heir to Bloodstone. Fond of liquor in any form. That's all there is to me."

"That is not true," I scolded. "What is your middle name?"

"Don't have one."

"Come on, every noble son has a middle name. Hell, Derrick has two!"

"Let's put it this way, my grandmother wanted to call me 'Nikkolas' to flatter my grandfather because *he* wanted to call me 'small corpse left in the woods.' My name is 'Riyan' only because my mother mimicked my shrieking baby cries to refer to me and the name stuck."

I imagined the wails of a newborn baby and I heard it. I smiled in disbelief. "Your name really is a scream?"

"Appropriate, isn't it?" he replied with a chuckle. "Since you care so much about names for some reason, what is *your* middle name?"

"Helia," I replied. Riyan silently mouthed 'Helia' and smiled afterward. "When is your birthday?"

Riyan glanced down at me and his cheek pitted like he bit it. "When is yours?"

"Last day of the year," I answered, raising my eyebrow as I looked up at him. "Answer the question. When is your birthday?"

Riyan avoided my eyes and dipped his head to avoid a tree branch as we walked into a shady grove. Hilda had gone through the trouble of packing us a basket and had mentioned today was special. She was a sweet woman, but she would not have put so much emphasis on our outing for no reason.

"Your birthday is today," I said with a smile. "Why did you not say so?"

Riyan's neck tensed under my arms. "My existence is nothing to celebrate."

My lips parted and my chest fell.

My birthday used to be so wonderful. The sun was December's fleeting friend, but I would run to the manor after a few hours of playing in the snow to find a warm pastry-braid the length of the entire dining table for Father's New Year's Eve party. I would get the first piece of the braid and a kiss from Mother and Father before the rest of the party guests clinked their goblets and sang songs for the rest of the night. I had looked forward to my birthday every year, but Riyan thought he was not worth what I had taken for granted.

Opening my heart to discover what I really wanted gave me the courage to entertain whims instead of plans. My first whim was to give Riyan a nice birthday for once.

Everyone deserved at least one good day.

Riyan walked between two trees and we found ourselves in a clearing with a large, grassy meadow surrounded by more trees and rocky hillsides. The meadow was a beautiful sea of blue-green grass underneath a cloudy sky. Riyan carefully stepped into the meadow, gently placing his feet in the lush grass below, until we were in the center of the clearing.

He sat in the grass, holding on to me with both of his strong arms as he lowered me down to his lap. I took in the crisp mountain air, listened to Riyan breathe, and rested my head against his thumping heartbeat. "This is lovely, Riyan."

"Just wait," he whispered.

The clouds parted and the full afternoon sun shined down on the meadow. As soon as the sun's golden rays touched the earth, the meadow exploded with red. I gasped—thousands of small crimson flowers opened their petals at once, making the meadow look like it was on fire.

"Bloodstone lilies," Riyan said. "They only open up for the sun."

I reached down and delicate lily petals softly brushed against my fingertips. They felt softer than satin and lighter than linen. I gently ran my right hand over the meadow and half a dozen lilies kissed my palm. My left hand swept over the flowers and the soft petals brushed up against the rough scar from the blood bond.

I slowly slid off Riyan's lap and into the flowers. I rolled onto my back and let the fresh-smelling earth and the red lilies envelop me as rounded clouds floated across the blue sky.

I laughed like the clouds tickled my belly. My chest was light and airy amongst the innocence and majesty of the Bloodstone lilies.

My only worry was when the next cloud would move in front of the sun and force the lilies to hide in the shade. I could not remember the last time I was so relaxed or…happy.

Bloodstone really was nothing like Hyton. I had no games to play, no one to lie to, and all I wanted was to listen to the whispers of the mountain wind and breathe in the scent of our land.

The lilies danced around me in the breeze. I ran my hands through the flowers as I spread out my body in the meadow. I was the First-selected, but I did not need the honor. All I really, honestly needed, was peace.

I laughed as I freed another secret—being honest did not have to be painful.

I sat up in the flowers and looked over at Riyan, who had a soft smile on his face as he watched me play in the lilies. His eyes sparkled as he looked down at me and the wind brushed his blonde hair around his forehead.

The clouds masked the sun and the lilies closed their petals. Riyan and I sat in the shade, listening to only the soft song of the wind through the clearing.

"Bloodstone lilies are very rare," Riyan said, his low voice adding to the peace instead of disturbing it. "You can only find them here. They aren't good for bouquets since they are so temperamental, but you can't beat the wonder of seeing them all open up for the first time."

I looked up at the sky to see when the cloud that kept me from the lilies would move on. I had only a few more seconds to wait.

"How have I never heard of this place?" I asked. "We have nothing like this in Ravenwood."

"People will only tell stories of Bloodstone that confirm what they already believe," he replied. "The rest of Lycaster thinks we are cold and mean with nothing else to offer, so no one bothers to find our good parts."

The sunlight broke through the clouds and the rubies of the earth bloomed again. Riyan smiled and motioned for me to come back over to him. I delicately stepped through the meadow, crushing as few flowers under my feet as possible.

I sat on his left leg like it was a seat made just for me. Riyan set the basket on his right leg.

"I don't know about you, but I'm starving," Riyan said as he opened the lid to the basket.

"Now that you mention it, I never see you at meals." I said as I peered into the basket. "Where do you eat?"

"At a trough with the other animals," Riyan joked. He pulled out a cloth bundle and undid the linen wrapping. His eyes widened and he smiled as he pulled out a bun topped with powdered sugar.

"I haven't had these in years," Riyan said softly. He glanced at me and held the bun up to my mouth. "Take a bite, you'll love it!"

I tentatively opened my mouth and bit into the bun. I expected the thick bread of the bun under my teeth, but my eyes widened as a warm, thick jam touched my tongue. The bread was hearty, but the jam was earthy and sweet without the tartness that normally came from berries.

Riyan chuckled and handed me the rest of the bun as he reached into the basket to get himself one.

"Buns filled with elskaberry jam," Riyan said before eating one of the saucer-sized buns in one bite. He smiled as he chewed and then swallowed. "Elskaberries grow just outside of the keep in the spring and Grandmother loves making jam with them. Sometimes she'd send a few jars to the academy and I would just eat it all with a spoon."

I raised an eyebrow. "You can use utensils? Look at you, you surprise me more every day."

Riyan laughed and I caught another glimpse of that dimple.

I indulged in another bun and Riyan had nine more. He glanced at me right as I licked sugar off my top lip. Those blue eyes did not leave my face and my cheeks heated up.

"You missed a spot," Riyan said. He reached over and swiped the corner of my mouth with his thumb. I caught a glimpse of the red jam on the tip of his thumb before it disappeared into his mouth.

I raised my eyebrows. "Did you really just—?"

"I don't waste elskaberry jam," Riyan interjected.

I rolled my eyes but still cracked a smile as Riyan reached into the basket again. Instead of another bun, he pulled out a leather-bound book with faded gold script.

Riyan smiled with disbelief. "I can't believe Grandmother snuck this in here." He held up the book to show me the cover—a gilded silhouette of a winged faerie stamped into the leather. I smiled, we had the same faerie book at Ravenwood Manor. Riyan opened the book and flipped through the yellowed and worn pages.

"Grandmother used to read this to me every night before I was sent away," Riyan said. He flipped a page and his eyes lit up. He turned the book toward me. "Look! My favorite—*Prince Haldar and the Giant!*"

His finger pressed on an illustration of a black-haired prince with his sword aloft as he rode on the back of a white wolf to slay the giant terrorizing his kingdom.

"Of course that one was your favorite," I said. "Very prophetic, Hero of Lycaster."

"It's every boy's favorite!" Riyan said with a smile as he flipped through the pages. "Prince Haldar has a magic sword and a talking wolf! The giant took his princess and kept her in chains to force her to be his bride, but Prince Haldar would never let that happen. So he rescues her from the monster that stole his…"

He trailed off as he looked down at the book. Maybe he was not much like his childhood hero after all.

Time to change the subject.

I gently took the book from his hand and flipped the pages until I found the illustration of a blonde faerie princess with flowers in her hair. She sat on top of a glass hill and tossed a golden apple to her true love, the dark-haired prince riding up the hill on his magic horse.

"*The Princess on the Glass Hill* was my favorite story," I said with a smile.

"The one where the princess chucks golden apples at the prince because she wanted to marry him?" Riyan asked with a scoff. "Ridiculous. Why would you like that one?"

I pursed my lips. "Because she got to choose who she married."

Riyan's chin dipped to his chest and he swallowed. He looked out to the meadow and took in a quiet breath. Guilt flickered through his eyes just like when we had sat in the Duke's garden.

I ran my hands along the leather cover of the faerie book. I had been so angry with Riyan for choosing me and destroying the life I had yearned for, but as I sat in the peaceful meadow with a belly full of elskaberry buns, I could not feel angry anymore.

And if I was no longer angry, I did not want Riyan to still feel guilty. Especially on his birthday.

I let out a breath. "I cannot blame you for choosing me. If I had the power to choose who I married, I would have picked the person I wanted too."

Riyan glanced at me and gave me a rueful half-smile. "And the person you wanted wasn't me."

I swallowed. True, but dwelling on that fact would make nothing better. Before I could think of anything clever to try to cheer him up, Riyan reached into the meadow and gently plucked one of the lilies from the grass. He placed the small flower on the crown of my head and worked the stem into my braid.

"What are you doing?" I laughed.

His cheeks rose with his smile. "Making you look like the faerie princess in the story."

He added flowers into my hair until he filled my braid with Bloodstone lilies. When he finished, he pressed his palms into the grass and leaned back to admire his work. A warm tingle crept up my neck and spread to my cheeks as he looked down at me. I looked away into the meadow, but he caught my chin with the side of his hand and turned me back to face him.

Riyan held my chin between his knuckle and thumb. I was frozen in place as his eyes gleamed with the same desire he had the night before.

"Don't you hide from me," he said in a low voice. "Not when you're the most beautiful flower in the meadow."

My heart pounded. Without taking his eyes off me, Riyan took my right hand into his and brought it up to his lips. I shivered as his soft lips kissed my skin again. He smirked and lowered my hand back into my lap and placed it on top of the book.

"Would you toss me a golden apple, princess?" he asked. "It's my birthday, after all."

He was not clever enough to fool me. The question was a plea disguised as roleplay—if I suddenly had the power to choose who I married, would I choose him? If I had the chance to know him as the person beyond the Beast, the Hero of Lycaster, or the Bloodstone heir, would I have happily married him over Derrick?

My first instinct was to lie and tell him I would choose him, but the warm light in my chest stopped me. Truthfully, I did not know if the warmth and comfort I felt with Riyan would have been strong enough to overcome my desperate desire for the crown.

If I was going to be honest, I could not give him the answer he wanted... but at least I could answer with what *I* wanted.

My stomach glowed with warmth as I shifted my hips closer to him and stretched my spine to reach as high as I could. "I can give you something better than an apple."

I placed my hand on the right side of his face and kissed him on his left cheek. His skin flashed hot underneath my lips. He held his breath and the muscles in his neck tightened as I pulled away.

My lips flushed. Riyan looked down at me with eyes so intense that he stoked my desire to kiss him again. I started to reach up when Riyan hooked his arm around my waist and pinned me down on his leg.

His voice was hard and strained. "You shouldn't have done that."

"Why?" I asked. "Riyan I was just—"

I cut myself off when I shifted my hips and felt the hard muscle underneath me. Riyan was not angry with me for kissing him, he was aroused.

My mouth watered as heat pooled between my legs.

I glanced across the empty meadow. No one was around, so what if I followed my throbbing heartbeat to see where our...*feelings* would go? Maybe we could even try to...

A twig snapped behind us. Riyan's head whipped around. His face was tight and his eyes vibrated as he stared at the line of trees behind us. His entire body tensed up as he held me.

"Riyan?" I whispered.

He sprang to his feet, picking me up and holding me tightly against his chest with both arms. I dropped the book and it landed in the meadow with a thud. Riyan's forearms squeezed into me with a fraction of his strength, but still hard enough that I thought he was going to crush me.

"Riyan," I squeaked, my chest cramped and tight under his grip. "The book—"

"Forget the book," Riyan said, his eyes darting back and forth as he scanned the trees. "Something is behind us."

A whistle sliced through the air as Riyan bolted through the meadow.

"Hang on to me!" Riyan shouted.

I flung my arms around his neck, locking my hands in place around each wrist, as Riyan shifted the weight of my body into his left arm.

He jumped and his body rattled as he grabbed onto rock. I squeezed my eyes shut as he scaled the side of one of the rocky cliffs with his free arm. He panted as he heaved us up as quickly as he could.

With one final pull, he dragged his chest and my curled-up body over a ledge. I kept my eyes tightly closed as he stood up. Riyan's chest heaved with his breath and he squeezed me with both arms.

"We are safe, Serafina," he said between breaths. "You can open your eyes."

I slowly fluttered my eyes open. Riyan stood at the top of a tall ledge, what would be nearly eight stories from the ground. I gripped my wrists even tighter as I dared to look down. The meadow of lilies looked like a large puddle of blood below us. Above us was the ominous peak of Nordingaard.

"Look over there," Riyan said as he pointed across the ledge. "It's Fraleigh's palace."

I looked into the distance at a small palace of shining gold that stood on a cliffside overlooking the Western Sea.

"Do you think she is there?" I asked.

"Most likely," Riyan said. "We should visit next time we need to borrow a cup of sugar."

I laughed, but Riyan's strong arms were still trembling as he held me. I looked down to the meadow and expected to see a wolf or some other beast chasing after us, but whatever we had run from was not there.

If it was ever there at all…

"Riyan, what did we run from?" I asked softly.

"No idea," Riyan replied as he looked into the clearing again. "I just have a sense of when danger is near."

"I told you a gentleman puts his body closest to danger!" I cried. "You held me out in front of you like an offering!"

Riyan chuckled, bouncing me up a little in his arms and holding me more securely against him. "Trust me, when you're in the wilderness, there is no safer place than right here."

I looked out at the breathtaking view again. I was grateful Riyan had rescued me from whatever was in the forest, but I could not rely on him to save me every time. I needed to be better prepared for danger the next time I stepped out of the walls of the fortress.

"I have one more surprise for you, Princess of the Lilies," Riyan said. "Let's go home."

Chapter Twenty Three
Dance of the Moon

Riyan kept me in his arms as he walked down the sloping backside of the cliff toward the fortress, not daring to go back into the meadow to retrieve his faerie book.

He constantly looked over his shoulder with stiff neck muscles and still breath as we walked. He would even stop in the middle of our conversation and scan the trees around us before deciding we were safe to continue. The muscles in his arms twitched like taut bowstrings as he held me.

"Part of being a soldier," Riyan said after the third time he stopped. "It's normal to just…be aware."

I knew what a lie sounded like, but I kept my mouth shut.

We passed under another grove of apple trees and I convinced Riyan to calm down long enough to eat.

Riyan set me down in the shade of a tree so I could stretch my legs and handed me an apple. He stayed within arm's reach of me, but allowed himself to lean on a tree trunk and pluck apple after apple from the branches to sate his hunger. I munched on my one apple while he ate each of his in three bites and tossed the cores down at his feet.

I studied the muscles hiding under his linen sleeves as he ate. Riyan had heaved us both up a cliffside with one arm in mere minutes and he had carried me for hours without complaining about the strain. My teeth pierced the flesh of my apple as my eyes roamed up and down his massive arms—his strength was more useful than fearsome.

I swallowed my bite just as Riyan realized I was staring at him. My cheeks flashed hot and I glanced down at the large pile of apple cores on the ground.

My lips were wet from the fruit's juice. "You told me you work up a big appetite as the fastest man in the world. Do you have an even bigger appetite as the *strongest* man in the world?"

Riyan responded with a half-smile and wink that made my stomach flip. He tossed his core into the pile as he swallowed his last bite.

He wiped the juice from the apple off his bottom lip with the back of his hand. "If I didn't know that I actually was the strongest man in the world, I would think you were trying to flatter me."

"Never," I said with a smile. "I could not risk your ego getting any bigger."

The sun hugged the treeline against an orange sky. Riyan scanned the trees and kept quiet for a few heartbeats.

"It's getting dark, we need to get back," he said as he stepped over to me.

He reached down and scooped me up again. I threw my apple core to the ground and my arms returned around his tense neck.

"I'm such a fool for not bringing my sword," Riyan said as he walked. He snapped his head toward the trees, but I had not heard a sound. Riyan's neck shook as he cleared his throat and continued talking as if he came back to reality. "That sword is really only good for giant attacks, though. I'm defenseless against anything smaller."

"Defenseless?" I patted his massive bicep—it was hard as a rock under my touch. "I do not think you can call *this* defenseless."

Riyan smirked. "Look who is being sweet all of a sudden."

"Only because you are acting like a gentleman." I poked his cheek. "You drop me again and the sweetness is over."

"I'll keep the gentleman act up as long as I can, then. You're sweeter than all those apples put together when you're nice and I'm going to savor it."

"Well, I am not nice to just anyone."

"Damn straight, I'm special."

I laughed and lightly flicked him on the jaw.

"My little sweetheart is gone!" Riyan cried with mock despair. "Oh well, it was nice for the thirty seconds it lasted."

Riyan picked up his pace as he raced against the dying daylight. Right as the stars appeared against the twilight sky, the blazing torches on the walls of the fortress peeked through the trees.

Riyan nearly ran around the trees and up to the gate. He gave the signal to raise the gate and we stepped into the safety of the fortress.

I looked around the courtyard. "Where is that surprise? I have high expectations after the Bloodstone lilies."

"Uh oh, the pressure is on," Riyan laughed as he lowered me to the ground. "You best get the blood flowing back to your legs again. Trust me."

I stood on the grass and rocked back and forth on the balls of my feet, cracked the joints in my ankles, and stretched my leg muscles.

Riyan took my hand in his and slowly led me around to the western side of the keep. The area normally hidden in shadows was lit up with torches. Three soldiers waited for us in the torchlight, including the captain of the Bloodstone army.

The captain held a violin and the other two soldiers had a lute and a wooden flute in their hands. The soldiers stood beside a square patch of dirt with tall torches on each corner that looked almost like…

"…a dance floor?" I asked.

"I told you I felt bad about ruining our first dance," Riyan replied. "So I paid this trio of degenerates over here to make it up to you."

"He called us degenerates, how adorable," said the captain.

"You're late, Bloodstone," said the short, round-faced soldier holding the flute. "We've been waiting out here for an hour!"

"Shut up," Riyan snapped. "I'm not paying you to complain."

My eyes danced from the carefully-placed torches in the ground to the three soldiers who looked at me expectantly. My stomach fluttered and I stroked my fingertips on Riyan's thumb as he held my hand.

"Today is *your* twenty-second birthday and you did all this for me?" I asked.

"Well, I did this for mostly selfish reasons," Riyan replied. "I figured taking you to the lilies and re-creating our first dance was the only way to get what I wanted for my birthday."

My lips parted and I let out a shallow breath. I was told my entire life that men only wanted one thing. Heat moved from my chest to my hips—maybe I wanted that *one thing* too.

I flicked my eyes up to his lips. "And what did you want?"

Riyan's eyes were soft and his hand flushed warm as it wrapped around mine. "I wanted to hear you laugh again."

I held my breath as my cheeks and ears flushed with heat. Riyan gently tugged on my arm and led me to the center of the makeshift dance floor. He took my hands in his and faced me, ready to dance.

"Play something nice," Riyan ordered. "Like something you would hear at the Duke's palace."

"Listen to him," the captain said as he held his violin against his shoulder. "Acting like we'd ever be allowed in the Duke's palace."

"You know what I mean!" Riyan barked.

The music started up off-key, but the three players eventually settled into the melody of a slow tune. Riyan picked me up in his arms and danced the steps on his own just like he had in the ballroom.

I learned quickly that Riyan's dancing skills at Annalisa's ball were not exactly hindered from all the wine. Even while sober, he still danced with heavy feet as he stepped in a small circle.

"Take a look at twinkle-toes Bloodstone over here," sneered the lanky lute-playing soldier. "You ever think you would see this day, men?"

The scar-faced captain snickered. The round-faced soldier's cheeks puffed and his flute squealed as he laughed. Riyan shot them an icy look. I tried to ignore the soldiers and appreciate Riyan's attempt. It wasn't a perfect dance, or even a good one, but he tried.

I needed to lift his spirits. "At least you have not dropped me yet."

"Lord Hyton probably danced with you a lot better than this," Riyan grumbled as he glanced away from me.

I lifted my chin to meet his eyes again. "Actually, I never danced with Derrick. The only other man I have ever danced with was Grigory Thornebow."

Riyan's nostrils flared. The soldiers below us laughed.

"And…how was he?" Riyan asked tensely, failing to hide his jealousy.

"Oh, he was not bad." I glanced at the ground, keeping my answer as low-key as possible. "He grabbed me a little too tightly, but his spinning skills were decent."

The trio of soldiers hollered with laughter.

"Damn, Bloodstone," bellowed the flute-playing soldier. "Even with a broken leg, Thornebow danced with your girl better than you!"

Riyan snapped his head toward the soldiers. If looks could kill, they would have all been decapitated.

Riyan held back his wrath for my sake, but the nice evening he had planned turned sour quickly. I drummed my fingers on his muscular shoulder and smirked. Riyan just needed to remind his soldiers who he was and they would play nicely.

"You know, Riyan," I said, "I think you have been a gentleman long enough."

Riyan looked back at me and raised his eyebrow. "Really?"

I batted my eyelashes and smiled. "I miss my brute."

Riyan flashed me a wicked smile and then gently lowered me to the dirt. He shot the trio of soldiers a devious look and their eyes all went wide. In half a second, the strongest, fastest man in the world pounced and took on all three of them in a flurry of fists and limbs. Riyan beat them while shouting every swear word I had ever heard, some I had not, and some I was sure he made up.

I bent over and held my belly as I laughed. The men attempted to grapple with Riyan, but he bested them all even while outnumbered. Riyan knocked the captain and the lanky soldier on their asses and then dangled the round-faced soldier upside-down by his ankle.

"Now *what* did you say about Thornebow and my girl?" Riyan asked with a low voice and a predatory smile.

"All right, you bastard son of a boar, I give up!" cried the soldier. "We have an offering! We brought grog!"

Riyan's eyes lit up at the mention of whatever grog was. He plopped the soldier on the ground and the other two soldiers handed him a huge glass bottle of mysterious brown liquid.

"Your liquid courage, *sir*," the captain said with sarcasm dripping off his last word.

Riyan gestured at the soldiers with the bottle. "If one of you pissed in this again, I'll tear your arms off." He took a big swig.

The three soldiers scrambled to get their instruments back as Riyan drank. Riyan lowered the bottle from his lips and handed it to the captain, who took a drink himself.

"All right, let's fix this," Riyan said. "No more of that pretty-boy shit. Play the song about the Man of the Mountain."

The Man of the Mountain. Legend had it a man took his bride to the top of Nordingaard to marry her, but she died along the way. He buried her at the top of the mountain and attempted to bring her back to life with magic. Skeptics said he died with her in the snow. Faithful believers in magic said he conquered Death itself.

But everyone could agree that whether dead, alive, or somewhere in between, the Man of the Mountain never left Nordingaard.

People of Ravenwood would plead to the mythical Man of the Mountain to save their own loved ones from Death, sang to him in the rain to get some of his magic, and built useless wells to make wishes in, hoping he would grant them.

In the spring, all the villages hold festivals in honor of the Man of the Mountain where beautiful girls dance around a fire to his song, vying to be chosen as a replacement for the lost bride in the legend. I had always wanted to dance with the pretty girls when I was younger, and maybe even be chosen as that year's bride, but Father had never let me. He hated the worship of the Man of the Mountain even more than the fanatical devotion to Ganora. Peasant nonsense, he called it. Nothing for a noble young lady to engage in.

Well, I was not a young lady under her father's ownership anymore. I was the future Baroness of Bloodstone—and I wanted to dance.

Riyan walked over and stood in front of me on the dance floor. The captain shot Riyan a wink. With a flick of his bow, the captain played a lively, folksy tune. The other two soldiers joined in and stomped their feet to the rhythm.

Riyan smirked as the music started up. "Watch this."

The captain sang the familiar song.

> *"There once was a girl both small and fair,*
> *Had fire in her eyes and raven hair,*
> *Stole my heart while dancing there,*
> *In the middle of the village square,"*

Riyan danced for me. He did not move in the confined and prescribed steps of a ballroom dance, but instead the jovial and fluid motions I had seen at festivals. He had a wild look in his eyes as he danced, showing off the strength in his legs and the quickness of his feet. I laughed and clapped along as the song continued.

> *"Come, girl, let's just run*
> *To a place where we'll be one*
> *I promise you that we'll have fun*
> *It's West of the Moon and East of the Sun."*

Riyan knelt down and held out his hand. I rushed to him as the energy of the music pulsed through me. He took my hand and spun me in small circles.

"Let's see Thornebow do this," he said.

The world was a merry spiral of light and laughter.

> *"We went o'er the stream, and then the hills,*
> *Faced too many of the mountain's thrills,*
> *Then my lover caught the chills,*
> *Death and I in a battle of wills,"*

Riyan let go of me and I found my bearings in the dirt as the world kept spinning. Soldiers cheered from the top of the wall and the tall square towers, all gathered to watch us dance. Normally I was too shy to perform in front of a crowd, but I was so happy I picked up my skirt and twirled for the audience. I finally had the freedom to dance to the old song and I was not going to waste it.

Riyan whistled as I kicked my feet and spun with my hair fanning around my shoulders.

"No, girl, can't be undone,
I won't stop till your life is won,
Don't you sleep until we've run,
To the West of the Moon and East of the Sun."

Riyan laughed and lifted me up. I wrapped my arms around his neck and he cradled me against his chest as we danced under the light of the waning moon. His heart pounded against mine. The light in my blood sparked harder than the night before and lit me up from my heart to my toes. Riyan's twilight eyes were on fire.

"I buried her there in the snow,
A greater pain I'll never know,
My tears did fall, my blood did flow,
And Death had gained her greatest foe,"

The light of our bond wrapped tightly around the stone casing around my heart. The bond glowed brighter as it squeezed the crumbling stone, breaking off small pebbles as I looked into Riyan's eyes. My heart pounded as I let myself give in fully to the moment.

A tiny golden rope pulled on my chest, beckoning me to get closer. The warmth in my veins was exhilarating, Riyan's smell was intoxicating, and all I wanted was *more.*

My heart thumped as my blood sang. *More. More. More.*

I placed my hands on each side of Riyan's face. Our bond grew warmer and warmer as I leaned in closer, erasing the coldness of the distance between us…

"Oh, girl, it was fun,
All my heart and soul you'd won,
But my love is never done,
I am West of the Moon and East of the Sun."

And I finally kissed him.

Our golden bond exploded with light the moment the soft heat of his lips met mine. The light sparked and glowed in the veins of my arms, then in my fingers, then all the way down to my toes. When the warm tingling sensation was too intense to bear any longer, I broke away.

The soldiers erupted into a chorus of cheers and whistles. The entire army must have come out to watch, but I did not care, I looked only at Riyan. Soft breaths escaped my flushed lips as he looked back at me. He was stunned, the stars twinkling in his eyes as he held his breath.

Right as I took a breath to ask him what was wrong, he grabbed the back of my neck and pulled me in to kiss me back. My lips were much smaller than his, but he kissed me like he was satisfied with anything I gave him and everything I was.

I weaved my fingers through the short strands of hair at the nape of his neck and grabbed tightly as he kissed me over and over. I softly bit his lower lip and he responded with a low chuckle that made my insides melt. He gave my thigh a firm squeeze, shifting me slightly up and forcing me to break the kiss with a small gasp.

"Go all the way, Bloodstone," cried one of the soldiers. "We want to watch!"

Riyan glared at his trio of degenerates and then swiveled his head to the wall and the keep's towers—he had not even noticed more soldiers had gathered. He turned back to me with a hungry look in his eyes.

"I think one brute is enough for you," he said in a low voice. "What do you say we go somewhere more private?"

My chest rose and fell with desire that escaped as a heavy breath. I could not speak, all I could manage was a nod.

A wolfish smile crept up Riyan's lips. He held me against him and ran to the keep faster than I had ever seen him run. I locked my hands around his neck and held on tight.

Riyan ran straight up the wall of one of the square towers and grabbed a stone with his right hand near the base of a second-story window. He climbed up the tower faster than he had scaled the cliffside. His breath escaped his nose in hot puffs and his mouth contorted in something between a snarl and a smile.

He reached the top of a third-story window and gave me a tight squeeze as he shifted his weight over to the left side. He kicked through the window, sending glass and the mangled iron of the panes into the room. I screamed from the thrill as he jumped in through the window. His boots hit the floor with a hard thud.

We had crashed into his bedroom. Riyan walked across the room, shards of glass crunching underneath his boots, and gently sat me down on the edge of his mattress. He towered over me, panting, hungry, and eyes on fire.

His voice was low and breathy. "Tell me what you want, Serafina. Anything you want, you can have it."

My breast raged in an inferno of heat and light. My back arched up toward him. My knees parted underneath my skirt. My heart pounded in my ears and between my legs.

I forgot about Ravenwood, or Hyton, or any promises or agreements I ever made with anyone. All I wanted or cared about was what my body yearned for. I would not lie back and accept my wifely duty. I would not cower while clutching a weapon underneath my pillow. I would get what I *wanted*.

I looked back up at Riyan and my hungry, flushed lips parted to speak.

"I want you, Riyan Bloodstone."

Chapter Twenty Four

Stay

The chilly mountain air crept in through the shattered window in Riyan's bedroom, but nothing could cool the flame burning in my hips.

I looked up at Riyan and waited for him to answer my call. The golden light of our blood bond pulsed with every heartbeat as it cried out to complete the enchantment.

Yes. Now. Please.

Riyan's chest heaved with his heavy breath. He reached to the back of his neck and his linen shirt dragged up the contours of his muscles. My eyes fixed on the sliver of skin that appeared at his waist and then traveled up the trail of reddish hair on his lower belly, to the muscles of his stomach, to the hair on his chest, and finally his collarbone as the shirt came off.

His strong and muscular stomach was right at the level of my eyes. I wiggled forward to sit on the very edge of the mattress as my eyes feasted on his naked chest. My fingertips dragged across the knitted wool blanket on the bed and lifted up as if they moved on their own. His muscles tensed as I lightly touched his stomach.

Damn. I had no idea the human body had that much muscle.

I let out a slow, admiring breath as my hand trailed down his skin. I caressed the hard line of his abdomen and then the soft line of hair underneath his navel as I moved further and further down. My fingers hooked onto the waist of his pants and I gave the fabric a little tug, but Riyan grabbed my wrist and held me fast in his iron grip.

"Not yet," Riyan said in a strained voice. "We have to warm you up first."

My lips were full and heavy as they parted. "Warm me up?"

"Just...I'm barely holding onto control as it is."

Riyan knelt down and I dropped my chin to meet his eyes—he was almost the height of a normal man. Riyan still held onto my wrist as his eyes blazed.

"I won't hold on for long," he said in a low voice. "And when I do lose control, you need to be ready. I don't want to hurt you."

I swallowed. The possibility of getting hurt had not crossed my mind.

Not that I cared.

Riyan let go of my hand and lowered his head to untie his boots. My hands crept across my leather waist cincher as my stomach fluttered in anticipation. I unlaced the cincher and my belly relaxed as it burned with need. Riyan lowered himself onto both knees and then his eyes met mine again.

"We're only going to do what feels good," he said. "If anything hurts, we stop."

I nodded. He gave me a little smile and then silently leaned forward. He took off my left shoe, then my right. His left hand wrapped around my ankle as his right hand explored up my calf, the rough skin on his palms catching the fabric of my stocking. He tried to lightly tug the stocking off and his brow furrowed when he failed.

I laughed softly and raised the hem of my skirt above my knees.

"Garters," I said with a smile.

"I suggest you untie them if you want to keep them intact."

The idea of him tearing off my clothes was thrilling, but I quickly unlaced both garters before I could decide if I wanted them destroyed.

Riyan caught my hands right as I untied the second garter and kissed them. He kissed my hands not with the respectful admiration of a gentleman, but with a passionate adoration that made my heart thunder.

Riyan gave my knuckles one last kiss and pulled my stocking off. His left hand wrapped around my calf, kissing the skin on the inside of my knee, then the side of my calf, then my ankle as he freed my leg to the chilly air. I shivered and gripped the sides of the mattress as he repeated himself on my other leg.

He rose after planting a soft kiss on my ankle and his fingertips traveled up the sides of my legs. His massive hands wrapped around each of my thighs and his thumbs pushed the hem of my skirt even higher up my knees.

He kneaded the soft flesh of my thighs and I could barely breathe.

Riyan licked his lips. His eyes gleamed with mischief as they met mine. "You've already seen me naked—why don't you return the favor? It's only fair."

He wanted to keep things fair, did he? How deliciously noble.

I smirked as my hands grabbed the hemline of my blouse. The fabric caressed my peaked nipples as I pulled my blouse over my head and tossed it to the side with a flick of my wrist. A couple of lilies fell from my braid and tumbled down my collarbone and my breasts.

Riyan's eyes widened when he looked down at my bare chest and he let out a shuddering breath. My confidence waned as he stared. I wanted to cover up my breasts with my arms, but I remembered Riyan's order from the meadow.

Don't you hide from me.

"I hope I did not disappoint." I squeezed my shoulders forward. "I know you must have expected bigger—"

Before I could finish, Riyan gripped the hair on the back of my head and forced my lips up to meet his. The slight tug on the roots of my hair was shockingly exhilarating. His other hand wrapped around the side of my waist and held me down as my back arched up.

He broke the kiss and his lips hovered over mine before he moved lower.

His hot breath wrapped around my neck. "Do you feel it too?"

I shivered. "Wh-what in particular?"

"The pull between us." He moved lower. "That burning inside that's guiding my every move. That gold fire."

His lips and the tip of his nose caressed my collarbone before he kissed me between my breasts, right over my pounding heart. "Right here."

The tongues of magical golden fire flared at his touch. Even though our bond burned me from the inside, I closed my eyes to savor the warmth of his breath on my bare chest. "Y-yes. Please keep going."

He dragged the tip of his tongue all the way down my middle and tasted my belly, only stopping where my skirt met my skin.

I opened my eyes and found Riyan looking up at me expectantly with both hands around my hips and his fingers gripping the waist of my skirt.

"I did get to see you," I said through heavy breaths. "It is only fair, after all."

Riyan chuckled low in his throat and tugged off my skirt and undergarments in one swift pull. The rumpled clothes smacked against the wall after he threw them like they had offended him.

Once I was naked, Riyan went quiet. He studied what was between my parted knees for a few breaths and his silence made my stomach cave in.

"Did you not study diagrams of women at the military academy?" I asked.

Riyan's eyes met mine and his eyebrows furrowed. "Any drawings of women I found were not for academic purposes." His gaze wandered back down to my hips.

"Do you…do you know what to do?" I asked. Maybe the pull of the blood bond stopped short of giving detailed instructions.

Riyan glanced up at me and the corners of his mouth turned up in an evil smile. He gently took my right hand, dragged it along my thigh, and held it above my pulsing desire.

"Show me," he ordered.

I took in a slow, sweet breath and closed my eyes. My fingertips sparked to life and I slowly stroked myself the way I did when I was alone at night. I licked my lips and dared let a moan escape my throat as I stoked my own fire.

When I used to touch myself, I would either imagine Derrick or that handsome school guard who used to sneak Annalisa treats. But as the sensation built, I opened my eyes and found the crooked smile and tight muscles of the only man I wanted to think about as I pleasured myself.

Riyan's right hand wrapped around my hip. His thumb gently pushed my hand out of the way and took over with soft stroking motions of his own. I melted into his touch.

"Like that?" he whispered. His breath kissed my temple.

I whimpered and nodded. I gripped the blankets as my heart raced. Riyan switched from downward strokes to circles and my legs opened up even more. My breath shuddered and he stopped.

Cruel bastard.

Riyan dropped his thumb and replaced it with the tip of his index finger, gently stroking my slit like he was knocking on the door.

"Please," I whispered.

"Only because you're being so sweet to me," Riyan replied.

Riyan eased his finger in and I whimpered. Just one of his fingers was nearly the size of two of mine, but my body not only accepted him, it begged for more.

"Do these happy little noises mean you like what I'm doing?"

I hummed in assent. My muscles pulsed around him as he stroked me from the inside. My stomach clenched as pressure built within me.

He leaned down and kissed me hungrily as I ground my hips in time with his hand. I gripped his strong arms to keep from spilling over too quickly. The calluses on his palm hit me *just right*.

"More," I begged into his mouth. "More, more, more."

"Now look who doesn't have any manners?" Riyan replied with a smirk against my lips. "I never was a gentleman, but you stopped being a lady the instant you entered my bed."

"Asshole," I whimpered.

"Oh, you're *bad*," he growled. "I'd better give you what you want before you get even nastier."

He eased in a second finger and lightning shot up my spine. I arched myself like a lyre as Riyan plucked my strings.

He picked up speed and sent me catapulting over the edge. My chest seized my breath from my throat as release rushed out of me like a rainstorm. My legs trembled, but Riyan did not stop.

"I'm about to fucking snap," Riyan hissed through his teeth. "You're ready for me."

I found my breath and gasped. I clawed his rock-hard biceps as my lower half shook with the tremors of my climax. I took in another breath as a cry built in my chest.

"Riyan!" I screamed.

The air shifted. Riyan's muscles loosened. All the control he had broke in an instant.

Riyan took his hand out of me and gripped my waist so tightly I could not breathe. He picked me up and threw me onto my back in the center of the mattress.

Before I could get my bearings, Riyan leaped on top of me and the wooden bedframe cracked under his force. The mattress fell through the broken frame and thudded to the floor.

My vision shook as the shattered bed hit the ground. Riyan propped up on his elbows above me. I caught a glimpse of his hungry and animalistic eyes before he dove toward my mouth. He kissed me, bit me, and stole all my air as he tasted the last drops of my screams of ecstasy.

He slid his hand under my back and jerked me into his chest.

He is going to snap her spine.

He gripped my thigh with his free hand and forced my legs open wider.

He is going to break her legs.

Riyan's chest pressed against mine as his hand left my thigh to undo his pants. My ribs bowed under his weight. My heart raced. I could not breathe.

He is going to crush her to death.

My arms were trapped between the mattress and his chest. I weakly punched him in the clavicle, but he did not feel me. I scratched at him as my lungs burned and I wrenched my lips away from his and gulped in a shallow sip of air before I pleaded for my life.

"Riyan!" I gasped.

His mouth found mine again and he kissed me even harder. He pressed his chest deeper into mine. My ribcage was going to crack just like the bed had. I struggled underneath him as much as I could but he either did not notice or did not care.

I finally understood why Derrick wanted me to have the dagger at all times. He knew brutes lose control. He was just trying to keep me alive.

Stars danced in the dark edges of my blurry vision. I turned my chin to the side to escape his lips and let out a final cry of desperation.

"I cannot breathe," I croaked.

Riyan threw himself off me with a short gasp and the room shook as he hit the floor. I let in a strained, shaking breath as my chest inflated. I laid my hand over my pounding heart as I slowly breathed through the burning in my lungs.

My back muscles flared with pain as I slowly climbed into a sitting position on the mattress. I took short, staggered breaths and tried to calm my frantic heartbeat.

Riyan kneeled on the floor beside the fallen mattress. His shoulders slumped forward and his hands gripped his knees—somehow his pants had stayed on. Tiny drops of blood blossomed out of the little cuts in his arms where he had hit the broken glass on the floor. His big eyes watered as he watched me struggle to breathe.

"Serafina, I'm so sorry," he said with a heavy voice. "I thought you were enjoying yourself. I didn't even know you were—"

He cut himself off. He squeezed his eyes shut and dipped his chin toward his chest. He took in a sharp breath and rose to his feet. He walked to the door with heavy footsteps, crushing glass beneath his bare feet without a flinch.

"Where are you going?" I asked, my voice hoarse.

"Outside," he replied, keeping his eyes bolted toward the door. "I don't belong here."

The golden light of our bond wrapped around my granite heart and tugged on the smooth surface. As the bond squeezed a new crack in the stone, my hand jolted up to reach out to him.

"Wait," I pleaded. My voice was stronger than before, but my stomach was still weak.

Riyan turned his head. His jaw was set tight but his eyebrows furrowed as he let out a breath. I curled my outstretched hand back to my chest and placed it over my heart.

"Stay," I asked.

Riyan turned his body toward me but shook his head. "How can you trust me after what I just did? How could you ever want me to touch you again?"

Because I just…wanted him to. Even if it made no logical sense.

The cold mountain air pricked my bare skin and raised the hair on my arms. I needed his warm body and strong arms around me if I was going to face another night with all my confusing feelings fighting each other in my head.

The muscles in my face relaxed but I did not take my eyes off him.

"Stay," I ordered.

Riyan's face softened. He carefully walked back to the plush mattress and eased himself next to me. All the tiny cuts on his arms had already magically closed up and healed. He laid on his side and curled his body to fit on the square mattress. Riyan rested his head on top of two pillows, his shoulders sloped forward and his back curved, and his glassy eyes looked up at me as I sat next to him.

"I never wanted to hurt you," Riyan said, his warm breath making the skin on my belly tingle. "Not on Selection Night, not now—"

"Do I look hurt to you?" I asked softly. For once, I was not lying—my pain and soreness had somehow disappeared.

The magic in my veins pushed me to touch him. He tensed as I gently placed my hand on his forearm, but then he relaxed after a heartbeat.

"You have my blood now, so it looks like you heal quickly too," Riyan said. He swallowed and his voice dropped to a whisper. "But you still scared the shit out of me."

I lifted up his heavy forearm and laid down on the mattress, placing his arm around my body like a blanket. I did not want to talk about what almost happened. The golden light swirling around in my chest only wanted closeness.

Riyan's eyes brightened a little as I snuggled him. His gaze wandered up to the top of my head and he let himself smile.

"You still look like my faerie princess," he said as he played with one of the lilies that managed to stay in my braid. His thumb dropped to caress my forehead and he chuckled. "If you were stuck on that glass hill, I wouldn't need a magic horse or any of that bullshit to save you. I would just punch the glass and shatter it so you could slide down into my arms."

A short laugh escaped my lips. "You cannot solve every problem by punching it, Riyan."

His fingertips caressed my back in long strokes. "I'm slowly starting to figure that out."

Riyan draped the knitted blanket over me but kept his arm over my waist and his hand on my back. I leaned into the pillow underneath my head and stared at the center of Riyan's chest. I watched his chest rise and fall, imagining that ball of golden light twisting around his heart.

The marriage enchantment was indeed special, but not like the Ashmore matrons had described. It had given me the ability to heal. It had even made me braver, more introspective, and, dare I think it, nonsensical.

I had already defied my rock-solid logic and reasoning by staying close to the man who had nearly suffocated me and I could not explain what drove me to want to touch him so badly. I had never felt that way about Derrick, or anyone else for that matter.

For some reason, Mother's words about fear and love being two sides of the same blade sang in my mind. Her ridiculous rambling made no sense the first time and it still made no sense as I mulled over it again. Still, that little spark of gold around my heart compelled me to make sense of it all.

"Riyan, what do you think love is?" I asked.

Riyan's chest stilled for a heartbeat, then he let out a long breath.

"Love is," he replied, letting the words slowly roll off his tongue, "when you realize you would do anything for someone because their life and happiness matters more than yours."

I hummed and kept staring at his chest. His logic was more sound than my mother's. Maybe I could take his word for what love really was.

My chest fell. I did not care about anyone else more than my own survival. I had closed off my heart to keep myself safe from pain, but I had never realized how selfish my protection was until Riyan spelled out what the opposite meant.

My defenses had all but crumbled and I had let Riyan closer to my truest self than I had ever allowed anyone in before, but I still kept him safely away from my heart. Even though he held me against him, I might as well have been on the peak of my own mountain far away.

Riyan's voice rumbled low in his throat as he spoke again. "I'll tell you a secret if you tell me one first."

I sighed and kept my eyes fixed on his chest as Riyan lazily stroked my back. The secret I was about to let out was ugly and cold, but I promised myself I would be honest.

"I do not love anyone," I said.

Riyan's hand stopped caressing my skin. I bit my tongue and closed my eyes.

"Not anyone?" he asked. "Not even Brietta Elvar? Or your parents?"

I let out a shaking breath onto my pillow and opened my eyes. I was only brave enough to look up at Riyan's chin. My lip trembled as another confession slithered out of me.

"I have not loved anyone since my brothers died."

My eyes stung with tears. I slammed my eyelids shut and clenched my fists in the knitted blanket. I needed to distract myself with Riyan's voice so I would not cry.

"What is your secret?" I opened my eyes and stared at the center of his chest again.

"Oh, uh," he stammered, "I drink a lot."

"That is not a secret." I unclenched my body and let a smile break through my lips. "I open up about my ugliest truth and you tell me that? How is that fair?"

"I…" He paused, then he cleared his throat. "It's not fair. You're right."

Riyan sighed. I waited for him to tell me what his secret actually was, but he gently ran his fingertips along my spine and settled into silence.

Just as my eyelids grew heavy, Riyan hummed the notes to the song of the Man of the Mountain. His low voice rumbled around me like a slow avalanche. I closed my eyes and smiled.

"I like your singing," I whispered into the pillow.

Riyan dipped his chin to rest on the top of my head. "Humming is not singing."

My head sank into the feathers of the pillow. I breathed in nectar and wheat.

"Where is West of the Moon and East of the Sun?" I asked as I stifled a yawn.

"It's another name for the peak of Nordingaard," Riyan replied. "It's the realm of beasts and monsters where magic warps trees and animals speak."

I yawned and started to tumble into the welcoming abyss of unconsciousness.

"I hate that place," I whispered. "It took everything from me."

The gentle tide of Riyan's breath sent me to sleep and his last words kissed me goodnight. "Me too, sweetheart."

Chapter Twenty Five

Monster

I woke up realizing I wore nothing but the memories of Riyan's lips on my skin.

Somehow I did not mind.

My arms were wrapped around Riyan's forearm and my cheek pressed into his skin. Riyan was sitting up in bed and looking out the broken window at the golden sunrise. Purple crescents drooped under his heavy eyes and his cracked lips pursed like he was holding back sickness.

I rubbed my eyes and shifted my hips. "Were you awake all night?"

He blinked like he startled himself out of a nightmare. "I was. I was thinking."

I pulled myself out from underneath Riyan's arm and sat up next to him. He did not move his eyes from the rising sun. My stomach twisted at his silence, so I gently placed my hand on his bicep.

"I admitted I was afraid last night," Riyan said. His throat bobbed as he swallowed. "I haven't allowed myself to feel afraid since the first battle with the giants."

I gave his arm a reassuring squeeze. "There is nothing wrong with feeling afraid, Riyan."

"If you're me, there is," Riyan said bitterly. "When I'm afraid, my body sabotages me. My blood ignites, my bones twist, my muscles scream, and I get bigger. The magic in my blood forces me to grow because it's trying to protect me from harm…but all it does is hurt me."

I furrowed my brow. "When was the last time you grew?"

Riyan turned his face from the window and looked straight ahead at the stone wall of the bedroom. "When I was fifteen. I was a little taller than General Hyton, but I was living a relatively normal life. Then we went to the first battle against the giants…and I saw so many boys my age and younger…"

Riyan's jaw tightened. His fists clenched so tightly his knuckles turned white. "I can't even talk about it."

Birds chirped outside as we sat in heavy silence. I could not imagine something so horrible that even *he* refused to talk about it.

"I may have lived, but I shouldn't say I survived that battle. Sometimes I'm still at the peak of Nordingaard, fighting those giants over and over again in my head."

I wrapped my other hand around his massive bicep and pressed my forehead against his skin. His tight muscles vibrated as he spoke.

"I never know if they will come back to slaughter more boys in my dreams, so sleeping is a fucking gamble. Sometimes I stay up for days and then force myself to drink an entire handle of grog so I can finally pass out."

My lips brushed against his trembling skin. "That sounds like hell."

His muscles tightened under my hands so quickly my heart skipped a beat.

"Being in this body is hell," he snapped. "I can't fit in most houses, I can't sit at the dinner table with my family, I can't even trust myself to *be with you* because I don't know my own strength. And that scares the shit out of me. But I know that if I get scared like I did in the past, I will grow and make everything worse."

Riyan's chest rose and fell faster and faster as he spoke. I held my breath as his trembling arm warmed under my cheek and my fingertips. His mouth twisted up in a snarl. "So I don't get scared. I just get angry and then I deal with the anger. That's how I've gone nearly seven years without growing. Life is already unbearable now—I *can't* make it worse."

I let go of his arm and backed off as he fumed. His jaw was tight and his eyes vibrated as he stared forward.

"Riyan?" I quietly called out.

He did not answer. He stayed still and unresponsive like he was not even in the room.

I bit my tongue and looked down at his tight fists in the blankets. Riyan had already broken his bed—I did not want to know what else he would break if he flew into another rage.

I thought of the last time I gave Riyan a small comfort and got an idea. I turned from Riyan and reached down to the floor to grab his discarded shirt from the night before. I shook off the invisible shards of broken glass and pulled the shirt into my lap.

I carefully placed my hand on top of his white knuckles and he released his grip on the blankets as he came back to me. I slid my hand into his and laid the sleeve of his shirt in his palm so he could see the flowers I had embroidered for him.

Riyan took a breath and looked down at the sleeve.

I traced the stitching of one flower with my index finger. "When you are afraid, look for the flowers."

"What is that supposed to do?" he asked.

"Calm you down," I replied. "Find your flowers instead of your rage."

Riyan gently brushed his fingers over the flowers. His chest and arms relaxed as he let out a slow breath. "Did you enchant the flowers or something?"

"Yes," I lied.

The light was back in Riyan's mischievous eyes. "You know the Duke made sorcery illegal, right?"

"I thought we established that Duke Hyton does not own me," I replied with a smirk.

Riyan plucked a crumpled and dry lily petal from my braid. He gently tapped the petal on the tip of my nose. "No one can own you, faerie princess."

Just as I thought he was going to pick more flower petals out of my frayed braid, he instead traced the curve of my cheekbone. I could not help but smile.

Days ago, Riyan said he chose me because I saw him. I had no idea what he meant then, but I finally understood—I saw his suffering.

Riyan just wanted a small reprieve from his life of torment—even if it was just a spoonful of jam, a kiss on the cheek, or a mended shirt. If all he asked from me was relief from the constant misery, I would give it to him.

Riyan smiled back at me. "Can I be selfish?"

I quirked an eyebrow. "How?"

His thumb trailed down to rest just below my chin. "Kiss me again."

My eyelashes fluttered down to my cheeks as he gently tilted my chin up. When our lips met, I led him into a dream instead of a nightmare.

A dream where no giants existed.

Hilda was spoon-feeding Astrid porridge at the dining table when I joined them for breakfast. Riyan had left the fortress to gather flowers for his mother so I could get ready for the reunion. I had stuffed my letters to Brietta and Annalisa in my pocket, but abandoned the Hyton dagger under my pillow again. Even though Riyan had lost control and nearly killed me, I did not want to carry it anymore.

What had constantly seeking protection really given me? Imprisoning myself behind stone and iron did not protect me from pain, but instead kept me from knowing sweetness, joy, or warmth.

Derrick's protection was not worth that sacrifice.

Hilda held up a spoonful of goopy porridge near her daughter's mouth. "Eat up, apple blossom, today is a big day! You finally get to see your boy!"

Astrid slowly and absent-mindedly ate her porridge. The blooms in her flower crown were wilted and mashed and she sat in a kind of chair I had never seen before—a chair with wheels instead of legs. Her wheeled chair replaced the bear throne at the head of the table. I sat on the bench across from Hilda, but Astrid did not even notice me.

Hilda tried to introduce me to Astrid after she had finished her mouthful of porridge. "Astrid, this is Serafina, she is a new friend who lives with us."

"Nice to meet you, Astrid," I said gently.

Astrid's grey eyes rolled over to me. She looked much older than thirty-nine, but seemed as though she was still a child. She reached over and touched my left hand with her bony fingers. She slowly flipped my hand over and revealed the tiny scar on my palm from the blood bond. She gently patted the scar and blinked twice at me.

Hilda's pink cheeks flushed even pinker. "This is a very good sign!" she nearly squealed. "She is in a friendly mood today!"

Hilda placed her hand on her daughter's back. "Serafina married your son. Riyan is grown-up now, Astrid. He wants to see you today!"

Astrid did not react to her mother and instead kept her eyes on me as she held my hand. She patted my hand again and then returned to her porridge.

My stomach fluttered with too much anticipation to eat a filling breakfast, so I left Hilda and Astrid to wait for them in the courtyard for the reunion.

Sweet morning air filled my nose as I stepped outside. The sun shone through wispy clouds and all the servants bustled around the courtyard, all seemingly realizing the importance of the day. Every servant and soldier avoided the battered tree trunk near the eastern wall. I rolled my eyes—I would get Riyan to move that damn trunk later so it was not in everyone's way.

Horses and carts passed through the open gate under the inspection of a pock-faced soldier. I handed him my letter to Annalisa.

"The recipient is a little testy," I said with a small laugh. "We may have an assassination attempt on our hands if this letter does not reach her fast enough."

The young soldier's eyes widened. He handed the letter to the first cart driver that was leaving the fortress. "Deliver this to Hyton Palace at once!"

"Why?" asked the driver. "I'm just picking up supplies from the villages. I'm not scheduled to go to Hyton for another week."

"It's the order of the future Baroness!" the soldier shouted.

The cart driver grumbled and drove south.

I bit my tongue from embarrassment, but still savored the small amount of power I held as a future Baroness.

As I stood at the gate, I spotted Nikkolas walking outside the walls. Hilda had assured me Astrid would not be ready to meet Riyan until noon, so I had plenty of time to ask the current Baron of Bloodstone what my life would look like as the future Baroness.

The young gate-guard stiffened and saluted me as I passed.

"Out for a walk, Baron Bloodstone?" I called as I approached.

Nikkolas glanced at me and slowed his pace. "Something like that. I know it will take some getting used to, but call me Nikkolas. I am quite unlike the Barons you are accustomed to, anyway."

I caught up to him and walked beside him. "Of course, I apologize."

"Do not apologize," he said. "You were well-taught. I am sure the Headmistress at Ashmore would have struck your hand if she heard you referring to a Baron by his first name."

"You are right," I said with a laugh as I thought of Headmistress Blackiston fainting in horror at my impropriety.

"I usually am."

Meadowlarks tweeted as I walked next to Nikkolas on a narrow dirt path that led into a forest. He was as quiet as a phantom amongst the trees and brush, his feet walking at a constant pace in a straight line but still avoiding every twig or errant pebble in his path. As abrasive as Nikkolas was, his stern face was an oddly comforting presence in the woods. He was every bit the cold and secretive man rumors painted him to be, but he strolled through his land as if he were part of it.

Nothing could harm a Baron in his own land, it seemed.

The forest opened up to a small clearing with narrow stones sticking out of the ground.

"Despite Ravenwood being our closest neighbor and ally," Nikkolas said, "you do not know much about our family, do you?"

I looked out at the rows of stones. "No, sir."

"Good," he said. "The Bloodstone nature is to keep to ourselves. It is a great burden, as you will see, presiding over the province that contains most of Lycaster's magic."

"I understand. Hilda told me about the red monster and the healing spring on the mountain."

Nikkolas's eyebrows raised with pleasant surprise. "Then you already have an idea of what you are dealing with. The mountain is dangerous. When

Astrid's...*incident* occurred, my sons tried to cure her. Fraleigh would not help, so they went out on their own."

Nikkolas pointed at a stone in front of us. "My eldest son, despite being my heir, went to the peak of Nordingaard and never returned. He is not actually in the grave, of course, but his wife is in the one next to him. She was the first-selected, just like you, and now she is dead. She was even pregnant with my heir and my son still decided to leave. Idiot."

A stone heavier than the ones in the ground dropped in my stomach. Nikkolas pointed to the next stone in line. "My second son, not caring that Bloodstone was his responsibility after his brother died, ran to the West of the Moon and East of the Sun too. His wife is buried there."

My eyes fixed on the headstone and my hands went cold.

"I ran out of sons, so I had to invest our magical little gift from the mountain as my heir. That massive bastard is the very last of my blood."

Nikkolas turned to me, his expression dark and serious. "You are Bloodstone's last hope. At first I thought my grandson succumbed to the curse that caused all my heirs to make moronic decisions when I saw he chose a tiny bride, but then I realized a smart girl like you can crack a nut like him. You can give Bloodstone the heir it needs."

My hands locked in front of my belly. "I understand the situation. The House of Ravenwood lost its sons and now my father is charged with high treason. The Duke could take Ravenwood at any moment."

"My, my," Nikkolas said with an amused smile. "Could you imagine Duke Hyton with direct control of both the magic and mystery of Ravenwood and Bloodstone? Oh, it would be catastrophic. Good thing I would not be around to see it."

I crossed my arms over my chest. "I know you want to secure Bloodstone's future and that we have a time limit, but I promise I am trying."

"Bah, a promise," Nikkolas scoffed. "Useless words that give me nothing. Unless you want the Hytons to gain unimaginable power from Nordingaard's magic, you are going to have to do more than just try."

"What do you want me to do, Nikkolas?" I snapped. "Take off his pants and jump on him as soon as I see him next?"

Nikkolas raised his eyebrows. "My, you really are Adalia's daughter. But, sure. And take care not to destroy my tower again, would you?"

I clenched my fists as Nikkolas suddenly walked away. Not wanting to be left alone in the eerie graveyard, I begrudgingly followed him down the dirt path for a few paces before Nikkolas spoke again. "Do you know what the biggest difference is between the Barons of the Northern provinces and the Duke of Lycaster?"

"No," I huffed, "not other than having more riches."

Nikkolas smiled down at me and took a breath. "We *really* love our wives. The Hytons cannot understand love like we do. They do not love, they consume."

The left side of my neck burned and I glanced down at the dirt path.

"As…*unbearable* as my grandson is," Nikkolas said with distaste, "I have a crumb of faith that the two of you can work. Hilda and I did, after all."

If Hilda was the rosy dawn, Nikkolas was the cool twilight—complete opposites, and yet their love for each other all but radiated off of them. However, their only struggle was a personality difference. Nikkolas could not crush Hilda to death.

I hugged my arms and looked up at Nikkolas's hard face. "Riyan and I are rather…mismatched. But you really think we can make it as Baron and Baroness?"

"You have to." His face darkened. "If not, both Bloodstone and Ravenwood will eventually fall to the Hytons. They *cannot* have access to our magic—not after what happened to Ilsa Ravenwood. The Hytons are monsters."

I hopped over a large stone in my path but looked back at Nikkolas. "What do you mean what happened to Ilsa?"

Nikkolas's eyes gleamed like patinated silver as we stepped into the sunlight again. "Even the Duchess herself could not escape the prejudice of being from a Northern province. When she was loved, she was a diamond. When she was envied, she was a half-giant. When someone needed to take the blame for a Duke's murder, she was a sorceress."

The walls of the fortress came into view. Was Nikkolas really saying Ilsa was not…?

"Ilsa was no sorceress," Nikkolas said with a smile that was as friendly as the snarling golden bear pinned to his cape. "She did not have the gift."

The gift? Before I could ask, a commotion near the gate stole our attention.

"I must speak with the Baron, by order of the Duke!" cried a familiar voice.

My heart nearly leaped out of my chest. I picked up my skirt and quickened my pace. Three Bloodstone soldiers blocked the entrance to the fortress where a silver-haired man stood. The man was alone, disheveled, and holding the reins of a tired brown horse.

"Father!" I cried. I could not believe it—Duke Hyton had pardoned him. He was safe and so was Mother.

Father's dark eyes warmed as I ran to him. I stood in front of him and smoothed the front of my skirt, looking as much of the future Baroness as I could.

Father opened his mouth to say something, but his eyes flicked above my head and narrowed. "An army, Baron? That would have been useful seven years ago."

I turned around. Nikkolas calmly walked toward us with his mouth in a tight line. "Baron Ravenwood, to what do we owe the pleasure?"

Father snorted. I whipped my head around to find a smirk on Father's mouth and pain in his eyes. "There is no Baron Ravenwood."

My stomach dropped. "W-what do you mean, Father?"

Father kept his eyes on Nikkolas. "As punishment for acts of high treason, the Baronage of Ravenwood was dissolved, making Ravenwood and Bloodstone provinces under the sole leadership of the Baron of Bloodstone."

My breath stilled in my throat. My heart did not even beat. Duke Hyton had finally decided on father's sentence for high treason, but if Father was no longer Baron, what did that make him? What did that make Mother?

Father reached into his pocket and pulled out his golden House of Ravenwood pin. The golden raven gleamed in the noon sunlight as he held it out to Nikkolas. "I got to keep my head, but I lost everything else."

Nikkolas looked down as if his silver eyes weighed exactly what the golden pin symbolized—full control of the Northern provinces. Before his tightly clenched fists could reach for it, a shriek of terror tore through the air.

"Go, you idiots!" Nikkolas shouted at his soldiers. All three soldiers turned on their heels and sprinted inside the courtyard. Nikkolas hurried after them as fast as he could and I only had to jog a few paces before I took in what was happening.

Riyan stood ten paces in front of the tree trunk near the eastern wall with a large bouquet of flowers in his hand and fear in his watery eyes.

Astrid trembled and screamed as she sat in her chair in front of him. Riyan took a step back and hunched his shoulders forward, but Astrid screamed like Riyan was going to attack her.

"Mother, please," Riyan whispered. He took another step back.

Hilda knelt beside her daughter and frantically patted her arm. "Astrid, it is your son, Riyan!" she cried. "Riyan is not going to hurt you!"

Riyan took another step back as his left hand grabbed his right sleeve—he was looking for the flowers. I took two steps through the grass to help calm Riyan down but Father grabbed my arm and held me back.

"Wait—!" Father ordered.

Astrid cried out and fought against her mother, desperately thrashing in her chair like she was trying to escape. Astrid swung her left arm into Hilda's chest and knocked her to the ground.

"Hilda!" Nikkolas cried as he rushed to his fallen wife.

Hilda did not move. I tugged against Father's grip to help Hilda up, but he pulled me back further.

Astrid's throat trembled as she looked up at Riyan with terrified eyes. "M-Monster!" Astrid screamed. "Monster!"

"Mother…," Riyan whispered. His voice broke. His eyes watered. He took another step back. Then another…

"Riyan, watch out for—!" I shouted.

But before I could finish, Riyan's boot caught the edge of the tree trunk and he fell backward into the eastern wall.

Boom.

A cloud of dust rushed toward me and Father threw himself over my back. I shut my eyes. Pain worse than the blood bond enchantment exploded in my chest. My veins were thorny vines of ice, glowing with biting agony in every part of my body. I screamed from the torture as Father's body shook on top of mine.

A single pained cry hit my ears and drowned out my own screaming— Riyan. The ground shook over and over with crashes like a thunder's rage. Shards of rock hit my spine where Father did not shield me.

Just as I clenched my teeth so tightly I thought they would crack, the pain slowly seeped away. My muscles were still sore and my heartbeat pounded in my ears, but I could finally breathe again.

"You bastard!" Nikkolas cried.

Father tried to keep me down, but I hurriedly fought my way up. I rubbed dust out of my eyes and coughed dirt out of my mouth.

I opened my eyes to chaos. Pieces of stone laid everywhere and dozens of soldiers sprinted to the eastern wall. Two maids ran to a screaming Astrid, took her out of her chair, and ran with her in their arms up the steps to the keep. Nikkolas kneeled next to his wife. Hilda was face-down in the grass with rocks and stones all around her. Blood poured from a gash in her head so quickly it stained her hair bright red.

A stone with a jagged edge lined with Hilda's blood laid next to her in the grass. The stone was larger than both my fists put together.

But maybe she survived. Maybe she just needed some help.

As soon as I took a step in the grass, Nikkolas cried out in pain. Like a bolt of crimson lightning, a gash cracked across Nikkolas's forehead—a twin to Hilda's. His eyes slammed shut from pain as his hand flew up to his head. The moment Nikkolas opened his eyes to see blood on his fingertips, his face contorted into a snarl and his body trembled.

His face snapped toward the fallen wall and his silver eyes lit up with fury. "I should have drowned you when you were born! I should have fed you to the wolves! You killed her! You killed my Hilda!"

My hands flew to my mouth. No, it could not be. Riyan would never—

I looked over where Riyan fell. My blood froze and my stomach dropped. Riyan's trembling body stood in the middle of the fallen bricks of the crumbled stone wall. His clothes were in shreds and hanging off his limbs. His hair had grown and fell to his shoulders. His muscles shook as tears streaked his face.

Riyan was as tall as the rest of the still-standing wall—at least fifteen feet high. My head would have only reached his knee. Riyan was no longer just the height of a peasant's house, or even merely twice my size…but the size of a giant.

In a heartbeat I understood—Riyan's magical blood in my veins had forced me to feel his pain, but while I stayed the same size, Riyan's fear had turned him into a monster.

He killed Hilda…and Nikkolas was not far behind.

But maybe I could fix it. Maybe I could stitch Nikkolas up and he would be better. Maybe I could calm Riyan down and—

I yelped as Father hoisted me over his shoulder and ran to the keep. "Wait!"

Father would not turn around, but I kept my eyes on Nikkolas and Hilda.

Nikkolas hissed in disdain as his shaking hands unfastened his House of Bloodstone pin. "Take it, you bastard! Take the Baronage and rot in the high hall of hell!"

With blood streaming into his eyes, Nikkolas hurled the shining golden pin at Riyan. Riyan's watery eyes only tracked the pin for a moment, but then he looked at me as Father took me further and further away.

"Riy—!" I screamed, but the rest of his name disappeared from my throat the moment Nikkolas collapsed next to his fallen wife.

I choked out a sob. The steadfast Baron and the kindly Baroness lied in a puddle of crimson, side by side, as their blood bond enchantment sent them both into Death's arms.

Father hurried up the keep's steps. Riyan blinked out a tear and then his massive shoulders turned away. His feet thundered into the earth as he sprinted toward the top of the mountain.

The keep's doors shut in my face—Riyan was gone.

Chapter Twenty Six
Over All Else

Riyan had disappeared the moment the earth stopped shaking, but Father did not put me down. He held me on his shoulder as he ran through the fortress keep, refusing to slow down even as he climbed the spiraling stairs and ran through hallways.

I gripped the back of Father's cloak as my chest rattled with dry sobs. I relived the past ten minutes over and over with each of my pounding heartbeats. Nikkolas and Hilda were dead. Riyan killed them. Riyan was fifteen feet tall. Father was no longer the Baron of Ravenwood.

Father pushed open a door with a grunt and fell to his knees. I slid from his shoulder and finally put my feet on the floor. I gripped my sleeves as I gathered my bearings. Dark bookshelves, tall windows, ashy hearth—we were in the Baron's study.

Father panted and looked up at me with his hands on his knees. "I was not sure I would make it up those steps, but at least you are safe now."

"Safe?" I cried. I gestured out a window that faced the mountain. "How am I safe? My husband is the size of a giant!"

My heart stopped. Riyan was the size of a giant. If he had nearly crushed me to death at his former height, I would not survive if we tried to consummate our marriage again. He would not even…*fit* inside me! An annulment was imminent.

Cold sweat slicked my palms, but I was too paralyzed with terror to dry them on my skirt. The safety of my marriage expired as soon as the full moon came around. Father was no longer a Baron, so *any* protection he could have given me had vanished.

I was twenty-five days from being at the mercy of the monstrous Hytons for the rest of my life.

My stomach twisted and acid crawled up my throat. Before I could vomit on the bear skin rug, Father shakily rose from his knees and moved to a large oak desk near the window. He hissed an angry breath through his nose and pulled out drawer after drawer.

My confusion forced my sickness back down.

"Father, what are you doing?" I spat as I walked to the desk. "Nikkolas's body is not even cold and you are rifling through his—"

"Was the army not the least bit suspicious, Serafina?" Father said as he yanked open a drawer. He pulled out a large black book and flipped through it—a ledger. Father tore through page after page as his eyes grew hotter with fury. "Legions of soldiers? Stockpiling enough food to feed Ravenwood for a month? He hoarded resources while my people suffered?"

"How dare you speak of him right after—!"

"Take a look for yourself, then!"

Father slammed the black book down on the desk with a huff. He dug in his pocket while I picked up the book and thumbed through a few pages. Sure enough, the ledger accounted for the salaries of a company of soldiers, purchases of crates of fruits and grains, and accountings of hundreds of jars of preserves, wheels of cheese, and cured meats.

The profits from the collected rents around Bloodstone did not match the exorbitant cost of Nikkolas's army and stockpile. As I flipped through the ledger, I noticed a consistent gap in the income that was the same every year—ten thousand marks.

I was never allowed to know much about money, but a discrepancy of ten thousand marks would only go unnoticed in the wealthy House of Elvar…or maybe the House of Hyton.

A flash caught my eye and I peered above the ledger. The House of Ravenwood pin glinted in the sunlight from the window as Father examined it with a hard brow.

His voice was distant. "I was a Baron exactly the way my father was—duty over all else—and still *nothing* I did was enough. I could have just…given Nikkolas this pin and everyone would have been saved. But then he had to die before he could make everything right!"

Father disdainfully dropped the pin on the desk. The pin clattered, but was not damaged.

I swallowed, remembering how Father repeated "duty over all else," to Erik and Endre before they rode away from Ravenwood Manor into the failed battle.

I forced the thought away and held out the ledger. "The numbers do not even out. Unless Nikkolas was getting ten thousand marks a year from somewhere else, his ledger is all wrong."

Father took the black book and scanned down a page before his mouth formed a tight line. "Hush money." He quickly flipped through the pages and his voice turned hard as a whetstone. "Twenty-two years of Hyton hush money."

My throat went dry as I stepped around the desk to stand next to him. "What are you talking about? Nikkolas hated the Hytons, he would never keep a secret—"

"For ten thousand a year, any man would," Father said with disgust as he tossed the ledger onto the desk. "Even though it was a *big* secret."

Outrage flared into my throat. "And you know what it was? You cannot keep it from me, I am—"

I almost finished with "I am your daughter," but a new answer formed on the tip of my tongue. I straightened my back and looked into my father's tired dark eyes. "I am the Baroness of Bloodstone. Tell me why the Hytons paid Nikkolas off."

Father's eyes shone as he looked at me, but then he scrubbed his face with his hand and stared at a nearby bookshelf. "That husband of yours is not really a half-giant."

I crossed my arms and scoffed. "Even Riyan knew that. Are you telling me the Hytons bribed Nikkolas into silence because they did not want anyone to know he was just a child of magic?"

"No, Serafina," Father said darkly. He pressed his palm on the desk and leaned in close to me. "What I am telling you is that Duke Hyton wanted everyone to believe he was a half-giant so no one would ask questions about who his father was."

Riyan…had a father?

Father must have read my thoughts through my knitted brow. His voice was sharp and cold as steel as he leaned in closer. "Riyan's father is General Ragnar Hyton."

I could have heard a feather drop in the silence that followed. I could not even hear my thoughts, or my heartbeat, or anything that could have connected what I had just heard with what I thought was the truth about Riyan.

As I compared the two men, I saw it—the blonde hair, the square jaw, the broad shoulders. I felt so foolish for never seeing the resemblance before, or for never questioning Riyan's story that he was merely formed from magic and had no father.

Riyan would have never lied to me, but then who lied to him? And why?

My lip trembled as my mouth hung slightly open. A question formed on my lips in one breath, but was replaced by another in the next breath. Finally, I pushed out the question that burned the tip of my tongue. "How?"

Father shook his head and kept his eyes on the top of the desk. "Those details did not tumble out onto Duke Hyton's pillowcase like the rest of the information."

I clenched my fists so hard my bones ached. "You mean Mother knows because she—"

"She is *privy* to certain information," Father snapped. He pushed himself off the desk and walked to the window. He placed his hands behind his back and looked through the diamond glass panes at the peak of the mountain that loomed above us.

I took a step toward Father and ugly, bitter anger rose up in my throat like bile. "How can you allow her to be with him? After everything he did to us? After he ordered…"

My voice broke and I snapped my jaw shut. My eyes stung with tears, but I stacked up my walls and closed the gate. I *refused* to cry.

I would not shed a single tear in front of the man who stood silently as my brothers took up arms to defend the province, who meekly sold off our family treasures to try to stop the bleeding, and whose wife made a fool of us all at Hyton Palace.

Father had been the Baron of Ravenwood, one of the great leaders of the Northern provinces, but his only plan for Ravenwood's salvation was the allure of a fourteen-year-old girl. I would have never worn the House of Ravenwood pin and led the province myself, but he and Mother had fully expected me to shoulder the burden as the Duchess of Lycaster.

Father let out a deep breath that fogged the glass in front of him and obscured his reflection. Although I could not see his face, I heard the tears in his voice. "Right after I married your mother, I watched my father die— trampled to death by his favorite horse. My mother fell to her knees right after, grappling at her face like she also had hooves stomping her skull in. I swore right then that I would do nothing to put my family in harm's way. So that is what I did for the rest of my life…nothing."

I loosened my fists. Father's shoulders shook, but he did not turn around. "When that horrible man ordered that Erik and Endre had to fight the giants, I did nothing, hoping they would come back…because I knew if I did something, Anders would make sure they never did. When he took your mother, I still did nothing, hoping I would not make the situation worse. But when he took you…I could not stand it anymore. I finally did *something*."

I swallowed and the anger in my chest softened, but did not completely disappear. Father's voice cracked as he fought sobs. "But as I sat in that cell in the Western tower of Hyton Palace, I realized that none of it mattered. Whether I did nothing or something, the result was still the same—I lost everyone I loved."

Metal kissed my fingertips. I glanced down—my left hand had wandered to the desk and stilled on the House of Ravenwood pin. I traced the raven's beak with my index finger as Father turned around.

His dark brown eyes were rimmed with red. "The question now, Serafina, is will you be like your mother and do something? Or will you be like me and do nothing?"

I did not like those choices—be the Duke's whore or be weak and trampled on. I did not harden my heart into stone to melt into a puddle of tears or cower at the feet of a tyrant.

I was a Ravenwood. I was going to survive.

I gritted my teeth and lifted the pin off the desk. My fingers curled around the golden crest as it rested against my scar from the blood bond. "Maybe I am not like either of you. Have you ever considered that?"

Father's shining eyes let only a single tear loose down his wrinkled cheek. His thin lips flicked up in a tiny smile. "I have wished for it every day, Little Ember."

My throat twitched with a fledgling sob, but I kept my mouth closed. I ran my thumb over the House of Ravenwood pin as my thoughts raced.

"If Riyan is General Hyton's son," I said slowly, "that makes him an heir to the House of Hyton."

Father nodded grimly. "The only other one. Anders has worried about his younger brother's impossibly powerful son for years. He would love nothing more than for the threat to disappear once and for all."

I swallowed. I had paid enough attention in history class to know the Dukes of Lycaster were not always the first-born son. Some ascended the throne because their elder brothers fell ill in childhood, others because the named heir died in battle, or…no, murder was never mentioned…but perhaps that was on purpose.

Just because the Ashmore matrons only taught us roses and smiles did not mean blood never stained the halls of the Hyton Palace.

Was General Hyton a real threat to his brother's throne?

General Hyton was never in line for the crown because he was unmarried and had no line of succession. But he did *indeed* have an heir, and not just any heir, the exalted Hero of Lycaster.

The cheers and applause of the crowd in Hyton city square rang through my mind again. Would thousands champion Riyan as a future Duke over Derrick? If General Hyton really wanted to usurp the throne, could he take a page out of his older brother's book and manipulate the peasants to believe Riyan was the better heir?

I imagined the crown on my head with Riyan at my side, but the glorious picture shattered in a heartbeat. No, Riyan could never be the heir.

Lycaster would only rally around a usurper if he had a solid lineage and that meant a blood bond. And since he was the size of a giant…our blood bond enchantment would never become permanent.

I was going to be the property of Duke Hyton no matter what I did. I clenched my jaw so tightly my head ached. Everything I had done to get the safety of the blood bond with Riyan ended up being for nothing. Playing in the lilies, dancing under starlight, kissing in the fires of passion…none of it mattered.

I nearly let myself believe I was just like Father—stuck no matter what I did—, but I refused.

A cooling breath passed my lips but my muscles hardened. I cast away Riyan's singing, the lilies in my braid, the sweetness of the elskaberry jam, and the warmth of his hand around mine. I had let myself live in a faerie story, but no more. I needed to focus.

Faerie princesses did not exist, after all.

I stacked all my knowledge of the House of Hyton like a deck of cards and then fanned it all out in my mind's eye. Duke Hyton was an unyielding bull who fixated on problems. Duke Hyton saw Riyan as a threat. Duke Hyton would do *anything* to keep control of Lycaster.

Maybe Duke Hyton would even let me keep Ravenwood…if he owed me a favor.

I raised the House of Ravenwood pin, holding the symbolic power of my home province in my very hand. I was the Baroness of Bloodstone, but only for the next twenty-five days. Once the full moon was high in the sky, my marriage enchantment would fail and I would be nothing again.

I could either go back to Hyton as little more than the smaller version of the Duke's whore…or I could arrive with the most powerful man in Lycaster feeling indebted to me.

My heart thumped heavily as everything clicked into place. Derrick had given me a lifeline, offered me a new blood bond marriage and leadership over Ravenwood. If Ravenwood and Bloodstone were under the control of one person, that meant whomever the Duke wanted to put in charge would have control of the Northern provinces.

If I took that lifeline, I could keep control of the magic like Nikkolas wanted, I could get Ravenwood the food and resources it needed, I could keep Astrid…

My breath stilled in my chest. Astrid. She had no one to look after her with her parents dead. She was going to end up the property of Duke Hyton too. He would not know how to take care of her. He could throw her into a cell until she starved to death…or worse.

I smoothed the raven's golden feathers with my thumb as I solidified my decision. I would take Derrick's lifeline—I would keep the magic, the North, and Astrid…

…the current Baron of Bloodstone just needed to die.

"Serafina?"

I looked up from the golden pin to Father's withered face, lines of worry creasing between his brows. He took a step toward me. "I know everything seems dark right now, but I will figure something out. I promise you—"

"Promise?" I said, my words colder than the mountain air. "Just like you and Mother promised me my brothers would come home?"

Father's throat bobbed. He opened his mouth to speak, but I cut him off. "I have heard many promises over the last seven years, but promises are just useless words that give me nothing."

I fastened the House of Ravenwood pin above my heart. The golden bird gleamed in the sunlight from the window as I flicked my eyes back up to Father. "You said Nikkolas had enough food stockpiled to feed Ravenwood for a month? Take it to them."

Father's brow furrowed. "Serafina, if you think I am going to leave you on this mountain like your brothers—"

He reached for me, but I stepped away. "Take a dozen soldiers and load up a caravan with as much food as you can carry."

He stepped closer. "Serafina, no—"

I crossed my arms and backed away. "Find the captain, the one with the scar on his face, and tell him—"

"I forbid it!"

"I am the Baroness!" I shouted. The silence that followed was thick enough to choke on, but I kept a tight grip on my arms and my shoulders squared. "I am the Baroness of Bloodstone and you are nothing. I will take care of myself and the Northern provinces."

Father nearly crumpled. "Serafina…why are you doing this to yourself?"

I stiffened my back and lifted my chin. "Like you always said, duty over all else."

My cold dismissal cut through him like a sword. He had to know distributing the food was not a real solution, but merely a reason to get him out of my way. Regardless, I had backed him into a corner. Baron or not, my father had always put the needs of the province first, and he would leave me on the dangerous mountain if it meant saving the peasants from starving.

Father nodded, accepting the command like I knew he would. He started for the door, but stopped when he was at my side.

He looked down at me with eyes like windows into his shattered soul. "Just remember where your heart is, Little Ember."

I snapped my head to face the window. Father's sullen footsteps faded behind me and the oak door to the study whispered shut.

I could never forget where my heart was. My heart was West of the Moon and East of the Sun, right next to the skeletons of my brothers.

The anger that had boiled up in my veins cooled to liquid steel. The walls and floor of the study turned into wafer-thin glass as I stood with the weight of my burden pressing on my chest.

I refused to think of Nikkolas and Hilda lying in the grass. I refused to think of Riyan's laughter or his hands softly stroking my back. I refused to listen to the tiny golden glow of my blood bond that flickered like fading candlelight as it was about to be severed.

My lifeline appeared like a rope amongst the forest of glass, leading me through the danger and despair to the Hyton dagger beneath my pillow.

I swallowed the hard lump in my throat and sent it down to the pit in my stomach as I leaned into my cold strength. Riyan was kind and gentle, but that was not enough to save me.

What a fool I had been, savoring his sweetness and forgetting why I had stacked up walls in the first place. But no more.

I was cruel steel. I loved no one. And that meant I was safe.

Over all else, I would give Riyan the reprieve from the constant misery he desperately wanted.

Part Four

Water
and
Light

Chapter Twenty Seven
Into the Darkness

The afternoon sun slipped behind the trees and bathed the fortress in cold blue dusk as I stood at my bedroom window. I kept a tight grip on my arms as Father's caravan of Bloodstone soldiers and carts piled high with supplies for the Ravenwood villages rolled through the fortress gate.

He did not even look back as he sullenly rode away.

Good.

I wiped my clammy palms on my skirt and let out a breath. Time to kill the Beast.

I lifted my pillow and found the Hyton dagger dutifully waiting for me. The blade gleamed with malice in the dying light from the window. My breath quickened. I did not want to kill Riyan, but I had no other choice.

Riyan's blood was the price of my security.

I swallowed my sadness and steeled myself. One cut. One cut and it would be over.

The stars emerged in the twilight as I tied the dagger to my garter once again. I stashed my needle and thread in my pocket along with my comb—supplies in case my journey in the wilderness took longer than planned. I dug through my trunk and found the small silver amethyst pendant and onyx choker. I was not going to raise suspicions by asking any of the soldiers for access to Bloodstone's money, so the few jewels I had could come in handy in case I needed to barter for supplies or bribe anyone into silence.

I took a deep breath and leaned into the safety of what Derrick had told me—Riyan had made enough enemies that no one would suspect I had killed him.

My heart grew heavy. Riyan had made enemies…but I had never heard him mention any friends. His grandparents were gone. His mother did not know who he was. His father did not even act like he wanted anything to do with him. Would anyone even care if the new Baron of Bloodstone just… never returned from the wilderness?

None of this was fair—Riyan deserved someone who wanted him to come back.

I shut the thought away. I could not fall prey to foolish emotions with the fate of the entire North on my shoulders.

I snuck down the tower stairs and out of the keep, being careful to stay within the shadows. Even though I was the Baroness, I was not sure the Bloodstone army was loyal to me. Besides, I could not imagine the Bloodstone army would stand aside if they found out I was going to assassinate their new Baron.

I pressed my back into the wall of the keep as the evening shadows made me all but invisible. The courtyard was mostly deserted. Nikkolas and Hilda had been taken away, hopefully to rest near their sons' graves. The rest of the staff were either tending to the distraught Astrid or sheltering in the safety of the stone keep in case the monstrous Baron returned.

Most of the Bloodstone soldiers gathered at the gate, but only two soldiers stood at the destroyed section of the eastern wall. I just had to wait for the change of the guard to sneak out of the fortress and track down Riyan.

Making sure the soldiers all had their backs turned, I silently ran over to the closest spot of the intact wall and pressed into the stone. The cold stone on my back made the hair on my arms stand up and my muscles shiver. Going further up Nordingaard would be even colder and I had nothing to keep warm with.

I looked over to the stream and noticed Riyan's cape still hanging on the line. In the daylight, the crimson cape stood out like a large warning flag, but it was much darker in the evening twilight. I weighed the risk of being seen against the risk of freezing to death, and I decided to rush for the cape.

I yanked the cape off the line and folded it in half to make it fit me. I wrapped the folded cape around my face and fastened it with the House of Ravenwood pin. The double layers of wool instantly warmed me and Riyan's smell enveloped me.

I bit my tongue as the tip of my nose stung. It was the last time I would ever smell nectar and wheat again.

My hands traced the stone bricks as I creeped through the shadows toward the crumbled wall. The two young soldiers held bows with notched arrows as they guarded their post. I flattened my body against the wall and waited for them to move.

"Is he coming back?" one of them asked the other.

"Dunno. Captain and a few others followed the trail of destruction up the mountain a ways. They didn't find him, but left him a few gifts to try to get him back to the fortress."

Gifts? What could possibly bribe Riyan? My ears perked up as the first soldier spoke up again.

"What's gonna happen if he never comes back? Are we out of a job?"

"Nah, Duke Hyton is gonna come up here and take it all over. We'll just be guarding whatever asshole he puts in charge."

At least the soldiers were prepared for what was going to happen, even if they thought I was an asshole.

The first soldier scoffed. "I give that asshole a month before Nordingaard takes him, too. I wouldn't be surprised if the big guy does show up just to eat him."

"He won't come back after killing his own grandmother. I would bet a month's wages on it!"

I held my breath and pressed harder into the stone. Even I saw how much Riyan loved Hilda. Listening to those moronic soldiers talk about him like he was a cold-blooded murderer made my stomach turn.

I swallowed the rising sickness but kept the rest of my body still. My fingertips tingled in anticipation against the rough stone and I pressed my weight into the balls of my feet.

"I don't want Duke Hyton up here," the first soldier grumbled. "I'm sick of the Hytons with all their money and power telling us all how to live. They wouldn't survive a single day in Bloodstone and the Duke is deciding who is going to be in charge after he sent us all off to fight the giants? Fuck that."

"What do you think a Duke does, you idiot? Of course Duke Hyton is going to tell us what to do. That's what they've done for hundreds of years!"

"I'd like to see Fraleigh put him in his place. She could come down from her shiny castle and hit Duke Hyton with a bolt of lightning!"

"Shut up, you've never even seen the Great Sorceress. You know she doesn't get involved in our business, anyway."

"Fine, *I'll* put him in his place. He makes one wrong move up here and I'll shoot an arrow through his fat neck!"

I pursed my lips. Duke Hyton was right. Not only did Bloodstone hate him, they hated anyone associated with the Hytons.

My stomach turned upside-down. Even if I did become the leader of the Northern provinces, the peasants could still hate me because of my allegiance with the House of Hyton. Would I have to utilize the Bloodstone army to quell revolt? I had no idea how to manage an army! Would General Hyton help me? Would he hate me for killing his son? Would he…thank me for getting rid of him?

As my head spun, I focused on the memory of the starving men and women beneath the Ravenwood and Bloodstone banners at the victory celebration. Their eyes were shining with hope as they looked up at me on the scaffold. If anyone could keep the Northern provinces from revolting against the Duke, it would be me.

All the more reason for Duke Hyton to put me in charge, and me alone. Everything was falling into place.

Heavy footsteps crunched in the grass. My chance to slip out opened up. I quickly checked to ensure the coast was clear and I darted through the gap in the wall and behind a tree.

My hands pressed against bark as I flitted from tree to tree with only moonlight illuminating my path. I slowly climbed up the craggy mountain following Riyan's trail of footprints, snapped tree branches, and crushed rocks.

I pulled myself up a waist-high ledge and pebbles clacked behind me. I whipped my head around and scanned the darkness. My heart raced as I pulled out the dagger. After a few pounding heartbeats, the air around me was still.

I let out a breath. I was just paranoid, but I kept the dagger out and by my side as I continued up the mountain.

I ran my hand along the rocky mountainside to find my way in the darkness, but I stopped when the sound of slow, heavy breathing filled the night air. My blood ran cold. I could barely see my hand in front of my face. Whatever lurked in front of me lay in wait in complete darkness.

The thin clouds covering the moon parted and the mountainside lit up in a gentle glow. My heart stopped when the moonlight revealed Riyan, sleeping on the ground only twelve paces from me. His back was against the tall rocky mountainside and his right hand splayed out toward his sword in the rocks. The remnants of his clothes laid around him and a large crimson cape draped over his stomach and legs like a blanket. His face was calm and his neck was exposed to the night.

He was so peaceful as he slept, but his new height was even more intimidating up close. His chest was the size of a mattress, his palm the size of a chair, and his biceps were wider than my whole body.

He was no longer my husband—just another giant to kill.

I carefully placed my feet around the rocks so I did not make a sound and kept my eyes on his sword. If I woke him up, he could grab that sword and cut me in half in a blink.

My heart raced as his breath warmed my legs. My hand trembled as it held the dagger.

Why, *why* did I have to kill him?

Riyan did not deserve it. The man who danced with me, fed me apples and jam, and filled my hair with lilies did not deserve to die. My eyes grew wet and hot, but I still refused to cry as I came closer and closer to ending his life.

The golden light of our bond crept up my arm and tried to force me to throw down the dagger, but I held fast to the bronze hilt. The warm rope of light burned into the stone around my heart and screamed out the truth of what I was about to do.

Riyan would never kiss me again. The heat of his body would never warm me at night. His hands would never run through my hair. His dimple would never send butterflies to my stomach. Our bond would sever and all the magical light that had freed me from my endless cycle of biting desolation and bitter rage would disappear.

I would live in the darkness forever.

But I had no other choice.

Cold granite shut out the light and I gritted my teeth. I could live in the darkness if it meant surviving. Riyan should have never chosen me. If he had just married Brietta like he was supposed to, Bloodstone and Ravenwood would be saved, Astrid would not be in danger, and Hilda and Nikkolas would have lived.

Riyan had to face the consequences of his actions. I had to fix what he broke the only way I could.

I silenced that pathetic golden bond and a numbing fog seeped down my body as I gripped the dagger. I stared at the muscles and veins in Riyan's neck as I decided where to strike.

Right across the throat, just like Derrick said. I strengthened my grip on the bronze hilt.

One cut.

One cut and it would all be over.

Do it.

DO IT!

I raised the dagger in the air. The steel blade reflected a shard of moonlight into Riyan's eye.

Riyan's eyes popped open and his pupils focused on me. My arm was still raised and the dagger was ready to slice into his throat. I gasped as his eyes met mine and I backed away.

Riyan's right palm slammed into the earth and the mountain trembled. I fell back into the rocks and dropped the dagger as he started to rise from the ground.

The sharp rocks cut my palms as I scrambled away from him. The dagger was useless since he was awake. He would catch me if I tried to run. I was trapped.

Riyan blinked and hissed hot air through his nostrils. He was half-raised and his cape had fallen off his side and pooled around his hips. Even in a sitting position, he was still taller than a grown man. Still powerful. Still deadly.

My heart pounded in my ears. My hands wrapped around the rocks beneath my palms. I could have thrown a rock at him and maybe slowed him down before he attacked me, but my blood froze in my veins and I could not move.

But Riyan surprised me. He did not reach down to attack me, he…laughed.

"You really were serious about wanting to kill me, huh?" His short bursts of laughter echoed off the mountain stone. "I just can't believe you didn't try sooner!"

He kept laughing. My fear morphed into confusion as I sat motionless in the rocks. Riyan was not angry, he had a thick tongue…oh no, he was drunk.

I quickly scanned the landscape and, sure enough, an empty glass bottle the size of my chest laid on its side near Riyan. So *that* was the bribe.

I clenched my teeth. What kind of sick bastard had the nerve to get drunk after killing his own grandparents? I unclenched and let out a breath, remembering Riyan's confession from earlier. He was not indulging or celebrating, he had pushed the poison past his lips as a tonic to sleep, or maybe even forget what he had done.

"But I thought you were smart, sweetheart," Riyan slurred. He reached for me with his massive finger like he wanted to tap me on the nose, but he clumsily just swiped at the air instead. "If you kill me, you die too. And then we'll *all* be dead!"

The numbing fog that had enveloped my entire body compressed into a tense grey cloud in my chest. I sat up in the rocks and leaned forward to hug my knees. "No, Riyan. If you die before our blood bond becomes permanent, the bond is just severed. I would…I would still get to live."

Shame rained down on my shoulders, but Riyan's drunken smile did not break. "And who told you that?" His bloodshot eyes flicked down to the dagger still lying in the rocks. With a heavy arm, he reached down and plucked the dagger between his forefinger and thumb. He held the bull's head hilt in front of his face for a few moments before booming out a laugh so forceful I thought he would cause an avalanche. "I'm an idiot! You *do* still love Derrick Hyton!"

He lowered the dagger and lolled his head to the side, resting it on his massive fist. He looked at me and smirked. "You didn't have to kill me to go back to him. I told you I would have let you go."

My lower lip trembled as I held the truth behind clamped teeth. No, I could not hide. Riyan at least deserved my honesty.

I squeezed my knees tighter into my chest and forced the words out. "Derrick was afraid for my life when I married you, so he told me that if I killed…if I severed our blood bond, I would marry the next leader of Ravenwood. Then Duke Hyton gave both the Northern provinces to the Baron of Bloodstone to punish my father for his high treason."

Riyan knitted his eyebrows and nodded his head against his fist, slowly piecing together everything I said.

I tried to swallow but my mouth was too dry. "Our marriage is going to annul because you are too big to…*you know.* I figured…either I go back to Hyton after the full moon as Duke Hyton's property and let both Ravenwood and Bloodstone fall to the Hytons or…or I make Duke Hyton indebted to me for killing you so he lets me keep the North and your mother—"

"Wait, hold on," Riyan slurred. "Why…why would Duke Hyton want me dead? I'm…I'm his hero, aren't I?"

I bit my tongue, but let the words fly free. "Because you are a threat to the crown."

"How? I don't want the fucking crown!"

He was drunk. I wished I had a better time to tell him, but he deserved to know. "Riyan, General Hyton is your father."

Riyan looked down at me with wide eyes. He did not breathe.

After three heavy heartbeats, he shook his head and let out a mirthless laugh. "The General…can't be my father. He hates me. I've been under his command for *twelve years* and he never once…"

Riyan silenced as I slowly nodded. "The Hytons want everyone to believe you are a half-giant so no one knows you are another heir to the throne."

Riyan snorted as he played with the dagger in his fingers. "So they want me eliminated. And pretty boy Lord Hyton sends a girl up the mountain to do his dirty work. What a dickless little—"

"He did not send me to kill you," I interjected. Derrick's jealousy bled into possessiveness, but if he knew Riyan was a Hyton heir, the stubborn bull would have done much more to kill Riyan than merely hand me a dagger. "All he asked of me was if I had to choose between my life and yours, I would keep myself safe."

Looking into Riyan's eyes as I explained how I had planned to murder him was torture, but I could not look away. "Duke Hyton…is going to take everything—the North, the magic of the mountain, your mother, me. I just thought…if I could have some control…I could make everything better—"

My throat seized before I could explain any more, but Riyan stared down at me with a trembling lip and shoulders hunched forward like he understood. He looked at me with clear eyes, as if the weight of my words had completely sobered him.

"When you take control," Riyan said quietly, "will you give me your word that you will take care of my mother?"

My word was no good. My silver tongue was its own dagger, cutting lies into the ears of everyone I had ever known. I could have told him anything and he would have drank it like poison, but since I owed him my honesty, I gave it to him.

I unlocked my hands from around my knees and opened my chest to the night air. "Of course I would."

Riyan blinked and looked to the night sky. Tears welled up in his eyes but he wiped them away with the sides of his thumbs.

He slowly reached over and limply held out his massive hand to where I sat. I wrapped my right hand around his finger as he helped me to my feet. He gave me a solemn yet sweet smile as he gently placed the hilt of the Hyton dagger in my hand.

My heart pounded as my fingers curled around the cold bronze. Riyan laid back down on the stony earth like I had found him and rolled his head to face me. His twilight eyes were bleak and lifeless.

"Do it," he said. "You deserve everything the Hytons promised you. You deserve…better than me."

"Riyan," I whispered. My lip quivered. My throat tightened with tremors.

"Please," he begged. "I killed my grandparents. I hurt my mother. I ruined your life. I refuse to continue living if it means everyone in my life suffers."

My chest sunk in and my shoulders squeezed forward. I could not breathe.

A tear slowly rolled out of Riyan's eye. "Make sure it's a deep cut so it won't heal, all right?"

My left hand clamped down on my trembling lips as my right hand gripped the dagger. I could make the one fateful cut and make both our problems disappear forever. Riyan begged me to do it. Derrick had empowered me to do it. Every ounce of sense I had screamed at me to do it.

But I was weak. I could not kill Riyan Bloodstone.

The triumphant golden light of our bond glowed down my arms and warmed my hand as it wrapped around the cold bronze. The bond glowed brighter and brighter in my fingers until they opened, releasing the dagger to the ground with a clatter.

I moved forward like I was being pulled on a golden tether. The light from the bond warmed each of my footsteps in the rocks as I walked to Riyan and then knelt in front of his face. His watery eyes were as large as each of my fists. His nose was as long as my hand. His breath hit my knees like a wave crashing into the shore.

I never thought his breath would give me relief.

"I cannot kill you, Riyan," I whispered. The golden light flushed in my lips as they formed his name.

Riyan's brow was heavy and his jaw was tight. "You shouldn't have to get your hands dirty, anyway." He raised up slightly and reached for his sword. "I'll do it."

The light shot through the veins in my arms.

"No!" I screamed. I caught his colossal forearm with both hands and dug my nails into his skin.

Riyan froze. His eyes moved from the sword to me. He blinked and a tear rolled out of the corner of his eye. "Serafina, just let me do one good thing in my life. Let me save you from myself."

My hands trembled around his arm, but I refused to let him go. Maybe the magic had poisoned my mind and dulled my sense. Maybe Riyan's beautiful voice had lulled me into a dream where nothing existed but red lilies and faerie stories. Maybe Riyan really did break me underneath him, crushing all my defenses and leaving nothing but raw vulnerability.

Whatever had happened to me, I leaned into the one thought that cried through my muscles, flowed through my blood, and punched through the stone surface of my heart.

The darkness did not exist as long as Riyan breathed.

My throat warmed as I spoke. "Riyan, I am terrified of what will happen after tonight, but I cannot face the next sunrise without you. You have to stay with me."

I gently released my grip on his arm. Riyan looked at me as tears slid down both his cheeks. I reached up and brushed his long blonde strands out of his face and tucked them behind his ear that was the size of my hand. I lowered my hand and slowly wiped away the warm tears on his cheeks. His chest shook. His throat twitched.

"Why?" he croaked in a hoarse whisper. "After what I did to you, and to my grandmother—"

"Because," I interjected, as if my lips moved on their own. Riyan kept silent as I rifled around in my head, searching for an answer that did not exist. Finally, I raised up on my knees and held the bottom of his trembling jaw in both my hands. I held my breath before the iron cage in my chest opened and released another secret. "Because you are the strongest man alive and…your strength and power is what I always needed. You have to be strong for me because I am so weak that…"

I was too cowardly to finish—I am so weak that I cannot survive without someone else's strength.

Riyan placed his hand behind me, his palm completely shielding my back. His satin voice caressed my cheeks. "I chose you, so this is all my responsibility. If you will not let me fix it, I will get someone who can."

I held onto his jaw like it was my new lifeline. "Do you mean your father?"

"No," Riyan replied, hard and fast. "He kept the truth from me for twenty-two years. I have no idea if he wants me to overthrow the Duke or if he's just ashamed of his monstrous burden, but I don't trust him."

He let out a long, slow breath that warmed my face. "Besides, he never mentioned my mother—not even once." He blinked and then glanced up. "We're going to Fraleigh."

My hands slid from his jaw and curled into trembling fists at my stomach. No one went to Fraleigh. Her only boon to the Dukedom was the blood bond enchantments every June. "But…she only serves the House of Hyton."

Riyan gave me a small smile. "Good thing we just found out I'm a Hyton. If magic made me grow, then magic can make me normal. We will make our blood bond permanent, I promise."

Of all the promises I had heard over my life, Riyan's was the first one I truly trusted.

I let a smile flick up on my lips. "Promises mean nothing, you know… unless you make them binding."

Riyan's soft smile grew enough to reveal his sweet dimple. "Then bind me to it, Serafina."

My hands pressed against his cheeks as I raised up on my knees to kiss him. My mouth was so small that I could only kiss his lower lip, but the golden bond that tethered us together sang in my veins as I bound him to his word. I stayed there for a moment, relishing in the small world that only had Riyan and I in it, before I pulled away to breathe.

A thin midnight cloud passed over the moon and stole most of its light. All I could see was Riyan's face in front of me.

His eyes sparked with life. He took a deep breath as he looked down at me and his low voice left his lips. "Serafina Helia, I—"

A rock clacked in the distance. Riyan swiftly pulled me into his chest. The steel of his blade scraped on the rocks as he drew his sword close.

"We are not alone," his voice rumbled against my face and hands. "Something is behind us on the mountain path."

His heartbeat slammed against my belly. I was not sure if anything was really behind us, but Riyan believed danger was near.

"As soon as the light of the moon comes back," Riyan said, "we are going to Fraleigh's palace."

His fingers wrapped around my waist and drew me closer until my cheek mashed against his skin. His long hair fell against my temple and nectar and wheat filled my nose again.

Riyan's voice was low and serious as he spoke. "I never wanted to take you up Nordingaard, but we have no other choice. General Hyton…he told me what lurks higher up the mountain, but nothing will hurt you as long as you stay *right here.*"

He pressed me deeper into his muscled chest for emphasis.

"You need my strength," he said in a quiet breath, "but if we are going to survive on this mountain, I need your bravery."

I wrinkled my nose. "You think I am brave?"

"The bravest in the Dukedom."

"Why?"

"You chose to stay with me."

I listened to Riyan's heartbeat slow down until it pulsed at the same rate as my own. Each beat echoed in his chest like the ricochet of a boulder falling off the side of the mountain.

Riyan's heart was strong. Riyan's heart was powerful.

But it was not a beast's heart.

Nordingaard blew a chill around us but I did not shiver in Riyan's embrace. The golden light of our bond warmed my chest as Riyan's slow breath warmed my back.

Even though the moon hid its light, darkness would never touch us.

Chapter Twenty Eight
Lost Boys

A deep growl echoed off the side of the mountain as Riyan held me against him. I gripped his chest and my fingernails dug into his skin.

"What was that?" I whispered. "Is it a monster?"

"Kind of," Riyan replied. "It was my stomach."

I could not remember the last time I had seen him eat. A giant his size could eat half a cow in one day. Or a whole sheep. Or a few people.

"What, uh…," I stammered. "What are you hungry for?"

"You." His wry smile brightened the night. "I'll eat you in a few bites and then pick my teeth clean with that ugly bull dagger."

I rolled my eyes and scoffed.

"I'll leave your left hand, though." His smile got bigger in his voice. "I'll send it to precious Lord Hyton so he'll have something to remember you."

"Stop it!" I hissed. I jammed my elbow into his ribs and he laughed like I tickled him.

"Well now I can't eat you," he chuckled. "You would give me the *worst* heartburn!"

His stomach rumbled loud enough to echo in my ears.

"Really, though," I said. "You need to eat and I have no idea how we can feed you."

"There is a village up ahead," Riyan said. "Can't you smell it?"

"No? You are not…smelling the people are you?"

"No! They are making bread!"

I bit my tongue as I tried not to laugh. "Where is the village?"

"It's a bit farther up the mountain in a place called the Beast's Pass," he replied. "It's on the way to Fraleigh's palace. As soon as the moonlight comes back, we'll head up there."

Did the villagers of the Beast's Pass know Riyan was their new Baron? Would they just see him as a giant and attack him? Or worse, would they see him as a murderer?

I knitted my eyebrows and patted his arm that was longer than my entire body. "How are we supposed to go into the village with you being so—"

"Devastatingly handsome?"

"Big. You will terrify everyone and start a panic."

Riyan sighed. "Worst case scenario, I grab you and run." He reached across his body and tugged at the cape around his hips. "But since I have my crimson cape, the people will recognize me as a Bloodstone and not a giant. Plus—"

He picked up a golden disc that looked like a coin in his massive hand. "—I also have this, if all else fails."

I glanced at the gleaming metal—the House of Bloodstone pin, proving he was Baron of Bloodstone. The Bloodstone army must have included the pin in their offerings to cajole Riyan into returning to the fortress.

I at least knew where the Bloodstone pin came from, but I had never seen the gargantuan crimson cape before. "Where did that cape come from, anyway?"

Riyan's body shifted like a small earthquake. "I found it wrapped around my sword. Those bastards just left Endre's Revenge on the mountain path and—"

My heart stopped. "What did you call it?"

Riyan was silent for a heartbeat and he cleared his throat. "You're supposed to name swords to give them more power and…well, I gave my sword a name with a real purpose."

Ten giant heads was my brother's revenge.

I could barely breathe. "You knew him?"

"Fought alongside him. Right until the end."

My lip trembled and I pressed on Riyan's chest, if only to keep myself from plummeting into the pit that had opened up in my stomach. Riyan must have sensed the shift in my body because he spoke again in a gentle hum.

"As far as the huge cape goes, I think Grandmother made it for me a while ago. She must have known that I would—"

Riyan cut himself off. His chest fell.

I gently rubbed Riyan's shoulder. Riyan's birth had caused Hilda to lose both her sons and the daughter she knew. Despite that, she had loved Riyan with all of her warm and gentle heart.

Riyan's love for his eternally sleeping grandmother sang through every one of his shaking breaths. If fear caused him to grow, then losing the person he loved the most must have sent him into a greater terror than any giant could. He had said the magic in his blood was supposed to protect him, but it had bent and twisted him until he made his own greatest fear come true.

The greatest cruelty of the world was that the deepest love meant the greatest heartbreak.

Riyan swallowed again and his muscles tightened around me. Maybe our bond whispered in my ears or the magic in my veins tingled with truth, but I knew what Riyan was doing all too well.

Eat the sadness. Lock it behind iron. Feel nothing. Dull the pain with smiling lies.

The clouds parted again and moonlight illuminated us in its soft white glow. I moved away from Riyan to give him room to rise from the rocks. Before Riyan got up, he handed me the Hyton dagger.

"Keep this thing with you," Riyan ordered. "As much as I want to pitch that ugly symbol of Lord Hyton's pride over the side of the mountain, you need to protect yourself in case anything happens."

As I raised my skirt and tied the dagger to my garter, the rocks shifted as Riyan stood up. I turned around and gasped. In the light of the moon, I could see him…*all* of him.

Any hope I had of being able to consummate our marriage vanished in an instant.

"Wh-where are your clothes?" I asked.

"What clothes?" he laughed. "You mean all those tattered scraps that fell off me as I ran?"

"You mean you have *nothing?*"

"Well, I was able to keep something."

Riyan picked up a small scrap of white fabric off the ground and reached out to hand it to me. The tattered scrap of linen was held together by white thread stitched to flowers. I ran my fingers along the petals I had stitched for him and smiled.

"It did not stop me from growing, but I do think you enchanted those flowers somehow," Riyan said with a smile. "They stayed with me even after…everything happened."

My heart fluttered. I put the scrap of fabric in my pocket along with my other trinkets and looked up at Riyan's naked body. "You know you cannot go to the village like this."

Riyan smirked and flexed his arms, the contours of his huge muscles defined in the moonlight. "Would the villagers not want to see their hero in *all* his glory?"

I rolled my eyes and scoffed. "We would get run out of the village."

"Run out by all the jealous husbands, you mean."

Riyan winked at me. He picked up his cape and tied it around his waist to cover his lower half. "Does this satisfy you?"

My cheeks flushed and I glanced off to the side as I remembered the last time he *satisfied* me. I kneaded the thick fabric of my skirt and tried not to think of what was hiding underneath the crimson wool.

Riyan must have taken notice of my red cheeks and he laughed. He sheathed Endre's Revenge—gripping the hilt with one massive hand instead of two—and fastened what used to be the back-strap of the sheath around his waist like a belt.

"Come here," he said with another laugh.

He reached down and wrapped his hand around my back. His fingertips squeezed into the sides of my waist and I yelped as he picked me up off the ground. He lifted me in the air and placed me in the crook of his left arm, cradling me against his chest. My legs rested on his forearm and my back rested against his massive bicep. I looked down, realizing in horror that I was higher off the ground than I had ever been.

"Riyan!" I shrieked. I grabbed fistfuls of chest hair and held on for dear life.

"Hey, it's only a little higher than when we went to the lilies and I need to keep you safe," Riyan said. "Plus, if I carry you, I can get you food sooner. Deal?"

My voice shook as I looked down at the rocks. "Fine. Just…do not jostle me around!"

"I won't. I'll be very careful, just like the other day."

Riyan took a cautious step up the path. I cried out in fear at first, but as he took one step after another, I eventually relaxed in his arm. Before I knew it, we approached a large, craggy gap in the mountain ridges.

The first rays of sun rose behind us, illuminating a tall wall that blocked the gap in the mountain pass. The wall was made from tree trunks and supported by thick logs that leaned up against the wall. Logs sharpened into spikes jutted out of the wall near the height of Riyan's eyes. The rocky path ended at a large wooden gate that did not look welcoming to someone of Riyan's size.

"This is the Beast's Pass," Riyan said. "Once you step outside their walls on the other side, we face everything Nordingaard has to offer."

"Why do they call it the Beast's Pass?" I asked as I looked in awe at the massive wall that even we could not see over.

"It's a bit of an ironic name," Riyan replied. "The village and its walls are here to prevent any magical beasts from passing through. The giants get around it by finding other ways down the mountain, but it keeps most of the monsters inside."

Riyan took a couple steps toward the wall and his booming voice reverberated off the mountain stone. "I am Riyan Bloodstone, Hero of Lycaster, seeking entrance to the Beast's Pass."

He refused to call himself the Baron.

A soldier in a crimson uniform carrying a torch appeared at the top of the wall. The soldier's eyes widened when he saw Riyan.

"By Ganora's mercy!" the soldier exclaimed. "It's him! Open the gate!"

Heavy clicking noises rang through the dawn. The two sides of the gate groaned as two soldiers on either side pushed them open. Riyan bent down and gently lowered me to the ground so I could walk inside.

The village was unlike any place I had ever seen. The dwellings were carved into the rocks and crawled up the mountainside above us. Holes in the dwellings that acted as windows and doors sparked with noise and movement. Thin women clutching bundled babes and small hands of wide-eyed toddlers left their homes and walked down the steep slopes toward me.

Murmurs of the villagers crept around in the morning air as more and more people filled the central path of the village. All eyes locked on the gate except mine.

I turned around. Riyan ducked under the gate and crawled inside. Dawn's spectacular rays illuminated him from behind as he arose. I held my breath as a halo of gold surrounded his hair and torchlight danced off the contours of his muscles.

He was magnificent.

The villagers gasped, some applauded, and dozens of people ran down from their homes to gawk in awe at the legendary Hero of Lycaster. A crowd of a dozen thin children dressed in rags tore away from their mothers' hands and ran to Riyan. Their wide smiles lit up their dirty faces.

The children all stood around their hero, their hungry eyes big with wonder. Riyan looked down at them with a cautious smile.

"Are you really him?" asked a young girl with blonde braids.

"In the flesh," Riyan replied.

"Why are you so big?" asked a toddling boy.

"Why are you so small?" Riyan asked with a raised eyebrow and a smirk.

"Did you really kill eight giants?" shouted a boy with two missing teeth.

"No, it was ten." Riyan sat down in the center of the village path and started telling the story of the great battle. Two children no older than five crawled into Riyan's lap as he regaled the tale. Mothers and old men gathered around him, captivated by his every word.

I was watching Riyan soak up the admiration when someone cleared his throat behind me. I turned around to find an old man with a long beard holding a cloth bundle in his hands.

"It's not much," he said, offering me the bundle, "but it's the least we can offer you, Madame Bloodstone."

The bundle warmed my chilled hands. I carefully opened it and found five flat loaves of bread stacked on top of each other. The bread was fresh, but it was not light and fluffy like the bread I was used to. Still, I was touched by the offering. If grain was in short supply in Ravenwood, it must be even more scarce in the farthest north anyone could live.

"Thank you," I said, "I will take these to Sir Bloodstone."

"No need," said the man. He gestured to Riyan and I turned around.

Laughing children climbed all over Riyan as he sat on the ground, their mothers offering him baskets of apples, bread, cured meats, and whole wheels of cheese. Riyan delightfully munched on every offering, his battle story pausing each time he had a new food in his hands.

The village was giving us all the food they had. I felt guilty for accepting, but my short time in Bloodstone had taught me that everyone showed appreciation and affection with food. Refusing the offerings would have been a huge insult—something we could not afford if we wanted to make it through the pass without conflict.

I bit into a disc of bread—it was coarse and I struggled to chew it. The bread did not whet my appetite, but it calmed my hunger pangs.

As I watched Riyan entertain the crowd, I noticed the cape around his waist was covered in mud and who knew what else. I turned back to the old man.

"If it is not too much trouble," I asked, "are there any scraps of fabric around? Sir Bloodstone recently outgrew all his clothing."

The old man chuckled and gestured for me to follow him. I stashed the bread into my pocket, even though they barely fit with all my other trinkets. I followed the man into a nearby stone dwelling where an old woman with tiny, crooked legs and a younger, broader woman sat on a small bed. Both women wore simple cloth dresses and their ash blonde hair was tied up in braids. The one-room dwelling consisted of only the bed and a small cauldron over a hearth.

"This is Madame Bloodstone," said the old man to the women. "Wife of Sir Bloodstone, Slayer of Giants. Sir Bloodstone seems to have a lack of clothing and needs some assistance."

The younger woman turned to the elder, who appeared to be her mother, and blushed. Her hand flew over her mouth to cover a giggle. The elder woman smiled warmly.

"By Ganora's mercy," the elder woman chuckled. She turned to her daughter. "Olga, go fetch some hides from the neighbors."

The younger woman nodded and quickly left the house. The elder woman patted the spot on the mattress where Olga had just been. I took the signal and sat down beside her.

"Your husband has brought great joy to our village," the elder woman said. "I lost my sons to the giants, as did many others here. Hearing that they were brought down, and not just by anyone, but one of our own—why, I've never seen so many smiling faces."

"I see." I gestured to the opening of the stone dwelling. "You would think the Duke himself came to the gates."

"Oh, not at all, dear," the elder woman chuckled. "Duke Hyton is wise enough to not come up here."

The elder woman, named Sigrid, and I began to talk. The soldiers outside of Bloodstone Fortress were not the only ones who harbored ill feelings toward the Hytons. Everyone in the Beast's Pass, and likely all of Bloodstone, hated Duke Hyton for sending their sons to die in the first battle.

Through Sigrid's watery-eyed story, I learned the Duke had sent only enough of his soldiers to fight one or two giants, but anyone in the Northern provinces knew there were at least three times as many destroying their homes and leaving trails of blood and screams in their wake.

According to Sigrid, Duke Hyton could have prevented the great loss, the famine, and the poverty if he cared enough about the Northern provinces to actually prepare for the first battle.

Olga returned to the dwelling with arms full of deer and rabbit hides. Some of them were freshly tanned while others looked worn, as if people had given Olga the hides off their backs. The three of us began sewing the hides together in a crude, but sufficient tunic for Riyan.

I moved my needle through the hides as the women gushed about the Hero of Lycaster being right outside their homes. A few more women trickled into the tiny dwelling, eager to do a favor for their hero.

We set up our operation so Sigrid and I were on the bed, Olga sat on the floor, and the three other women sewed the end of the tunic outside the doorway. As we sewed, all the women talked about the giants, about Riyan, and about life in Bloodstone.

From what I heard from the women as they sewed, Bloodstone was similar to Ravenwood—dead sons, hungry bellies, and nothing to give them hope… except Riyan. To hear them talk, you would think that Riyan took on the giant army himself. No praise of the Hyton army, the General, or the Duke left the lips of the women of the Beast's Pass. If what those women said was what everyone else in Bloodstone believed about the battle, then Duke Hyton's plan to endear himself to the people of the North using Riyan had failed. Riyan alone held the glory of the victory, not the House of Hyton.

We completed the hide tunic after an hour. The length of the tunic stretched from Sigrid's bed all the way out the door and was held together at the top with a long rope. The other women gathered up the tunic between them and walked out into the main road.

Olga lifted her mother off the bed and walked outside the dwelling. I followed the women outside and found Riyan playing with the group of giggling children. The children climbed up and down his arms and legs and he would grab them, drop them, and catch them mid-air as they shrieked in delight.

My stomach fluttered when I noticed a big-eyed toddler sitting in the palm of Riyan's hand. I walked over to pick up the child, balancing him on my hip as I gestured to the tunic in the women's hands.

"Sir Bloodstone, the people of the Beast's Pass offer their gratitude for your acts of heroism!"

Riyan looked from the laughing boy he dangled upside-down by the leg to me. The dimple appeared again as he smiled.

"You made this?" Riyan gently placed the child on the ground, who scampered over to his waiting mother. Riyan lowered his shoulders to look the women of the Beast's Pass in their faces.

Olga walked up to Riyan's face with her mother still in her arms. Sigrid smiled warmly and reached up, gently touching the right side of Riyan's face with both hands and giving him a kiss on his cheek.

"Thank you for avenging my sons," she said with tears in her eyes. She kissed him again. "For Ivar."

The giggling boy on my hip grew heavier as Sigrid kissed Riyan for each of her sons. Ivar. Fenris. Asvin. Leiv.

Four. Sigrid had lost four sons. Riyan's eyes shone and his muscles tightened with each name. His big blue eyes watered and he started to say something, but then more women rushed forward in a small mob. The women, young and old, frantically thanked Riyan, each one standing on their toes to kiss everywhere on his face they could reach and crying out the names of the lost.

Harald. Aemund. Brynd. Einar. Vigon. Candyr.

Names of boys that never grew into men. Names that never knew honor under the Duke's reign.

Until Riyan gave it to them.

My lip trembled and my tongue tingled behind my teeth. I wanted to add honor to two more names, but I did not want to cut through the crying mob. I did not want anyone to see or hear what I needed to do.

I gave the sweet baby boy on my hip a final nuzzle before I handed him back to his mother. I pulled the small discs of bread out of my pocket as I noticed two large wooden statues guarding the gate into the magical realm like sentinels. I silently walked down the path in the center of the village to the carved statues of two females and stood in front of them alone.

The statue on the left was carved with a faint smile on her lips and her hands held out as if giving a gift. The statue was decorated in chains of summer blossoms and had what I could only assume were bunches of deep-red elskaberries at her feet. The idol was none other than the Great Sorceress herself, although the people of the Beast's Pass had depicted her as much more loving than she was in real life.

The statue on the right, however, bore no trace of affection.

Ganora's statue had a hard brow and a firm mouth with her hands held in tight fists at her sides. The people of the Beast's Pass were much more generous with her offerings than with Fraleigh's. The terrifying statue had dried apples, loaves of bread, and even small scraps of meat piled up at her feet. Even with most of the giants defeated, the villagers did not take any chances angering the fabled queen of the mountain.

I turned from the statue of Fraleigh and stepped in front of Ganora. I looked up at her hair and eyes painted a chalky white. Father would have scolded me for what I was about to do, not only because Ganora worship was pure villager foolishness, but also because she was responsible for the slaughter of the boys. She created her giants and sent them after our people. She mixed innocent blood with snow and destroyed the Northern provinces under her fists.

But as I tore the bread into ten pieces and recited every name I had heard as I dropped piece by piece at her feet, I did not honor Ganora—I honored the fallen. If the Queen of the Giants could hear me, then she would take the offering as a reminder of each young life she stole.

I created a pile of bread until I had one flat loaf left in my hands. I tore the loaf in half and my chest shuddered.

"For Erik," I whispered. "For Endre."

I laid the halves of the loaf next to each other on top of the pile of offerings, side by side.

My breath hitched. My lungs burned. I had not said their names in seven years.

The corners of my eyes stung and just as I thought a tear would escape for the first time since I was a child, two heavy fingers laid on my shoulder.

"I never took you as a Ganora worshiper," Riyan said as he knelt behind me.

I glanced up at him and furrowed my brow. "The offering is not for her, it is for them." I gestured back to the rest of the village. "If piles of offerings make them feel safer, then why not? Besides, I could not think of a better way to honor the fallen boys than to do something to prevent any more of them from becoming prey to the giants."

Riyan let out a breath and rubbed my shoulder with his thumb. "You could see it that way, but you will never catch me on my knees offering that monster anything. Well, except maybe my boot up her—"

"Sir Bloodstone!"

Riyan and I turned around. Olga held her frail mother in her arms but looked up at Riyan.

"Before you go, you have to make a wish!" Olga gestured with her blonde head toward a well near the Fraleigh statue. The stone well was also decorated with chains of pink and white flowers.

Riyan shot me a half-smile. Might as well indulge in the village foolishness.

Riyan stood up and walked over to the well. Children danced around him as he knelt beside the ring of stone. Riyan glanced down into the water and looked back at me. With soft eyes, he wrapped his massive hands around the stone and lowered his head into the well. His low whispers echoed off the stone and then he pulled himself out. He stood up and gestured to the well. My turn.

I took his place, pressed my hands on top of the rough stone, and looked down into the dark well. I blinked at my reflection in the still water. I had not wished in a well since I was a child, and even though my logical mind knew it was all peasant bullshit, my heart fluttered with excitement. I stood on my toes and leaned as far into the well as I could, making sure only the water could hear my whispers.

"I wish to stay with Riyan." The whisper tingled my lips as I spoke.

I smiled at my reflection and pulled myself out of the well. I did not dare look back as I walked away, but out of the corner of my eye, I could have sworn the water glowed white.

The villagers all cheered and waved to Riyan as he stood near the gate with his new hide tunic folded up over his arm. I raised my arms and Riyan picked me up by my middle and held me against his chest again.

He held a bunch of fat elskaberries in his right palm—a snack for the journey. Riyan took a step toward the open gate into the wilderness, but he stopped and looked back.

Riyan stepped over to the Fraleigh statue. He leaned down and tipped his right hand, rolling the juicy berries into Fraleigh's wooden palm.

"For Hilda Brina Bloodstone." He let out a breath from his nose as his throat muscles tightened. I leaned into his chest and listened to his heartbeat slow to a low thump. I could almost taste the sadness he held back.

"You can let it out, Riyan," I whispered so only he could hear. "As soon as we cross the gates, you can honor her the way you want to. Where no one else can see."

"I don't have enough liquor for that." Riyan set his eyes north and walked back to the gate. The villagers all cheered and said their farewells as Riyan faced the open gate with me in his arm.

With one step, we entered the magical wilderness. I was ready to see monsters, the Queen of the Giants herself, or even the legendary man trapped on the mountain, but nothing appeared.

"So what did you wish for?" Riyan asked as he walked up the mountain path.

"You know I cannot tell!" I laughed. "If I tell, then the wish will not come true."

"Here you are again, surprising me with your faith in peasant bullshit."

I poked him in the chest. "Do not mistake desperation for faith, Riyan."

I expected him to retort back, but he cleared his throat and took a slow breath. "Grandmother actually believed in wishing wells. I could almost… hear her in my ear when I had my head in that well. Sounds crazy but…she was proud of what I wished for."

I swallowed and glanced out into the blue morning sky. The mountain clouds swirled above us and birds sang in the crisp air.

Riyan hugged me close to him. "Let's just hope that well magic isn't all peasant bullshit."

His voice broke on his last word and he stopped on the mountain path. His heart thudded against my head. Tension rumbled in his chest.

I placed my hand in the center of his chest. "Riyan, are you all right?"

His voice was quieter than I had ever heard it. "She taught me to read."

He turned his head toward a grove of tall trees and walked over to them. "Every time I got hurt, she kissed where the injury had been—even though magic had already healed it."

He knelt under the canopy of branches with sunlight dappling his golden hair and lowered me to my feet. "Every available maid was too terrified to nurse me, so she fed me goat's milk through a flour sack. Every two hours. Even though Grandfather thought she was crazy."

Riyan pressed his palms into the ground and hunched over. His eyes swam and his brow knitted. Our bond pulled beneath my chest and compelled me to go to him.

I walked between his arms with my face just under his. His massive body shook and his eyes darted back and forth as he stared down in the grass.

"She went through *so much* just to keep me alive and I…"

My blood glowed in my arms and they lifted up. I stood on my toes and wrapped both arms around his trembling neck. I whispered that her death was not his fault, that it was a horrible accident, but that did not stop the tears that wet my hair and shoulders.

No birds sang. No wind rustled the leaves. The only sound echoing off the mountain stone was Riyan's short, bitter sobs for Hilda Brina Bloodstone.

I nuzzled my cheek into his throbbing neck and bit my tongue as my own chest started to shake. Our bond rattled around my heart and forced me to remember every memory of my brothers I had shut away.

Erik pulling my hand away from the fire. Endre dangling upside-down from a tree while Erik shouted at him to get down. Endre whispering bad words at the dinner table. A frog in Erik's boot. Scars on Endre's knuckles. Mud pies. Nursery rhymes. Stories under candlelight.

I leaned into Riyan as the bitterness of my brothers' absence spread through my body like rot. My arms tightened their embrace and our bodies nearly melded. His sadness was a barb behind my eyes. His guilt was a boulder in my stomach.

His grief and mine mirrored, but I still could not cry.

Chapter Twenty Nine
Troublesome Sons

When Riyan's chest stopped shaking and I wiped the last tears from his eyes, he stood up and changed into the tunic I made for him. I sat down and picked at the grass as Riyan dressed.

Riyan sniffed once and then the air around him shifted. He hardened back into the Hero of Lycaster the moment he fastened his sword back around his hips.

I tore through a blade of grass as I bit down on my own sadness. I wanted the last time I said my brothers' names to be when they heard them from my lips as they rode away from Ravenwood Manor, but I was weak. The moment I broke that bread and said their names, their deaths finally cemented in my soul.

I ripped apart another blade. My stomach was hollow and dark, like I was fourteen again and staring blankly at Mother and Father when they told me Erik and Endre would never come home.

Riyan muttered under his breath as he shook dirt and muck off his crimson cape. I looked up from the shredded grass in my hands. The darkness in my belly lifted as soon as I saw his annoyed face glaring at his cape that was covered in dark stains.

Riyan murmured about the cape being clean enough and wrapped it around his shoulders. His face twisted up in irritation as his meaty hands fumbled with the cape near his clavicle. A glint of gold passed through his fingers and he growled in frustration as he failed to secure the cape.

"Damn this stupid, tiny…," he grumbled. He hissed out a breath and his big eyes flicked down to me.

A smile cracked across my dry lips. He did not need to ask. I pushed up from the ground and raised my arms. "Come here."

Riyan knelt in the grass and leaned forward so I could reach his shoulder. He held out the House of Bloodstone pin and I took it—finally, someone was ready to accept the role of Baron. I stood up on my toes and poked the pin through the crimson wool near his right shoulder.

I caught his dimpled half-smile out of the corner of my eye as I worked the pin through.

"Looks like my sweetheart is back." His voice was a ribbon of satin against my ear. "You've come a long way from trying to stab me a few hours ago."

I smirked. "You sure?" I poked him in the clavicle with the pin. He did not flinch, but he chuckled low in his throat.

"You can't hurt me." He said with an edge of impending mischief. "It just tickles."

Riyan took advantage of my raised arms and quickly ran the tip of his finger up the side of my ribs. The sensation forced an explosive laugh out of my throat before I turned and smacked his hand away.

Riyan laughed. "I can't decide who I like more, my sweetheart or my little ball of fire."

"Tickle me one more time and I will make that decision for you," I said as I fastened the pin shut, "because you will never see the sweetheart again."

I ran my thumb over the bear of the pin. The metal chilled my skin. "Why the white bear?"

"The House of Bloodstone chose the white bear to represent strength and stability," Riyan replied with an eye-roll. "What a joke. I'm probably the most unstable man in Lycaster."

I smirked. "Probably?"

He leaned forward and matched my smirk, his eyes gleaming with more mischief. "Don't make me step on you, Ravenwood."

I stuck my tongue out at him and Riyan questioned how a naughty girl like me made it out of Ashmore. He picked me up and rose to his towering height, stooping his head so he did not hit the tree branches above us.

He stepped out from underneath the trees and back onto the mountain path. A flash of red rustled in the corner of my eye as Riyan tugged at his cape with his free hand.

"The crimson color of the House of Bloodstone has a sensible meaning, at least," Riyan said with a smile. "We wear bright crimson capes so others can find us if we get lost on the mountain. Not that I am particularly hard to find."

I laughed. "The House of Ravenwood wears dark green for the opposite reason. We want to blend in with the woods, unseen. Disappearing into our surroundings is our goal."

Riyan's big blue eyes glanced over to me. "Sounds sneaky."

I crossed my arms and leaned into his collarbone. His honey-colored hair brushed up against my shoulder as my fingers traced the House of Ravenwood pin securing my own cape. "It does, which is why we have a *false* reputation of ambition and deception."

"So what's with the raven, then?" The snark building in his throat gave his voice an iron edge. "You like poking around corpses?"

"No!" I shrieked. "The raven symbolizes intelligence and resourcefulness! We do whatever we can to survive."

"And you wonder why Ravenwoods get the reputation of being sneaky and ambitious? You might as well put a scowling weasel holding a knife on your crest."

"Asshole," I hissed. I looked away from Riyan into the endless evergreen trees and brush around the mountain path. The birds warbled in a lower pitch. The air was too still. I half-expected a troll to hobble across our path when Riyan's chest rumbled as he murmured.

"You have something else to add?" I snapped.

"All I was saying was that you can't disappear."

"Explain."

"If the Ravenwood goal is to disappear into your surroundings, you failed miserably." His thumb stroked the side of my knee as he held me. "You're the most beautiful woman in every room. You practically glow."

I bit my tongue and my cheeks burned. "Really?"

"Of course," he said, like it was obvious. "Your mother is a close second, though. *Damn.* If that's what you're going to look like in twenty-five years, I'm the luckiest bastard ali—"

"Please stop talking."

He and Duke Hyton had similar tastes. A chill crept up the base of my spine. If Fraleigh could not help us and my marriage annulled, I might as well get shipped off to Hyton Palace wrapped up like a present.

I looked out to the faded dirt path to keep myself from vomiting. I could only see forty paces ahead from my position at Riyan's chest. I tilted my head to the blue sky to see a flock of black birds flying past us. My eyes flicked down to the top of Riyan's blonde head. I wanted to see what he saw.

I patted Riyan's chest. "I want to be taller."

"Well, short stuff, we can ask Fraleigh for your own little growth spurt when we get to her palace."

"No, I want to see more." I gently tugged on a strand of blonde hair that brushed his collarbone. "Sitting on your shoulder should work."

"You screamed the first time I picked you up and now you want up on my shoulder?" He let out a short sigh. "All right."

Riyan held me around the waist again and lifted me onto his left shoulder. My hands gripped his cape underneath me as I settled in right next to his neck. My legs dangled near his chest as I steadied myself. I leaned my right shoulder against the top of his head as his long hair fell into my lap.

My eyes were even higher than Riyan's. The sky was bigger. The trees were shorter. The mountainside looming over us was even less intimidating. Mist curled in the distance. Wind kissed my cheeks. I closed my eyes and tasted the air—the crispness of the magical wilderness mixed with nectar and wheat.

Riyan's step hitched on uneven ground. My stomach lurched as I wobbled backward, but Riyan's left hand caught my back before I could fall.

"You're scaring me up there." His palm pressed into the left side of my ribs and hips. His fingers curled across my back to grip my right side.

I glanced over at his arm that curled up to hold me in place on his shoulder. Even he would get tired if he held me like that the entire journey. I worked my hands through his tangled strands of hair falling on my lap and got an idea.

I dug through the pocket of my skirt until my fingertips touched the sharp tines of my silver comb. I took the comb out of my pocket and gently raked through his hair.

"I don't think I need to look pretty for Fraleigh," Riyan said wryly.

"It has a purpose!" I laughed as I untangled a few strands.

Once I had banished the tangles, I quickly braided a few strands of his hair together like a rope. I held on tight to the braided hair with both hands.

"There!" I said into his left ear. "Now you do not have to hold me."

"Have to? Maybe I wanted to hold you." He hesitantly removed his hand from my back and lowered his arm. "At least you found a use for all this damn hair. I was never allowed to have hair this long. General Hyton always chopped off my hair himself—"

He cut himself off. I waited for him to say anything else about his father, but he kept silent.

The mountain ridges around us grew shorter and shorter as we followed the setting sun and ascended the path. Birds stopped singing. A hairy goat with curling horns stood in the rocks and watched us with a too-knowing eye. I held tighter onto Riyan's hair as we walked further into the wilderness.

I looked west. Through a break in the rocks, golden needles speared the sky in the distance. I placed my hands on top of Riyan's head and lifted my body to get a better look. The golden needles were really spires on top of gilded towers—Fraleigh's palace.

My cheeks rose with my smile and I dared let myself indulge in a taste of hope. A flicker of excitement rushed through my veins. My fingertips curled on top of Riyan's head and my nails grazed his scalp.

Riyan squirmed and his head jolted back. I gripped onto his hair and held on before he steadied his shoulders again.

I laughed. "Big, tough Hero of Lycaster has a weak spot, I see?" I gently scratched again for emphasis.

Riyan's neck and shoulders trembled like he fought a shiver. "One of many."

"You know, I never heard exactly how you earned that title." I gripped the braid-rope and settled back on his shoulder. "The Duke told the story of the battle at that celebration but first I heard from Grigory Thornebow—"

"Grigory Thornebow?" He spat out the name like a curse.

"His younger sister was a year below me in school," I explained. "He sent her a letter after the victory and then told me about the battle himself when we danced at the Suitors' Ball."

Riyan scoffed so forcefully that I bounced up on his shoulder. "I still cannot believe he danced with you."

"Each suitor is *supposed to* dance with each bride at the Suitors' Ball."

"Hey, I wasn't allowed to go," Riyan retorted, defending himself against my barb. "General Hyton said I would have scared you girls half to death."

"As opposed to only scaring *me* half to death when you just appeared unannounced on Selection Night?"

"In the army, we call that risk management."

"In the real world, we call it cruel."

"Well, it's a good thing I didn't go," Riyan said with a lighter tone to his voice. "I wouldn't have let Thornebow dance with any of the girls at all. Probably would have caused a riot."

I remembered Grigory's hand pressed into my back and my chest against his. I could still feel his breath on my ear as he hissed about Riyan's beastly heart. I gulped, remembering how hard Riyan threw Grigory into the palace wall the night of Annalisa's ball and threatened him.

"Why do you hate Grigory?" I asked. "He seemed nice enough when we talked."

Riyan's shoulders shifted slightly. His jaw tightened against my side. "Serafina, nice boys don't get sent to the military academy."

"What do you mean?"

Riyan took a step up a rocky ledge. "Noble families normally send their sons to Heaston, right? At Heaston, they recite poetry, drink tiny goblets of wine with their pinkies in their air, and brag about how rich and powerful they are. It's a rite of passage for noble boys, but for the more…troublesome sons? Well, it's off to the military academy to break them out of their bad habits."

"But *you* were sent to the military academy."

Riyan's cheek rose with his wry smile. "I never said I was a nice boy." His fingertip traced the side of my leg underneath my skirt until he touched the bare skin of my thigh. He laughed as I smacked him away.

His smile faltered and his shoulders drooped with a long exhale. He raised his hand again but gently held my ankle between his thumb and forefingers. I let him.

"Despite being my…my father, General Hyton encouraged the other cadets to be a little…ruthless when I arrived at the academy." His voice was lower and more thoughtful. "I was the youngest kid there by a few years, but that didn't mean I got any mercy. None of those other delinquents messed with me after I grew a couple of times and could beat them into a bloody pulp."

I leaned my arm against his earlobe and hummed out a breath. He had to fight even as a child…and his father wanted him to. The memory of Duke Hyton beating his son bloody flashed through my mind. Maybe General Hyton was not so unlike his brother after all.

Riyan absent-mindedly stroked my calf with his thumb. "About three years after the first battle with the giants, Thornebow showed up after he got kicked out of Heaston. Oh, he was such a little prick, always bragging about how much money his father had."

Riyan's voice grew quieter and darker. He stopped stroking my leg. "One day, Thornebow got caught in town with a girl. That girl got to talking and it turned out Thornebow had…*interacted with* a lot of girls in Hyton."

"How?" I asked. "Even boys have to be chaste to go through the marriage enchantment. Grigory could not have been with girls in…*that way*, right?"

"Some men will go as far as they can before Selection Night with girls they think don't matter," he replied flatly. "But…he was not with them like you think. He was hurting them."

He took another step up a steep ledge and I gripped his hair. "Hurting them?"

"They had, uh…bruises. All over their wrists and necks."

We walked in silence again as I waited for Riyan to explain, but he stayed quiet.

Morbid curiosity burned behind my ribs, but I was not brave enough to ask. What was Annalisa in for?

My heart sank. Grigory could do whatever he wanted to her—no law kept a man from hurting his wife, even if it was generally frowned upon.

I let out a breath. Annalisa would never let someone like Grigory hurt her. If she could walk up to Riyan and threaten to stab him, she would not be afraid to fight back against a smaller man like Grigory. Besides, I remembered her wide smile as she had danced with Grigory at her ball and how Grigory had rushed out to the garden to protect her from a drunk Riyan. Maybe the military academy really did straighten Grigory out and he had changed his ways.

Riyan maneuvered around a grove of pine trees. "Have you ever noticed how Thornebow walks with a limp?"

The edge of an evergreen branch brushed my shoulder. "I tried to be polite about it. He said it was an old battle injury."

Riyan scoffed. "Of course he would say that."

"Why? What happened?"

Riyan smiled against my ribs. "General Hyton used to make us fight each other on a weekly basis to prove our strength. Since I guess he liked to see his son dominate everyone, General Hyton one day ordered me to wrestle every cadet one by one."

"But you were so much bigger than the rest of the cadets! That is not fair at all!"

"Life isn't fair." Riyan shrugged hard enough to bob me upward. "After I heard what Thornebow did, I wrestled with him, just like General Hyton wanted me to do, but then..."

Riyan's smile grew even bigger. "...I snapped his leg in half."

"You *what?*"

"He deserved it." His smile even reached the deep tones of his voice. "Everyone saw me do it. General Hyton didn't allow me to hurt anyone outside of his orders, so my punishment was severe."

"*You* were punished? But he was the one hurting those girls!"

"Like I said, life isn't fair."

"What did your...what did General Hyton do to you?"

Riyan turned his head slightly to look at me. "Do you remember that bridge we crossed the other day? The one over the river separating Hyton and Bloodstone?"

I nodded.

Riyan clenched his fist in front of his chest and each of his knuckles cracked. "First, the General made me get up before sunrise to cut down two trees and carry each log over to the bridge. Then, he ordered me to destroy the first supports on the bridge—those stone columns on the Hyton end of the bridge, you know? A few hours later, it's sunset, my palms and knuckles were bleeding from breaking the stone apart, but I still wasn't done. I had to support the bridge on my shoulders all night."

"All night?" I exclaimed.

"All night, and all the next day," Riyan said proudly. "So many horses and carts drove over me, and General Hyton made all the soldiers run across the bridge over and over the next morning. I can still feel the pounding of their footsteps on the back of my head sometimes…well, all of them except Thornebow's."

I imagined Riyan underneath the bridge—waist-deep in river water, his shoulders red and bleeding from the stone, and dust falling in his face with every stomp of a foot or trot of a horse.

My heart was heavy from the image, but Riyan laughed. "This troll eventually was allowed to emerge from under the bridge. All I had to do was replace the supports with the logs I had cut down—easy enough. But Thornebow didn't get off so easy. That leg was in a splint for a year. He had to switch from being a swordsman to an archer so he could stand in one place and shoot his little arrows from a distance instead of being in the action like a real hero."

Riyan's fingers gently wrapped around my calf to hold me in place as he stepped over a fallen tree. A spark of fear jolted up my spine—he could close his fist and break *my* leg if he wanted.

He must have sensed the tension in my calf muscle because he let go of me as soon as he returned to a steady gait. The moment his fingertips left my stocking, I wished they would return.

"Do you think Grigory learned his lesson?" I pictured speckled bruises on the insides of Annalisa's fair wrists. Acid crept up my throat but I swallowed it down.

"If not, he knows I will teach him that lesson again," Riyan said with a smirk. "I had a little…conversation with him the night of the ball. Told him that if I heard *anything* happened to the Duke's daughter, he could say goodbye to his other leg."

I glanced at his smirk, knowing his dimple was on the other side of his face. Annalisa could handle her own, but Riyan was so…*gallant* that my chest swelled with an airy heat. I brushed some of his hair away and leaned over to kiss him on the temple. My lips let out an appreciative hum against his skin and his eyelashes fluttered closed, savoring it.

If only Annalisa knew Riyan was looking out for her, maybe she would not be so eager to shove a knife in him.

Riyan stopped near the bank of a sparkling stream that blocked our path. Withered and moss-covered remnants of an old wooden bridge laid in disarray on either side of the stream.

He reached up with his left hand and secured me. "Hold on tight, sweetheart."

Even though he would not let me fall, I still gripped the rope of hair as Riyan ran to the edge of the stream. I closed my eyes as he jumped over the water. His feet thudded into the earth with a boom and the ground trembled.

I opened my eyes. Over the tops of the trees, the golden spires and gilded turrets were so close I could make out small windows in the towers. As I admired the distant palace, my eyes flicked up to two black birds flying toward us. The birds beat their wings against the blue sky like they were in a panic. Their glossy black beaks pointed down at Riyan.

Ravens.

I tugged on a strand of Riyan's hair to get him to look up. His head tilted back and one of the ravens dove toward us. The bird nipped at the fabric around my wrist as it flew over Riyan's shoulder. I squealed and drew my hand against my chest.

"Did it hurt you?" Riyan asked. He turned his head toward me as much as he could without knocking me off his shoulder.

I rubbed my wrist. "No."

The raven swooped around Riyan's back and perched on his right shoulder. Riyan turned his head just as the bird pecked his neck.

"Little shit!" Riyan cried. He swatted at the raven with his right hand and it fluttered up in the air to dodge him.

The second raven, larger than the first, swooped out of the sky and perched in my lap. I screamed, but did not dare move.

"Just hold still," Riyan ordered. "I can't swat it away without knocking you off my shoulder. It will go away once it realizes we aren't rotting corpses."

The large raven ruffled its feathers and croaked at me. The gurgling from its throat and clips of its beak were not the normal call of a raven. I listened closer.

"*Se-ra*," croaked the raven. "*Se-ra.*"

I screamed and my knuckles hit soft feathers as I knocked the beast off my lap. The raven flew up and joined its smaller companion as it circled around us in the air.

"It talked to me!" I cried. "It knew my name!"

"I told you things got weird up here," Riyan said, using his left hand to hold on to me and his right to swat at the birds in the sky. "Go away! We don't have any food!"

Both ravens squawked and screamed as they flew around Riyan's head.

"*Se-ra! Se-ra!*" they called.

Riyan cried out as the larger raven bit his right ear.

The ravens talking to me and knowing my name made me so exposed, so vulnerable, so seen, that my chest shook and my stomach opened up into another hollow pit. I slammed my hands over my ears to shut out the ravens, closed my eyes, and buried myself as deep in Riyan's hair as I could.

Riyan's voice was close enough that I could hear him through my blocked ears. "If I can't kill these things, I'll have to outrun them."

He reached up and held me again and then his body lurched forward. His hair flew back behind me as he sprinted faster than any human or animal could travel. I kept my eyes squeezed shut and braced myself in his hold, gripping any bits of his hair I could snag in my hands.

The cold mountain air whipped me in the face. The muscles in Riyan's neck throbbed against me. The only sound that touched my chilled earlobes was his panting breath that shuddered with each of his thundering footsteps.

After a few minutes, Riyan slowed down to a trot, then his shoulder loosened as he slowed down again. I shivered from the chill of the run, even with my wool cape still wrapped around my shoulders. Riyan lowered his hand from my back, but I still gripped onto his hair with iron hands.

"You're going to want to open your eyes now," Riyan breathed.

I cautiously fluttered my eyes open and tilted my head up toward columns of golden light. We reached Fraleigh's palace.

The sun kissed the horizon and illuminated the gilded splendor of the home of Fraleigh, the Great Sorceress of Nordingaard. A field of tall white flowers surrounded the palace, the last breath of green with nothing but snow and rock further up the mountain. The field was bare except for the palace and the flowers. Nowhere for anyone, or *anything,* to hide.

The palace had three tall gilded turrets topped with the golden spires I had seen earlier. The only apparent entrance was two doors and the front of the palace painted in beautiful swirls of gold leaf.

Riyan's chest was at the level of the thick stone arch above the palace doorway, which had "*Ipse Dixit*" carved into the stone and embellished with gold paint. On each side of the huge double wooden doors were two knockers in the form of ugly troll's heads with a golden ring in each of their mouths.

Riyan gently placed me on the ground in front of the doors. I stumbled and wobbled as my feet touched earth again. The gold and grass spun around me and my head buzzed. My body bore the toll of not sleeping for two days.

We had no time to rest, though. I shook my head and pulled my eyes open wide. I would sleep after Fraleigh made Riyan the size of a man.

I looked up at the doors. As huge as they were, Riyan could not fit through them, even if he crawled. A cold breath escaped my lips and my hands curled into shaking fists.

I had to face Fraleigh alone.

Riyan knelt down and eyed the doors. He gave me another sweet half-smile and hooked his finger around one of the heavy rings.

"I believe in you, Sera." His satin voice wrapped around my heart alongside our magical bond that glowed brighter than the palace in front of us.

Riyan let go of the ring and it hit the wooden door with a loud boom. The knock echoed inside the palace. One by one, footsteps pattered toward the door from the other side.

My palms started to sweat in my fists. My heart pounded.

I had one chance to convince Fraleigh to help us. One shot to make Riyan normal-sized.

And if I failed, I belonged to the Duke.

Chapter Thirty
The Golden Palace

I held my breath as the door of Fraleigh's gilded palace opened.

I expected to see Fraleigh's golden eyes and luminescent skin, but instead a young woman with warm brown hair peeked around the heavy wooden door. The woman's crystal blue eyes grew wide when she saw Riyan kneeling in front of the palace doors but still towering over us both.

"Riyan?" asked the woman.

Riyan smiled. He held up his massive hand and gave her a wave. "It's been a long time, Rosaline."

Thorny green vines crawled through my veins as Riyan's eyes flashed like he took note of Rosaline's full-figured frame.

Rosaline's voice was more casual than I expected. "Fraleigh wondered when you would come."

I furrowed my brow. Fraleigh knew everything, did that mean she knew Riyan was a Hyton heir all along? Was she sitting comfortably amongst her riches while Riyan suffered for years, tapping her sharp finger against her chin as she puzzled why Riyan had not figured out the truth of his lineage to seek her help?

If Fraleigh knew Riyan was a Hyton, it seemed that Rosaline woman knew also.

I clenched my teeth as Riyan kept his eyes on Rosaline. "She's going to have to speak to Fraleigh for me. I think I'll have to wait outside."

I turned to Rosaline. "I am Baroness Bloodstone, his wife." More envy blossomed out of my voice than I wanted, but I kept firm. "I need to see Fraleigh as soon as possible."

Rosaline glanced at Riyan then back at me. I ground my teeth behind tight lips as I silently dared her to say anything. After a heartbeat, Rosaline shrugged. "All right, I suppose she is in a good enough mood to receive you."

Rosaline opened the door wider and gestured for me to follow her inside. I jutted my chin in the air and took a single, powerful step inside the palace, but the glory of the entrance sapped the rest of the confidence out of me.

The polished stone floor and rows of columns flanking the entrance reflected the glow of gold like man-made sunlight. Gilded friezes of winged beasts crowned the walls. Filigrees of gold curled on the tops of each column. At the center of the room was a staircase that spiraled upward, the railings gilded and shining so one could ascend with the touch of gold at every step. Extravagance. Luxury. A testament to Fraleigh's power and influence.

The door closed behind us with a loud bang and shut Riyan out. Rosaline stepped forward and led me through the foyer. Instead of taking me up the staircase like I expected, she turned right and led me through a small and unassuming wooden door.

I followed Rosaline through the door. We entered a conservatory with large windows looking out on the Western Sea. Unlike the Duke's conservatory, the room was circular, with plush purple benches attached to the wall underneath the massive windows.

My heart stopped when I saw Fraleigh. She wore simple grey robes and no jewelry aside from her golden collar. She sat on one of the benches with her legs tucked underneath her and looked out at the pink and blue sky surrounding the setting sun over the peaceful waves.

"Your majesty," Rosaline said calmly, "you have a visitor."

Fraleigh slowly turned her head to face us and her golden eyes blinked in soft surprise. Her face stiffened when she focused on me.

"Ah, Baroness Bloodstone," Fraleigh said cooly. She turned toward me but stayed on the bench with her hands folded neatly in her lap. "I am surprised you took so long to come."

Fraleigh nodded to Rosaline, dismissing her. Rosaline bowed to Fraleigh and then disappeared out of the same door we came through.

A sharp chill ran through me when I realized my tired mind forgot my manners. I quickly corrected myself, clumsily dropping into a kneel and bowing before her.

"Get up," Fraleigh clipped.

I placed my hands on my leg and struggled to heave my exhausted body back up. I stacked each part of my spine as I reverted back to all of Ashmore's lessons in proper posture. My head buzzed with exhaustion, but I folded my hands in front of me and presented like the perfect lady I was trained to be.

"Your majesty," my voice was cool and respectful, "I seek your help."

"I only serve the House of Hyton," Fraleigh said.

"Riyan is a Hyton heir. I only ask for your magic to help him."

"He is a Hyton heir, but you?" Fraleigh said with a wicked smile. "If you want my magic, I require…payment."

Payment. I instinctively grabbed the side of my skirt and held the lump of my stashed goods. I fumbled in my pocket and pulled out the amethyst pendant. I held the jewel out in front of me and my arm trembled with a mixture of fear and fatigue.

Fraleigh's eyes widened slightly, like she did not expect me to produce anything valuable. She reluctantly stood up and she approached me so gracefully she could have glided on the stone floor. She took the pendant in her hands and her head quirked up like she had heard something.

I held my breath, trying to detect the smallest noise, but I heard nothing.

Fraleigh slowly walked back over to the bench. She sat down and tossed the pendant onto the cushion next to her. She crossed her legs underneath the long fabric of her robe and looked back up at me expectantly.

"Go on," she said with almost a sigh.

"Y-your majesty," I stammered, "as you know, my husband is afflicted with…with magic."

"Afflicted?" Fraleigh said with a laugh as she leaned back and lounged against the window. "How can one be afflicted with magic?"

"He was always large, you see," my voice trembled even more. Why was she asking? She knew everything. I gulped, trying to swallow my fear down. "Now he is the size of a giant. We need him to be smaller."

Fraleigh smirked and raised her thin eyebrow at me. "I think you are the first woman in the Dukedom to want a smaller husband. What do you mean by smaller?"

My voice was stronger. "I mean the size of a normal man."

"Well, he is not a normal man, now is he? Why would I make him a normal man if he was never one to begin with?"

My cheeks flashed hot and I clenched my fists. "Because we still have not consummated the marriage. It is impossible at his size."

"Nothing is impossible," Fraleigh said as she picked at her long fingernails. "Sounds like you have not tried hard enough to make it possible."

"I was trying." Anger churned in my stomach and lashed up at my throat. "I was almost crushed to death trying. I know you did not tell me I would be a satisfactory bride like you did my classmates, but that does not mean I deserve to suffer an annulment!"

In the fog of my fatigue, I had abandoned my training in manners and proper reverence. I did not have time to talk in circles or for game-playing. I needed Riyan to be the size of a normal man *immediately.*

Fraleigh did not look at me and continued examining her sharp fingernails.

"Serafina, really," she said with a smirk, "many young ladies are dissatisfied with their husbands after Selection Night. You will just have to bring yourself to consummate your marriage with the man who selected you, just as every other noble woman has for centuries."

"This is different and you know it!" I shouted. My blood boiled in my veins. My tongue was a steel blade. My bones were iron. I refused to show fear or weakness. "You know everything. You know what happens if my marriage annuls. Duke Hyton will *own me!*"

My voice hitched. Fraleigh's golden eyes flashed for a moment. I wanted to bite my tongue and shut down before I looked even weaker in front of Fraleigh, but I only had one chance to convince her to help.

Fraleigh had told me I was manipulative and an excellent liar, but I could not trick her into giving me what I wanted as I could with others. Those ancient golden eyes saw right into me.

If I wanted help, I needed to show her the real reason I needed her magic.

I let out a shaking breath and imagined myself on Duke Hyton's balcony.

My heart stopped and my vision swirled. Fatigue burned the backs of my eyes. Duke Hyton's imaginary hand slithered around my waist. His sharp breath stung my nose. His thick fingers weaved through my hair and yanked me down into the pits of my darkest fears.

"*Just like your mother,*" the invisible Duke whispered in my ear.

I crossed my arms in front of my shaking chest and found Fraleigh's golden eyes. I stacked my spine again. I pulled myself out of the pit.

"You cannot let him own me." My desperate whisper left my lips like a tiny fledgling bird.

Fraleigh's face broke for only a moment before snapping back into stillness. Pity. Understanding. A glimmer of hope.

My nails dug into my sleeves as I clutched myself into a false safety. "I know you cannot imagine the Duke owning you, being as powerful as you are. But…but I will not survive. He cannot turn me into *her.*"

My mother. Weak. Powerless.

Fraleigh's eyes glistened amongst a face of iridescent stone. I held my breath. Fragments of granite clung to my weak heart as it pleaded with each beat.

Please, Fraleigh. Please save me. Please save us.

Fraleigh's shoulders dropped slightly. She tilted her chin up. The corners of her mouth turned up and her golden eyes flashed.

"You can figure this out on your own, Serafina," she said.

Fraleigh made a dismissive motion with her hand. Rosaline appeared next to me, having entered the room some time during our conversation.

"She is ready, Rosaline." Each of Fraleigh's words was a fist to the gut. "She has a long journey ahead of her."

My blood ran cold. She refused. I was doomed.

Rosaline gently took my limp arm. She met eyes with Fraleigh and nodded once before leading me out of the conservatory. My feet followed her out, but my eyes stayed on Fraleigh. Despite how badly I hoped she would reconsider, she stayed still with her fists in her lap as she watched the sun die behind the sea.

The conservatory door shut with a thud. I expected Rosaline to turn right toward the front doors of the palace, but instead she turned left to the golden spiral staircase.

"Look, I could get into trouble for this," Rosaline said in a hushed voice, "but I'll do it for Riyan."

I followed Rosaline, who had shards of my hope shining in her crystal eyes, up the first step. We climbed the gilded staircase and she led me through a corridor decorated with rich tapestries of fair-haired men and women. Rosaline quickly snuck me through another door and up a tight set of spiraling stairs until we reached the top of one of the towers.

Rosaline stepped toward one of the arched windows and gestured for me to stand next to her. She pressed one palm to the glass and pointed up with the other.

"You need to go to the top of the mountain," Rosaline whispered. "Fraleigh is not the only being who can wield magic. Find Daigen."

Daigen. Each syllable sounded like salvation.

"What is Daigen?" I asked.

Rosaline exhaled and rolled the answer around in her mouth before she responded. "He's the size of a man, but he's red and has the horns and feet of a goat. Just…just find him. And don't take 'no' for an answer."

The terrifying red monster from Astrid's paintings. The very same creature that cut Riyan out of his mother when he was born.

"This…Daigen will really help us?" I asked.

"You don't have another choice," she replied. "Trust me, I've worked for Fraleigh for years and know more about magic than any other mortal in Lycaster. I can't use magic myself, but I know the three beings who can. Fraleigh, Daigen, and—"

"Ganora," I finished. My breath turned to ice in my lungs as I said her name.

Rosaline's eyes turned grim and she let out a breath. "I hope you find Daigen first. He's tricky, so keep your eyes open."

I imagined a horned red monster would not be too hard to find amongst the snow.

Rosaline took her hand off the window and gestured for me to follow her back down the stairs. The tower door creaked open and we carefully snuck through the corridor, each of our footsteps a whisper on the wooden floor. She led the way down the staircase and we silently crossed the grand entrance. As far as I could tell, Fraleigh was none the wiser.

Rosaline opened the door for me and we stepped out into the evening air. Riyan was sitting in the grass and surrounded by the white flowers. He was even taller than me when sitting down and Fraleigh expected me to just *figure out* how to consummate our marriage.

I should have known nearly five-hundred years of unlimited power would turn her cruel. Maybe she did not even have a heart.

Riyan noticed us and smiled. He rose from the field and came over to kneel in front of us.

"Did it go well?" he asked. Hope swam in his eyes.

His optimism was an arrow in the chest. Rosaline and I exchanged glances.

"We have a new lead," I replied. "We just have to travel a little farther."

I was not ready to tell him our new destination was the home of his worst nightmares.

Riyan gave us a half-smile and then shrugged. "Not a problem. I can get anywhere quickly. We have time."

We did not have time. Sure, we may have had twenty-four days left until the marriage annulled, but time would slip away from us faster than Riyan thought.

Riyan pulled out a small circle of white flowers from behind his back. He reached over and gently placed the flowers on top of Rosaline's head. Rosaline gasped and her crystal blue eyes sparkled.

"You remembered!" she cried. Riyan gave her a dimpled smile. Green fire burned in my chest.

I tried not to stare at Riyan's gift as Rosaline turned to me. "I wish you luck, Serafina. She's hard to understand most of the time, but Fraleigh does indeed know everything. She'd never tell you that you could figure out your problem if it weren't true."

I doubted that. Fraleigh was only angry with me for my insolence. She clearly had no real faith that I could find a way to make Riyan a normal man.

Rosaline blew a goodbye kiss to Riyan and turned back inside the palace.

She peeked out from behind the wooden door and looked me in the eyes. "By the way, any woman who would confront the Great Sorceress for her husband like you did is *much more* than just a satisfactory bride."

My mind was too exhausted to accept the compliment and the door painted with gold spirals closed on us. Riyan held out his hand and I looked up at him—our new silent signal that I was ready to go.

A smile blossomed through the fatigued muscles in my face as his fingers wrapped around my back and he picked me up. He placed me on his shoulder and gave me a moment to settle in.

My exhausted heart fluttered when Riyan reached up and held my leg again. I leaned my body against the side of his head as he gently stepped through the flowers. The gentle swaying of his shoulders started to rock me to sleep. My eyelids were heavy as lead but I kept my focus on the white flowers below us that danced in the evening breeze.

"You can make flower crowns?" I asked. Both my hands wrapped around his braid—my lifeline in case I lost the battle to unconsciousness.

"Rosaline taught me how," Riyan replied. "Her family lived in a village by the fortress and sold flowers during hard times. I felt bad for poor little Rosaline, so young Riyan was their best customer. I would walk down to the village and buy flowers from her every day to give to my mother."

I smiled, picturing an unnaturally tall blonde boy skipping into the fortress with a handful of blossoms.

"Was Rosaline your friend?" I asked.

"The only friend I had before I was sent away," Riyan replied. "I'm glad she's working for Fraleigh. She looks like she's finally being fed well."

Fraleigh definitely was not wanting for food, or anything else for that matter, from the looks of her golden palace.

"Your friendship with her paid off," I said. Friendship. Just friendship. "She helped me when Fraleigh would not."

"She always was sweet," Riyan said. "So what was your new lead?"

I looked down at the white flowers. My mind danced along with the thin green stems as I tried to tactfully tell Riyan we needed to hunt down the magical creature that cut his mother in half and gave him life.

"Oh, we just have to find Daigen," I said, like the subject was as inconsequential as choosing what to eat for breakfast.

"What is this Daigen and where is he?" Riyan was as blunt as a cudgel.

"He, well," I struggled to make the news more palatable, "he can use magic, and we will not take 'no' for an answer—"

"Sera, you don't have to coddle me." Riyan interjected. He stopped in the middle of the field and turned his head a little toward me so I had the full attention of his left eye. "I'm a *soldier.* Tell me where we need to go and what I have to do."

I took in a long, slow breath. "Daigen is the red monster who freed you from your mother's womb."

Riyan's blonde eyebrow raised and his eyes softened. "And where is he?" he asked, but his eyes glistened like he already knew the answer.

"West of the Moon and East of the Sun."

Riyan's neck muscles froze. His fingers trembled around my leg for a heartbeat. His shining eyes hardened into cold steel and he looked forward. All that lay in front of us was a massive upward slope of rock and snow.

"Then so be it," Riyan said. His sword rattled against his leg as he took the first step forward. He gripped the hilt of Endre's Revenge with his right hand as he bravely walked toward the battleground of his nightmares. "Let's just hope those ravens weren't a bad omen."

I swallowed. Ravens held a special place in my heart as my family emblem, but the rest of Lycaster saw them differently.

Ravens were bringers of Death.

Chapter Thirty One
Feathers and Fire

The sun had died and the sky darkened into a rich blue, turning the snow on Nordingaard's peak a soft periwinkle. The moon was nowhere in sight, but the snow was still bright.

Riyan's soft padding footsteps in the grass field outside of Fraleigh's palace had turned into mighty crunches in the snow as he marched up the slope. I glanced down at his bare feet, which had turned scarlet as he stomped through the powder.

"Are you cold?" My breath left my lips in a swirl of mist. I let go of Riyan's braid and tugged the crimson wool tighter around my body.

"I'm fine," Riyan replied. His shoulders shivered. "I slept outside in the dead of winter for nearly seven years with nothing but a handle of grog to keep me warm."

I pressed myself against his head and neck, hoping I could give him just a little of my body heat.

"I u-used to love winter." My teeth chattered. "Snowball fights, ice-skating, sledding…but the best part was coming in from the cold and snuggling up by the fire. I would sprawl out in front of the hearth like a cat, letting the heat envelop me. It was like a hug."

"Sounds nice," Riyan grunted. "Please, keep bragging."

"Being grumpy will not make you any warmer!" I nudged his cheek with my head. "Talking keeps my throat from freezing."

"And as we all know, it's my *top* priority to keep that throat of yours pristine."

I kicked my heel into his chest, but it was so weak he probably did not even feel it. "Anyway, I said winter *used to* be my favorite. Then I went to Ashmore. We spent so much time locked up that sometimes I did not even recall what month it was. Winter lost its bite. Spring lost its shine. Summer meant nothing other than one class of girls was married off and a new crop of young brides would arrive at the end. Years just became muddled blurs—like a jar of water you clean paint brushes in."

"You paint?" His breath formed a small cloud before it disappeared.

"No, as much as the matrons tried to force me to be good at it. I hated getting greasy paint on my hands." I pulled the cape in closer to my chest. "But that memory of the disgusting glass jars of grey water stuck with me."

I looked out at the expanse of white broken up only by scraggly pine trees. "Sometimes I saw the world like I was looking through that glass jar— everything was murky and colorless. Other times I felt like I *was* the glass jar. I could have made something beautiful, but instead I was full of cold waste."

"You *are* beautiful." His voice was stronger, his heavy footfalls in the snow punctuating each word. "Nothing about you is a waste."

"Only because *you* say so," I replied. "When you are brought up to be only a bride, you are nothing until you are married. Then someone else decides what you are. Duchess, Baroness, mother…none of that is what I am."

The snow around us reminded me of Ilsa's infamous icy beauty. She was a Duchess, whore, half-giant, traitor, sorceress…but only because others said she was.

The most harrowing part of Ilsa's tale was not her alleged misdeeds, nor that her shining beauty was destroyed, but that she died without anyone knowing who she really was.

"And…what are you, Serafina?" Riyan wore a smile, but his voice was still heavy.

Dozens of words spun in my head. Daughter. Friend. Rival. Liar. Manipulator. Plotter. Lover. Enemy. Murderer. Failure. Each vibrant word mixed with its opposite, swirling together until it resembled nothing but bleak, grey water in a jar.

A jar of nothing.

I snuggled into his hair and took a deep breath of nectar and wheat. "I have no idea. I survive…that is all I do. Does not make me much of anything, does it?"

A loud squawk echoed all around us. I looked up, two black birds flapped their wings and darted back and forth in the rocks above us.

One of the birds flew right for me.

"*Se-ra! Se-ra!*" it screamed.

The demented ravens had returned. I pulled the hood of my cape over my head and closed my eyes.

"*Se-ra!*"

A sharp sting sliced through my right side.

Pain stole my breath from my lungs. My eyes met a dark sky. The crimson cape fluttered around the edges of my vision as I plummeted to the ground.

My back smacked against the snow. The shock of the impact rattled my bones. My face hit the snow over and over as I rolled down the slope. The left side of my body crashed into stone, but pain screamed from my right.

What felt like a cold black fire ignited from my right side. I screamed through gritted teeth and pressed my hands to my side, but black flames spread through my veins to the rest of my body.

Over the sounds of the pain roaring in my ears, footsteps dragged through the snow, panting breath grew closer and closer, and just when I thought a hand gripped my shoulder, the raven screamed again.

"*Se-ra!*" The cry was as horrible as Death itself. "*Se-ra!*"

Feathers beat against my face as the raven marked me for the reaper. My body was consumed with invisible flames. I bucked against the stone and writhed as I burned alive.

Dread seeped through the black fire. Truth escaped its iron cage as the rest of my body burned down. I came to Nordingaard to kill, so Nordingaard was going to kill me.

Nothing I did not deserve.

"Sera!" The voice was louder, clearer, and desperate. Riyan. "Where are you?"

I wrenched open my jaw and screamed in response. The earth rumbled under me like it was going to crack open and swallow me whole, but then two hands scooped me out of the snow and raised me up to the sky. Riyan held me against him, but I was still burning. I thrashed and kicked his chest and arms.

"It's a fucking avalanche!" Riyan cried.

Riyan cradled me in his left arm and pressed me into his chest. He jumped and yanked us up the mountainside as rock crashed like a raging ocean below us.

My back arched in an impossible curve as I burned and then my stomach dropped as I slipped out of Riyan's arm. His hand caught me around my waist before I fell and I screamed as his fingers pressed into my right side.

"Almost there, Serafina." He was pleading. *Pleading.*

Riyan pulled us over the edge and took off in a sprint. Riyan's heart pounded against me as I writhed in his arms. I punched him, kicked him, and gnashed my teeth—fighting through the pain as much as I could.

"Riyan," I spat out, "I am sorry."

For trying to kill him. For failing to manipulate Fraleigh. For thinking he was just a drunk and a brute.

For not giving him a chance from the beginning.

"No, don't you say goodbye, Serafina." His breath warmed my body against the bleak, dark fire.

Riyan stopped and quickly lowered me to the ground. Cold, dewey pebbles pressed against my back. He gently, yet swiftly, removed the cape around my neck. He slid his hand under my back and lifted me up off the ground as the cape disappeared from my shoulders. My whole body shivered and convulsed.

Riyan's voice shook. "Sera, I need to take your clothes off. You have to get in the healing spring."

"No!" I cried. I squeezed my eyes shut tighter and bared my teeth as my limbs fought against the pain. Water would not put out the black fire. I would rather die by flame than drown.

"I will not let you die too!" Riyan cried.

I cracked open my eyes. Black streaks stained his chest from where he had held me. I removed my right hand from the side of my ribs and looked at my palm—it was completely stained black.

I closed my eyes. My body went limp. He still thought I was worth saving.

"Scared…," I whimpered. "I am…so scared."

"If you can be brave, I can be brave." Riyan's voice was like a trumpet's call across a field. Strong. Shaking. Desperate. "You're going to take a swim and I'll talk about my first battle with the giants. Deal?"

I opened my eyes. Riyan knelt over me, but I could barely see his face. My vision faded. Nordingaard swirled into a hazy grey, trapping me in the nothingness like I was in that jar of paint water.

"Deal," I whispered.

Right as the word left my lips, Riyan's strong hands ripped the leather waist cincher off my torso with one tug. He tore off my shirt, my skirt, and then each of my stockings and shoes. I was cold, naked, and exposed as I convulsed blindly on the rocks.

Splash. Warm water closed its jaws around me, but I was no longer in the grey paint water.

The world had turned as black as Death.

Chapter Thirty Two
The Bloodbath

My body was an empty shell drifting in the dark abyss. My arms and legs dangled around me, weightless. Water gently lapped the sides of my eyes. My hair softly brushed against my shoulders and my back.

My eyes would not open. Breath escaped my barely parted lips in soft puffs. My ears were submerged and I listened to the rhythmic, underwater rumbles of another life in the water with me. Skin brushed against my back. Muscle held me steady in the water.

Another low rumble disturbed the water and tickled my skin. The vibration was not a twitch of muscle or a flutter of breath, but a smooth, strong voice.

"I was fifteen…"

My eyes opened. I was in a rocky, snow-covered plain and looking up at a tall mountain pass. The tall rocks on either side of the pass loomed menacingly. A thick white fog rolled between them onto the plain before dissipating into the chilled mountain air.

Hundreds of boys holding pitchforks and axes quietly moved about, all wearing the plain grey, brown, and green garb of farmers and villagers. A small group of no more than two dozen stiff-backed soldiers in the blue uniforms of the Duke's army stood at attention in front of a tall man with white-blonde hair—General Hyton.

Suddenly I was right beside him. His sparkling Hyton Blue eyes were at the level of mine, but that was impossible. He towered over me…

"Any minute now, the first giant will smell us and appear through that pass," General Hyton boomed. "Once the first giant falls, aim your swords for the weak points of the body: ankles, the backs of the knees, the wrists, and especially the neck."

A man stood one head taller than the rest of the group. No, he was not a man, but a boy. The only boy amongst them. A red cape fell from the shoulders of his uniform—Riyan. Teenage Riyan stood at attention with the other soldiers. His face was steel, yet fear clung around his shoulders like an icy mist.

I wanted to walk over to him, but I could not. I had no feet. Or legs. Or even hands. I floated as if I were air around the groups of men. I could not speak. I could not touch anything. I could only watch helplessly as young Riyan trembled amongst the men around him.

The soldiers split into two groups, one moving to the east and the other to the west, until Riyan stood alone in front of General Hyton. Riyan may have been substantially taller than the General, but he flinched as the General approached to stand in front of him.

If I had hands, I would have put one on his shoulder.

"You know what to do," General Hyton said. "Meet with the Ravenwood boys and lead the Bloodstone militia."

"Yes, General," Riyan said with a salute.

General Hyton lingered in front of Riyan for another moment, a tiny twitch of his lower lip the only sign that he was anything other than stoic. He blinked only once before turning away and walking to the eastern group of his soldiers.

A flash of white. The world shifted. I was next to Riyan and watching him speak with two dark-haired young men wearing green capes—Erik and Endre.

I gorged myself on the sight of them, taking it all in bit by bit. Endre's messy hair and unlaced shirt. Erik's crooked nose and focused, black eyes. How Endre chewed on his lip. How Erik stood exactly three inches taller because *of course* they had measured.

If I had eyes, I might have cried.

Erik had his shoulders back and one hand on his sword while Endre held his arms and looked up at Riyan.

"The General said to wait for the first one to fall," Riyan said. "Then rush forward and attack the weak points."

"Really?" Endre asked, his mossy eyes twinkling with mischief. "Like this?"

Endre rushed into Riyan, knocking him off balance and toppling him onto his back.

"Little shit!" Riyan laughed as he hit the ground.

Endre quickly stood up and fumbled for his sword at his side. He drew the sword and pointed it at Riyan's heart with his arm wobbling slightly from the weight of the thick blade.

Riyan laughed at Endre and raised his shoulders off the dirt. "Not the chest, this isn't a duel." Riyan moved the tip of Endre's blade to point at his neck. "The neck is better, but you need to do it fast or else—"

Riyan kicked Endre's wrist and knocked his sword out of his hand. Riyan jumped up and grabbed Endre around the waist and hoisted him over his shoulder. Endre bellowed with laughter.

"Damn you, Riyan!" Endre laughed. "Maybe we should just leave you with your own kind and forget this battle all together!"

"Will you two stop?" Erik snapped. "I dealt with your antics for days, but this is serious! The giants will attack any minute!"

Riyan lowered Endre to the ground and back onto his feet.

Erik stomped over to Endre and glared at him with a hard brow and wide eyes. "You take the west flank!"

Endre picked up his sword and sheathed it with a glare at his elder brother.

Riyan quickly drew his own sword and held it out as if it were just another part of his arm. "Remember, Endre, this isn't a Heaston duel. It's kill or be killed."

Endre gripped the hilt of his sword. "Hell, I know. This blade is just a little thicker than I am used to. Have to adjust."

Riyan snickered. "Yeah, I bet you're used to working with something much smaller."

Endre's brows furrowed for a moment before he threw his head back and laughed. "Fuck you, Riyan! Bet I still kill more giants than you. Just because you have a bigger sword does not mean you know how to use it!"

He ignored Erik's glare and jogged to the western group of Ravenwood sons.

Erik turned to Riyan. If I had a body, I would have shrunk away. Even seven years of absence could not erase the memory of that cold, black glare.

"Really? You have to act like a jackass *now?*" Erik snapped.

Riyan swallowed. "It just takes the edge off the stress…that's all."

Erik stepped in front of Riyan. His black eyes were glassy, but his stoic face did not break. "You may be an unintelligent brute, but I know you can count. The Duke did not send enough soldiers. This is going to be a bloodbath."

Riyan's lip trembled but he did not blink. A grim affirmation.

"Promise me, Bloodstone," Erik's voice broke but his shoulders stayed strong, "promise me as a future Baron, as a *man,* that no matter what happens, you will save Endre. One of us has to become Baron Ravenwood after this is all over, and it needs to be him if I fall. Someone has to look after our little sister."

Riyan looked down at my eternally serious elder brother and took a breath. "I promise."

A flash of white and the world shifted again. A foreboding rumble echoed through the mountain pass. Soft thunder slammed into the ground once, then again and again.

I gathered my bearings—I floated next to Riyan. His eyes were wide with terror and fixed on the foggy mountain pass. With a blink, I was suddenly in his head—seeing everything through his eyes.

A giant appeared through the fog. Its flesh was clods of earth pressed together to form a body. It had a round head, big ears, and stringy black hair that fell over its milky white eyes. It sniffed through its crooked nose and growled, its bellow like the sound of boulders scraping together.

A few boys from the Bloodstone and Ravenwood militias held a long rope tightly between them at the opening of the pass. The giant stomped forward and caught the rope on its right foot. Instead of tripping, the giant pulled the rope like it was not there and yanked the screaming boys into the rocks.

The giant slowly turned toward the screams. With one swipe of its huge, lumpy arm, it picked up one of the crying boys in its hand and went back into the pass, disappearing into the fog.

Another giant crashed through the trees in the west, three more following behind it, carrying axes and clubs. Five more stomped through the east, each with weapons in their hands.

The army was surrounded.

Suddenly the story did not play out like a portrait, but instead in quick images, sounds and feelings.

Flashes of grey and red. Glint of steel. Bones snapped. Boulders crashed. Sky-shredding screams. Prayers for salvation. Boyish throats crying for their mothers. Iron and sweat in the nose. Blood on the lips, then the tongue, then the throat.

I tasted the blood. *Tasted it.*

Another flash. A giant carried off a man in a green cape, who whacked at its left arm with his sword. The giant and Erik then disappeared into the fog.

Another shift in the memory. A loud boom echoed through the plain. One giant laid face-down in the rocks. Riyan, Endre, and the Bloodstone and Ravenwood sons rushed to the beast and hacked at its body with all their strength.

Riyan and Endre sliced their swords over and over at its neck. The giant's clear, sparkling blood poured out of the gashes. As soon as Riyan or Endre managed to make each cut, the wound completely sealed up seconds later.

"What is happening?" Endre screamed.

"Its blood is made of magic!" Riyan yelled, his teeth coated in blood that did not taste like his. "It's healing too quickly, but keep trying! Keep trying!"

The giant's fist slammed on the ground and knocked Endre and Riyan into the snow. Riyan tried to get up, but he was not quick enough to stop the grey hand launching toward the dark green cape. The giant grabbed Endre by his cape and pulled him up in the air.

Endre dropped his sword and he dangled. He choked, grabbing at the neck of the cape with desperate hands and trying to undo the raven clasp. His eyes bulged and his face turned purple.

"Endre!" Riyan cried. He reached a crimson-stained sleeve up.

Endre desperately reached down to Riyan, his once mirthful eyes filled with panic and tears, but it was too late—the giant already had him up too high. Endre's eyes rolled back and his violet face lolled forward. The one-eyed giant pulled Endre's body into its fist and stomped toward the fog.

Riyan chased after him. He panted. Tears formed in his eyes. He whacked at the giant's leg with his sword. Crystal clear blood poured out of the wound before sealing up seconds later. The giant may have only had one milky white eye, but it still did not even look back at its attacker. Riyan hit it again, but did not slow it down.

"Hang on, Endre! Please!" Riyan cried, desperate tears leaking onto his cheeks.

General Hyton appeared and pulled Riyan away from the giant with one arm and held his sword in his free hand.

"Stop, Bloodstone!" General Hyton screamed up at him. "You're going to get killed!"

"I made a promise!" Riyan cried, pulling out of the General's grip and turning to the giant. "I can't let him die!"

"No! That's an order!" General Hyton shouted.

"I don't care!" Riyan cried as he sprinted toward the fog.

A hard thump flew into Riyan's back as the hilt of General Hyton's sword made contact. Riyan fell forward and crashed into the ground. Snow mixed with blood on Riyan's tongue. His muscles burned. Pain flared through his blood like blades. Cold tears stung his tense cheeks. His wool uniform tore at its seams. His bones cracked and re-mended. His scream shredded his frozen throat.

The pain was unbearable, made only worse by the barbed emotions sinking into the base of his brain and spreading through his body like a disease.

Terror. Weakness. Hopelessness.

Then his mind became a spiraling pit of grey, swirling storm clouds, barren of happiness, devoid of faith, or truth or light.

Guilt. The storm was guilt. He felt it in every nightmare, every breath, every heartbeat, and it screamed at him.

Your fault! Your fault! Your fault!

Hands clapped onto Riyan's arms and shocked me out of the darkest depths of his mind. Riyan still refused to open his eyes, but I recognized the voice that commanded dozens of soldiers to haul Riyan to safety.

"Come on, boy!" the General roared. "You will not die on this mountain! Come on!"

Blood stained the snow. Tears streaked the dirt. Rocks dragged against raw skin. Muscles and joints ached. The screams got quieter. The snapping and crushing sounds softened. Everything faded into blackness again.

Then another flash of white.

I was outside of Riyan's head and floating around the peak of Nordingaard again. The foggy mountain pass poured fog out of its maw. Cold air whipped through honey-colored hair.

The taller, meaner Riyan that I knew stood in his uniform, towering over the dozens of the Duke's archers behind him, including Grigory Thornebow. General Hyton stood with his archers but had his Hyton Blue eyes fixed on Riyan.

Riyan had both hands gripped on the hilt of Endre's Revenge that he held aloft and ready. His muscles were tense. His chest heaved with his breath. His teeth were bared and gritted tight. His twilight eyes vibrated with intense focus on the mountain pass.

The first stomp thundered through the pass. Then another. The giant emerged from the fog, blindly following the smell of fresh meat.

"Come here, you fucking bastard," Riyan growled.

The giant took one last step and Riyan's feet sprang forward like he set off a trap.

Riyan roared like a lion freed from an iron cage. His boot kicked into the giant's lumpy stomach. Magical grey flesh boomed as it hit the snowy plain. White knuckled fists gripped the sword's hilt. Steel gleamed over the fallen grey mass.

Chop.

Chapter Thirty Three
Smoke and Charcoal

My eyes fluttered open to thousands of twinkling stars in an inky black sky.

My chest released a breath from my flushed lips and the mist curled like a phantom above me before disappearing into the night. Steam slowly writhed toward the heavens as warm water met cold air, each curve and bend lit from the calm blue glow of the water.

I was in the healing spring—free from Riyan's nightmare.

The warm water pulled at my submerged skin and my head rolled in the direction of its pull. Riyan sat next to me in the magical hot spring, guarding me as I floated above his arms. His face and chest were lit up by the cerulean glow of the water. His eyes were fixed on a faraway point, vibrating slightly as he stared. The muscles in his arms twitched under the water, ripples from each movement disturbing the calm surface of the spring.

The healing spring was full of enough magic to give Astrid pictures of her own memories when she bathed in it. The magic must have done the same for me, throwing me into Riyan's head and showing me every cry, ache, and bloody scream that plagued him when he closed his eyes. The spring sent me to Riyan's memory and brought me back, but Riyan was still fighting the giants. I needed to pull him out.

"Riyan…" I whispered.

Riyan's eyes sparked back to life and looked down at me.

"Shh, Sera," he hushed. His hands rose underneath the water to support my back and legs. "Not so fast, you still need to heal."

The black fire was gone, but a soreness remained on my right side.

"How much longer do you think I need to heal from a raven attack?" I asked.

"I don't know, and I don't know how but…" Riyan's voice hitched and he swallowed. "You were poisoned. Your blood turned black. It's…it's even still coming out of you."

My right hand tingled as it floated in the water, sensing something cold and devoid of magic dissipating under my fingertips. Riyan's forearms tensed as I slowly brought my right hand to my side under the water. The coldness grew thicker as I pressed my palm against an open gash near my ribs. Poison leached out of me and yet I felt no pain.

My lips parted with wonder. I was not sure how a raven could have poisoned me, but Riyan still knew how to heal me.

I looked up at Riyan, who held no amazement in his sad, wide eyes. Although his face was despondent, his arms were still strong as they guarded me against every threat Nordingaard had to offer.

"You saved me," I said softly.

Riyan's sad eyes hardened. "I'm the reason you're here to begin with. This is all my fault. I should have just looked for Daigen myself. I should have kept you safe at the fortress. All of this is my fault."

"Riyan, no." The water pulled me toward him like it was alive. I gave in and rolled into the pull. "None of this is your fault."

"Yes it is!" Riyan snapped. The surface of the water rippled like it cowered from the power of his wrath. "You said so yourself back at Hyton Palace. Had I not ruined the Duke's plan and just married Brietta, you would be living in luxury at Lord Hyton's side right now. You wouldn't be stuck with someone three times your size, or forced to kill me to save our families, or starving in the wilderness, or poisoned!"

I felt the pull again, but I realized it was not the magic of the water, but the glow of our blood bond wrapping around my heart and tugging me toward him. The water carried my fingertips to his chest. His stomach muscles tensed under my touch.

"Riyan—"

"I have hurt you so many times, Sera," he interjected, "and every time you have come closer to your death. Everything bad that's ever happened to you happened because of me!"

The golden bond crushed the shards of granite still clinging to my heart.

"Endre's death was not your fault!"

Riyan looked down at me again, his face frozen with shock and his eyes glistening with sadness. His hands trembled underneath me and the water rippled.

The magical water lapped in my ears and brought Endre's bright laughter with it. The stars above me were freckles on his cheeks. The steam above the spring carried his scent of mint and fresh smoke.

"You made the last days of his life happy." Hot tears rimmed my eyes. "You trained him. You gave him confidence. You were with him until the end."

Riyan softly shook his head. A single tear fell from his eye. "I still should have been faster. I still let him die."

My nose and throat burned.

"Riyan, the magic took me to your memory," I croaked through the pain in my throat. "I saw the whole battle. You did everything you could."

"Like that matters," Riyan said. His lip trembled, but his jaw was hard and tight. "Ravenwood is going to shit because its last heir died on my watch. I broke my promise."

Erik's voice was low in my ears. *"Someone has to look after our little sister."*

My eyes stung and my voice shook. "You did not break your promise."

Riyan's shoulders slumped forward. I pictured hands steepling in front of a serious, pensive brow. I looked up, the midnight clouds were as black as Erik's eyes. My hands curled into fists under the water and I gripped my big brother's cape again. I smelled tea leaves and charcoal.

"All Erik wanted you to do was protect his family." I struggled to get each word out, fighting the magical mist building up around my eyes. "He would be so happy to see you taking care of me because…because he loved me. They both did."

My throat seized. My chest shook. I blinked once and then a bead of water like a warm diamond rolled from my eye. Then another. Then another.

Pieces of the crumbling granite around my heart fell and disappeared in the chasm of my bare soul. Each one of my tears filled the chasm, giving it the gift of raw emotion, of love, of life.

Sobs cracked off my tongue. Tears dripped off my chin into the water. Riyan cradled my head in his palm.

"And I miss them so damn much," I sobbed, "because I *loved them*. But you made me remember them. You made me feel them again, even after I had shut out their memories and their love for seven years."

The golden bond burned brighter. Riyan must have felt it too, because he pulled me into his chest. Skin against skin. My wounded body against his wounded soul. Our blood bond forged from ancient magic glowed so brightly it engulfed my heart and shone in Riyan's eyes.

The golden glow warmed my heart and took away the pain of my sobs. My voice was soft, clear, and strong as I spoke. "You saved me."

I blinked through my gentle tears and calmed my sobbing chest. I smiled, warm and true, as I took in Riyan's handsome face that glowed in the light of the spring. His face was soft, his damp blonde hair curled at his collarbone, and he looked down at me with tenderness. As we sat in the magical hot spring, my raw heart surrounded by the illumination of our bond, I finally saw Riyan Bloodstone for who he truly was.

He was a stone fortress—pretending to be the valiant champion and the perfect killer. When the tides of his gentle passion beat down the stone walls of his prison, he freed himself to his true nature. He was both kind and fiercely protective. He was both humble and a show-off. He was both strong as a mountain and weak as a crumbling bridge.

Riyan was a mess of impossible contradictions—and that is what made him a wonder.

His right hand broke through the surface of the water. He caressed the side of my face with his thumb and water from the spring ran down my cheek along with my tears.

"They talked about you all the time." His voice broke. "I barely made it into our Selection class with my mid-June birthday, so I had joked about marrying you. Erik wanted me nowhere near you, but Endre secretly gave me his blessing to choose you."

A laugh rippled in my sore throat.

The corner of Riyan's mouth flicked up for a moment like he wanted to smile. "After that first battle, Duke Hyton said I grew too big to marry an Ashmore bride, but General Hyton convinced him to let me back into Selection Night after my victory. I'll forgive him for never admitting he was my father for that alone. I never would have even *seen you* without him."

He stroked my cheek again. His touch was like a kiss.

"And I wanted you the instant I saw you through that magic mirror, but when you put on that raven tiara, I could almost feel Erik Ravenwood kicking me in the ass to remind me of my promise to look after you. Everything about you was so impressive, so wonderful, so *right,* that I thought I was doing the first good thing in my life by choosing you.

"You did." I smiled up at him. I pressed my hand against his chest and he relaxed. The golden glow passed through my skin into his. His into mine. Back and forth for eternity. "When you chose me, you saved me."

Riyan finally smiled back and his dimple appeared. "Before you, my life was so bleak and dark, like I was living in endless night. Every time you say my name is another break of dawn. Your touch is daylight on my skin. Your guiding light brings me out of my nightmares, out of the churning black sea, and into a future I want to wake up to."

Riyan cupped my cheek and jaw with his forefingers. He leaned down as he held me and his breath warmed my bare chest. His face was a kiss away from mine.

"When I look into your eyes, Serafina, I finally see the sun."

I leaned into his touch—his warmth, his honesty—, but then tension pulsed through the water. Our bright bond of safety and happiness faltered and revealed a crack of insecurity.

"But every time you are hurt, or edge closer to your mortality," his voice was darker, shakier, "the endless night wraps around me again. I never know if I am the hero you need or the monster you have to slay."

I let out a slow breath. My soul was bared and undefended. Even though the golden light consumed my entire body, a magical presence in the water swirled under me and crept through my open wound at my side. The presence was even older than our ancient blood bond, but it worked its way through my blood as if it knew me.

The magic rattled around in the open iron cage where I had kept all my secrets and dragged the ugliest one out. The secret clawed its way up my throat with the magic pushing it to escape and I opened my lips to free the truth.

"Riyan, you are not a monster—"

An ancient voice in my head finished the secret for me.

"—*but you are, Serafina.*"

Invisible icy hands with claws of flame gripped my mind and pulled me out of my body, under the water, and down, down, down where no glow of a blood bond or the magical healing spring could touch the darkness.

"*You cannot hide anymore,*" said the ancient voice.

Darkness. Nothing but darkness. I could not move. I could not scream.

"*I see you, Serafina Ravenwood.*"

Chapter Thirty Four
Little Ember

West of the Moon and East of the Sun—a place without day or night that transcends the mortal confines of good and evil.

The mythical land of the legends was not the snowy peak of Nordingaard like Riyan had said. No, it was the chasm of darkness where I was held.

A creature with an unseen face held me in the darkness. My head hung back on my limp neck as the rest of my body was still as a corpse. My heart did not thump, my chest did not rise or fall, and I was completely helpless against the creature that held me underneath its breath. A thin arm held my hooked legs and another braced my shoulders. I looked up at the vast darkness as I searched for the rays of the sun or the glow of the moon.

I searched in vain, knowing deep within my blood that no light would reach me. I was in the chasm between the sun and the moon—a place where time could not touch.

All I heard was echoes of water and all I saw was a smothering blanket of ink, but I did not feel isolated from the world I had just left. Instead, I felt as if I hovered above it all like I was floating, looking down at the entire world in the darkness, and waiting for whispers of knowledge to reach my ears so I could pass judgment.

The potential of knowing all things was exhilarating, but I still did not know exactly what held me in its stiff embrace.

I tried to hum through my frozen throat and call out to Riyan.

"*Your silver tongue will do you no good here,*" the ancient voice whispered. The voice was both cold and warm, both cruel and kind. "*You cannot lie to me, Serafina. I see everything. I know everything.*"

I wish I knew what held me.

"*Time does not reach the bottom of my pit,*" the voice replied. "*Although enough of it has passed above me that the name I had was lost to the wind.*"

Helpful.

The thin arms, untouched by age or rot, gripped me in something between a clutch and a cradle. "*But here is a hint: I cry into the loops of infinity; I mourn for millenia; I give gifts to the worthy; I fight Death.*"

If my heart were beating, it would have stopped. The Man of the Mountain held me. He captured me as a replacement for his lost bride.

"*No one can replace her,*" the voice hissed. "*Though many have tried—thrown their daughters bound and gagged into my waters as sacrifices, run to me and begged for my gifts, stolen my tears or fell into my chasm and were lost.*"

I was lost.

"*No, Serafina, you are not lost. You are found. Seen. Wanted.*"

And yet, the Man of the Mountain called me a monster.

"*Because you are one. And you need to see the truth.*"

Light exploded around me. Golds, whites, and pinks swirled until I floated above the dressing room at Hyton Palace. A snarling beast in a green dress attacked Annalisa. A wide-eyed maid helped Annalisa off the ground and led her to a far corner of the room. While everyone else busied with Brietta's dress, the maid dabbed black-stained tears from under Annalisa's eyes with a white handkerchief.

The Man of the Mountain pulled me into the corner with them and Annalisa opened up like a rose under sunlight. Her weeping heart poured tears in my mind and her shattered spirit released the truth as plainly as if it were written on parchment.

"No point," Annalisa sniffed to the maid. She forced her chest still as her eyes leaked. "I am not marrying a prince. My father does not care about me.

My friends cannot use me to get to Derrick anymore. I am just…worthless to everyone."

The word pounded through Annalisa's mind like a heartbeat.

Worthless. Worthless. Worthless.

"She considered you a friend. She faithfully kept your secrets for years and covered for you in times of trouble. Yet you struck her down when she was at her lowest."

I hated seeing Annalisa cry, but I had to do something. She hurt Brietta.

"She was not the only one who hurt Brietta."

The world swirled into gold and blue. Derrick laid on top of Brietta on a velvet couch. Both of them stared at each other with wide eyes and white faces as they came out of a fog. A door slammed open like a clap of thunder.

"There it is!" Duke Hyton roared. He grabbed Derrick by the back of his collar and yanked him off Brietta to drag him into the ballroom. The door slammed shut, trapping Brietta with the aftermath of whatever had just happened.

Brietta laid motionless, wondering why her hips ached. She pressed against the velvet couch and sat up. She hissed through her teeth as pain sparked between her thighs. Sitting had never hurt before. Brietta slowly lifted the hem of her skirt up until she found spots of blood on her thigh. Her undergarments had disappeared.

Brietta dropped her skirt and stared at the swirling yellow wallpaper in front of her. The gravity of what must have happened settled in the bottom of her stomach as her mind spun to try to explain the unexplainable.

She shook her head slightly, if only denying to herself what had happened. No, it was not supposed to happen that way. Not with Derrick, not on a couch, and not where she could not remember.

The cold words of a broken Duchess crept down her spine. Welcome to hell, meat.

Tears had just begun to blossom in the corners of her eyes when the door clapped open again. A roar more horrible and cutting than the Duke's tore through the room.

"How could you? You ruined everything!"

"You manipulated your best friend to bear the shame of an annulment for you and then you shamed her when she needed you the most. Ice cracked beneath her

feet and you shoved her into the frozen depths because you wanted to give her a taste of the nothingness you feared most."

I…I never knew how much Brietta was hurting. Had I known…

"But you didn't stay to find out. You made her your villain instead of facing the fact your little plot had failed…"

Green bled over blue. Dark wood overtook gold. Teenage Derrick trembled under the eye of the sharp-faced girl in front of him as he stood in the foyer of Ravenwood Manor.

"You stalked that boy like prey. You lied to him for seven years."

Ravenwood Manor faded into a dark hallway at Hyton Palace. Derrick kneeled in front of a potted plant alone while the revelry of his twin's ball raged without him.

Cold tears stung his cheeks after his stomach purged his sickness into the dirt. His golden coronet was dull. His Hyton Blue cape fell over his shaking back as he sobbed. His hands were stained with soil. He did not know how he ended up on top of Brietta Elvar, but he refused to let Uncle Ragnar's monster take his Serafina because of it.

"You used pure, young love as nothing more than a weapon to get what you wanted."

I had to be Duchess. Everything I did, I did for Ravenwood.

"LIAR!" the Man of the Mountain roared. *"You are manipulative and an excellent liar, all right. You were even able to manipulate and lie to yourself."*

I had no answer for the ancient man. I let his magic sweep through my body and scrape out all the ugliness and dishonesty, but I had nothing left to give him. Nothing except…

"You never cared about Ravenwood."

Any air I had left in my lungs disappeared. I never had a plan to help the people of Ravenwood. I never thought about how I would feed them, nurture them, or make them whole. I just wanted to feast on their praise and adoration like I had in the Hyton city square.

I wanted to eat their love because I was starving.

"Duchess, Governess, Baroness…the title never really mattered to you. You wanted the height of a crown and the weight of an iron fist. The world was made to step on you, so you cut the world off at the ankles."

I was small and weak. Born to be nobody but a bride and nothing but property. I wanted to stand taller, look men in the eye, and be my own mountain.

I did anything to feel stronger—forging a friendship with the wealthiest girl at Ashmore, fabricating a romance with the heir to the Dukedom, and soothing the Beast so he kept his arms around me.

Yes, I had done monstrous things to those foolish enough to get close to me. All my love and safety disappeared the moment my brothers rode away from Ravenwood Manor, and I just wanted it back. Was that really so wrong? I just wanted to be more than nothing.

"I exist beyond the mortal notions of right or wrong, Serafina. All I see is the truth."

Shades of red flashed in my eyes. The burgundy wine Riyan and I shared on our wedding night. His crimson cape swaddling me as I laid down in the Bloodstone carriage. A delicious red Bloodstone apple in his hand. A bead of sweet elskaberry jam on the tip of his thumb. Soft vermillion petals of lilies gently placed in my braid. Riyan and I's blood like liquid rubies binding together under the centuries-old enchantment.

Red. The most beautiful, passionate, and warm color ever mixed on a palette, grown on a vine, or streaked across the western sky. A flush of desire. A signal for the lost. A banner for the broken.

Red.

"You fell for Riyan Bloodstone because you wanted his strength and his power. But when you realized you could not control him..."

Red turned into cold bronze.

"...you tried to murder him in his sleep."

Moonlit steel slashed through the red. Hands broke apart. Wine spilled. Crimson wool shredded. Jam turned sour. Lily petals withered. The apple rotted.

"You are his sun, the only light in his world, and yet..."

A raven-haired woman shrouded in a dark cloak stood over me. Her hazel eyes were sharp, but the dagger in her hand was even sharper. No trace of regret in her face. No mercy. She raised the dagger over my head as cold tears crawled down my cheeks like icy mud.

The monster's blade did not stop at my tears. The menacing steel thirsty for my blood plunged down and stopped just short of my neck. My eyelids would not close. I stared frozen and wide-eyed at the hardened face of the raven-haired monster as if I were sentenced to an eternity of staring into a dark mirror.

"Even after all your treachery, he still begs for your life."

Darkness smothered me again and banished the monster. Distant echoes of water against smooth stone pinged in my ears. The sound turned warmer, lower, and I tasted the sorrow of the words sung in another world. Each deep note was a heartbeat, each vibration a lifeline, and each syllable a kiss that transcended time.

"No, girl, can't be undone," Riyan sang, "I won't stop 'till your life is won. Don't you sleep until we've run to the West of the Moon and East of the Sun."

Even though his desperate plea cut like a knife, his song ignited the golden light around my unguarded and tender heart. The light warmed my throat and my lips until it freed me to speak. "Do not torture him—punish me for my lies and my wrath, not him. Let me go back to him. Please. Just let me be his sun again."

I still could not see the Man of the Mountain, but I heard his smile in his voice. *"Sometimes I use my gifts to grant wishes that come from the heart. I did not forget that you wished to stay with Riyan."*

My wish from the well. He did hear me.

The glow of the blood bond dampened into darkness. The Man of the Mountain removed his arm from underneath my legs and placed his hand in the center of my chest. His ageless touch pressed through my skin and bones until it gently whispered against my raw heart.

The tiny ember that awoke after Derrick and I's first kiss blinked to life within the red flesh of my still heart.

"Serafina Helia, the Little Ember."

Childlike laughter jingled like bells. A tiny raven-haired child ran around us. She had an innocent smile flashing across her face and golden rings like sunfire around her pupils.

"Your father failed to protect you. Your mother fell prey for you. So you sharpened your tongue into a forked sword and cloaked yourself in deceit to keep anyone from stomping out your fire."

The giggling child grew into a slender wisp of a girl staring out the windows of Ravenwood Manor with cold eyes and folded arms.

"But in keeping everyone else out, you suffocated your ember in stone defenses. Even still, your spirit remained inextinguishable. Your fire was dormant, just waiting for a breath of life…"

The raven-haired girl grew into a woman dressed in white. She leaned into the embrace of a dark-haired man in black as he kissed her. The tiny ember in my heart pulsed red.

"…and little by little, the defenses chipped away until the truth drove out the lies."

A man with long golden hair, larger than any man imaginable, sat in a pool of glowing water and held the raven-haired woman in his arms. He cradled her against his bare chest, the top of her head pressed against his cheek, and he breathed in time with her slow, but unfaltering, heartbeat. The ember warmed to gold.

"And since your blood is already filled with my magic, I will grant the wish of Riyan Bloodstone."

"Riyan?" My voice echoed through the chasm. "What did he wish for?"

I swore I could see the Man of the Mountain's smile in the darkness. *"He wished to keep you safe."*

The Man of the Mountain pressed his thumb against the ember, not snuffing it, but instead igniting it into a white blaze.

"Now you will never again defend yourself with stone or iron. You wield a power stronger than steel or silver."

The white blaze crystallized into fractals, each one shining like a flaming diamond in my heart. The brilliant flames pulsed out of my heart and seared my blood with a pure white power.

"Take my gift and shine, Little Ember. Shine like my bride once did."

The Man of the Mountain's hands left my body and I slowly floated up. The darkness dragged against my skin like honey as I ascended the chasm. A pinhole of white light directly above me lit my way. A moon at midnight.

Low, slow waves of a vast ocean crashed against my skin. The wave was not forceful and cutting like seawater, but soft like a cloud.

No, it was not a wave, it was a breath—warm breath that smelled like nectar and wheat. My right arm reached up as the light in the darkness drew me up closer to freedom.

Whispers of voices swirled around me as I floated—all those who were trapped in the place West of the Moon and East of the Sun with no gift to free them.

Two hands laid on my shoulders, but I did not startle. They were not the ageless hands of the Man of the Mountain, but young, feminine hands—soft and caring like they belonged to a friend.

"The Queen of the Giants is hunting you," said the feminine voice. "Take Riyan and run."

The hands gently pushed me up closer to the growing white light until it completely enveloped me.

Then no space existed between the sun and the moon.

Chapter Thirty Five

Guardian

Rising, falling. Rising, falling. Into infinity for eternity.

The world was only white light. I faced down into the expanse of a blank canvas, a blanket of glowing snow, or the inside of the farthest star, and gently rose and fell in the air.

The Man of the Mountain said he gave me a gift, but the flaming diamond he placed in my heart gave no sign of life, no spark of power, nothing.

My tender heart beat in my chest. Time could touch me, wherever I was. I focused on my heartbeat, each soft pound another second on the ticking clock, and let my throat hum. Air from my lungs warmed my throat and I found my power in his name.

"Riyan."

Hot air kissed the top of my head and ruffled my hair around me. The soft caress of coarse hair tickled my belly. My fingers drummed against the white expanse and the touch of relaxed muscle answered my call. I took in a breath and smelled nectar and wheat.

I closed my eyes and shut myself in the darkness. My heart sang out a wish. The sun needed her moon.

My eyes fluttered open. Instead of stars shining in the night sky, small crystals embedded in a rock wall glowed right in front of my nose. All I could see were those crystals with their cerulean glow like freckles on a stone face, but underneath the aroma of minerals and crisp water was nectar and wheat.

I looked down—I was lying on my belly on Riyan's chest. A heavy weight pressed on my back and legs. I caught the edge of Riyan's wrist in the corner of my vision—both of his hands held me securely against his chest. I stretched my legs out and the wool cape shifted on my bare skin. I was still naked but for my cape covering everything below my neck like a large blanket.

I wiggled slightly out of Riyan's hold and propped myself up on my elbows above his softly thumping heart. Riyan was asleep and his massive chest rose and fell underneath me with his peaceful breath. Hot air from his nose puffed down on me with each exhale.

I looked past his head to find a small mouth of a cave with the healing spring just outside. Just short of the immediate edge of the hot spring, where smooth pebbles covered the ground, was a thin layer of sparkling white snow.

I had not seen the crystal cave when we were in the spring together. Riyan must have found it and squeezed himself inside while I was with the Man of the Mountain. I crawled out from under his hands and sat on top of his heart. The roof of the cave was so low I could almost reach up and touch it.

The cold air chilled my bare breasts and belly as I admired the hundreds of glowing crystals, but I was too dazzled by the mystical beauty to care. Some of the crystals were as small as my thumb while others were as large as my forearm. The light from the crystal constellations bathed us in the same blue-green glow of the hot spring as we sheltered together.

My eyes dropped from the crystals to the cave floor. Next to Riyan was a tiny stream of water that flowed out into the hot spring. The stream went all the way up into the cave and disappeared in the darkness. On the other side of the trickling stream was a pile of what used to be my clothing along with the Hyton dagger.

I flicked my eyes back up to Riyan's handsome sleeping face. The top of his head was pressed against the rough cave wall and his crimson cape was bunched under his head to act like a pillow. His chin pointed toward his chest, but his face was turned toward the mouth of the cave like he was still on watch.

I leaned forward and placed my hand at the bottom of his strong jaw. My heart swelled and my breath stilled. Every one of my muscles tingled with energy, each sinew strong and lithe, and all I wanted was to join my body with his.

Fraleigh said I could consummate my marriage on my own, even though I thought it was impossible. Maybe the gift the Man of the Mountain gave me was what I needed to make it happen.

A low fire burned below my stomach and stoked the diamond flames in my heart. For the first time, I did not just want to make obligatory heirs—I wanted *babies*. I wanted fat, smiling babies with golden curls plastered to their foreheads and big blue eyes.

I raised up to kneel on Riyan's chest and I brought my hand to the other side of his jaw. I stretched my spine forward and kissed him on the chin right below my right thumb.

"Riyan," I whispered, "wake up."

A muscle feathered in Riyan's cheek, but his eyes stayed closed. I placed another gentle kiss on the other side of his chin and his chest rose with a long breath. I would kiss away his nightmares if I had to.

I reached up and softly kissed him on the soft skin of his lower lip. The fire in my hips spread through my whole body until my heart pulsed pure *want* through my veins.

"*Riy-an*." Each syllable rolled off my tongue as I sang out his name.

Riyan's eyes fluttered open and then grew wide when he saw me. "Sera! You're awake!"

His hand cupped my back and his calloused palms tickled my smooth skin. His surprise brightened into elation as his chest pulsed under my knees.

His voice was as soft as a moonbeam. "I thought you wouldn't wake up."

"Well, I am awake now." My voice was low and sultry. Riyan's muscles tightened underneath me and his pupils dilated.

"Serafina, what are you doing?" His voice was also low, but like a warning instead of an invitation.

I placed my hands on top of my knees and subtly squeezed my breasts closer together with the sides of my arms. "I feel…much better after my rest."

Riyan's eyes focused exactly where I wanted them to, but then they wandered lower to the right side of my ribs. He shook his head slightly.

"You think what happened to you was a rest? Serafina, you were asleep for two days."

My heart stopped and the fire below my belly cooled. I glanced out of the mouth of the cave. Night still surrounded us, but I could not see the moon. Time did not touch the dark chasm with the Man of the Mountain, but two whole days had passed while my mind was in his hold.

My lip trembled as I struggled to find the right questions to ask.

"Two days," Riyan repeated. "I could not wake you up, no matter what I tried. After the sun set on the first day, I figured the magic of the spring wanted you to sleep so you could heal. I kept you with me the whole time."

Riyan's fingertips gently stroked the right side of my ribs. My skin was smooth as butter with no trace of a wound. Riyan reached back with his left arm and propped up his head as he looked at me with a gentle half-smile.

"I sang to you, combed your hair eight times, talked about everything and nothing for hours, and when my throat was sore from the constant noise, I listened to your heartbeat just to make sure you were still alive."

His eyes flicked up to the top of my head. "I also, uh, made you a little present."

My hands floated up and my fingertips touched soft petals. I carefully removed a circle of flowers from my head to admire it. The crown was a complicated braid of vines with tiny blue flowers with heart-shaped petals. Riyan had weaved the vines together in a strong bond, letting the blue blossoms show on the outside edge of the crown.

Riyan smiled. "I went through four of those because the vines were so delicate they kept snapping."

My cheeks flushed as I admired the crown. "What kind of flowers are these? I have never seen anything like these before."

"I hadn't seen them before either. They were growing up the side of the cave and I thought they were pretty—pretty enough to make into a 'we've been married for a week' present for you, anyway."

I put the crown back on top of my head and then pressed my hand over my full heart. Riyan's cheek's flushed pink, even under the cerulean light of the crystals, and he glanced at the trickling stream in the middle of the cave.

"I needed something to give me hope," Riyan said. "The half moon came, so I knew it had been a week since our marriage started and…it made me miss you even more. I concentrated on making the crown and pictured you opening your eyes surrounded in flowers. I don't know, I was desperate. It was the longest two days of my life."

Two days. I had never slept for that long before, not even when I was confined to my bed in the days after Erik and Endre died. The Man of the Mountain took me West of the Moon and East of the Sun not only to show me what a monster I was, but also that Riyan was my protector and guardian.

Gratitude filled my chest along with warmth from a tender heart that fluttered only for him. "I cannot believe you took care of me for two whole days."

"Of course I did," Riyan said with a small laugh that shook under my knees. "You know, when I was younger and still clinging to the hope of being in Selection Night, I would dream of what my life would be like once I got my promised Ashmore bride. I used to imagine being around my gorgeous, naked wife *all the time*. Well, nothing like the past two days was anything like I had fantasized."

The fire ignited under my belly again. I let my head fall to one side and batted my eyelashes at him. My heart thudded. Blood pulsed in my hips with a gentle heat.

My breath was warm and heavy as I leaned forward so Riyan's eyes were the same level as my own.

"And what did you use to fantasize about?" I whispered. I kissed him on the cheek. My clavicle pressed against his strong jaw. My peaked nipples brushed against the tight muscles of his neck. "I am just dying to know."

Riyan's throat bobbed and his voice was strained. "Interesting choice of words."

I hummed against his cheek as I kissed him again. His muscles tightened underneath my legs and his heartbeat slammed into my knees.

"Since I am fully healed, we are alone in this nice, cozy cave, and Fraleigh said nothing was impossible…," I whispered into his skin. I placed another kiss on his cheek, making a trail of kisses down to his lips. "We should try sex again. Fraleigh thought we were not trying hard enough and Rosaline did say she knows everything…"

I let myself trail off, giving Riyan a pause to answer. He took a tense breath.

"You remember what happened last time." His voice was as dark as the night.

I pulled away from his face and sat on my knees again. Although Riyan's eyes devoured me, his jaw was set tight and unmoving. He was afraid of crushing me again, but Ashmore taught us how to fulfill our marital duties while on top of a man.

"You can stay on your back this time." My fingertips traced circles around the muscles of his chest like I was stirring tea. "So I will only gasp for air in a good way."

I wanted Riyan to reach up and touch me, but he kept both his hands pressed against the cave floor as he propped himself up on his elbows. His eyes darkened as they raked along my body.

"You don't get it." His voice was low in his throat. "It's not going to fit, and if you try, I am going to rip you in half."

My chest rose and fell. I could make my own determination if he could fit—it was *my* body, after all. I turned my head to see if I could make a visual judgment when Riyan caught my cheek with his fingertip and forced me to face him again.

"No," Riyan commanded. He did not blink. He did not breathe. "Just wait until I am normal-sized. We'll find Daigen eventually and then you can ride me until your legs fall off. Deal?"

Eventually. I bit my tongue and studied Riyan's tight muscles. If I had wasted two days being asleep, that meant we only had twenty-two days left until the next full moon. Rosaline had warned me that Daigen was tricky and he could elude us for weeks.

"We do not have time to find Daigen," I pleaded as he dropped his hand to the cave floor. "We need to try or else our marriage will annul."

My heart pounded as I pictured going back to Hyton as the Duke's property—trapped in the House of warring bulls forever. I could hear gossip pricking my ears, smell rotten perfume masking the odor of lustful sweat, and taste endless draughts of wine to drown my sorrow and rage until I faded into the fog of numbness and died inside.

I shook my head quickly, forcing myself to remember that I was with Riyan and not at Hyton Palace. "Duke Hyton cannot own me. I have no idea what he will do to me in that palace with all those awful people—"

Riyan silenced me by gently tugging my wrist forward. "Come here." His voice kissed my shoulders as softly as wool.

I followed his gentle pull and crawled forward a little. He let go of my wrist and wrapped my crimson cape around my shoulders. His heart still pounded underneath my legs and his eyes burned with desire, but he placed his hand on my back with the touch of a protector.

"I want more than anything to fuck you and it's torture." Riyan's tone was quiet and calm, but strained like a wolf on the end of a leash. "I wanted to tear that little green dress of yours to shreds the instant we were alone on our wedding night. When you kissed me in the field of lilies, I almost threw you into the flowers and tore into you right there. I might have even done it had we not been attacked."

Riyan's body warmed underneath me and his heart beat faster and faster despite the calmness of his voice. Every muscle was tight, like he struggled against invisible chains that pinned him down to the cave floor.

"But we know what happens when I lose control," he said. Memories of the shattered bed and cracking ribs flashed through my mind. "I won't be gentle with you, I *can't* be…and I know I would kill you."

His throat bobbed and his lip trembled. His fingers weighed on my shoulder.

"That desperate, longing fear that consumed me for two of the darkest nights of my life is all that stops me from giving in to how my body begs for yours. I am more afraid of losing you than I am of the giants, the Duke, or even my fucking father. I will not lose you. I *cannot* lose you, so stop begging me with those big hazel eyes to let the beast out."

I clutched the cape around me. My fists trembled underneath the crimson wool. "But what if Duke Hyton—"

Riyan raised his right hand and caught my chin on his knuckle. He held my face still while his eyes bore into mine.

"If Duke Hyton does what?" Riyan growled. "We will quench our thirst for each other when the time is right, regardless of what moon hangs in the sky. If that man tries to lay a single greasy finger on you, I will tear his head off with a flick of my wrist."

I gulped.

"He would still enforce the law," I whispered as my jaw trembled against his hold on my chin. "He would not let the other Barons think anyone was above him, especially you. He would see it as a move to usurp the throne and send his army to get me if it meant keeping his control over the Dukedom."

Riyan smiled enough to show off his dimple and then chuckled low in his throat. "I have an army too, sweetheart. Not that I would need them."

He loosened his hold on my chin and stroked my cheek with his thumb. I closed my eyes and savored his sweet touch like it was another bite of a Bloodstone apple.

"He can keep his stupid throne so long as I get to keep you," he whispered.

I smiled against his thumb and opened my eyes. Riyan's face was soft with his promise. He gently tapped the end of my nose with his index finger. "Be patient, Serafina Helia."

A giggle like butterfly wings escaped my lips. He asked for patience, and yet he looked at me with his sparkling eyes, flexed his muscles underneath my legs, and whispered every promise my frightened little heart needed to hear. The more he spoke, the more I wanted to meld our bodies together and satisfy our blood bond that ached for permanence.

The golden light sparked as I nuzzled Riyan's thumb. The light blanketed my heart and fanned its warmth through my arms and legs. My shoulders sighed down. My jaw loosened. My fists unclenched.

My handsome guardian of the crystal cave gave me a gift more valuable than any riches, stronger than any magic, and more powerful than any crown. For the first time in seven years, I finally felt safe.

"I still want to find Daigen," I said. I flicked my gaze to his lips and then up to his twilight eyes. "If only because feeling you *under* my legs and not *between* my legs is pure agony."

Riyan laughed and lowered his hand from my jaw. "Then I suggest you slide off my chest before you make me any more…excited." Riyan nodded toward my pile of clothes on the other side of the cave. "Some of your clothes should still be intact. Get dressed while I, uh, calm down."

I held the cape closed around me as I climbed down from his chest. I carefully stepped around Riyan's sword and hopped over the tiny stream bisecting the cave.

I inspected the pile of rags that used to be my clothes. My shoes were fine. My skirt was mostly intact, but the waist was gone. My waist cincher was completely destroyed. My blouse and my stockings were in tatters.

As I sorted through the scraps, Riyan sang a low tune about various unappealing sights to get his blood flowing back into his head.

"*Toothless old crones fighting over dried prunes.*"

I took the torn fabric of my white blouse and tied the ends together in simple knots, making a long piece of fabric. I laid that long piece flat across my breasts and wrapped it around the rest of my torso before tying it securely at my waist.

"*Bag of kittens drowning in an icy river.*"

I tore excess fabric off my stockings but kept everything from the ankle-down intact. I took one torn stocking and made it into a belt to secure my skirt. With the other, I tied it around the Hyton dagger and tied it loosely around my hips. I folded and wrapped the cape around me and clasped it shut with the House of Ravenwood pin.

"*General Hyton screaming in my face.*"

As Riyan sang, my mind fell back to the chasm with the Man of the Mountain. His low voice had surrounded me, singing the ancient song of lost love as he begged for my life. I stared at the crystal wall and as the memory of hands on my shoulders and a female voice whispering in my ear sent a chill down my spine.

What would Riyan think of my journey West of the Moon and East of the Sun?

"Riyan, are you…calmed down now?" I asked.

"Oh yeah, that last line did the trick," he responded.

I turned around. Riyan was reclining on his side as he watched me get dressed. His balled-up crimson cape was at his elbow along with the House of Bloodstone pin and Endre's Revenge was lying in front of him.

"Riyan, when I was asleep, I heard a voice."

He smiled. "Mine? The talking and singing worked?"

My heart fluttered. "Yes, but…I also went somewhere else. Somewhere between worlds. The *real* West of the Moon and East of the Sun."

Riyan furrowed his brow.

"I met the Man of the Mountain." I folded my hands over my heart. "He forced me to see all the terrible things I had done…and I am so sorry that I—"

He shook his head. "Don't worry about that. What about that voice you heard?"

"It was a woman's voice. She warned me."

He raised an eyebrow and pressed his palms into the dirt, ready to rise and crawl out of the cave. "What did the voice say?"

I swallowed. "She said Ganora was hunting us. She told me to take you and run."

Riyan's brow hardened. He turned his head toward the dark depths of the cave and hissed out a breath. "I don't trust it. That voice could have been Ganora herself, wanting us to flee like cowards because we're seeking out magic."

"And if it was a real warning?"

"Do you want to go back?" He looked back at me with softer eyes. "We can go back to the fortress. You can stay safe there while I finish the journey—"

"No." My hands curled into loose fists over my pounding heart. Even though a chill crept through the crystal cave, my blood was luminescent with warmth. Maybe the gift the Man of the Mountain had given me was pure bravery, because I did not want to leave Riyan's side for a moment, even if it meant facing the dangers of the mountain's peak.

Riyan nodded. "As you wish." His eyes turned icy and his jaw set tight. "We're going to find Daigen, I won't let Ganora scare us away. If she dares to send her remaining giants after us or even so much as shows her face…"

He gripped the hilt of Endre's Revenge. "…I'm going to kill her."

Chapter Thirty Six
Footprints in the Snow

My thumb ran over the embroidered flowers in my pocket as Riyan prepared to leave the safety of the crystal cave to search for Daigen.

Fat snowflakes slowly fluttered to the ground outside the mouth of the cave. Each crystal of snow sparkled in the cerulean glow of the magical hot spring before melting into the steam rising above the water.

I hooded my cape over my head to try to keep warm, careful to not crush Riyan's sweet wreath of blue flowers around my head. I had tied my onyx choker around my neck to keep the skin under the satin ribbon protected from the frigid air.

I let go of the scrap of fabric in my pocket and wrung my hands together to increase blood flow. My comb, mirror, needle, and spool of thread were lost to the mountain when I had tumbled through the snow, so all my worldly possessions were tied to my shivering body.

Riyan pulled himself into a sitting position near the mouth of the cave. The top of his poor head scraped the roof of the cave even as he hunched over. Endre's Revenge was sheathed and secured at his hip. I had helped him fasten his cape around his shoulders, but his hide tunic on his lower half was his only other cover against the cold.

Even though he was cramped, Riyan's eyes still danced with wonder at the glowing crystals all around him.

"When I moved all those boulders to uncover the cave, I was surprised to find all these crystals in here," Riyan said with a hint of wistfulness in his voice. "These are illegal."

"Illegal? Why?" I asked.

Riyan looked back at me with a glimmer in his eye. The blue-green glow highlighted the contours of his handsome face. "People thought they could use them for sorcery."

He glanced up at the roof of the cave, scanning the glowing stones instead of admiring. He set his eyes on one and grabbed the crystal embedded in the rock. With a strong tug, he plucked it out of the rock wall and handed it to me with a smile. "A magical stone for my magical bride."

My cheeks flushed as I took the crystal in my hands. The stone was the size of my palm and vaguely heart-shaped. The glow of the crystal soon faded, but it was still a beautiful deep blue stone. I stashed it in my pocket along with the embroidered flowers.

I looked out of the cave and into the glowing water of the hot spring and then out onto the bright, clean snow. Only…not all of it looked so clean. I noticed some indents in the powder that looked like footprints near the mouth of the cave.

My eyes followed a trail of footprints that were slowly disappearing underneath the falling snow. The footprints stamped in the powder looked like someone had walked to the mouth of the cave, stood there, and then retreated into the wilderness.

My stomach dropped. I certainly did not make those footprints and Riyan's feet were much too large to leave prints that small.

"Riyan," I whispered. "I think someone has been here."

Riyan's head whipped around and peered out of the mouth of the cave. He crawled over and shielded me with his body. He squeezed his shoulders through the jagged, narrow opening of the cave and rose to his feet outside. He unsheathed Endre's Revenge and examined the fading footprints.

"You're right," Riyan said in a low voice. "Those are bootprints. I knew we were being watched before. A man has been here—or something pretending to be a man, anyway."

I dared to step near the mouth of the cave to get a closer look. Daigen could not wear boots on his hooves, although he could have used magic to change his form. We came to the top of the mountain looking for him, but maybe he was also looking for us.

Something was panting and running toward me when the ravens had attacked me further down the mountain. And I swore a hand had grabbed my shoulder…was that Daigen too? Had he been following us? Was he the one tripping on rocks on the path behind us?

Could have been Daigen, could have been a number of strange creatures that lurked on the mountain. But what if—it was impossible, but…what if Derrick had climbed the mountain to rescue me?

I wrapped my hand around the cold bronze hilt of the Hyton dagger. I could almost taste the bitter bite of the metal as my thumb ran over the bull's head. No, Derrick would never set foot on Nordingaard. But the memory of his hand tangled in my hair and his breath over my lips as he whispered that I was his flashed through my mind and suddenly I was not so sure.

Derrick was not the anxious boy I had met in Ravenwood Manor seven years ago—he had grown into a true Hyton bull. He was powerful, he fixated on problems, and he did not stop until he got what he wanted.

He was exactly the kind of man who would go to the place West of the Moon and East of the Sun to save his lost bride.

Riyan cleared his throat. "We need to move. If these prints are our only lead to Daigen, we have to follow them before they disappear."

He scooped me up in his left arm again. He held me close to his chest and shrugged his shoulder so his cape fell over my body. He tucked the wool cape around me and left only my face exposed to the cold.

The waning moon hung high in the sky and the sparkling snow softly crunched under Riyan's footsteps as he followed the footprints into a grove of trees. Each snowflake tingled my skin as it melted into me. The leafless branches of the trees around the spring were warped and bent like they were frozen in place during a moonlit dance.

Snowflakes dusted my eyelashes as I looked through the dark and twisted trees for any sign of movement, but everything was still in the midnight glow. No twigs snapped, no pine needles rustled, and even the wind held its breath as Riyan carefully walked through the realm of magic.

The trail of footprints disappeared into a tall rock formation that stretched as far left as I could see through the snowfall.

"Fucker must have hidden in the rocks," Riyan growled. "You think he would be excited to see me after all this time. I bet he would be shocked at how *big* I've gotten."

I rolled my eyes at his terrible joke, but my stomach was hollow from fear. Riyan crept in the shadows of the tall rocks as he kept his eyes low. I scanned the rocks at my eye level, looking for any trace of red.

Our path sloped upward. Endre's Revenge gleamed in the moonlight. The night was too quiet.

Riyan's head snapped toward an open snowy field to his left. His heart pounded in his chest even though his breath went still.

He did not have to tell me what caused him to freeze in place. In the distance were two towering boulders with an ominous fog billowing between them.

We were at the battlefield where my brothers died.

"Sera, I need to warn you now," he whispered through a tight throat, "when the giants come, don't scream."

My trembling hand instinctively gripped the hilt of the Hyton dagger, as if it could do anything against a giant.

"They'll smell me and think I'm alone, so they won't come after you as long as you're quiet," he said, sounding as if he had to force each word out of his lips. "*Don't scream.*"

I let go of the Hyton dagger and slipped my hand into my pocket to find the scrap of embroidered fabric. I traced the flowers with my thumb, willing myself to not let fear overcome my sense.

The first stomp echoed even through the suffocating calm of the snowfall. The earth trembled. More thunder rolled like a slow stampede.

A group of giants was coming through the foggy pass.

Riyan's muscles shifted and he lowered his chin. My heart pounded in time with his, but instead of my body seizing in fear, it vibrated with energy.

"Here they come," Riyan said in an exhale. "Hide, but don't make a *single* sound until you're safe."

He gently placed me on the ground behind him. Even though my heart sang out with a white light, beckoning me to join in the fight somehow, I scrambled to the rocks and pressed my body behind as much stone as I could.

The round, grey head of the first giant emerged from the fog. It turned toward us and stomped forward with its milky white eyes on Riyan.

I bit my tongue and ordered my body to be quiet like Riyan had said. A white-hot claw crept up my throat and held it closed for a heartbeat before it vanished.

I blinked and brought my hand up to my neck where the searing sensation had lingered for a moment. I had no idea what had just happened, but I knew deep in my blood that the last thing I was about to do was scream.

Riyan stood in front of me with Endre's Revenge ready and thirsting for giant blood. The Hero of Lycaster did not lunge, he did not run, and he did not charge. His bare feet were planted firmly in the snow and his crimson cape fluttered around him in the wind as he waited for the perfect opportunity to strike.

The hunted suddenly became the hunter.

The giant's horrible growl made my skin crawl. Two more giants appeared in the distance behind it. The first giant stepped closer and closer…

…but Riyan was ready.

As soon as the first giant was within arm's reach, a war cry tore from Riyan's throat as he swung his left fist at the giant's head. His fist met the giant's head with a crash like a strike of lightning and the giant toppled to the snow.

Boom. The giant's body rocked the earth and I gripped the nearest rock to stay steady. White powder flared high into the air around the giant from the impact.

Riyan quickly stood over the fallen giant, grabbed a fistful of its thin black hair, and jerked its head upward. Endre's Revenge sliced through the frigid night air and cut through the hard flesh of the giant's neck. Sparkling clear blood spilled onto the snow.

Riyan held the giant's head in his fist and hurled it in the direction of the other two giants. The head hit the giant on the left, smacking it in the chest with a deafening crack and knocking it to the ground.

The earth shook again, but I did not grip onto my rock. Riyan charged for the still-standing giant and my fingertips left the cold stone, my heart pounding as every fiber of my body compelled me to join in the fight.

My feet softly crunched the snow as I marched forward. I did not know why I had left the safety of the stone, but the diamond in my heart from the Man of the Mountain sparkled with power and forced me to keep going.

I was twenty paces away from Riyan as he attacked the second giant. He decapitated the second giant with a snarl, and just as he turned to eliminate the third as it rose from the ground, his eyes widened in terror and he froze. The last giant had one large, milky eye—the giant that killed Endre.

Riyan stood still as the giant slowly stomped toward him, but my entire body ignited. Seven years of rage that I had shoved behind granite and tried numb through a fog of apathy roared to the surface of my heart.

Tears that were so hot they were nearly boiling lined my eyes. Tongues of white flames surged from my chest to my arms. Searing outrage consumed my entire body.

I had loved no one. I had torn my life apart at the seams. I had nearly destroyed every speck of light in my life to shield myself from the pain those fucking giants had caused.

But no more. I was a scream of morning light, strong as a diamond and tall as the sky.

Riyan's sword was not Endre's revenge, I was.

The giant raised its massive fist to swing at Riyan, but its arm cracked as a single word pulsed through my mind and body.

Burn.

My temples ached and my heart pounded, but I refused to yield. The blood that flowed through the giant's crumbling arm glowed as white-hot as my rage. Its gray clods of flesh burned red before they fell to the earth and sizzled in the snow. The giant's milky white eye went dim as I incinerated it from the inside.

Burn. Burn. BURN.

The giant sank lower and lower to the ground, its mouth open and releasing a strained growl of pain, before it disintegrated into smoldering ash on the snow.

My muscles screamed in pain but vibrated with power as I stared at the pile of ash that had killed my brother. My blood was molten bronze. I exhaled and I swore steam curled out of my nose. The crystal in my pocket glowed with warmth against my leg.

Riyan's eyes turned from the fallen giant to me. His chest rose with an amazed breath as he awoke from his worst nightmare. A smile crept up his mouth as his left hand gripped his forearm.

"Sera, I felt that in my blood, I felt you…" His voice broke, but his smile never faltered. "You, you're a…"

Even though the word was stuck in my throat, I finished his failed sentence in my mind.

Sorceress. The Man of the Mountain had made me a sorceress.

A flash of white light blinded me for a blink. Talons of ice wrapped around my throat and suddenly my feet left the snow as I floated in the air.

Riyan's eyes went wide. He looked up.

"No!" Riyan yelled. He lunged forward but an invisible force held him at the neck. Riyan grabbed at his throat to fight off whatever held him back, but he failed to throw off the power.

I grappled at my throat but felt nothing but my cold skin as I was pulled higher and higher in the air. As soon as I was at the height of Riyan's head, I slowly spun around to find a pair of huge, glowing ice blue eyes.

I blinked as I struggled to breathe, taking in everything in front of me. Face as grey as a frozen lake. Snarling smile of sharp teeth. Scream of long, white hair. Necklace of bones over a tunic of blackened hides.

Ganora. The Queen of the Giants.

Her voice was dark as the bottom of a well. "Look at this, another little sorceress." She dangled me in the air with her invisible power, as if she were a cat playing with a mouse.

I gritted my teeth and channeled the magic of the diamond in my heart, but Ganora's magic was so cold not even the hottest fire could dampen it. I kicked and thrashed in her grip as my lungs burned.

"Ganora!" Riyan choked as he struggled under her invisible hold. "Let her go!"

Ganora did not take her eyes off me. "Do you know what happens to little girls who become sorceresses?"

The icy talons tightened their hold on my throat. Tears leaked out of my eyes as I desperately sucked in bits of air through my teeth.

"Don't hurt her!" Riyan cried.

Ganora's glowing eyes snapped to Riyan. "Not so powerful now, are you? You took my giants—now I take something of yours."

Her magic snapped my windpipe shut. My eyes widened as the stars danced.

"Please!" He begged through his gasps. "Anything you want, you can have it, just let Serafina go!"

The temperature plummeted as Ganora's power ebbed around me—sizing me up, weighing my value. I clawed against the invisible talons around my throat, fighting with every glimmer of magic in my veins, but her power completely smothered mine.

She smirked. "The biggest and strongest man alive is offering me anything I want for the little sorceress? How interesting…"

"Anything," Riyan pleaded.

Ganora chuckled low in her throat. "I want you, Riyan Bloodstone. Drop your sword."

Endre's Revenge hit the snow with a quiet thud. A second thud—Riyan had fallen to his knees.

My head buzzed and the corners of my vision went black.

"You can have me." His voice broke but his throat was unobstructed. He was free from Ganora's force. "Just spare her."

My head lolled forward as the world went dark.

"Your life for hers?" Ganora crooned in delight. "It's a deal."

The talons released me. Air rushed into my mouth and filled my chest. My cape fluttered around me as I plummeted to the ground. My face hit the cold powder, but I only barely noticed the cold prickling my cheek as I struggled to breathe.

Riyan's strong hands helped me to my feet. My legs were weak and trembling as he held me up.

"I'm so sorry, Sera," he said softly. Tears trickled from his eyes. "I was supposed to keep you safe and…"

My hands trembled but my throat stayed frozen. I tried to fight back, but the magic in my blood dampened. Somehow, the power the Man of the Mountain had given me could not stop Riyan and Ganora's agreement.

As if nothing could sever the bond Riyan had just made. His life for mine.

Even if no one could change what was about to happen, I still wanted to scream—no.

No, it was not fair. No, you cannot leave me. No, I cannot be alone again.

I grabbed onto his fingers and desperately clung to him as my head throbbed in pain. My throat was sore, but my magic still refused to let me speak.

Once again, I stood motionless with a frozen tongue and a shattered heart as my life crumbled before my eyes—powerless to do anything to stop it.

Riyan's eyes scanned me frantically, taking in every last detail of my face and body. Even though his gaze ate me up like his last meal, his eyes swam with guilt.

"Go back to the fortress, Serafina," he said, his satin voice shredding more with every word. "Take care of my mother, try to…try to be happy…and…"

Riyan reached up and tore the House of Bloodstone pin from his cape. His crimson cape fell from his shoulders onto the snow. He opened up my trembling hand with his finger and slid the pin into my palm.

"…take charge of the Northern provinces," Riyan finished. "You don't need me, you don't…"

Riyan trailed off as soon as my lip trembled. The cold golden pin bit the center of my palm. I did need him. I needed him not for his strength, or his power, but for his heart. I shook my head as I refused to let him leave me alone in the darkness of the world again.

Riyan held me even more steadily. "You are the Baron, Serafina, and not because I say you are, but because *you are* powerful. And if anyone says otherwise…you have an army."

Against my own will, I nodded. Tears broke from my eyes and streamed down my face.

Riyan smiled softly. I trembled as I savored every last second I had with him. My eyes frantically swept down his golden hair, his square jaw, and his strong brow and nose. I quickly memorized every groove of his chest, every muscle in his arms, and every callus of his hands as he held me. I took a deep breath of nectar and wheat.

Riyan's lips parted. "I love you."

Our golden bond cried in both triumph and agony. Riyan kissed me on the top of my head. He let his lips linger there for a moment and took in a deep breath.

My hands floated up to reach for him, like I had gripped onto Erik's cape long ago and silently begged him to stay. But just like my eldest brother broke away from me and walked to his doom, so did Riyan.

I turned around and my desperate eyes followed him as he approached Ganora.

The words sat on my tongue with wings raised, ready to fly to him, but my throat was still. I had enchanted myself to stay silent, but the words soared through my heart and to my veins, the power of each one holding me down to the earth.

I love you too.

Riyan faced Ganora, their eyes the same level, but he refused to look at anything but me. He gave me a little smile as one last goodbye.

Ganora grabbed Riyan by his jaw with her sharp hands. She leaned closer. Just when I thought she was going to kiss him, a wicked smile crawled across her face.

"You are going to be useful," she said. "Sleep, Bloodstone."

Ganora opened her mouth. Her breath like a wicked blue frost spiraled out of her throat and into Riyan's mouth and nose. The light went out in Riyan's eyes before they rolled back into his head. He went limp and collapsed into the snow with a ground-shaking thud.

I wanted to scream, but my enchantment still kept me silent.

Ganora knelt next to Riyan's lifeless body—as if he were nothing more than a mass of muscle and bone. Her icy eyes met mine and she quirked a devious smile.

A dare—she wanted me to try to take him back.

Just as my fingers flexed toward my dagger, Ganora placed her hand on Riyan's back and a flurry of snowflakes swirled around them in a vortex. The powerful flurry blew my hair back. I kept my feet planted and leaned into the cold. I nearly took a step forward when the biting cold faded and the snowflakes vanished—taking Riyan and Ganora with them into the night.

I blinked once, then twice, wishing with each flutter of my lashes that Riyan would return from the darkness, but after three agonizing seconds, my heart sank.

The only noise through the silent snowfall was the whip of the wind through the craggy ridges at Nordingaard's peak. The danger was gone and the enchantment in my blood released its hold on my throat.

I fell to my knees in the snow and sobbed. My tears boiled as they left my eyes but slowly stung with fury as they rolled down to my jaw.

He was gone.

I raised my face and my eyes found Endre's Revenge lying in the snow— useless without the only man who could wield it. Riyan's cape wrapped around the steel blade as it crumpled in the wind. The Bloodstones wore crimson to be seen on the mountain, but without it, how would I ever find Riyan again?

I slowly rose to my feet and stepped into one of Riyan's footprints in the snow—the last remnant of my only love.

My feet planted firmly in the indentation as if I could somehow siphon the strength from Riyan's last stand. I pulled the scrap of fabric out of my pocket and traced the three flowers, each one marking a promise I had made.

Take care of Astrid. Try to be happy. Take charge of the Northern provinces.

I transferred the House of Bloodstone pin from my palm to my pocket. The North was finally mine, but the triumph was hollow. Even still, I accepted the burden to honor Riyan's last wishes.

I would lead the Northern provinces, I would take care of Astrid, I would try to be happy…but I did not know how I could be without him.

A flash of red caught my eye and I snapped my head toward the most beautiful color in the world. The waning moon illuminated a red face with curved black horns and golden eyes peeking out between the snowy rocks.

Daigen.

Power surged through my veins again, lighting me up inside like a forest fire. I squared my shoulders as the diamond in my heart ignited with truth. I finally knew what I was and what I wanted.

I was a monster—a beast born of grief with sharp teeth and razor claws who tore through anyone who got in her way. The monster no longer had a heart of stone, but she never went to sleep. She was still starved of love and her one love was just taken from her.

A new monster prowled Nordingaard and she was hungry.

I kept my huntress's stare on Daigen's face in the rocks as I slowly slid the embroidered flowers back into my pocket. The crystal in my pocket still glowed warm under my touch as my heart pounded in my wrists and my ears.

Cold bronze met my white-knuckled grip and I snarled out a breath. I raced through the snow to Daigen with the Hyton dagger in my fist and an enchanted flame in my heart. Not only would I not accept "no" for an answer, I would accept nothing less from the magical beast than Riyan's freedom.

I kept my focus on Daigen's scarlet face as his eyes widened. He launched from the rocks and his red legs ending in hooves ran through the snow, but the starving monster only ran faster.

Blood. Wine. Apples. Jam. Lilies.

All I saw was red.

THE ADVENTURE CONTINUES IN...
THE SORCERESS OF
LYCASTER
COMING SOON

Acknowledgements

Firstly, thank you for reading. I'm so grateful I got to share this story with you and I hope you're ready to continue the journey.

To my editor, Hina at Faemance: You cracked the hard shell of this story and always told me the truth. Thank you for helping me make it shine.

To my alpha readers, Abigail, Erin, Georgie, Lauren, and Magda: Thank you for listening to me for hours as I rambled about my fantasy world. Thank you for still talking to me even though I might have lost my mind.

To J.B., Riyan's biggest fan: Thank you for sprinkling some sweetness in.

To my parents: Thank you for sending me to college to get more knowledge.

To Lesa, my mother-in-law: Thank you so much for believing in us and for all your support.

To Erik, my brother-in-law: I'm sorry.

To Darren: Thank you for believing in this weird side-project I took on. "Slaking." Are you happy now?

To my brothers, Hunter and Cade: I love you into eternity, you little shits.

To my daughter, TJ: Thank you so much for understanding that "Mommy is working." I hope I've shown you that you can scale the mountain and take your power like I did.

To the BookTok and AuthorTok community: Thank every single one of you for your support, for your guidance, your spicy takes, and for teaching me how to self-publish. I couldn't have made it here without you.

To the Oklahoma State University Agricultural Communications program: Thank you for giving me an editor's eagle-eye, Adobe software finesse, and the work ethic needed to take on the giant of self-publishing.

Lastly, to Ryan, my hero: Thank you for your unwavering support, your geographical expertise, your fiery evisceration of my plot holes, and shouldering every one of life's burdens so I can stitch up my soul and shine like you knew I could. Thank you for keeping me safe.

About the Author

Perci Jay was first inspired to write when dealing with those pesky emotions that came hand-in-hand with training bras and boys not texting her back. After 16 years of ideas, Perci composed a dynamic love story full of tragedy, sacrifice, and spicy scenes that make her pray her parents never buy a copy.

When not chasing her toddler, Perci is watching "Beauty and the Beast" for the millionth time, debating the finer points of morally grey men with her husband, and running at an excruciatingly slow pace around her neighborhood in the heart of Texas.

www.percijayauthor.com

TikTok: percijay_fantasyauthor

Instagram: percijay_fantasyauthor

Twitter: @percijay_author

Pinterest: PerciJay

Discussion Questions

1. Is Serafina an unreliable narrator? Did you ever think her narrative was not telling the truth?

2. Serafina describes her "stone walls" and "iron bars" that she hides behind, but when does she let herself feel vulnerable with someone else?

3. Do you think Serafina was justified in her actions? Do you think sometimes she went too far?

4. Why does Serafina lie? When does she lie?

5. Which characters do you think are hiding something?

6. Did you have one opinion of a character in the beginning of the book that changed by the end? Which characters?

7. How do Serafina, Derrick, and Riyan show affection differently? How are they similar?

8. How did Serafina change from the beginning of the book to the end?

9. Why do you think Riyan was quick to forgive Serafina after she tried to kill him?

10. Do you think Serafina and Brietta can salvage their friendship?

www.ingramcontent.com/pod-product-compliance
Lightning Source LLC
Chambersburg PA
CBHW030107310726
48970CB00004B/1176